Sorrow churn
Deep within it does reside
Pushing you towards homicide

Retribution I command
Into you it does expand
This thing you can't withstand

So scream if you can
Slow to understand
Been there and I always have

Dreading your fears
To you they do adhere
And becoming a prison cell
Your neverending living hell

Sweet is my embrace
Propelling you towards disgrace
Constricting your breathing space

Punishment I demand
Gaining the upper hand
Destroying this your wonderland

So scream if you can
Slow to understand
Been there and I always have

Dreading your fears
To you they do adhere
And becoming a prison cell
Your neverending living hell

Hell to you I bestow
You're beginning to overflow
With this my final death blow

Moving slowly master hand
Hourglass out of sand
Welcome to No Man's Land

So scream if you can
Slow to understand
Been there and I always have

Dreading your fears
To you they do adhere
And becoming a prison cell
Your neverending living hell

Wayne Heath
"Sweet Sorrows"

PROLOGUE

1

Having a great deal of time on their hands, and being a relatively closed society, all vampires were natural gossips. The old proverb that stated that one could trust only the dead with one's secrets did not take into account the vampire. They lived on secrets as much as on blood. They were avid voyeurs by nature. And what was gossip—and vampirism—but the act of subsisting on another's life? The slayer knew then, accordingly, that the story circulating around the East Village and parts of SoHo and Prospect Park had been embellished many times over and bore little if any resemblance to the truth. Still, he was prepared for anything. What else could he do? He could no more predict an unstudied vampire's reaction to an affront than he could pick through the tatters of downtown hearsay and determine the ultimate truth—if indeed, one existed.

In any event, Empirius, the proprietor of the Abyssus, a lower Lower East Side nightclub, and master of the hive of vampires contained therein, invited him in graciously. The slayer bowed low and kissed his ring. "Your Grace."

"Welcome," Empirius said in his sibilant whisper. He was impeccably dressed in a grey Armani suit, a red silk blouse, and a gold papal cross pinned up tight under his chin. His dark blonde hair was combed straight back and tied in a three-inch ponytail, noticeable when he canted his head to one side like a curious cat. His eyes were tiny but brilliant, the large black irises reflecting the light of the many votive candles like chips of flint. His smile showed a row of perfect teeth. "You look most...disarming tonight, Master Alek."

The old vampire had enough class not to say anything in response to the slayer's long-coated appearance, but he could not quite keep a malicious splinter of glee out of his bloodshot eyes. Already he was thinking of what outrageous tales he would spin for his thralls after this night was done. A slayer here to brush against the souls of the outcast in his coat and cloak of long hair, a warrior who wore his armor on the inside, Death, not Red but black and white—white-faced and black-clad, the lottery cast. But for whom? his eyes asked.

The pit was crowded tonight. The humans served and were served among the stained-glass images of redemption and repentance, the low stone altars and statues carved with sensual reverence. Spare, white-pale bodies like slaughtered swans lay here and there, alive, or nearly so. "Take me," they said to the slayer mistakenly, and "My blood is young." Others lied. "I've never been tasted" and "A virgin's nectar is the sweetest". It was their thoughts, their living emotions, as much as their words that the slayer encountered as he made his way to the bar.

The club was a swamp of incense, sandalwood or clove or some such sweet smoke undercut by the hot metallic tang of blood and passion. The slayer spotted a beautifully androgynous vampire bleeding a mortal boy perhaps no more than fifteen years. The boy's white flesh looked nearly translucent, the ropes of his young veins strained near to the point of collapse. It was probably his duty to intervene, except that from the gleam of old knowledge in the vampire's eye, the boy was probably a tenfold safer in its arms than on the street or in the overfilled holding cell of the communal NYPD bullpen downtown.

Still, the sight of the vampire's languid slat-ribbed whore sent a shiver down the slayer's spine. He'd been outside this crowd too long. He supposed he'd begun to believe on some subconscious level the esthetic tales of cinema vampires and vampire novels, the black cloaks and garlic and coffins and casual murders. If the vampire race were that stupid and evil it would not have survived this long. Were it not for his vampire, the boy, like so many other whores in other parts of the city, would probably be leading a miserable life as a slave to vice and one human pimp after another.

The slayer moved on.

Salvatori was behind the bar tonight. Greased and pinstriped, he looked as much the part of the Sicilian good fellow as Marlon Brando ever did in his heyday. He nodded at the slayer's approach and started the workings of a Long Island Ice Tea before the slayer shook his head no. Sal's eyebrows peaked. On duty?

"Good crowd?" the slayer asked, coming abreast with the bar.

"Always. Someone new every night. Don't know where they all come from. Masochism seems to be the thing. Must be the new city legislative."

"Possibly. So who's new?"

Sal shrugged. "No new vamps, just victims. Everyone wants to be a victim." He dropped his voice to a whisper and glanced around conspiratorially. "Personally, I think they just want to feel sorry for themselves, if you know what I mean."

Sal was a monster and a murderer, but no liar. There were no new vampires here that the slayer was consciously aware of. Disciples, yes, there were always those—deviants and lowlifes and groupies behind the mask of sanctified stone and veil, mortal prostitutes who serviced their masters' needs in exchange for the rare sweet high of blood loss that could be achieved through no known conventional drug. Then there were those who believed that if they commingled with the vampires they might somehow mystically gain the rare genetic factor that permanently separated the breeds. But nothing save the young boy from earlier was suspect here. Empirius ran his hive like a militia, with strict attention to etiquette. He never allowed rogues to remain within the walls of his establishment for long. Bad for business. If it got around the East Village that he was letting the psychotic muck of vampire society into his hive, if bodies started turning up in the Hudson or under bridges, the mortals were more apt to pilgrimage to some of the safer uptown clubs to get their fixes. Something like that could ruin a reputation.

Which led to another line of thinking.

"Where's Akisha?" the slayer asked.

Sal shrugged. "With Empirius?" He was shooting seltzer into a glass, trying to avoid talk and trying unsuccessfully to be casual about it. The slayer knew Sal had no more love of police than any of his mortal associates had during Prohibition. And with Coven there was always an added aspect of danger.

"Empirius is alone," the slayer stated. "Don't fuck me around, Sal."

Sal looked up, afraid. "Probably she's upstairs, sulking over some young god of a child. You know Akisha." He moved evasively to the side to attend a newcomer.

The slayer let him go. There was no reason to detain the barkeep over what was obvious. If he knew Akisha—and he thought he did—Salvatori was probably right. Among other talk in the Village was rumor that Akisha was phasing herself out of vampire society. The once proud and arrogant Black Queen was skulking free of her admirers' attention like some aging Hollywood actress craving the dark to hide her many shames. Some said it was age; other said she had changed since Empirius's victory in slaying the mad vampire cum alchemist Carfax and taking his queen as his own. It was rumored that Akisha wept for the first time in two centuries the day Carfax was destroyed. Was it not so far-fetched then to believe that her subsequent forced bonding to Empirius might have caused her enough bitterness to want to tarnish the name of her new lover with a few heinous crimes?

Darkness flickered at the tail of the slayer's eye and here she came, the mistress of the hive, the devilless herself, like something conjured by thought alone. She looked twenty-five or thirty, dressed in a black leather motorcycle jacket, short shiny-black pageboy hair contrasting beautifully with her skin, smooth and poreless like the best Han jade. Her left nostril was pierced through with a length of narrow chain that found its glittering way to her left ear. Empirius's mate had been experimenting with the industrial look so popular these days in the club and sub-culture scene, yet even so, Akisha had managed to loose nothing of the regality of her rich old *shugo* blood. Her eyes moved analytically across the room, then snapped around to find the slayer sitting alone and conspicuous in the center of her lover's hive.

"Alek," she said, coming upon him immediately. "It has been a long time, hasn't it? Business or pleasure?" She raised one raven-black brow in blatant challenge.

And he wanted nothing more than to answer her with a gentlemanly smile and respond the latter, but the night was wearing on, the random murders in the East Village accumulating, and the Coven's business could be put off only so long.

2

The long darkly-paneled room above the club was respected by all in the hive as Akisha's private space, a place of uninterrupted retreat where the Queen of the hive could lock herself away when her thinking grew too complex for distraction or she wanted to be alone with one of her boys. According to the stories the slayer had heard, not even Empirius was welcome here. So it came as something of a surprise when Akisha invited him up.

She lit a single candle and set it on the mantle as the slayer wandered soundlessly down the chamber. No less than four paintings of Akisha lined the gallery at the far end. The oldest was an ornate Romantic nude, possibly Matisse, except the colors looked too dark. A Klimt then. Changeless eternal Akisha. In every incarnation she had the same narrow hips and small high young-girls breasts, the slender long legs and warrior's muscle tone, the same somber dark eyes and shimmering fur-like hair. The second portrait was a Weimer Berlin, by the slayer's educated guess, this one a fully clothed Akisha in SS uniform. Long hair scraped back and severe, she stared out of the portrait with damning eyes, expression grimly defiant in a 1930's world that had gone mad around her. The third was a 1960's-style psychedelic kitsch of red and purple with a mermaid Akisha superimposed over a blazing red sun presumably going supernova on her.

The final painting was done by the slayer himself, with Akisha very much like she was right now, dressed in black satin and steel, her hair an arrogantly streaming cloak at her back. Although a product of the Absolute Realism school the slayer belonged to, the picture showed Akisha as only one of her own kind would see her, eyes diamond-hard and predatory and scarcely able to hide an ages-old lust.

Without ado, or excuse, Akisha went to a low stone divan and lay down over the gracefully slumbering body of her newest interest. A college boy he looked like, someone scarcely out of his virgin skin where vampire whores were concerned. His body had not yet acquired the gaunt paleness or loss of muscle tone so evident of an old hack. Holding the young man's body like a strange, Eastern-inspired Madonna, Akisha lapped at the rivulets of blood coursing down his face from the crown of barbed wire the slayer assumed the Queen herself had affixed to his shaven head.

The slayer shifted uncomfortably, turned away and began wandering among the tomes of Akisha's vaulted library, glancing at the swirl marks of fingerprints on ancient leather spines, the French and Portuguese and Cantonese gold leaf wearing to near illegibility. He let out his breath and sucked in the cottony scents of parchment and old oil paint and blood and sex in the room. He sighed. He was suddenly weary. At the end of the room he turned around and studied the living fresco before him. "Tell me, have you and Empirius been fighting again, Akisha?"

The young man stirred in his sleep and Akisha made motherly cooing noises until he was still again. She kissed his cheek like a young girl biting into a new golden fruit. She said, "He is master, I am his wench. Really, Alek, what is there to fight about?"

The words were meant to sound unbothered, but the bitterness in Akisha's voice was unmistakable. In many ways, the slayer could not blame her for that. Vampire society was by its very nature a primitive, essentially patriarchal setup. Males guarded their harems of females jealously, with the blood-bonded females forcibly dependent on them, especially during their periods of Bloodletting, a condition that struck them annually and transformed them into creatures little better than frenzied lionesses. It made them captive inside even the lenient circles of their own kind. Feminism and independence were difficult to cultivate in a race so dependent on its second half. Were something terrible to befall Empirius, Akisha would be forced to find another master to bind her or die on her own, unbound, within a year. But she could have done worse in the slayer's opinion; she could be bound to a far crueler master than Empirius. She could still be bound to Carfax, who'd had trouble discerning the difference between friend and experimental guinea pig. So in many ways she was right in her rage, but wrong in its direction. After all, to say Empirius cherished her was to say night is dark.

The slayer shook his head. "You're being evasive, treating me like police, Akisha."

"Are you in uniform?" She smiled with smeared red lips. "I think you are. You are like the Stazi now, or the Gestapo." She sucked in a breath, filtering a world of tastes through her Jacobson's organ, laying his intentions—including the forty-two inches of oiled steel under his coat—completely bare. "Yes," she said, her eyes slipping shut. "Like Gestapo, the sword is almost drawn."

It was difficult to guess if she was talking figuratively or not. The slayer approached her, his leather greatcoat drifting ambient as wings around his ankles. Akisha lifted her attention to meet him, her eyes gleaming in the dark as if she would welcome him to her little personal orgy if she could. If she thought he would stoop to that level. So beautiful were those eyes, like black pearls. The slayer went to one knee before the divan and put the back of his hand to her white cheek. He tried to see into her but Akisha's age and power prevented his penetration. Her motorcycle jacket was unzipped and he followed the chain around her neck to the miniature sickle of obsidian dangling between her breasts. It glimmered there like a talon and he found himself all but mesmerized by it as he spoke. "Are you in your period, Akisha? Tell me."

Akisha dropped her eyes to her beautiful young victim. Like the others, a crimson swan. Yet he breathed, his life's rhythm steady and content. A look of profound insight seemed to hover at the edges of his expression. Undoubtedly he was having the deepest, most evocative dreams of his young life. Like some worshiper of the water pipe in a London opium den, a bomb could have fallen over the city and he would remain undisturbed in his mistress' playground of the mind.

"Does it seem that I am?" Akisha asked innocently.

The slayer glanced aside and said, "The city is understandably disturbed by these murders. Missing children, rumors of bodies picked clean of meat, of blood. The police are calling it Vulture Murders. You can imagine." He found himself whispering as though her victim were a young child in need of his sleep. And surely he was; how else would he endure yet another night of so dark a passion with his mistress? The thought caused a stir deep in the slayer's belly and loins that he put aside immediately as ridiculous. It was nothing but emotional shrapnel from another life. "This thing—it could have repercussions. The stories...I'm only seeking the truth."

She watched him intimately. She smiled. So near and tainted with her lover's life and her face gained such wistfulness the slayer sometimes wondered if only he ever saw in it. "And so the Coven sends forth their gallant knight-errant to slay the dragon. How old-fashioned. What about the other possibility? This *is* New York City. Human beings are still capable of deviant behavior, or has the Coven forgotten that?"

"That possibility exists," he admitted. "I'm not certain if they suspect someone or if they merely feel the need to investigate. But either way, it's become my problem."

Akisha reached for him. He closed his eyes and followed her presence as it closed in on him over the prone body of the child. It glowed darkly, her presence, like a living cloak. He shifted his weight and moved his hand down an inch. He automatically brushed the hilt of the sword under his coat.

Akisha's bitterly sweet lips hovered an inch from his throat. "You still don't trust me, do you, Alek? So long I've known you, known all your secrets and not spoken a word. But you will not trust me..."

He waited in defiance of her words. No razor-sharp instrument slashed his face or cut his lip or throat. He opened his eyes and there was just Akisha in all her cold black-and-white beauty. He shook his head and looked away. "You have the Book of Deborah on that shelf over there," he said. "One of the Apocryphal books. It was edited from the final text of the Bible in the Tenth Century by King James."

"You are changing the subject."

"No...this is the subject."

"What? Censorship?"

"Yes," he said. "No one ever has the whole story. Only fragments, rumor. But rumor is dangerous. A rumor can destroy a man. Or a species."

Akisha locked her jaw.

He touched her hair compulsively. Oriental silk—real when so much else was not. "Tell me the story. Tell me who is murdering these children. I have to know, Akisha. I can't walk away otherwise."

"Empirius," she said, closing her eyes, "does not harbor rogues."

"Perhaps he does not know this one well enough."

"Empirius knows everything about everyone."

"Then perhaps Empirius is being set up by someone wanting his downfall?"

Akisha laughed. "With Empirius gone I would be sole ruler of the vampires here until I became again bound. My period is in three months. Do you think I am doing all this terrible murder so Empirius is ruined and I am widowed and powerful for all of ninety days?"

He shook his head at her wryness and wound a lock of her hair around his finger. He sensed her cold—her sudden thrill of fear of him because he was one of the few threats she still continually faced in her unchanging, uncomplicated life. "I think you know much," he said. "You always did."

Again the innocence like a little-loved veil seemed to fall over Akisha's face. Her sudden look was feverish, almost desperate to speak. And yet she held it all in check. "I think," she said after a moment, "that you should join us tonight, unseen. I can tell you no more than that."

3

As the slayer wandered down the streets he noticed men and women walking past on either side, completely unaware of what moved in their midst.

It was late Sunday afternoon and the tourists were emerging from Broadway matinees and dinner at Mama Leone's and being safely bussed back to their suburbs in Jersey and Connecticut. There was a young mother with a little girl standing outside of the Winter Garden Theatre where it seemed *Cats* had been playing forever. The little girl, whose eyes had been turned forlornly to the wintry grey sky only a moment ago, suddenly dropped her gaze and centered it on him.

And for one spare moment he saw himself through her eyes— long black hair, thick like fur, falling around a thin white face and two black eyes, a long leather coat, the swift sensuality of a snake or monster or something just as alien. He caught himself like a vain man with the annoying habit of studying his reflection in every mirror he passed and tucked his conscious eye back into the pocket of his own flesh where it belonged.

The girl's eyes widened. What did she see? Only a tall strange man all in black? Or was it death-in-waiting? If only he could know. The girl turned to tell her mother something, but already he was gone, dissolved back into the onrushing current of society where the carpet of concrete could usher him along anonymously toward the place where all his decisions would be made in only a few hours.

4

"The day before He suffered to save us and all men, he took offering in his hands and looking up to heaven, to you, his almighty Father, he gave you thanks and praise. He broke the bread, gave it to his disciples, and said: Take this, all of you, and eat it: this is my body which will be given up for all of you. When the supper had ended, he took the cup. Again he gave you thanks and praise, gave the cup to his disciples, and said: Take this, all of you, and drink from it: for it is the blood of the new and everlasting covenant. It will be shed for you and for all so that sins may be forgiven. Do this in memory of me.

"My people, let us proclaim the mystery of faith. Our Father, we celebrate the memory of Christ, your son. We your people and ministers recall his passion, his Resurrection and his Ascension, and from the many gifts you have given us we offer to you, God of glory and life eternal, this holy and perfect sacrifice: this child of God who is now the body of Christ and the cup of eternal salvation which is His life's blood."

For a moment Empirius glanced down at the young human man bound to the blood-blackened altar at the center of his club. The look clouding the young man's eyes was one of utter acceptance and submission. Not forced worldly misery as like so many of the children who visited the club and mingled with the damned. This was not pretend. He was one of the Elect and proud to serve as such. He was one with the people. Empirius smiled on him in the smallest, most meaningful way. Then he took up the steel knife lying beside the chalice on the pall and, with that gesture, dragged the instrument across the young man's throat. Blood pumped out of the open wound, washing the dark altar stone, darkening it farther. The young man gulped compulsively as his life pulsed out of his body in thick almost-purple pulses. Empirius placed the chalice under the torrent of blood and filled it halfway to the rim with the hot crimson liquid. When the air became charged with the radiant fragrance of life eternal, an audible sigh ran through the congregation of vampires gathered for Mass

"Jesus took bread, and blessed it, and broke it, and gave it to his disciples, and said, "Take: eat, this is my body, broken for you." And with that and a surgeon's precision, Empirius sliced deep into the meat of the boy's thigh.

5

Alone in the aftermath of Mass—by now the others had returned to their warrens and city apartments—Empirius knelt down before the altar and sipped the remaining blood off the stone. The warmth entered the frozen labyrinth of his cold-blooded body like a mere whimper compared to the raw primal roar of a true feeding, a true death. No matter how many times he tried to convince himself that the mechanics of the Mass might indeed be the redemption he and his people had so long sought, he could never overcome his contempt for the difficult process, the Election, the policing of slayers and the Coven and all the things that existed to deaden the hunt to him and to his fellows. Cursed by memory and by age, he still recalled the sweet burning rage of the predatory hunt and kill, the food of victory. For all the many miseries his state of existence had cost him, the days of mankind's ignorance and the vampire's absolute freedom were ingrained in his makeup for all time. The boy had died thinking he would return as one of them, and that was well enough. It was better that the children died thinking so, less chaotic, but unfulfilling too. Even as his fingernails dug into the soiled stone and his lips sought even the smallest warmth remaining, specters of past victims surrounded him, mocking him with their ultimate victory: the great and ancient Venetian vampire lord Empirius was scrabbling at the blood of the dead like a starved creature!

He sat back quite suddenly. A door had closed at the back of the vacant club, the sound as great as a gunshot in the silent chamber. In the corner of the catwalk that circumvented the pit a figure materialized, dark on dark, too dark for even Empirius to recognize it at first. He jerked backwards a step and narrowed his eyes. "Who's there? Akisha? Salvatori?"

And then the figure stepped forward, and the darkness came off of it, and Empirius felt the laughing, mocking ghosts cluster about him to witness his doom.

6

The slayer stepped forward, a hand on the hilt of his sword in the event Empirius drew a challenge, and began the slow descent down the stairs into the pit. The slayer knew it would have been over much faster in a surprise attack—faster and far tidier—but nowhere near what he wanted. A dead vampire, no answers to his many questions. No.

"Ah...Master Alek."

The slayer sighed. "I thought perhaps it was one of your young thralls, one of their perversities," he whispered. "But you?" He tilted his head. "Empirius?"

The vampire's pose relaxed. In less than a blink of an eye he went from absolute guard to absolute openness, as if he'd come to the conclusion that there was nothing to defend, no reason to panic and work his persuasions now. He would not beg. The slayer knew that.

"How did you see?" he asked, taking a step forward in defiance of his fear. "Where were you? Not among the Mass? You couldn't have seen—"

"I saw through your eyes, Your Grace."

Empirius laughed appreciatively, wiping the blood from his face. "And I did not even feel your presence inside of me. God bless him, Amadeus must be a proud Covenmaster to have such an acolyte as you, Master Alek."

The slayer drew his sword on reaching the bottom of the pit. It all but sung in the spare light of the city filtering in through the stained blue glass of the windows. For the first time in many years, the slayer felt its streamlined weight in his wrist and elbow. Quite absently, as if to put off the task at hand, he glanced sidelong at the intricately engraved asps entwined in white jade that made the hilt of the Double Serpent Katana. There was a story that the wielder of this katana would one day be a ruthless hunter.

He said, "Why, Your Grace?" He shook his head. "Your reputation was admirable. Mortals donated their blood and bodies to your flock every night. You wanted for nothing. Why bring yourself to *this*?"

Empirius smiled as he considered his blood-soiled altar. Dressed now in his papal robes and dark purple mantle as he was he cut the figure of an ancient like few vampires could. It was his eyes; the age was less a parody in them than most. When he spoke of the Crusades, the Reformation, war, it was with a jaded wisdom not to be found in any but the oldest of souls. He said now with muted amazement, "Do you know, Master Alek, that many of my flock have grown to consume flesh with little or no problem? Even some of the elders?"

"I noticed. Why do I care? Why do *you*?"

Again Empirius laughed, this time with disgust. "When God put you together, my slayer, He was kind and brilliant, to be sure. And because of that fact, or perhaps despite it, you are an ignorant creature. You, the dhampiri, have never had to subsist on blood. How could you know the wonder of what you beheld this night?" He spread his hands as though to bestow a benediction. "The glory of it?"

The slayer stepped forward and Empirius's attention automatically snapped to the sword at the slayer's side. "What I beheld was a *felony*. What I beheld could easily raise a third Inquisition. I fail to see the religious significance of *that*."

"I am curing my people with salvation."

"There is no salvation for us," the slayer whispered. "There is only control. Don't make excuses."

"I am not. You want answers to my intentions. I am merely

giving them to you."

The slayer let out his breath; the temperature inside the club was so low it plumed like a ghost in the dark. For a moment the clockless silence seemed to echo to the very height and breadth of the building. "And," he said, "do they believe that—do they believe that your communion will save them?"

"Why do you care?" Empirius mocked him.

"I don't. I just want to know."

"Vampires believe no more in heaven or hell than mortal men. No angels or devils make themselves apparent to us, no matter what the paperback lies say," Empirius answered. "I am sorry if this disappoints you, slayer, but it is true. It is all a matter of Faith."

"And do you believe in your salvation?" the slayer whispered.

"I believe as much in my faith and my purpose as the Pope does his."

"And what does *that* mean?"

"Nothing," said Empirius. "It means nothing. You did not come here to duel in philosophies with an old man. You came here to fulfill your master's will. So let it be." Unlacing his fingers, the old vampire genuflected before his altar and placed his ear to the bloodstained surface of it. He closed his eyes, his mouth a straight line of determined surrender.

For a moment the slayer was disoriented and he wondered if Empirius was working some form of influence over him. A large part of him stood ambivalent to the whole thing, and that part wondered wistfully if there would be a happy ending after all. But a greater part knew the answer to that question. There were no happy endings, just inevitable conclusions. The Coven would not have taken notice of this situation if anything but this type of work were required. The vampires policed themselves. The Coven made it so. If justice were not meted out, the mechanics by which the vampires had come to terms with Rome and human civilization would be jeopardized.

Yet that wasn't enough this time. Jesus, Empirius was all but a celebrity in his people's minds. The slayer had to reach much farther this time—for a fault, for the desecration of a perfect human life. The young body of the sacrificed boy had been picked clean by the congregation, the blood drained like a wineskin. The slayer closed his eyes and reformed the child's face in the private slideshow of his mind, his drowning face, the belated regret stamped so cruelly on his features. And with that vision, he asked himself why he had waited until the end, what madness had held him sealed to the spot outside the club. And in response to *that* he swept forward with the dangerous catlike grace so long ingrained in his makeup and training and took a handful of Empirius's hair in his fist and jerked the sharp of the sword across the back of Empirius's neck and closed his eyes and heard nothing but blood flow and fingernails screeking on altar stone in a dying death grip, and the sound filled his head like a migraine and pained his teeth.

7

Akisha sat bolt upright in the black satin bed she shared with her bonded mate, and her involuntary shout was a wolf howl of both agony and release.

8

The letting of blood stained the walls and floor of the club like paint across an artist's loft.

The slayer went to the bar and uncorked a bottle of White Russian, pouring three-finger's worth into a glass stein. On the floor lay the body of Empirius, mangled in death and beauty. Another swan, but slaughtered, this one. It lay crumpled and fetal and awaiting the strange funerary practices of his kind—the loving evisceration and ritual consumption of the vitals and fluids, the butterflied flesh allowed to smolder in the rising day—the practices the slayer himself could scarcely remember they were so strange.

He took a quick pull off the whiskey bottle and then went to retrieve the severance where it had rolled just behind the altar. He dropped it into the gunnysack tied to his belt under his coat. The will of the master, of the Coven, be fulfilled, he thought as he heard the slam of the body that had fallen to the floorboards above his head, the rat-like scratch of fingernails seeking purchase in pain and release. Akisha would survive her freedom like she had survived her bondage. Akisha, in her cunning, had outlived nations.

Her revenge was complete.

The Coven's will fulfilled.

Taking the bottle, the slayer retreated to the door of the club, his eyes full of liquid night and a hand pressed to his mouth to stop the first cup coming back up his throat.

Chapter 1

1

A letter from His Eminence Cardinal Henri Guiseppe, Special Attendant to His Holiness and Chairman of the Vatican Historical Council to Father Joshua Benedictine, Representative of the New York Branch of the Vatican Historical Council, postdated February 11, 1962:

Brother Joshua:

It pains me to be the harbinger of news that things do not go well. It seems that for every loose thread we cut, two more appear to take its place. Last night I discovered one such loose thread is a vampire of Genevan descent by the name of Father Paris, a priest of the Order of the Sacred Heart. I do not know how he escaped our most excellent detection, but he absurdly poses as one of us, and has apparently been living under this guise since the first Inquisition.

What's more, the brothers have discovered certain documents missing from the vaults. Among them, most disturbingly, the Ninth Chronicle.

Understandably, this discovery has caused us more than a little concern. Our investigation of the theft has left us to believe Paris has a number of agents and human familiars at work at undermining our work both in Rome as well as in the States.

At this juncture, knowing that the Final Purge is

rapidly drawing near, I have decided to take drastic measures to protect our interests. Paris and his agents must be eliminated, the Chronicle returned to us immediately. Through my sources I have determined that Paris has in fact sent the Chronicle on to New York City and will be meeting with an agent of his circle by the name of Byron. I formerly ask that you set your Covenmaster to the task of rendezvousing with this vampire and his hellspawn master, since I can think of no better agent than your "white angel" to accomplish the near impossible. The VHB has issued you a line of credit for your convenience and shall hold a seat in abeyance for your most austere presence at the conclusion of this mission. As in any war, casualties are expected and expendable.

Time is of the essence. Our duty must be carried out in the name of God at any costs. I will remain here and dispatch any and all remaining agents, as well as any others who might have been made to believe the information contained within the Chronicle without the book as proof. Though there are always unforeseen difficulties, I am confident the book will be in my hands and Paris's head upon the slayers' altar within the week. Should any other complications arise, I will notify you at once.

Yours in Christ,
Henri

2

New York City, Present Day

In the end it was a typical Braxton show, big and gaudy, Manhattan fare for the socially overfed, but dull, uninspired. Passionless. Sexless. Twenty-five pieces filled the Wallace Wing of the gallery, every one of them a toothache. And the guests no better, there not to see but to be seen. What had he expected? It was no longer 1957 and in the world of painters there were no more explosions of passion. Chagall and Picasso had taken it all. Bauhaus was dead, Impressionism commercialized.

Awash in an ocean of rosy mortals he moved, sipping from a sauterne, nodding at the witty comments and praises, the theoretical center of attention. He saw crones garroted by Bette Davis boas, men in vampire suits. The diamonds hurt his eyes. He had thought of canceling the show, but, Jesus, you just didn't cancel a show with Braxton, a show you'd had scheduled for over two years, not unless you were ready to admit your life was over.

Hot in here. Someone murmured the damning word Bosch on looking into his only favorite and it was enough. It was over. He went out into the night.

Cold, but he liked it, breathed it in deeply. Snow tonight, maybe tomorrow. It would make the city look almost clean. He walked, enjoying his great escape. He let his coat fall open, undid his hair to float behind him in his wake like a veil. Better. Mmm. The air was almost sweet. Who would notice the void he'd made?

He was in sight of the East Village now. It stretched away beneath him, the last bit of purple evening clinging to the street and the sloping roofs of the shops. He heard the rush of battle rap in passing, the hydroplaning of too many expensive cars piloted by uptown hoods. Italian and Middle Eastern cooking vied for dominance over the street. He passed Oriental and Armenian green grocers closing up shops, and most looked up at him, offered him a customary Village nod or an *Evenin' Meesta' Knight* if he'd shopped recently. He nodded in return and moved on, his tall narrow reflection stalking by in the shop windows.

Crossing Madison to his studio, he glanced up the hill at Sam's Place where it teetered on the Upper Westside and was almost a cafe, thought of stopping in for a nightcap, and then moved on. Not tonight. It was that time of the month again and he needed to make a pilgrimage to the Covenhouse, unburden himself, and it wouldn't do for him to have his mind all muddied up by a Wallbanger that had no immediate intention of letting him go.

He let himself into the studio, shed his greatcoat, let it fall to the hardwood floor in a heap. Next came the black Nehru jacket and the blood-drop brooch at the throat of his shirt. Vincent greeted him in the dark with his glowing green eyes. He scooped the cat up and carried it with him to the ass-wide galley kitchen at the back of the renovated space. Vincent meowed, his one orphan ear twitching toward the fridge like a signal. He poured the cat a platter of milk, a glass for himself. Touch of Vermouth. He took one sip and sent the rest down the drain. No. Not tonight, damnit, he reminded himself. He sighed. Do it.

With the studio lights still out and only a weak filtering of phosphorescence from the sodium lights on the street to cast Vincent's shadow as big as a tiger on the wall, he stepped up to his bedroom on the undivided upper level and pulled open the closet door. He spent a moment picking at the newest bloodstain on the battered and creased greatcoat, then slid it off the hanger and shrugged into the creaking twenty-five-pound mass of leather. From the space below the floorboards he exhumed the leaden gunnysack and affixed it to his belt. He pulled forth the katana last, pausing briefly to stroke the intricacies of the pommel's engravings.

He frowned. Something wrong somewhere...

He knelt down on the floor, the sword between his knees, the tip grooving yet another hole in the naked oaken floorboards. He balanced his mind, sharpening it. The wood was warm and solid under him, the sweat cold on his brow, the silence heady and unbroken. Acrylics and turpentine and lead-kohl and the presence of those many who had lived and worked and died here clung like incense to the walls. He shrugged it all off.

He felt his mind drift and pierce the distance. He felt it *see*. He rose up and up like a spire, and then he was high above the city and floating, flying, bodiless, a thrill cold like death in his heart and throat.

It was going on a little after midnight and the lights of the Chrysler Building and its old adversary the Empire State had already been turned off, but the rest of New York City glowed like a rare collection of jewels. He saw towers corkscrewed to sword-points. He saw cabs, cars and limousines moving up and down the glittering canyons of the streets and avenues. He saw, beneath those streets, subways rolling and rumbling like a whole subterranean city. He saw clubs, restaurants, cafes and hotels open and cramped warm with life. He saw people strolling along sidewalks or staggering drunkenly or drugged. He saw fencers and hustlers and prostitutes plying their trades. A voyeur like all of his kind, he saw behind the curtained windows of a million apartments, and there he saw people staring at the gospel of their flickering television sets; he saw them read and fight and mate and despair in what they perceived as their safe and private hostels. He saw that, in the duration of a minute, someone died, someone was born, and someone else murdered. He saw and was witness to the whole of this filthy, beautiful, unkempt city throbbing with human life laid so open and naked to his special vision. But though he saw it as if with a minor god's omnipotence, he found with time that his attention was inescapably drawn to a triviality—a new snowfall gathering like sapphire on the backs of carriage horses and on the battered tarpaulin of the children's carousel in the center of Central Park.

He lingered there a moment, but only that. Addictions came in all forms. With a last long look at the almost full, dirty-red Hunter's Moon hanging low in the sky over the city, he returned to himself and opened his eyes. He was warm and calm now and all the knots were loose. He stretched, letting that stretch take him to his feet.

Slipping the katana into the lining of his coat, he moved to the web-frosted window that looked east over the clogged arteries of the city. In it was February, almost Valentine's Day. He saw so clearly tonight the filth and the evening and the cold beauty of a modern city built on ancient bedrock. The misty tops of skyscrapers jabbed like a collection of glittering weapons into the soft underbelly of a stormy night sky.

Vincent jumped to the windowsill, startling him. Silly animal. He set the cat down and slid the window open. Then he himself leapt, catlike, to the narrow ledge outside, not teetering, balancing himself expertly between the empty, frozen flowerpots. He crouched low, the snow slashing his face like swords, numb to the cold. Glancing sidelong, he saw Vincent looking out at him with curiosity.

He shook himself, breathed in the white cold and the spicy fumes of the city and the filth and the blood and the life and the death of the night. Then he, Alek Knight, artist and slayer, creator and destroyer, dropped—primly, silently—to the alley floor forty feet below his window.

3

The Covenhouse: It was a lovely grande dame of a Colonial house erected by the Plymouth Colony in 1624. A stony monolith with neat black shuttering and black scrolled trim on the porch and cornices and cupolas, Alek could easily imagine it glowing with romantic yellow candlelight to ward off the chill of the Atlantic, its warmth folded as secure as hands around the Separatists' children, huddled together in their hand-sewn cloaks as they formed an attentive horseshoe around the priest's bench. It was gilded with frost now, the house, adding to its gingerbread charms.

Alek dusted the snow off his coat and went inside. He looked around at the stone-faced walls and timber buttresses and rugged, heavy furniture. Home, he thought as he did every time. I've come home once more. He let out his breath. The rooms were artfully Spartan with a many-roomed Colonial closeness that made them cozy despite the lack of bric-a-brac. Bookshelves bore books. Mantels supported simple amber-glassed Tiffany lamps. Nothing here not worth its weight in use. On the foyer desk was the mail that still occasionally came for him here. He passed a brief eye over it as he worked open the buttons of his coat. Stupid. He had not lived under the Amadeus roof for more than twenty years, not since he was a boy and a ward of the Father's. Stupid also, he realized. After all, one of the Father's favorite idioms was that a ward of Amadeus was forever. No matter where he traveled in this world of mortals he need never stop learning, need never cease to be a disciple of ancient wisdoms far and wide.

From the drawing room came the static sounds of a TV with no volume and voices pitched low, squabbling whispers, the tapping noise of wood on wood. Company. A meeting of some sort. Running a hand through his hair to smooth it as best he could, he went to investigate the noise. To his utmost surprise he found practically the entire Coven assembled in the Father's drawing room. He stopped in the threshold. For some reason, the sight of so many slayers there, standing or sitting on the chaise lounge and sofa and matching chairs, talking, smoking, and playing dominoes or watching TV did nothing to waylay the curiously ascending feeling of dread he was experiencing all night.

Five of the seven acolytes, including himself, who comprised the New York City enclave of slayers and made their homes here in the city were present. The overall impression was of a relaxed, even casual, gathering. At least until Alek stepped through the door and encountered their hooded, fixed expressions.

There was Aristotle, the tech-obsessed young one who, when duty to the Coven wasn't calling, hid away in his home all day making things out of plastic, scrap metal and electronic circuitry. He glanced up from the game of Mahjongg he was playing alone on the desk by the door and gave Alek a look. Over on the chaise lounge, Takara, the magnificent Oriental warrior dressed in a dark, subdued suit dress like the mild-mannered magazine editor she usually was, lowered the back issue of Cosmo she was perusing. Strapping, mute Robot with his piercing black eyes noticed him next, turning fully away from the Maxfield Parrish-inspired painting over the fireplace mantel he was studying. After him came the slow, thorough scrutiny of Kansas, their resident duster-wearing cowboy, perched on a window seat and trick-chambering rounds in his vintage .45 Colts. And finally—Eustace, the Father's newest and youngest ward, seated on the floor in front of the silent TV with his history book open in front of him. *The Waltons* were on and the boy seemed more interested in the adventures of the mountain clan than in his homework. And not at all interested in the newcomer, apparently, for spare moments after Alek entered the drawing room, the boy was once more absorbed in John Boy's current dilemma.

Not so with the others. For a long moment Alek felt torn between either slipping wordlessly past them or holding his ground in the face of their collective scrutiny. He opted for the latter. He knew someone would eventually let him in on the secret, though it was never a comfortable task, waiting and facing down the others. Held together by the aims of the Coven but having little else in common, they were not a particularly close bunch of souls, nor prone to loyalty to one another, or to him. Diverse, distinct, and divided by age, race, and religion, the only thing holding them together was their tainted blood and the aims of the Coven. And the Father. Yet, over the years and decades of his indenture to the Coven, Alek had found certain responsibilities falling upon him, a few arbitrary muscles flexed now and again, as if the Father were trying to instigate him as some new axis of power in their midst. But if that was what the Father was doing, he was probably wasting his time. Slayers cared little for each other's company and even less for his own.

He never discovered the source of their communal dislike for him. Tonight though, feeling a curious doom fluttering at the edges of his awareness, he felt their revulsion in particular and found it disconcerting.

Takara, her almond eyes peering out of the flawlessly cold and smooth planes of her face, said, "You were called, whelp. Damned took you long enough to catch on, though." Alek inclined his head, feeling, as always, like a little boy under Takara's scrutiny. He wished he could say that was because she was like the grandmother he had never had, except she had never taken him as a young boy on her knee for a story or given him a jelly foldover like grandmothers were reputed to do. She did give him a broken arm once from an excellently executed pinion when he was fourteen years old, though.

"I'm sorry. I was distracted tonight."

"Dumb as shit," Takara said, going back to Cosmo. Aristotle, who studied Alek's every move with blatant jealously and worship, opened his mouth as if to pave over what Takara had uttered, then closed it dutifully, blushed, and went back to his game of tiles. He might worship Alek as his model, but Takara was like a surrogate mother to him. A cold, Kali-inspired mother, to be sure, but a mother nonetheless.

The other dhampiri did little better than she. Kansas pulled the silver-skinned Colts out of his armpit holsters in a blurring series of quick-draws. Robot went to peruse the Father's vast bookshelves. Eustace, after a moment or two of silence, turned up the volume and started to repeat the dialogue on the TV.

Alek shrugged it off. So he *was* being called, after all. His feelings were neither a premonition nor malcontent. It was simply the Father pressuring their mental link. Now he knew for certain that he would like nothing better than to escape the house. But the Father was calling him and it was time to face the music, so to speak. He turned away from the others and headed down the long sparsely lit hall that led to the butler's pantry and unlocked the basement door with the key he kept on his wallet.

Querulous frowns, unspoken whispers. He could hear them even now, or imagined he could. It never ceased to amaze him how much slayer society mimicked that of the greater vampire hives, the conceited clichés and ever-scheming circles. He knew a scarce moment after he left the room tongues had begun to wag without restraint.

Poor Eustace, he thought, breathing in the dry hallowed smells of the cellar stairwell leading down into the lower mysteries of the house. It wasn't like when he was a kid and your ward mate was your brother, your blood. Things had changed over the years. Brotherhood, family, Coven—these things seemed to mean less to the newcomers to their little enclave. Little passion remained in the heart of the average slayer; mostly the work was treated with a surgeon's careful yet ultimately impersonal attention. Eustace would probably grow up disillusioned by the whole mess and ask for a desk job before he was thirty years steeped in his craft. The thought made Alek sad. Between the two of them, himself and his chosen brother Booker, they'd been hellions even among their peers.

The flagstone steps, cut giant-wide into the New York bedrock by unrecorded Puritanical chisel and hammer, led him down into the loins of the house. And as if he were still a child, or perhaps only because he was in his child's mind at the moment, Alek counted them to their end. Forty-five. A step for every year of his life. He put out his hands on the last step and felt the warm, ancient wood under his fingers. The heavy double doors groaned cantankerously as he pressed against them. Then again, Father Amadeus always spoke of them as if they had more character than most individuals. Board planking from off the stern of the *Mayflower*, or so the stories went. He opened them with deference on the Great Abbey.

As a child looking on the wonder of it, the Great Abbey had reminded him once—and still did—of the pictures of Camelot he'd seen in storybooks, a richness of tapestries and brass and weeping mortar in flagstone. He found the high grisaille panels in the stonework ceiling almost immediately, two to each side over the narrow side chapels, and each with a gem of colored citrine stone in its scored center. He stepped inside the nave and was bathed in the hellfire of those precious skylights, the only source of light here save the pylons of lighted candles in iron sconces on the walls. The cobbled promenade rushed down and away to the center of the nave and was flanked on either side by spiraling Corinthian columns, slender stone giants that rose inexorably upward to meet the ancient bedrock dome where clans of bats regularly roosted, raised and suckled their young and flexed their silent bronze wings. Below, where he stood, the nave littered out to where the Coventable was set in the shadow of the dais.

Alek moved toward it. Smooth, seamless rosewood, un-nailed and unsanctified. In the Great Abbey there were no mosaic puns on the Bible, no Stations of the Cross crowding the walls, no odor of myrrh or palm leaves or Eucharist to be found, nothing to make an unholy jeer of their violent crusade. The only attempts at comforting the empty spaces were the various swords enshrined in the blood of their masters, and the tapestry art: those lovely, wonderful portraits enshrined in silk, a mythology of figures who had in their toils and talents entered the histories of the Coven and became a part of its eternal making. They looked down on him out of their banners as if to weigh their lives against his own, all of their faces stern, their mouths brutal slashes set under the fierce glitter of ancient eyes, eyes so like those in the portraits which still hung in many New England houses, eyes which followed you everywhere you went in the room.

How small and insignificant he felt in their presence. His sword arm was a passable thing, but hardly the stuff of legend. And his own particular psi talent was a cringe in the face of so many of the others' accomplishments. Book's laborious achievement in controlled pyrokinesis was almost an art in itself, and Takara— well, some of the things he had seen her do went without explanation, almost without description. Alek was not so colorful as all that and he doubted he would ever accomplish anything so illustrious as to win himself a tapestry out of which he might silently weigh another.

The promenade took him to the foot of the raised altar, and there he began to climb the altar stairwell, his dread momentarily blotted out by the wonder and reverence he never failed to feel here. From a distance the altar bore the illusion of a meandering honeycomb. Close up, however, it was a leviathan. He had to squint and crane his neck all the way back to take in the more than eleven thousand vampire skulls fitted abstractly together, as if with a gifted child's artistry of architecture: sunken, irregular cavities and cultured pyramids and towers. But the configuration of the Coven altars were not important, only that they exist to hold the remains of all these deviants. The golgotha's vastness and power could humble even the greatest of slayers. But New York was an old city, his Coven one of the first of the Vatican's New World Foundings, and there had been time for this grand creation.

On the little altar table he lit a votive candle, felt its small, uncertain warmth grow on his face and hands. Most slayers pilgrimaged little, preferring to harvest and amass their offerings. But he was not most slayers. The impressions the others gained from the harvests were only a vague dream, a nagging sensation they forgot within moments of the kill. He worked the skull from the sack and peeled away the residual flakes of skin and straw-dry strands of hair still clinging to it. And with it he filled a cavity between two tiny childlike skulls. Then he stepped back, scrubbing his hands on the breast of his coat. The impression this time was ugly. He saw curious things—skeletal men and women dancing, their limbs jerked by wires like some kind of marionette-torture while a mountainous landslide of blood flowed like paint in the background and covered everything in a simmering Pompeii-inspired burial. The last thought to flicker through Empirius's mind before the final darkness took him.

Alek shivered and regarded the altar instead of the image, her aged splendor. Thousands of empty eyes containing almost half a millennium of darkness stared sightlessly back at him. Innumerable lifetimes. History. He had a fantasy of himself sliding down through a pair of those eyes, of becoming the leviathan itself, and then being slain by the sword wielded by his own hand.

"Shit," he whispered, "no more Vermouth for you, old man."

He shivered once more, but helplessly this time. He'd feared the altar once, the way a child would. But then Amadeus, ever patient, had taken him before her one day. *Fear her, my acolyte? Why she is the symbol of our great Covenant with the children of men, that the horror and slaughter of our brethren during the Inquisition shall not be repeated. The altar--do you see?—is that supplication, the tower which crawls ever upward together with her sisters all over the skin of this world, working towards that final day when at last the glorious face of Peter's church will not be denied us and absolution for our many sins will be ours. She is our salvation. Are you now so afraid of her, my best child?*

He never feared her again, only what she contained. He'd never feared anything, if he wanted to be honest with himself, except the Father's disappointment. He'd read the books of the Covenant and he had taken upon himself its bitter truths and its ordinances and priestly vows of celibacy and obedience. A good student, he memorized every word of the diatribe and fought the secularism which had threatened the core of the Coven in the early seventies. Faith had been lost, and found. But some things, like ceremony, preserved. Many slayers said the New York City Coven was old-fashioned, its Covenmaster too static to push his acolytes through the tribulations of the new millennium—and yet their enclave was more successful statistically than all of the other Covens put together. So perhaps there was something to be said for being old-fashioned.

He genuflected and sent up a short prayer for Empirius's soul, then turned and descended the steps to the nave. And there he stopped.

Father Amadeus sat in the shadows at the head of the Coventable, his hands pinnacled under his chin, his eyes cast downward upon an ancient jade chessboard crowded with tiny figures shaped in silver or bronze as animals. Horses for knights and mice for pawns. The kings and queens were cats with sparkling green eyes. They'd played chess in the past, he and the Father, yet never with this antiquated set. For a moment the little board intrigued Alek, frightened him, and stopped his concentration.

The Father looked up as Alek approached. His appearance was that of a man of thirty-three, the age at which he had ceased to age, the same as Alek. Yet his face and hands and his flood of wintry hair was bleached to the whiteness of bone and his unevolved skin contrasted like marble against the blackness of his habit, so much so that most of him seemed suspended in the dark, ephemeral, unnatural. And old. He lifted his pale lapis blue eyes and Alek felt the mental tug binding his thoughts to something far vaster, far older than his own mind.

These are bad times, Amadeus said.

Alek frowned. Yes, there was something wrong, terribly, horribly wrong. This silence, the chessboard with its unfamiliar army—

"Peace," said Amadeus. His silk habit shivered as he rose from his seat. Standing now as he was, no creature could help but be awed by the Covenmaster's presence, his erect, aristocratic form rising like a statue of stone and obsidian from the floor, immovable, fearful in its Giovanni-touched beauty. Alek frowned, his mind engaged in memory and loss so deep and profound he found he had to cast about for a suitable reason. Finding none, he finally fixed on the disappointment of the Braxton show earlier that evening.

The Covenmaster moved toward him with hypnotic grace and touched the back of his long claw-like fingers to Alek's cheek, dispelling those thoughts. The feeling was ash, a freezing burn that emanated like an aura of light from the tips of Amadeus's fingers. Alek found it impossible to turn away, frozen as he was in the glare of those silvery eyes, the glitter of such bone-hard fingernails on his flesh. Amadeus smiled knowingly and Alek felt the blood rush to his face, his heart pounding in his ears with a rhythm that he realized after a moment was mimicking that of his master's.

"Beautiful," the Covenmaster said as his misshapen talons whisked across Alek's cheek. Then he dropped his hand. Alek looked away, mortified by the simple word. His master went to the edge of the nave and began lowering the rutted wagon wheel chandelier on its rusted orange chain. It fell in painfully rusted increments until it hung like a wreath before the altar. Alek had long wondered where that wagon wheel had roamed, what lands it might have covered before it had come to reside here. How had it come to be here, of all places?

"Questions. Always questions," Amadeus answered his thoughts. He produced a tinder wand and rasped it against a bedrock wall. "Like Socrates, Alek, the gadfly, the flea in the ear of the magistrates. It is both your blessing and your curse. To thirst for knowledge is like to open oneself up for the addiction of blood." It wasn't quite a reprimand; the Father's voice was too amused for that. He lit the candles in the rusted arms of the wheel, turning the wheel as he worked. Those hands—they were like birds in a ritualistic dance, and Alek found it nearly impossible to believe that this man, Amadeus, the teacher to so many slayers, had never seen a day in his whole long life.

"Something's wrong," Alek said. "Something *is* wrong. You've summoned me. Why?"

"The others—they have told you this?"

"Yes, but—"

"You knew before that. You always know, nein?" Amadeus's wand guttered to white smoke. He dropped it to the Coventable. He swayed like a white medusa toward Alek, stopping only when they were eye to eye, their shoulders nearly touching. Alek hesitated. Some great sorrow clung to the man like a rank aura.

What must they look like? Two versions of the same man but that one mirrored the other negatively. And that other younger and darker and less perfect one? His thoughts were enfeebled by a nameless terror clinging to his mind like the bats to the walls of this abbey. Here they were, two men who were so alike and yet so unforgivably separated for the moment. Alek reached, imperfect mind and imperfect soul, for the cloister he knew so intimately and found only a somber place unpeopled by memories. For a moment he panicked in his isolation. Never had it been like this between them, never—

"Father?" Alek ventured. "What's wrong?"

"You were always my best disciple."

The thought made Alek want to collapse, vomiting. He wanted

to ask more questions, demand answers and reassurances, but he felt Amadeus's hands again on his face, seeing it more completely now, melting to the flesh and form so that they were like two marble statues seeking reconnection. Those long skillful hands moved slowly over his cheekbones and down into the hollowed valleys of his cheeks, fluttered over his lids and eyelashes so gently he did not blink or turn away. "Alek. My Alek," Amadeus said. "My beautiful eternal one. My magnum opus."

Normally he loved to hear his name on Amadeus's tongue, the harsh tenderness of it, the way the Father's old-world accent accentuated the last syllable and carried it down into a click. But not like this. Not with weariness. Not with regret. He did not want to be called a magnum opus as if...

Alek closed his eyes as Amadeus's mind brushed lightly, deftly, against his own. This was old magic. As a child he'd lain across the Father's lap after their daily sparring matches, and with his brow slicked with diamond sweat, Amadeus had touched him like this, seeming to worship his face and the sharpness that had come into it too quickly in his youth. Alek had felt the Covenmaster's mind then, those terrible first needling which had ached hours afterward, making his mind a swollen cavity filled with the things of Amadeus. But after so many years they were old links now, moving inside each other with all the deftness of ancient lovers.

I speak to you now of secrets.

Father?

Of dark things. Dark times. We must prepare. I shall not be with you much longer, my most beloved.

Alek's heart fluttered against his ribs like a frantic bird battering itself senseless against the bars of its cage. For a desperate moment he tried to break the link, to turn away his mind so the Covenmaster would not see his sorrow, but inside this strange private world there were no doors so easy to find. He was trapped, ashamed.

Peace. I have had a vision...

But Alek's mind broke down into a helpless confusion and he felt Amadeus withdraw in response, unable to settle amidst the fear. Alek blinked against his stinging eyes, pulled away physically and mentally from his master's touch. "I don't understand. What's going on? What are you saying?"

Amadeus shrugged, the gesture horrid, accepting. "You can do nothing to stop this now. I have seen the things to come and they will not be thwarted. The curse of the Seer. It was said in the old world that the Cyclopes of ancient Greece traded one of their eyes to see the future, but the gods cheated them and all they saw were the time of their own deaths—"

"Goddamnit, don't tell me stories!" Alek said, leaning against the table. "Just tell me what you saw!"

The Father's dead white eyes floated to a point just beyond Alek, as if he was seeing a vision being played out on the pale body of the altar. "I saw as always I do in visions: I walked in a familiar place I did not know the name of. I saw—light and shadows and animals running and music and heat and blackened crimson. And I saw a figure in black, his eyes wild with the bloodlust. And then a midnight sun rose upon my eyes, deadly in its brilliance, and I did not know another day. I knew only the darkness that is alien to us all."

Alek shook his head. Amadeus spoke of death. "I...I don't understand."

"Nor do I. But when has that mattered to prophecy?" And with that he simply returned to the table and his seat and his game. Just like that. Fertig. The end.

But no. This was stupid. They were immortal, or nearly so. They were the dhampiri, the refuse thrown from a tryst between a vampire and a human female. They watched from the accursed circle of their kind as the earth devoured the sons and daughters of man all around them. Friends, family—time took them all and left behind only cavities, while they went on and on without respite into the uncertain tunnel of the future. And Father Amadeus, who had fought perhaps longer than any of them, would be there among them, for them. Amadeus was always there. He had to be. If he were not, Alek and the rest of the dhampiri would probably all go mad without his direction.

Amadeus's hand rested atop a little silver horse. "If only that were so, my beloved. If only I could be at one with my brethren forever. But the map of my life has been marked. I have been selected to pursue the greatest mystery of all."

Alek wanted to scream at the bullshit of all this metaphysical hocus-pocus and noble double-talk. Death was death. And death without absolution was damnation. The Father was wrong. Wrong. Because if Amadeus was to die, it meant that his head was going to be taken. And nothing had the power to take him unaware, no human, no vampire—

But a Judas?

Amadeus glanced up as if hearing the thought.

Alek felt an urge to go over to him. Instead he went to the other side of the board and looked more closely at the little animals. His mind was numb.

"Perhaps," said Amadeus, moving the horse forward, "Someone among us this day may be a Judas." He shook his head. "Strange, but the face is not known to me. There is a curious force afoot, Alek. It hides it from me. My path is chosen, that is all I can say."

Alek shuddered. Was he a fool to feel this? He was no longer a child, he did not want to fear like one, and yet he was afraid. As afraid as an orphan child. How old they were, he thought, and yet how young they remained.

"We have a young one to welcome tomorrow," Amadeus whispered. "A promising kinetic. Intriguing. His name is Sean Stone and I want you with him. Watch him. Your eyes will be mine. I have informed him that he will be apprenticed to you." Amadeus looked up. "For the experience."

Alek toyed with the hilt of his sword, running his fingers up and down the engravings. "Is he some kind of agent?" He thought about it. A new recruit—some sniper from one of the more liberal hives. It made sense. Let this Sean Stone walk into the trap of his own free will. One false step and he would be prey. If he raked a hand over the altar, Alek could find the heated presence of over a dozen assassins executed in the last twenty-some-odd years by his hand. And now perhaps it was this one's turn to join the altar he was supposedly helping to build.

"I must know for certain," Amadeus explained, abandoning the game a second time, this time to sit back and nod solemnly. "We are, after all, something of a dying breed, are we not?"

Alek nodded obediently.

"Now, I must know: will you do this for me, mein Sohn?"

"You know I will."

"Very good." With the slightest ghost of a smile, Amadeus stood and put his thumb under Alek's chin, urged his face up to the level of his blind gaze. He smile grew both in sorrow and wonder. "Now, no more ruminations on grief, child. I must know if you are prepared to take my place in the event that you are needed. I have to know you will be strong for me."

The spit dried in Alek's mouth and for a moment he could do nothing but stare numbly at his master's narrow, questing gaze. Covenmaster. He shook his head slowly as feelings—mostly utter raw, bone-vibrating terror—began to filter back into the byways of his body. "Father," he stuttered, "Father, you—you said this was many years off, if at all, you said—

"We don't have many years anymore, Alek. Are you ready?"

"I—I don't know, this—it's so sudden."

"You know."

"I would try, Father, you know that, but—"

"You must. Close your eyes. Come into the dark with me. Into our secret place."

What he was asking now, not just duty but communion, the sharing of souls, was so much like lovemaking, yet so alien to it too, so much more than it. All of it was so overwhelming. So much so, that instead of falling into the old rhythms they had laid down decades earlier, Alek simply stood there, stunned and swaying, hanging in a place where there was no will, no decisions, no *self*...

And in that place the Father came to him quietly, his hands falling like ashes upon his acolyte's shoulders. Amadeus pulled him close, so close they breathed nearly as one and whispered the words of the communion. "Blessed are they who come to my table and partake of my supper. Blessed be... "

No, the Father's vision was wrong. Everything was so fucking *wrong.* He was here to leave his offering and play a friendly game of chess with his teacher, not learn of his demise, not be told he was next in line for this horrendous responsibility. Covenmaster. When had the world gone so horribly wrong?

But then Amadeus smiled as sadly as an angel and held him for he was quite incapable of standing on his own and stroked his acolyte's cheek, murmuring the soft terms of endearment that had so comforted Alek as a child. Amadeus kissed him as though to savor him, long and lingering, drinking his acolyte in with his mouth, taking the salt from his cheeks, the fear from his words, offering only the breath of comfort on his face, his throat.

At the little place behind his ear Alek felt the tips of a delicate set of teeth graze his skin. He shuddered, thinking of how a big cat breaks the neck of its prey, yet his shudder of expectation did nothing to slake the Father's desire, nor did he want it to. It had been so long. Alek closed his eyes and held on and remembered how awkward he'd felt when Amadeus had first offered him this thing. Twelve, he'd just turned twelve, yes, and it had been the first time in their daily sparring bouts that he had met every deft move of Amadeus's sword with his own. They had come together corps a corps that day, in utter symmetric perfection, true warriors, both of them. And Amadeus, himself breathless, cheeks ruddy with the raw blood of exaltation, declared Alek ripe for that privilege the Covenmaster offered only his most beloved and devout student.

And with those words he'd urged his best student to lie back helplessly on the Coventable. Alek had complied at once. Why shouldn't he? What had he to fear from the man who had saved his soul? The man he loved, the man he desired more than anything real or imagined that the world could offer him? And then came the touch of the master's mouth taking him, the delicate prick of a kiss under his chin. He remembered sweating in sudden panic, wary of those teeth and this passion and fearful that their relationship would change somehow and Amadeus would not seem the same to him afterward.

And yet once more the Father had shown patience with him, his touch deft and kind and passionate and fatherly. He'd been so foolish in his dread, Alek supposed, to fear a little innocent communion, the mingling of blood, and with it, minds. But the scars of his childhood had still been raw, in some places, still bleeding. Their relationship had changed after that, yes, had gone fathoms deeper, become a separate entity almost as if they had breathed a living soul into it.

Amadeus held him down against the table, kissed the familiar mark in the hollow of Alek's throat, rasped it open with his sharp catlike tongue. Alek caught his breath and shivered, felt the Father's hand drift over his hammering heart as if he would catch and calm it. "My beloved," Amadeus sighed, his tongue like cut glass against the wound. "More than anything ever before, more than anything will ever again be mine. My blood. My soul. My beloved." And now those teeth, primitive and long and deadly as sin, were in his acolyte's vein, and with every throb of Alek's rapidly beating heart, he could feel his master drinking, drawing nourishment from this chalice he knew so well, drawing life itself, and he found quite unexpectedly that he did not care that it might be killing him. At that moment life seemed like nothing but a barrier standing between himself and the ultimate knowledge.

He reached out blindly and sent a cotillion of little animals scattering across the Abbey floor. He clasped something enormous and sweet and suffocating above him and held to it with both hands. His eyes were half-masted, running over, seeing the light of the candlelit wheel grow brighter with each passing, beating, bloodred moment, the supernova of heat branding his face like the tearfully white fury of the noontime sun.

Amadeus. He must hold to Amadeus for whatever time they had now. He groaned inwardly. He wanted to die for Amadeus. He wanted to mourn for all they had, all they would never have, the lessons, the tomes of wisdoms, the words spoken inside their minds and out. On the midnight of his fourteenth birthday Amadeus had taken him to his first opera and made him sit still until it was over and he was in love with the Bohemian forever. Then afterward, they'd gone to the country and found and bled a rabbit in an act of passion that Alek had thought never to share with his master. *We are all of two minds*, said the Father that night with absolute wisdom. Remember your lessons; they are the clay of your soul.

We are all of two minds.

Two minds...

Amadeus drew back, his tongue skating his bloodstained teeth as if to savor this gift. But it only made Alek feel sad and small. Of all the wards in the world that Amadeus had raised up in the Coven, the men and women, the eternal beings with their eyes full of holy fire, why him? Why was he special?

You were always in my dreams. I loved you before the founding of the Earth. I shall love you always.

"Always..." Alek echoed and watched in awe as the Father skated one long glasslike fingernail over his own unscathed whiteness of throat, an invitation and a summoning. *Take this and drink. For it is the blood of the new and everlasting covenant. Do this in memory of me, my love.*

He dwelled in darkness as he rose up and kissed his master in sadness and reverence, even as those kisses deepened into blood and ceremony. He cleaved to darkness, a blind man, because in the dark he and Amadeus could be the same.

4

From the very beginning of time her kind had had its rules, its holy commandments of conduct both with mortals and within the circle of its own kind. Perhaps once, in a time before recorded history, vampires had lived by their own simple codes of ultimate freedom which might have been summed up in the phrases Do what thou wilt and Judge not lest ye be judged yourselves, but if so, it was a time long since passed. Her kind—When had it come so close to the surface of human existence?—had traded in such basic primal rights of predatory survival for the comforts of human companionship. Human responsibility.

But she had no such responsibility, except where she chose it. She was of pure breeding and it showed in the unique doll-like pallor of her face and hands. Her eyes burned under the fiercest of manmade lights. Her skin singed at the touch of iron. But most importantly, her Glamour was powerful. She could be whatever her client wished. She could control his reality to some extend. She only wished she could control the hunger in all its trembling, nail-biting fury.

"The fee," said the middle-aged communications marketer down from Boston on business this weekend. He had claimed earlier at the Fox and Glass on Broadway that their latest venture was a combination of classical and avant-garde music his firm was hoping would catch on with the post-MTV crowd. Whether or not that was true was not her concern, though she let him talk. Whether or not he spoke the truth about himself was even less her concern.

"Let's not talk about that now," she muttered, her voice groggy with hunger. She could barely get out the words. It had been so long. She'd held back, been a good girl for so many nights, too many nights. And it was, after all, almost the middle of February, the anniversary of the greatest death in her long life, and she celebrated it yearly with all the religious fervor of a pagan priestess on an equinox. "This is your night," she told him. "Your fantasy." She unzipped her motorcycle jacket. "Anything you want."

He told her his desire. His mortal blood was thundering through his veins. She could hear it from across the vast Marriott hotel room like a crest of water tumbling off a cliff, seething and boiling among the stones. What he wanted was not so unusual. Yet he spoke of it hesitantly. Most of the clients she'd met felt that since they'd paid their money they owned her for the evening, that they were entitled to do whatever they liked. And they did. Or tried to. They just didn't understand what kind of asking price their requests come with. This man was different only in that he was an obvious novice. For him this would be his initiation into a life he had only ever dared dream about until now. Not since...since the time...she frowned...since the time his mother caught him with those skin rags under his mattress and beat him to within an inch of his life. Her frown leveled out to an impersonal smile as they went to bed. She slipped the links of chain off the catches on her jacket and bound him tight as a collared dog to the bed frame as she whispered innocuous little obscenities into his ear. By now his heart was triphammering at every pulse point in his firm if aging flesh and making sheens of sweat stand out like silk on his face and brow. If he was only a few years older she might fear he would suffer a coronary at any moment.

She licked his brow and lips and chin.

He slid his hands under the jacket and pinched her nipples. "I have protection," he murmured thickly, some final attempt at good sense before he plunged over the rift and into this new and exciting nightlife.

She smiled. "I trust you."

"It's for me."

She kissed his dry, chapped lips. She could feel his heart throbbing in her mouth, as if it had somehow been relocated there. She bit his lip until it bled and she could taste his wasted life on her tongue. "Don't worry," she said. "I have nothing you can catch."

He was oblivious. He reached for her, trying to slide his hands over her nakedness under the leather jacket, then his kisses. But she had lied. Tonight was not what he wanted. Tonight was what she needed. The death she celebrated.

She pulled away abruptly and heard his gasp, felt his body shudder as it reached instinctively for the soul drawing away from him. He looked disappointed by his failed fantasy. But for her there was no physical or spiritual pleasure in the act of sex with a mortal, nothing but the unique sensation of life alive and throbbing and so near and open to her insatiable hunger that she had to swallow it whole and make it a part of her or go mad from the want of it.

She moved slowly, tantalizingly, up his body, leaving the prints of her lips on his belly, his chest, his throat. Beneath her he lay as still as a corpse. She could tell he was trying to control himself, trying to be a good lover. Undoubtedly he had used the same technique for years as he waited patiently for his wife to reach some semblance of satisfaction. Tonight, however, all that wasn't necessary. There was no need to wait. She was ready for him, ready. She dropped painful little kisses over his naked flesh until there was no more resistance left in him, until he cried out, his body writhing beneath her, suddenly brought back to life. It was then and only then that she grasped his chin in her hand, turned his head sharply to the left, separating the most fragile of tiny bones and the long vital spinal cord, effectively rendering him paralyzed from the neck down, and gave him a razor blade vampire kiss.

"Paris," she whispered thickly through the flow of his crimson warmth.

5

The following day, Booker Jefferson arrived just before noon for their ritualistic midweek lunch date. Alek stood up from his easel at the sound of the well-tempered engine revving under his window and stretched, felt his spine crackle in a dozen little places. Just as well Book was here early; these primaries were going nowhere but in the circular file.

Alek grimaced at the forcefully erotic scratchy image of a nude holding forth an iron apple while tendrils—possibly electrical cables, he hadn't decided yet—trailed out and upward into a vast toothy skybound machine. Braxton would probably shake his head when he saw it, tell him how hackneyed it looked, and then he'd do his little J. Jonah Jameson-style fit and dance and pull Alek's

University Grant off the ticket. And then his career would be over and it would be back to bussing tables and tending bars in Lower Eastside dives for one, Mr. Alek Knight.

He shrugged. Too bad. Without a second thought, he stripped off his wire-frames and pinched the bridge of his nose until the headache that had been forming behind his eyes for the past two hours passed. He got up, reached for the black wool topcoat draped across the living room futon, and headed downstairs. Book waited, his Jag purring like a mechanical panther. Alek dropped into the passenger side and slammed the door hard enough to rattle the driver's side window.

"Do that again, will ya? I think you missed an axle or two."

"Sorry."

Book shook his head. Alek looked him over. Book was the most infuriating man in the entire world, pressed to the nines, alert, ready to make a clod of Einstein with his next miracle of science. Or otherwise out-charming all those ladies in those tight-ass Andy Warhol-inspired uptown cafes he frequented. He looked forever elegant, even in jeans. Alek despised him bitterly. He wore his denims and a tan London Fog this hazy afternoon, an aviator scarf swirled carelessly about his neck and camel-leather driving gloves on his tapered, long-fingered hands. The smell of hospital oils mingled with his spicy cologne.

He smiled apologetically and tugged at his pert little slayer's ponytail. "I've been in surgery since six this morning."

"Poor baby."

Book laughed. "The Panda?"

"Of course."

"You look like shit."

"Why thank you, Doctor. Is that your professional opinion?"

With a dandy grin, Book put the car in gear and arrowed straight into Fifth Avenue traffic. Alek had known the man since they were eight years old, growing up together in the Covenhouse, and he knew for a fact that Book's one weakness was a fast car. He had never endangered their lives, but he always made Alek feel as if they were finalist in the Indy 500. Book steered with his left wrist resting on the wheel, his right hand balanced on the eight ball gearshift. His mulatto-tanned profile was marred by four streaks of flesh several shades lighter than the rest of his face.

"Your cat?" Alek asked.

"That's what I'm telling everybody."

"What happened?"

"Bastard took me from behind." He reached up and pulled his scarf and turtleneck down. Alek spotted the throb of Book's pulse beneath the half-healed bite mark. It was going to leave quite a scar.

"Ouch."

"That's what *I* said." Book said. "Shoulda been there to hear what *he* said when I paid the fucker back for it."

Scars were a strange thing for his kind, since they faded away everywhere on their bodies but their necks, as if to serve as a reminder that they could lose their lives as easily as their quarry. The oldest of their kind bore veritable colonies of bite and slash marks and postured them during Coven Circles like status symbols or badges of honor. Alek scratched absently at the mark in the hollow of his throat. Most of his own scars were deliberate, not accidents at all. Kisses from Debra, though Amadeus had done his best to conceal them.

"Maybe I'll finally get to show up those snobby elders next time the Father holds Circle, hey?" Book said.

"Oh good, then you'll really have a scar."

Book laughed, tightened the scarf. Then he got serious. "Anyway, what's going on? I drop into the Covenhouse this morning to catch the buzz I missed last night—I mean, Perlman played Carnegie last night and how many times in a lifetime do you get to see *that?*—and there's Robot, y'know, just being spooky, and I tries to be friendly and he just about rips me a new asshole. And I was like what the fuck...?"

"Politics. I'll tell you about it after I get something in my stomach."

Book grunted and spun the car onto Hudson Street and slid into a parking slot moments ahead of a silver Ferrari. Alek swallowed down his heart and got out.

Cinnamon and soy weighed the air like incense as they walked shoulder to shoulder along the narrow sidewalk. Book's stomach growled. There were many Chinese restaurants in the Village, all of them good. But the Panda Bear Paradise was a favorite because the chefs worked in a large open window where the patrons could watch them perform their alchemy. The waitresses too were a sight, all of them outfitted in long black hair and red kimonos like lovely fallen angels. Intriguing. A Cantonese ballad tinkled overhead, and the warm scent of Hunan spices and steamed bamboo mingled with the hot cooking sake coming from the kitchen.

"Lawdy, am I hungry," Book complained.

"You're always hungry, brother."

"Hey, cut me some slack, brother. Some of us have *real* jobs, you know."

Alek gave him a friendly elbow.

A slender Oriental hostess grabbed two menus and held them to her chest. "Usual spot, Book?"

"Please."

She led them down a short flight of stairs and seated them beside a small gurgling fountain filled with pennies. The water and the soft flutey music made some of the tension leave Alek's shoulders. The hostess handed them menus and quickly left. A moment later a busboy set water glasses each with a slice of lime in front of them.

Alek set the menu aside without looking at it. Book glanced at his and then set it on top of Alek's. The owner waited on them herself. Book ordered Burmese ginger beef and a Diet Coke. Alek asked for only a glass of sake, but Book added an order of Kong pao chicken to it. Alek thought to protest, then changed his mind.

"Not hungry, brother?" Book said as they were brought a basket of wantons. He took one and dipped it in the tangy sweet-and-sour sauce before taking a big bite.

Alek shrugged.

"You never eat." Book finished off the wanton and reached for another. "Your poor, weak stomach."

Alek unfolded his linen napkin, smoothed it over his lap. "You make up for me."

"Don't worry: I will."

The waitress returned with their drinks. Alek sipped his sake, enjoying the bitter scorch it brought to the back of his throat. He placed his hands in his lap.

Book polished off another wanton. "Something's up."

"Just tired. I didn't get much sleep last night."

"You look like you went ten rounds with Harvey Wallbanger."

Alek ran a hand through his uncombed, unbound hair. It felt like fizzled, exposed electrical wires. He remembered waking up this morning with a hellacious headache, hangover or misery he wasn't exactly sure which. As it turned out, he'd slept the night in his clothes sprawled across his loft bed in the studio, which proved that at least he had made it home. But past that it was anyone's guess what had happened or how he'd gotten there. Feeling effectively like shit, he sipped the hair of the dog. He grimaced; it only made the four Tylenol he'd dry-chewed earlier come alive in his mouth.

Book gave him a puritanical look.

Alek glared back at him. "It's not like I have a problem. Okay?"

Book raised his hands as if to fend off an affront. "Hey, okay, just being your doctor."

"Well don't."

"Shit, man, everyone's strung tight as a goddamn bow these days. What the hell happened last night?"

For a brief moment Alek considered telling Book everything: the gathering, the words the Father had spoken, the prophecy, and the sheer absolute unrelenting terror he felt at the thought of leading the Coven. He and Book had had no secrets as children, had spent hours beneath their bedcovers together, whispering over comics, tuning in the radio to the Sox, gossiping, giggling innocently over dirty jokes they'd found scribbled on washroom walls. But he and Book had not been children in a long time, and if Amadeus chose that the Coven should know the truth, he would hold a Circle for that purpose. Really, it wasn't Alek's decision to make.

He finally recalled now, somewhat hazily but with a fair amount of conviction, that after their communion the evening before, the Father had broken down the gathering and sent the others home with an announcement of reconvention in twenty-four hours to welcome the initiate, this Sean Stone fellow. "Someone new coming in and we're the official welcome wagon, you know the routine."

Book frowned like he wasn't at all convinced that was the main reason for the gathering but said nothing more about it.

Alek sipped his sake and tried not to shrug guiltily in response. He could spill his guts, he supposed. Hell, it might even make him feel better, but he didn't enjoy watching the pity burning there in Book's black eyes, as if he were thinking his brother was some poor white-bread Brooklyn-bred lush who couldn't get his goddamn life together. So let him find out on his own. Lushes were known to be unreliable, weren't they?

The waitress brought their food, setting two enormous platters down in front of them, then left as quickly as she had arrived. Book put steamed rice all over his plate and spooned the entrees on top of it. He waited until the waitress was out of earshot before he spoke.

"I got Eustace."

Alek took the rice from him. "He's a good kid. A little slow, but he has dedication." He served himself some chicken and a little beef. "From the Midwest, right? A runaway?"

Book nodded between mouthfuls. "Mother's dead. His daddy was a shotgun preacher. You know how that goes."

Alek felt cold; the food stung his mouth. The pattern again. The dhampiri were not destined for happiness. It was a fact Alek had come to understand a long time ago. They fell from one kind of death to another—death of spirit, death of reason. Some, like he and Book, found the Coven and were thus saved from themselves. Others were lost forever. Like Debra.

Alek said, "The Father gave me this Sean Stone character."

Book choked, coughed, wiped his mouth with his napkin. "Jeezus, no wonder you're sulking. You have my condolences, brother."

Alek arched an eyebrow. "That bad?"

"This is strictly hearsay," Book said, pointing his fork, "but I heard he drew a six-inch switchblade smile on some dumb punk in a downtown bar." Book leaned forward, dropped his voice to a conspiratorial hush. "Then, believe it or not, brother, he *drank the kid's fucking blood.*"

Alek had to all but sew his jaw back into place. "You're shitting me?"

Book smiled, wagged his head No shit.

"So he's a bad seed."

"Bad seed? Way it's being told among the brothers, he's the whole fuckin' crop."

Alek was silent and busy pushing his food into artful patterns on his plate while he tried to take hold of all this new information. Who was this Stone character, then? A sniper from one of the Coven-decimated hives? He tried to imagine this whelp imbued with God alone knew what kind of power creeping around their Covenhouse. Either the Coven as a whole had gone mad to let in this crazy, or someone was serious about marking Amadeus. He supposed he could appeal to the elders, maybe even Rome herself, but that would take weeks. And what good would it do, ultimately? Circumstantial evidence was just that. Unpat. Even a Covenmaster could not halt the flux and flow of the Coven over a vision of paranoia, no matter the power of the Seer. Such was the nature of politics—and religion, unfortunately—to push even the supernatural to the back burner in the name of social evolution. Alek had heard that the Vatican had begun disavowing its exorcists in the very same manner. What would come next? An extraterrestrial origin for vampirism? Or maybe the disease theory again?

Book rubbed his hands on his jeans and took a long sip of his

Coke. "So, when are you and Mr. Pleasantries getting together?" Book's voice broke his train of aimlessly wandering thoughts and brought him back to earth. "Tonight, I suppose." Alek picked at a fragment of chicken. It was almost too spicy, like medicine. He reached for his sake, finished it. He pushed his mostly full plate away. The spices were turning in his stomach. "You?"

Book nodded, grabbed the ginger beef platter and refilled his plate. "Though I'm sure we'll probably spend the whole night at Dairy Queen talking history of Catholicism over shakes. You know how whelps are the first time out."

"I remember."

"Robot and me spent the whole night at a marquee on Delancey Street watching a triple feature John Ford fest. They say you never forget your first time out. Or your first kill. You remember your first time?"

Alek shivered. Darkness and the odor of blood and metal commingled on his tongue. Communion was done in blood song and wafers were made of steel. So hot in here, the air prickling his skin. Suddenly he wanted the cold and the open city. He needed to see the winter sky.

"Alek?"

"What?"

"You remem—"

"That was a long time ago, Book. A lifetime ago. I really don't want to talk about this anymore."

Book looked hurt.

"Look, I'm sorry if I seem sulky; I'm not being good company, I know. But I really don't want to talk about this anymore right now."

Book brightened. "All right, we'll talk about something else. I have an extra ticket for *La Boheme* next Saturday at the Lincoln Center if you want. You know how I hate seeing the ending all alone..." He paused, the last of his rice on his fork. "Go home, brother. You're not yourself."

"Good advice, Doctor." Alek stood and reached for his coat.

Book finished the last mouthful and pushed back his chair. "Drive you?"

"That's okay," Alek said, dropping a Washington onto the table. "I need a walk."

"Well, man," said Book, forever the klass klown, even now, "while you're out get yourself a Damocles cross and a whole lotta garlic if you're gonna be hanging with that dude tonight."

Alek shook his head and couldn't help but smile.

6

The carousel: it was garbed in its wrinkled and weatherworn tarpaulin skin, its shiny-worn animals stuck in time like worshipers around a dead high altar. Alek studied it from a bench, letting the cold bite through his coat with its fierce little terrier teeth.

A carriage horse clip-clopped down the asphalt trail winding through the park, passing darker avenues in the trees that undoubtedly concealed any number of dangers. The lovers in the carriage were silent and busy, as if their passion had magically pushed back the darkness and the ghosts haunting the garbage-strewn paths. The carriage approached, then rumbled away into the distant roar of the city.

Above, Alek could make out a few of the brighter stars through the haze of light and air pollution that constantly blanketed the city in an unhealthy golden brown atmosphere. Sirius. The jackal that called the Nile to crest. He watched the star grow brighter like a lighted hole punched through black paper. He rose only when the reddened sun touched the tops of the cityscape. Nightfall. The coming dark meant the junkheads and staggering homeless and all the monsters would emerge soon.

He shrugged, coughed, his throat as raw as sandpaper. His muscles felt shortened and his stomach ached hollowly. Maybe, he reflected, if he'd tried to exist on something other than his usual cataclysm of caffeine, booze and aspirin he'd be better suited to tonight. Right now, though, the thought of food turned his stomach inside out.

Tonight.

He and the new one would not spend tonight at Dairy Queen. He knew that. It would be a disaster. He knew that too. He felt it murmured in his bones. He sighed. For Amadeus. He would endure for Amadeus. Like the Christ that had presently forsaken his race, he would suffer for love.

But first he needed a drink before this hell night began. He picked himself up, shook the new snow from himself, and headed uptown toward Sam's Place.

7

"Bout time, man," called a bored Bronx voice when Alek stepped into the studio sometime after midnight, Vincent shooting between his legs like a beast afire. The voice came from a street-smeared blonde figure draped all over his futon and reading his latest issue of *The New Yorker*, a hand trailing on the floor.

Alek slammed the alley side door and eyed this pretentious stranger stupid enough to break into a slayer's apartment. Were he among the more impulsive of his kind, the hood would be eviscerated and sitting on the floor in a puddle of his own gore right now. Lucky for the stranger, Alek preferred explanations first. He checked the door's many locks, but none of them looked jimmied or otherwise tampered with. He returned his narrow-eyed attention to the stranger. "Who the hell are you and how the hell did you get in here?"

The stranger, a child really, peered up, eyes slanting dubiously. There were hard and metallic, those eyes, and around them the sculpture of the boy's face was like a Michelangelo angel with a particularly nasty turn of mind, cherubic and feral. One pale eyebrow arched evilly. He looked to the open industrial window facing out over the alley and tapped his temple with a forefinger, grinned, giggled, showing a mouthful of heartlessly perfect teeth he'd filed to absurd points.

Well, that just about left no question as to who or how. Alek let out his breath and relaxed his light instinctive battle stance—but only a little. He estimated the child to be about sixteen and tried hard not to hate him too completely. Only a whelp in the Coven, like Eustace. A psychokinetic—and probably psychotic—result of crossed genetic codes that had no business knowing each other. It wasn't his place to judge, but something about the kid made the hair want to stand on the back of his neck.

Alek clenched his fist, let it go, looked around his studio. The centerfold art of all his *New Yorkers* had been torn brutally from their spines and lay scattered across the length of the studio as if a tornado had passed none too subtly through the alley wide space here. Alek watched with a dry mouth as Sean delicately stripped the copy he held of its Andrew Wyeth.

Alek closed his eyes and swallowed hard. He let it go.

"Rip it up, man. Shred it *gooood*..."

Alek opened his eyes. "What?"

Sean's face sharpened wolfishly, a gem of saliva glittering with obscene brightness at the corner of his grinning mouth. He laughed. "Ain't you never heard no bitchin' rap before, man? When you from, man?"

Alek dropped the coat off his shoulders, shivered as though he were completely naked now. "I'm afraid I'm not much into the moderns, Mr. Stone."

"Stone Man to you," Sean corrected him. Then he mellowed, laughed, eyed the stereo at the far end of the studio and the riffled collection of records on the table beside it. "Man," came the Stone Man's voice like a javelin, "who the fuck is Joe Jackson?"

Alek shuddered, let it go, and went to the closet to get his leather greatcoat and sword. He briefly considered using the weapon on the stupid, unlearned little bastard, then thought better of it. It would only make a bigger mess of the studio. "No one you'd keep company with," he said.

Sean watched him with feline eyes. "Man, what is it you *do* here?"

Alek hooked a scarf around his neck, jerked it tight. "Do?" He turned around. "I sleep here. I eat here. I paint here. I do the things you do in a studio apartment."

Sean yawned theatrically. "Father said you got an 'old soul' or something, so I guess you're like older than fucking dirt. Probably were here back when the fuckin' Redcoats landed, right?" When he received no reply to that assumption, he shifted his weight and put his dirty, unlaced sneakered feet up on the glass coffee table next to a veined Han jade amphora, one of his prized possessions. Alek held his breath, but the amphora stayed intact for the moment.

"So you do, like, what? McFarlane stuff?"

"Excuse me?"

Sean rolled his eyes ceilingward. "You know, man, Todd McFarlane. You do comics or what?"

Alek pointed to the oil over the futon, a surreal Neolithic piece that had made the cover of *Le Jour* in Brussels two years ago and had gotten him that Braxton grant he'd very soon be bereft of if he didn't come up with something salable pretty soon.

"Yours?" the Stone Man asked.

"Yes."

Sean studied it thoroughly. "You in counseling for this, man, or what?" he asked.

Alek slammed the closet door, a crack like a jagged hair magically appearing along the plank wood. "I would very much hate to interfere with your methodical trashing of my home and life, Mr. Stone, but are you ready?"

Sean grinned, pulled himself up with enormous ceremony. Like so many lanky young kids, he looked taller and more impressive on his feet: over six feet of squealing paten leather, jangling zippers and blinding moon-white metals. Delicate chains grew mystically from Sean's earlobes and disappeared up his nostrils. His eyes looked to be smeared with lipstick. As he moved, his coat slit open like a skin to reveal a wide link of bronzed trophy teeth hanging to the dead center of his dirty black T-shirt. Sean's mouth twisted into a sneering grin. "Smokin', man. Let's...get...it...on!" He narrowed his eyes to glittering black slashes, pinning Alek like a punk thinking to roll some homeless sot.

Alek blinked and automatically threw up a thin impromptu field of mental protection as he felt something build in the room between them, something like the sizzling foreboding supposedly felt by a victim before the strike of lightning. No good. A desert-hot ghostly hand brushed past his cheek and punched the dust shield of the Neolithic on the wall, sending two crazed zigzags through the Plexiglas that looked suspiciously like a couple of S's. Initials?

"Shit, man, did I do that?" Sean laughed a high, cackling laugh.

The sound of it made Alek think of soft, padded rooms in a high-end mental asylum for the criminally insane. He ripped the scarf away, lest it become an impromptu noose. Oh, he prayed, for a chance to escort the kid to Greystone himself. He remembered the prophecy and then reconsidered the possibility of it ever coming to that, if the whelp wouldn't be destroyed long before.

Running a hand through his hair and down over his face, washing away all his suspicions for the moment, he went to the alley side door. "Let's. Go. Stone," he said, holding the door open for his young charge.

Sean stopped laughing and smiled like a kid told he had full run of the world and had every intention of running it like an amusement park with free rides. "Yes, massah. Whatever you want, *massah...*" he said, skipping ahead of his teacher and out into the night, nimbly, like a summoned strigoi or dancing demon loosened from a pit out of some remote corner of Dante's legendary hell.

8

Club Bauhaus had a monopoly on the other private pleasure clubs in the inner city. It was located a mile from SoHo, in the middle of one of New York's older, shabbier Bohemian communities. But because it was not the Lower East Side, like the Abyssus, or located on the river like many of the other ones, it had the advantage of attracting the business class as well as the usual menagerie of lowlifes.

"Fuck, man," Sean said, loping after Alek over the broken walk, "So how old are you?"

He just didn't want to let this lie, did he?

"Old enough," Alek answered distractedly as he strolled toward the looming black mass of battered industrial brownstones at the end of a half-forgotten dead-end street.

"A hundred?" the whelp asked.

"Nope," Alek said, stopping where a pile of ancient reeking garbage crouched in the curb and a length of dirty police line dragged in the gutter like a mark of demarcation. He looked up, past the rat-infested grime, and took in the sight of the club.

Originally an abandoned warehouse, the building had been converted into a disco by several young ambitious capitalists two decades earlier. But when that craze died, so did the club. It passed through several hands and incarnations before being bought by the present owner, Jean Paul, a Paris-born vampire with an indelible taste for real estate. After several months of interior redesigning the dive had reopened with a new name and a new attitude. Converted into a goth-punk haven with live music, a dance loft and an exclusive "Members Only" area for those humans with more esoteric tastes in entertainment, the club had quickly developed into the hottest place in SoHo to hang out in and be seen.

As usual, a crowd of impatient patrons waited anxiously on the sidewalk outside. Most were wealthy, thirtysomething businessmen in fifteen-hundred-dollar lounge suits with young women in designer dresses and stiletto heels on their arms. The club catered to mistresses, not wives. Morals and convention were checked at the door.

Crowding them for space were the goths and Generation X-ers with a great deal less money or hope. But just the same, here they were seeking a path and an escape in the club from what they saw as the rigors of Church and Government and whatever other institutions they presently felt were cheating them of life and pleasure. Their look was a mix of black leather and faded denim, Victorian finery and post-grunge regalia. Jewelry and makeup was cheap and slathered on in excess like a masquerade behind which these disillusioned children of the night might hide their true faces.

In many ways, Alek found himself sympathizing with the younger generation. Most were bright and sensitive young people trying desperately to cope with a world that had learned to hate its youth. Lonely and disillusioned, they had created a whole subculture not unlike the renegade youth of the sixties and seventies he was more familiar with. But unlike those lost souls, these young people were basing their rebellion and inner culture on decadence and death and the overdramatic plights of the vampires they unknowingly shared their world with. Their view of vampirism came from erotic novels and cheap B films, not the real thing. As he edged through their numbers, he couldn't help but wonder what they would make of the real thing.

A three-hundred-pound vampire named Erebus jealously guarded the entrance to the club. Dressed entirely in black, with skin like polished ebony, Erebus exuded an air of barely-restrained menace and arbitrarily controlled all admissions to the club. His word was law. Bribes meant nothing to him, nor did social standing.

Alek nodded at the doorman. The vampire crossed his arms— they were as thick around as Alek's thighs—and grimaced with a mouthful of gleaming white teeth as he took in the slayer's long hair and coat. So brave, and yet his eyes registered threat almost at once when he realized who it was. His smile fell, perhaps because he was remembering his painfully close shave five years earlier with Hanzo's blessed blade. "Jean Paul ain't expecting you, man," Erebus said.

"Then announce me," Alek told him.

"You got an awful lotta fuckin' balls comin' round here," Erebus said in a last-ditch effort at bravery.

"That's not all I have," Alek said, lifting his coat aside for a moment.

Erebus stepped back hastily, holding the door open for Alek and his charge with all the spirit of a true gentleman. He and Sean swayed wordlessly through the door and into the club.

Alek paused, letting his eyes change to accommodate the dim interior. The spare moody glow of the black lights and the swirls of tobacco and clove smoke made it difficult to see. The ever-present pound of industrial heavy metal played at the very threshold of pain made conversation impossible. Sean's whoop of bright-eyed excitement was silent in the hot, deafening roar of sound. For a moment it seemed possible that the whelp was simply going to shoot right into the mass of patrons and disappear. Alek caught him by the collar. *Wait*, he mouthed sternly to the kid. Sean's dazzling silver eyes narrowed. He looked about to protest. *Sit*, said Alek and pushed the kid into an empty chair.

Nobody noticed them. Nobody cared. The goths, the norms and those somewhere in between crowded the dance loft and the promenade below as busily as insects crawling over a corpse. They moved frenetically to the eardrum-splitting rhythms of the house band, a quartet of body-pierced, tattooed delinquents who were either vampires themselves or were just keyed up on enough junk to have a similar predatory look in their eyes. Alek cared neither way; he wasn't here to talk to the musicians.

Accompanied by a backbeat that wouldn't quit, Alek descended the narrow stairway leading to the basement, his nerve-endings on fire at this level. At the bottom of the landing stood another figure beside an ornately carved door marked *Members Only*. Here was Mako, a small, slender male with near-mahogany skin and greased hair and too wide of a smile. Though he looked no more exotic than an eighteen-year-old Asian-African mix, he was closer to a thousand. And a Moor. He loved cops no more than Erebus, but like the gatekeeper, he was wise enough not to court an affront with a slayer.

"Jean Paul in?" Alek asked the vampire conversationally.

Mako blinked, white eyes flashing in his dark face as he took in the sight before him. A slayer. And he was asking if his boss was in tonight. Normally, the members of the hive were obligated to defend their master to the death from possible harm. But in this case, Mako had decided that discretion was indeed the better part of valor. "Sure," he said. "Yeah. When's he not? But he ain't havin' guests tonight."

"I'm not a guest," Alek said, brushing past him, "I'm the Coven."

There were a dozen cocktail tables scattered about the private chamber of the master of the hive, with perhaps a dozen vampires and twice that many human whores and lackeys present. A barkeep furnished the humans with wine and brandies and the vampires with bottles of some of the finest imported and domestic animal blood in the world. To the rear of the room, upon a small raised dais, was the entertainment for the night, the living crucifixion of a young girl by a small rat-faced vampire dressed all in black Reaper robes. For a moment Alek was confused by it all; then, studying the crucified girl more closely, he realized she was really a small slim woman dressed all in Alice in Wonderland frills, not a girl, and certainly not human. Gabriella, Jean Paul's favorite. He recognized her now, her lewd prettiness. Shrugging, he looked past the patronage and found a small aristocratic man in a white suit and red tie strolling toward him, brass-headed cane in hand.

Jean Paul. He had the disarming, boyish looks of the young-old Richard Geere and the fashion sense of a true Parisian—and was well-known in many circles to use both of them to his full advantage in business as well as pleasure. "Quite the appetite whetter, is it not?" Jean Paul asked, indicating the bleeding body of his thrall on the cross. As always, the hivemaster's approach was direct, no quarter given, like a man with nothing to hide.

"I wouldn't know," Alek answered, looking away from the display. He was conscious of breathing through his mouth since the start, a reflexive action to keep the scent of blood from making him sluggish. An old trick of Amadeus's.

Jean Paul lowered his eyes seductively. "A necessary evil, you understand."

"How so?"

"Have you yet tasted the vintage, monsieur?" His hand snapping out, he snagged a cocktail glass on a waiter's tray in passing and offered the elixir to Alek.

Alek let out his breath and instantly regretted it. The "vintage" smelled disgusting, flat and lifeless and metallic. "Hart?" Alek asked as his Jacobson's organ was assailed by the abusive odor of the stuff.

"The most repulsive substance in the world, next to cow's blood," Jean Paul said, taking a sip and making a face. "'Tis shame it is as nutritious as it is. I'd much prefer to tear out the throats of the poor creature's murderers. But until the day the Coven is no more, we endure." Jean Paul nodded toward the dais as he escorted them both to a table near the back. "And we do the best we can to summon our desire." He added this with a smile that baited Alek's response.

Alek refused to rise to the argument. He sat and took in the performance instead. All or most of Jean Paul's thralls were painfreaks and this was his typical display of guilty innocence. Many of the vampires, including the late Empirius, would—and did—scoff at the Parisian's incessant propriety and strict attention to law. It was almost a caricature, as if Jean Paul believed that good behavior would gain him a privilege or three. Not that it would not. Alek had known the vampire since he opened the club in the early nineties, and though no unexpected deaths had turned up in or around Club Bauhaus, nothing said that the Parisian was not a hunter in some other remote corner of the city. If he wanted to, Alek would have had no trouble finding out about Jean Paul's nocturnal prowls; he knew souls out of every walk of life in this city, from Chinatown all the way up the peninsula to the Long Island Sound. But why press for the slaying of an all-but-model vampire citizen?

"Your 'desire' is being contained within these walls, is it not, JP?" Alek asked as he glanced askance at Gabriella's bloody, sensual display. Of course, what Jean Paul's subjects did in the privacy of their own circle was entirely their own business. Alek had seen enough in other clubs, both hive and human, to consider this a regular kindergarten class.

Jean Paul sat back in his seat, the back of his chair characteristically to the bricks like Wild Bill Hickok obsessed with being taken from behind. His eyes lowered, this time not in seduction but in subdued surprise. "Why, have you heard otherwise?"

Alek smiled. "No. But if you had answered any other way, JP, I would have started to worry."

The Parisian relaxed. "So your most welcome visit is strictly friendly?"

"Actually, I was wondering if you knew of anyone who might want Amadeus out of the way, besides yourself."

Jean Paul let out his breath and closed his eyes. Raising a hand, he held up two fingers for a human waiter to see. 1982. His favorite vintage. The year he slew the hivemaster Antony and claimed the dead vampire's harem queen as his own. Gabriella had been bonded to him ever since. "You are being less than subtle."

"I don't have time for subtleties, Jean Paul. Don't ask me why. I just need to know what the word on the street is."

Jean Paul thought long and hard before speaking. One did not simply jabber on about anti-Coven feelings in the inner city, not unless one wanted to be associated with some of the meaner, less orderly hives. They were served the bottle some spare moments later. Alek's eyes strayed incessantly to the performance until at last Jean Paul's incipient whisper brought his attention back around. "There was a demonstration two nights ago, a small one," he said as he poured them both a glass of rabbit's blood. "Animal blood thrown at Erebus, a few proclamations. I believe they were whelps from upstate who seemed to believe we had sold out to the Coven. Ridiculous sentiments, of course. Without it, where would we be?"

Jean Paul stopped speaking. He heard it too.

Alek canted his head to the side as he acute sense of hearing picked up the row downstairs, barely discernable beneath the bass-thump of the music. "Shit," Alek said, standing up and nearly overturning the table. "Keep me informed," he told Jean Paul, and then he was gone.

Unfortunately, by the time he made it back up to the club, the whelp was already gone, a patron was draped over a table with a razor blade smile, and one of Jean Paul's angry thralls was pointing toward the alley side door where a motorcycle was snarling to life. Alek made it just in time to find Sean popping the clutch on an antique Harley Davidson and pouncing forward, the bike carrying the whelp up and over the hills of the city and into the sterile holocaust of midwinter in raw breaths of blue smoke and cooking rubber. From a distance, Alek saw the whelp laugh and toss back his head, his lion's mane of jaw-cut yellow hair becoming a river of molten gold under the one-eyed Martian gooseneck Village lamps. "*We are the Children of the Night, man!*" he cried as he took a corner at an impossible angle. "*Listen to our bitchin' music!*" Sean's voice lengthened into a werewolf bay, a ruthless sound that echoed out to silence in the far distance.

Goddamnit him to hell.

Alek made it to the roof of the club in minutes. Soaring like a bat, he crossed the thirty- and sometimes fifty-foot drops separating the buildings with a single leap on a northeastern-bound flight toward the Atlantic, following on the heels of his psychotic acolyte. Most but not all of the buildings in this part of the city were level with the tops of the next in line. He jumped the alleys between the structures with little effort and even less thought, sending off multiple motion detectors on roofs and gables but never slowing or stopping even a moment to catch his breath, cursing himself for trusting the little bastard to behave himself.

The bike, meanwhile, carried his acolyte deeper into the Eastside underworld of rotted buildings gothic and eyeless with glass, twisted projects and derelict cars, X-rated babylons and Asian groceries too afraid to stay open after dusk when all the monsters came out and too poor not to.

The brainless fool was on the road for almost a quarter of an hour when it happened the first time. Sean whooped as he reined up his machine at the blinking intersection of Grand and FDR Drive. Alek watched from the top of a project as his hands caressed the ignition and the cycle growled impatiently. His jackal-like mouth slackened open, tongue flicking over his teeth and making them shine like wet little pearls. *"Oh yeah, man, oh fuckin' yeah!"* he bellowed as he picked up on the first insinuations.

Leaping down to a Bank Four building, Alek felt the first stirrings—a dull prickling in his nape and in the small of his back, as if a wire were being thrummed across the length of his spine.

"Yeah, man!" Sean's glassy gaze returned to the road ahead of him, shoulders bunching and flexing, tough, coiled muscle writhing like a nest of snakes under his paten leather hide. He gunned his machine and eyed the alley directly across the street. *"There we go, baby, there ...we...go!"*

His metal-plated beast screamed.

Howling, Sean peeled out at whiplash speed and rounded a corner into a dead waste of lightless alley space. Alek clambered down the fire escape of the building and watched. The Harley's shiny Cyclops's eye splashed over orange clay brick and a gallery of arcane graffiti, finally picking out the two figures at the back of the dead end space. A girl, her sharp bones scarcely protected by a punk mini and a battered leather jacket, had a junky hanging against the wall. A moment after the light hit her she turned, black painted streetwalker's eyes catching the invasion of light and sending it back like the aquamarine eyes of a Siamese cat.

Her mouth and chin were as scarlet as the flimsy little white dress she wore.

Such a dirty trick, Alek thought. Vampires did not read their half brethren the way they did their own. In a vampire's powerful and delicate psyche the dhampiri were as blank slates to them as the mortal human beings they preyed on. Blank until that final moment of total understanding, when it was far too late for them. Alek, like many of his kind, had learned that with time and stealth many never had to know they were hunted at all. It had often been his method.

But Sean was going to be a bastard about it.

He rode his mount to a skittering halt and booted down the kickstand, leaping from the machine like a fair angel of destruction falling to earth. He smiled at his quarry, brandishing his katana like a baton. "Here, kitty, kitty."

The little vampire hissed and showed him her cattish teeth.

"Aww, nice kitty. Nice kitty, kitty." Sean cut her.

The girl fell against the wall like a smashed insect. She growled, eyes flashing up at her slayer like bits of broken glass.

Sean kicked the carcass of her dead john. "Bad kitty. Bad, baaad kitty. Lookit the mess you made!" He sliced her face.

The girl crumpled, hissing in and out of her mouth and the side of her cheek. Sean giggled like a wicked little boy and kicked her over, knelt down beside her, and licked the junkie's blood off her mouth. The vampire bit his cheek. Sean swore and bashed her skull against the pocked asphalt floor of the alley. She writhed like an eel. Sean punched her in the cheek. She lay still at last, watching him with her oily, tearless eyes.

"Such a very bad kitty," Sean growled, gasping as if he'd been running ceaselessly for hours. He smiled, licked his teeth like a lion. "Want to share some kitty with me, little girl?" With his sword he sliced the front of her dress open. The material hissed apart to reveal bruised ribs and too-thin skin and the heaving chest of a fevering, unbound female. "I'll be the best you ever had..."

Watch him, Amadeus had said. Your eyes will be mine. Yes and watch he had. But he couldn't watch this. Not this—slaughter. Dropping down from the fire escape, Alek zeroed in on the kid.

Sean grinned, looked up, glee fleeing in favor of blatant horror. "What the fu—?"

Alek smashed a controlled palm-heel strike into the center of Sean's chest, lifting him up and off the girl and driving him into the darkness beyond. Sean cannonballed into the dead end wall, a geyser of purple blood streaming out of his mouth and nose from a ruptured spleen. He slumped, pale eyes fluttering to rise and meet those of his master's in blatant confusion. Alek snarled, leapt forward like a shadow, and wrenched the sword from his student's idiot grip. With his free hand he covered Sean's face, narrow sharp finger bones burrowing deep into the soft pouches of flesh under the whelp's puzzled eyes. "You want to fuck someone? Fuck *me*, you dickless little whelp," he said, shaking the kid like the bag of waste he was and covering him in threads of spittle. "*Stupid, shitty punk. Judas. You've learned nothing. You know nothing.*"

He raised the little shit up. Sean groaned, a low nasal sound with the vice of bony fingers crushing the cartilage of his nose and sending the blood back into his throat. The whelp's black-lacquered fingernails raked Alek's cheeks, caught like bats in his hair; his legs pedaled uselessly. Alek smiled. So light and flimsy, like a wicker marionette that could be shattered to hopeless splinters within seconds.

Yes.

Amadeus was sure to live forever then.

But he had his vows. He wasn't yet Covenmaster. He didn't yet hold the privilege of judging his brethren. God help Sean if he ever did. Disgusted, he cast the whelp into a small cluster of trashcans with a noisy splash of dented tin and flat, dervishing lids. Sean whimpered and blinked his disbelieving eyes where he lay among a month's worth of refuse.

Alek flung aside the whelp's sword and turned away, his teeth locked so perfectly together he tasted his own blood in his cheek. He drew his own sword and crouched down over the girl's laboring body. He brushed blonde strands of hair from her face. The beauty under her fear surprised him, made his fingers tremble a little when he put the back of his hand to her ruined cheek. His touch seemed to stop her labored breath, her pain, her panic. He sensed great distance, time and knowledge...

Her face jumbled and ran like rain. With effort be wrenched his mind away, a mind that so wanted to live inside of others, his vampiric mind. He murmured meaningless words of closure and comfort as he buried his hands in her hair and jerked his sword gently across the exposed bow of her neck. Somehow, another beheading seemed an unnecessary evil. Her body collapsed with the slightest of murmurings, like a sleeper awakening or only returning to dreams as her life bled away into the cracks of the pavement.

Sean sat up and screeched thinly, the sound like that of a starved beast robbed of its meat. Alek spun around, his sword barring his own throat in defense. But the punk had not even moved out of his position; he only smiled at Alek, then glared at the sword lying at Alek's feet.

Alek stamped his foot forward over the sword, but the weapon was being summoned with astonishing mental power. He skated off the steel and went to one knee with a grunt. The sword skipped effortlessly along the ground and into Sean's hand like a pet returning eagerly to its master.

Then the whelp's body shot upward, casting off tin lids like discarded bits of armor. His face writhed as he charged, legs scissoring, shoulders bunching into the precise arc of his swing.

"Don't," Alek said. Sean came anyway.

Alek parried the blade in passing, shouldered the dumb shit away from him. Both Sean and his blade clattered to the alley floor.

"Whelp," Alek growled. He stepped in and effortlessly butterflied his katana. Sean's necklace of teeth chittered down and pelted the ground around him like rain. Sean looked up. Fear, he would see now, he thought, a silent plea—

But Sean only smiled, laughed. "Fuck me, you're crying," he said. "The mighty Chosen One is crying like a fuckin' baby!" He rolled to his feet, still laughing. His laughter whined on the concave undersides of the trash can lids, made a noisy coven of crow arrow out of their roost in the city's hidden heights. "You are righteously tipped, man, you know that?" Sean cried. "Righteously fuckin' tipped!"

Alek touched the warmth on his face. Tipped. A profanity. Slander. Tipped was Debra, not him. Filth. It was all filth falling from the filthy mouth of a little shit with no judgment and no sense. How he hated Sean, the little Judas, his mouth already sweetened rottenly with the kiss of death.

He stepped in and slapped Sean across the face.

Sean spanked against the brick wall, his laughing face seizing up into a corpselike rictus. One hand tentatively explored the spayed red mark on his face. "You hit me," he said with astonishment. "Tipped motherfucking bastard, I can't believe you hit me! Nobody hits the Stone Man! *NOBODY!*" His eyes shrank to screws.

Alek stiffened. In his mind he saw a plate-glass dust shield spider, he saw a sword skating along the ground as if drawn by a powerful magnet, he saw, in the boy's mind, a sharp black-pointed pencil streak off a desk and stick like a dart in another boy's eye. He leapt backwards as he felt Sean's vengeful spirit claw reach for him. He raised his arms and his mind in an impromptu shield as it tried to envelop him.

The loosened psi talent hit his barrier and halted. Alek shuddered violently, felt it coil back onto itself.

Sean's eyes narrowed to mere threads as he bore down with the unleashed fury of his mind. Alek grunted as he was rocked back against the wall by the crushing weight of the boy's psi. Christ, he couldn't do this, couldn't hold back this kind of titan force trying to shove him through three feet of bricks.

The air shimmered with distortion like heat rising off the deadpan of the desert at high noon. Slender black cracks trickled up the flanks of the derelict tenement building on his left. A window on the third floor burst into diamond rain. A fire escape fastened to a wall squealed as its metal bones were methodically reshaped. The soft, dying, warbling bodies of pigeons pelted the ground from the broken clerestory high above them like wadded-up masses of tissue...

The idiot. He had no idea what he'd unleashed. Sean's psi was coupling and expanding between them and before very long, Alek knew that even with all his experience he would not be able to balance it. He wasn't certain what would. And when he was spent, what then? He could imagine the sphere of psi breaking apart like a glass meteor, sparks of wild energy set free-wheeling into the night to fall like rampaging stars all over the city. And the brunt of it, the body, falling back on the source, into Sean Stone. In its present state the energy would have the power to punch the heart from his chest and twist his limbs out of their sockets with the ease of an angry child dismembering a doll. Would serve him right, too.

But no such pleasure. The power had to be dealt with, had to. It was Coven law. His law.

Alek closed his eyes. It was always easiest to work in the dark, to see as Amadeus saw. In the dark there were no limitations. The mind's eye was infinite. And with infinite care Alek extended a beckoning finger of his own empathic talent toward the swarm of angry energy. It came eagerly. Alek's finger expanded, became a full talon that cradled the wild globe of loosened energy with gentle reverence.

Then his mind spiraled up, pulling free of the bruised alley. It drifted weightlessly over the cold black sea of the city with its many blinking eyes and patchwork of street-stitchery and its monoliths of glass and steel and its people wise and ignorant. And there, in that place, invisible and powerful, Alek cast the titan force deep into space where it would spin and soar and gather momentum for all eternity.

The exercise sucked all the energy from Alek's body, and he crashed, gasping, to his knees. He brought his hands down very slowly, breath hitching, dying in a long hiss of release. Relief.

The new emptiness in the alley felt vast. Christ, what a mess they'd made of it.

Alek pushed himself up using his sword as leverage. He staggered forward unevenly, with all the careful precision of the chronically ill. He was spent. Sick. He headed toward the figure of his acolyte kneeling in the center of the alley.

The whelp moaned, sick as a dog, sick as hell itself.

Alek smiled. Good.

Sean fell forward and Alek caught him.

9

The vampire waited until the two slayers were gone before emerging into the bluish neon moonlight pouring in through the shattered clerestory window of the tenement building she called home. Behind her, the light cast the fallen beams into suggestive crossbones relief. She walked to the edge of the open ledge, her shadow sweeping along the cluttered floor to meet her like an attentive retinue. She looked down. The alley stank of cardboard and standing water and the aftereffects of the war—wet steel, shed blood. Death. Death most of all. She did not enjoy the smell, not now, not when it emanated from the dead body of the unbound female. Already the flesh and bones had begun to decay, she was so old.

She studied the remnants: black leather jacket and white chemise gown, alluring, ancient, intriguing. But it was what the johns the vampire had fed on had seen in her eyes. Survival of the fittest. Adaptation. The coveted philosophies of the Ancients and the modern Darwin. The female had been only a girlish thing, like the vampire herself, but not really. Too old. An antique doll, centuries old and beautifully preserved.

But not now. Free now.

In too many ways, she was bitterly jealous.

She was dressed in the garb of the evening before, the dusty leather mini, the jacket with its bloodstained chains. But as though she wore a gown of white and gold, she brushed her fall of ragged hair off her shoulders and studied the slivery disk of the moon overhead. It was full as it ought to be. Full as it had been the night Paris died.

She blinked. Last night she had tried her best to not look at the man on the bed at the Marriott, his lifeless body as shiny and ephemeral as snow in the moonlight, the telltale track of her teeth from his crotch to the gaping black hole in his throat. As she had removed the cash from his wallet on the bureau—three or four hundred dollars at a quick count—she had felt a curious pang she could identify only as guilt. But it was a passing thing. It was their way, hers and others, their purpose, their divine will to embrace the cannon of the predator and swallow the weak-minded and the faltering. It was a drama as old as time itself.

She'd stuffed the money into her jacket and took his watch as well. She thought she might be able to pawn it at the shop on Jerome Avenue for maybe forty or fifty dollars, and every little bit helped. Anything to help her survive to finish the mission. The wedding band he wore she crushed in her fist and slung into a dark corner of the room. Some things no one deserved to own.

The vampire shifted and the chemicalized city wind shifted with her as she considered the war so recently waged. Survival. War among predators. It was a drama played out well between the two slayers, the dark one so like a stony embodiment of Hades and the sickly colorless one with the madness and the taint of early death in his blood. Their souls were clear as colored glass to her. The pale one had a spirit as inky as tar. The dark one was red. Red with crimson lines of fire at his fingertips and behind his eyes.

His priestly eyes were like Paris. But she knew that already. She had known that for a very long time, in the long years she had studied the slayer.

The vampire closed her eyes, and in her ragged memory her Paris put an iron knife with a papal-cross hilt of black onyx into her hand. Now she drew it out from under her dress and tested its weight. She heard her Paris's words, his plea, and she nodded. She remembered the undying love of his lips, his hands. She remembered the vow she had made. All these years and she had had no way to fulfill it. Until now. She looked at the knife in her hand and she thought about the slayer, that tall icy soul all in black with the face of his murdered sister. These two things, the slayer and the knife, were her destinies, then. Finally. After so many years, it was all beginning to come together. She had the knife.

Now all that was left was the slayer. Opening her eyes, she searched for the moon among the black clouds and between the tall stone monoliths, yet she was blinded by the crimson lines of his power impressed on her eyes like the veins of the sun at dusk.

10

The dolphins blazed blade-grey in color, sleek and cold, like perfect little silver crescent moons. There were two of them poised over the curling green waves of the ocean. The window was more of a seascape than anything else, a frozen mosaic of painted glass shards puzzled together by the same hands of the Puritan who had cleaved the bedrock under the house and set his mark in stone forevermore. The window claimed no place and no time; like all true art it made no excuse for itself.

Through the grey dawn gloom Alek watched the dolphins come alive. He lay perfectly still and waited for the window to fill with light. And it was only then, when it was beautifully illuminated, that he moved a hand out over the pattern of the old eiderdown quilt under his fingers. This morning it felt almost unfamiliar.

No, not unfamiliar. Only lately unvisited.

It had been a long time since he'd lain here in his cell and felt the comfort of a hand-sewn coverlet about him, a long time since he'd awakened to the sight of the dolphins growing brighter and bluer as the eastern light cut through the panes of glass. It had been a long time, too long, since he'd spent the night beneath the protective wings of the Covenhouse.

A kiss of sapphire sun touched his cheek and he felt strangely animated. He pushed himself up, propping his head against the headboard of the bed as he resettled himself. The old horsehair mattress shifted slightly under a weight it knew too well. And gradually, as he watched, his cell grew to silent life all around him, the dust, the fabrics, the cherry wood finishes rubbed to raw bone. Cells. The bedrooms of the Covenhouse were called cells. Amadeus's designation for them, and it would sound ridiculous in any mouth but his. The cells were simplicity itself: a rustic iron framed bed, thick lion-pawed table and chair, working gaslight, fireplace, armoire and bookshelves. That was all. The walls were eggshell alabaster and unadorned; the window was art and it was enough.

Sometime in the night while he had slept a fire had been lit in the hearth. It was gone to white, sweet-smelling cedar ash now behind the iron guard. About a dozen years ago he and Book had installed working electricity and central heating in the old mansion. Still, the Father's habits died hard—if, that was, they ever died at all.

Alek settled back and lazily half-closed his eyes, trying hard to recall the peace of this place, his childhood home, this gentle abeyance away from his human life. He frowned as it escaped him. He didn't feel well, not at all. His stomach roiled emptily and there was a sour, singed taste in the back of his throat. He was forced to swallow hard against a returning wave of nausea.

An overuse of psi could do that.

Or else it was just Sean making him violently ill.

Sean. If there was any justice in the world he would be busy hurling his brains out in the nauseous throes of an overextended psi for the next three days. Yes, that would be perfect. That would be justice.

The night before, when Alek had carried his burden into the house, the whelp had been unconscious and his body had felt like a slack mass of rubber in Alek's arms. His loony, Machiavellian eyes had been closed, making him seem absurdly angelic. Deceptively innocent.

So sad that he could not feel tenderness for such a face, he'd thought at the time. Such a tragedy that such beauty must be trapped inside with such an ugly soul. But Alek had dropped the tragedy down onto his bed without ceremony, turned away and vomited in the bathroom. Then he had instinctively sought his old room.

"Ah no, what is it he has done to you, beloved?" Amadeus had been waiting for him there. When the sickness passed and he was able to stand, Amadeus put his palm to Alek's hot cheek for many moments and they spoke in images as only artists can. Then Alek, exhausted, sank onto the bed as Amadeus undressed him as if he were still a small child and lay down beside him, giving him his warmth and words and blood.

In time they slept. And Alek dreamt. And in the dream he was covered in spiders and unable to escape their webs.

Alek pulled himself up, weaving a little, his arms steadying himself against the bedpost as the room slowed, then settled itself down properly. After a while he made himself walk off the nausea like a seasoned drunk would a hangover.

The morning light cast itself in unbroken, dusty banners on the western wall of the room and picked out a book here, there. Alek fingered the volumes as he went along, read the names. Calvin. Paracelsus. Chaucer. Pliny the Elder. Cornelias Agrippa. He pulled down a volume at random and felt its ancient weight in his hands. Volney's *Ruins of Empires*. He carried it with him under his chin like a schoolboy and circled the room twice before he stopped in front of the Colonial armoire. He gently pulled open the antique double doors. Gabardine habits were folded into dark uniform stacks on the shelves, the skins of a younger Alek Knight still here, as if he'd never grown up and went away from the Covenhouse at all. As if a younger Alek Knight would walk in at any moment with his stack of study tomes and put on his glasses and one of the gowns before tackling the Father's lesson plan for the day.

Some fragile understanding, tenuous as a silk thread, fell in. And all at once he realized what being chosen of Amadeus truly meant. His was the only cell in the vast old house left unchanged, undisturbed, after all this time. Unused. Enshrined. As if Amadeus hadn't a doubt in his ancient mind that Alek would one day return forever.

Covenmaster, he thought.

Covenmaster Alek Knight.

He frowned, shook his head. Absently, he touched the mark on his throat. The wound had healed, yet it stung still.

He looked at the musty stack of habits and wondered if it was possible to slide into those skins of the past, now, almost thirty years later. And looking, his breath hitched softly, then died in a little sigh. His fingers came away from Amadeus's mark and inched into the armoire. Alek put Volney on the table behind him so that he was free to take the impish thing at the back of the armoire in both hands. Raggedy Andy in his pale little face and faded blue sailor's uniform smiled up at Alek. He'd been Debra's once, a long time ago in a time of strife and confusion. Like the carousel and the cheap little gold ring hanging from the rusted chain around the doll's neck. Debra's. Wicked Debra's. He buried his nose in the red yarny hair, and yes, he could smell her still, feel the stickiness that time and handling had put into Andy's hair by childish fingers.

He slid the ring on the chain off the doll and put it on his ring finger. Stuck. Why not? Debra had worn it on her thumb it had been so big at the time. Now it fit him exactly and he realized he couldn't pull it off. He looked around the room, feeling all the fragile threads falling into him now, an enormous wed spun in years and distance, heavy with time and surely full of power.

"Coelum non animum mutant, que trans mare current."

The voice was like the gush of wind at his back.

Alek quit pulling on the ring and closed his eyes. "'Those who cross the sea change the sky, not their spirits.' Horace. *Epistles.* I remember, Father."

"You forget nothing. Unlike so many."

Alek turned slowly, raised his eyes to the Father. "Why don't you simply kill him?"

Inside the casting of the door Amadeus stood like an ancient warrior prince, his face all chiseled ice, his loosened white hair trapped on the rough grain of the alabaster wall in a frosted web. Over his forearm was a Covenmaster's black silk habit. He stroked the length of fabric lovingly, like the hide of a great conquest. "Kill him. Kill the prophecy," he reasoned. "And would you do this for me, my best child? A single word from me and you would bend the Covenant itself to preserve my life?"

Alek tightened his hold on the doll. "It is not in my power to destroy the boy, but Father, you've lived so long. You could summon the Vatican Council, reason with them—"

"Do you," Amadeus said with complete judgment, "believe I covet my life so that I would try and correct destiny like an Orpheus? Or manipulate my child like a human parent?"

Alek dropped his eyes.

"I would. I should—nein?—for my life is the Coven. But the Coven will live after me. Through you, my son. You will be the soul of the Coven in my stead. Do you see? My blood lives in you even now. We are one. And I will live again after my own death, only it will be another face, another pair of hands and another heart beating, but beating the blood of Amadeus still."

"Immortality."

Amadeus nodded. "Yes, you see. You see best of all. Like a blind man sees."

Alek's mouth twisted against the tears and he tasted them in the back of his throat like bad liqueur. Immortality. But it was all just a bad joke. Immortality was for gods, and music, and legend, not the damned. Not for those whose heads could be removed and whose souls cast off the scales into hell.

Amadeus smiled. "Memento mori."

Remember that you must die. Ovid? Martialis? Alek couldn't remember. His mind was clotted with grief made all the worse because it could not be completely grasped yet for its lack of true presence, of arrival.

"Beloved, we are merely immortal. Not eternal," said the Father. "You too must one day die."

Raggedy Andy fell through Alek's fingers and hit the floor dustily. But the ring on his hand remained, flashing. Of course he would die one day. They would all die. Like Debra had died. Like the thousands they'd slain had died on a thousand other nights and like thousands more still would.

"You doubt," said Amadeus.

"I fear."

"The weight of this—"

"—will crush me."

"Der Unsinn," said Amadeus. "Do you remember the night I found you in the park, holding to your sister, afraid even to speak? You were in my visions long before. As a child I saw you standing in the night in your black hair and bloodied steel. The Chosen. I was led that night to you. Drawn to you. Drowning in love for you. My journey's end."

Andy smiled up at Alek, demure, a tease who knew all the answers. Alek crossed his arms, almost shuddering. "It's morning," he said and his voice sounded curiously empty to himself, as if like the past and the things in it, coming from a long way's away. But here now. Arrived. "I have to go now, Father. Braxton will be up my ass, my studio's a goddamn mess, I—"

Amadeus touched his cheek.

Alek flinched and looked up. He hadn't perceived that the man had even moved.

Amadeus flinched in return, but it was only the flash of the ring catching his light-sensitive eyes. He said, "It is the morning of your ascension, my most beloved." He reached, his fingers melting against the thin bones of Alek's face as if he would mold them as everything else.

My master, Alek thought helplessly as Amadeus's fingers fell down over his eyelashes and down farther to the mark on his throat. And then he was there, nuzzling, making Alek's skin shiver with the familiar intimacy of it and making him recall all they had shared last night, every intimacy, as if it were their last night together. We are one, he thought with serene wisdom. Never before, he wanted to say, never before have I felt this. But in the end he did not, for he knew it was a lie.

"Finish your affairs in the world this day," said Amadeus. "Gather yourself and the things most you value. I give you today. And then you will come to me at midnight in your faith and your loyalty and I will give you the Dominatio, and it will be my greatest act. Verstehen?"

Alek shuddered within and without. *Dominatio.* To absorb another's soul through the ultimate partaking of blood—to *become* that person, to let that person become you. For a moment his whole being rebelled against the concept. So much so, that he almost shied away from the Father's touch.

But the Father was patient, as always. "Do you trust me, mein Sohn?'

"You know I do. It's just—"

"I shall recede."

Again he shuddered, but this time in mind-numbing horror. Recede in the Dominato. To let one's soul die...

It was horrible and beautiful at once, this gesture.

Amadeus smiled as he pressed the habit into Alek's hands, and when his voice came a moment later it had no fear. In fact it purred with perfect fulfillment, the finish of a promise too long denied. "Go now," he said, "yet return to me, my beautiful slayer."

Alek nodded and turned to leave his cell, to do as the Father had requested of him. But in the end he faltered, one foot upon the threshold, and turned back abruptly. Desperate. Was there any way to show this man his grief? Amadeus. Father, brother, his best friend in all the world. He would never know how much his child wanted to die for him. But because he could not, because it was not his time to die, Alek only returned to his master and kissed him, a gift and a covenant.

Then he left.

11

"Mister Knight?"

He'd been standing there with his hand in the mayonnaise jar, watching the girl on the street corner for almost twenty minutes. Punishing heels and phony bloodred hair lying limp and cold on her leathered shoulders. A wood crucifix at her throat. One of the children of men gone to darkness and running. A child of the night now, though her black painted streetwalker's eyes would not shine in the dark and she would not live forever. Perhaps a few months on the brutal back of this devouring city. No more than that. Somebody's daughter. Sister, even.

The girl posed for a passing john in a blue sports car and Alek noticed that beneath the girl's cheap rhinestone-encrusted jacket her thin, cold little dress was red. Red.

Debra's color had been red.

But Debra was gone—

"Mister Knight?"

He let the chintzy curtain fall back over the window and wandered back across the studio to the galley where Eustace was helping him pack boxes. Not that he needed the help, mind you. All the important things he'd managed to collect outside of the Coven would probably fit into half a dozen suitcases. The rest the new owners of this shitbox could have, the evil green sofa and the Formica-and-cinderblock coffee table some SoHo residents called shabby chic industrial, the card tables and the faded bed sheets and the rest of the mess he'd managed to make of his human life.

He looked at the few things of importance here, his tools of the trade, easels and canvas stretchers, the weapons, the pair of commas he'd never learned to use. The ring he still had not gotten off his finger. Soap, oil, mayonnaise. Nothing worked. Nothing. He washed his hands at the sink, watching the tarnished gold flash in the harsh overhead light. He owned so little—but then, what were possessions but chains to bind a soul to earth when he might fly—?

Fly with me, Alek, please?

Debra. Her voice. Her plea from so long ago.

He closed his eyes and shook his head, wondering if he was losing it, the stress of the past two days too much. He waited, hoping breathlessly for the voice to fade, then let out a long sigh of relief as her special laughter eddied away into darkness inside him. His eyes ached as if with headache and he felt a strange, lagging sense of disorientation. He looked again at the ring, tried to twist it off, but realized it would probably have to be cut away.

"Mister Knight, sir?"

His blinked and the undeparted faraway feeling cracked at the edges. Shaking away the remnants, he regarded the debris of his life scattered across the counters and the tall young man placing it all with such gentle reverence into brown boxes. Trying to make points with the new authority, a cynical part of his mind whispered, though he knew for certain it wasn't the truth. Eustace just wanted to please. He was simply too damned honest and too damned simple to have any alternative devices.

"What's this, Mister Knight?" he asked as he held up an object.

"Alek, please."

"What's this, Mister Alek?"

He smiled, took it from the boy's hand. "Tortillion," he explained and brushed the rubber tip against the boy's nose. "You use it to rub lead into the grain of the paper for a better blending of values."

"Laws," said Eustace, taking it back and observing it like a newly discovered species of otherworldly life. "Don't got nothing like that in Morningvale. Why do you get better value mixing lead with grain?"

Alek shook his head, almost amused. "I'll teach you sometime. Like to draw, son?"

"Sure. Houses and horses and things. Whatta these?"

Alek reached across the island and took the shabby deck of cards from him. "Tarot. They tell the future. Sometimes. Though not for me. A friend gave them to me in the summer of '69. Everyone was into it back then." He riffled the cards, came up with the High Priestess, the conceiver of mystery. Truth be known, he seldom consulted the Tarot; the cards never seemed prepared to reveal anything of any real importance. It was almost as if they knew him for what he was and resented the fact that to tell his future would occupy them for far too many years.

He scowled over the top card, one finger ringing the High

Priestess's portrait with her casually juggled moons and stars. All wrong. When he'd split the deck he'd anticipated the face card of the Hermit to embody the new position he would be entering into tonight—at the very least the Hanged Man for his act of surrendering his professional life, such as it was, to a priest's order. The cards were probably as muddled as ever. He set them in a box. Useless things...

He squinted as his mind swelled suddenly with the dark shadow of laughter and a promise of grief. Of revenge. Debra would do anything if it meant returning to him to wreck her vengeance, anything at all. He felt her hands on him, he felt his own heartbeat in his left hand, he felt—

Eustace spoke his name with some concern but he scarcely heard the boy. He had to drown that fucking little-girl laughter, drown it before it drove him insane. He went to the cupboard and poured himself a three-finger whiskey, downed it too quickly and scorched his mouth raw. He threw the glass tumbler into the sink and watched in satisfaction as it cracked into a dazzling rain of false diamonds.

He laid his forehead to the cupboard door and moaned. Sean was right. He *was* coming apart. Tipped. Hmm. Some Covenmaster. He wanted to weep, almost thought it would help, but he knew from too much experience that his tears might fall forever but they would bring with them no relief or release.

"Mister Alek...Mister Alek, you look badly ill."

He shook his head. Carefully. There was an abrupt, sullen ache like a stab wound in his left temple. He touched it meditatively. Migraine. Half head. Come to me, he pleaded. Please, come and destroy me or else go and leave me in peace...

But Debra remained an ambient ghost, always prepared to torture him but forever beyond his reach and command. Fool. He was a damned fucking fool to believe he could summon her. Debra, wicked Debra. In life she'd been an unbound dhampir the likes of which even Amadeus could not hold back. But in death she was a goddess. Why did he try?

Vermouth. White Horse. Wormwood for the brain. Anything was better than this madness.

He tried to twist the ring, failed. Felt like it was fucking *soldered* onto his hand. He wished he'd never found it or that damned doll. I should throw 'em off the top of this building, he thought. Or maybe the Empire State. Yeah, that'll work. He lifted the amber bottle and saw with horror that it was empty. When had *this* happened? It had been half-filled only a moment ago. He looked at it long and hard as if the image would change suddenly like an optical illusion. But the bottle remained stubbornly empty. And his headache was worse, so much worse.

Female laughter crested in his head, as rusty as hellish old bells. It hurt so bad.

He was supposed to go to Amadeus as a priest in just a few hours, and there was no hair of the dog to make him right. He was all pain, all laughter, all bones and hair and ragged fabric like a doll with faulty craftsmanship. Amadeus would touch him and he would simply fall to skeletal pieces like a smashed jigsaw, his pieces scattered across the length of the Abbey like the fragments of the tumbler at the bottom of the rust-yellow sink.

"Oh fucking hell..." He turned around and checked the time. The clock over the sink was only now plodding toward ten. He had time to visit Sam's Place, and if he did not he would make time. He dropped the bottle into the sink and swayed past Eustace and his studio and all the fucking repulsive Bosch jobs hanging from the fucking repulsive walls, all the women with black steel cable hair and the machines eating their makers, and if this didn't make him right, God help him, nothing would.

12

"Mister Alek?"

He paused partway up the hill and looked back down at the Village. What once had seemed quaint and glowing and as opulent as stained glass only looked tired and defeated. Overindustrialized.

Industry, that's all it was—empty and soulless and inhabited by minds as flat as those of store mannequins. Urbanized industrial rich. No sun. No night. No inspiration. He realized with something close to panic that he was living in the middle of the very fucking thing he'd once looked upon as a parentless child and abhorred. It was no wonder he could no longer paint. How the hell had this happened?

"Mister Alek...wait up!" called Eustace as he came loping up the street and took him by the arm. "Where're you going, Mister Alek?"

"An errand."

"Can I come?"

"No."

"Please?"

"No."

"I'll be real quiet, I pr—"

"No! I said no! Are you on stupid pills?"

Eustace jerked. His eyes were young and afraid.

Fucking lunatic, what had he done? Alek reached out, carefully, and gathered the boy under his arm. This was no good. What was wrong with him? What the hell was going on? "I'm sorry, son," he said. "I—"

He paused. He felt it first in his back, and then a rush in his neck and jaw. Something coming their way. Down that alley across from them. He looked at Eustace. Eustace only looked back. He was innocent. No blood there. He and Book would be getting together pretty soon, but Alek didn't think he needed to ask how it had gone the other night. Dairy Queen, obviously.

"Wait here," he said and crossed the street to where a pair of crumbling tenement buildings stood side by side, so close their ornate stone cornices nearly necked.

Dark here. While waiting for his eyes to adjust he drew his katana, brought it up under his forearm into the ready-strike position. Paranoia? But of course. Vampires were especially capable of vendettas. And they were as good at hunting as their hunters. He felt for the presence with his mind, sensed its retreat. Oh no you don't, he thought. You're following me and I'm just in the mood for you tonight!

He stepped into the alley, felt the presence retreat all the way to the far back. Useless. This alley, like the majority of the Village alleys, was a flat dead end. He sidled against one wall and stalked the creature, his feet making no sound on the dirty asphalt. He deftly avoided the stacked boxes and mounds of refuse scattered down the throat of the alley. A rat scrabbled loose from one mound of garbage and skittered between his feet to reach the next. He ignored it. His eyes narrowed, crawled over the darkness and the rearing graffiti-covered city walls.

There…a shadow fluttered like a wing not a hundred feet ahead and a little to his right. He stopped, gauging its size and speed. Small. Childlike. Christ, but he hated doing the kids.

A pair of catlike eyes studied him out of a pocket of utter darkness, red and reflective.

"Who are you?" he said, swinging his sword overhead. "Speak, and I might not cut you apart."

He was about to corner it when it did the unexpected and strode gallantly forward like a priestess cloaked in awry shadows. He did not move, did not react. The sword and his arm were suddenly disconnected for the first time in his life. His instinct, for either flight or fight, was gone. His breath was gone. The alley of which he'd been the expert on only a moment ago whirled around him in a lightless tempest. Bosch. Bad melee of studies in half-light. From somewhere on the avenue came the severe throb of music. Rhapsody of my heart, he thought.

But then everything grew still and devoutly quiet before the phantomlike figure floating toward him, the face the finely chiseled chinabone craftwork of a doll, the hair frayed black flaming silk, the mouth red, the eyes red, Snow White, Rose Red.

Alek's mouth rasped open over no words and no voice. He dropped his sword; then he himself dropped to his knees.

Debra had returned at last and she was going to kill him.

INTERLUDE 1

1

His earliest memory was of a pallid room, the last in a long line of pallid rooms that came to be his and his sister's prison for the first eight years of their lives. The dorms of McEnroy Home slept four apiece and in each corner of each room was an iron-framed bed with a white chenille spread and white pillows. Drapes and valences were colorless and sexless and the air of the Home smelled perpetually of cold hospital antiseptics. And then there was Ms. Bessell, the dorm mistress, and in his earliest memory she was scolding some kid—his name was Louis or Lenny or something—because he had gotten a bloody nose from picking it and there was blood on the white laundered spread now and the blood was bright and warm and fascinating to Alek, a single island of life in the midst of the apocalypse of seamless whiteness.

These were the things he remembered first, the things that stood out in the most distant part of his mind.

It was said that it was the Home cook who'd found them, he and his sister, swaddled in newspaper and cradled in a cardboard box on the back stoop of the Home under the eaves. No note or keepsake, so went the story, only themselves, waxen foreheads touching, their faces androgynous and similar. The eleventh set of twins forced upon the Home that year, the social worker in charge of their case scratched the surname Knight on their records in true Dickensian tradition and yanked their given names, Alek and Debra, from the skin rag hidden in the pencil drawer of his desk. After that, he handled them in terms of paper only.

It was Cook, a big dark woman with a great laugh and the fearsome habit of smoking lavender cigars, who saw to it that the twins were not separated and placed with their own sex. And in time they came to occupy their own room exclusively, though Cook had little to do with that. The year was 1950 and even though postwar America was prospering from overseas fortunes and Ipana toothpaste ads were telling the baby boomers that in America no child had so bright a future, twins were still especially difficult to place and it wasn't expected they would be. So this token by McEnroy Home was like a consultation prize.

But it was more than that. Cook knew it; they all did.

The twins were special. Magic, some said. Some said things about the twins that scarcely deserved imagining. They learned all their lessons quickly because they were clever, and they made everyone think of them as thoughtful because they were. But there was a subconscious degree of separation between them and the other children of the home. They were almost never seen apart, and their soft, silent looks weighed things between them constantly. But to the other children who could not hear their thoughts they were simply a mystery. They did not exchange secrets in the showers, did not pass or receive notes during class, did not join any of the playground clichés that grew and constantly reformed. And the torment the older Home children wrought upon the younger—the books knocked from desks, the legs outstretched in aisles, the pillowcases full of shaving cream, the braids knotted and dunked in school ink—these things somehow passed them by completely. Cook called them her little blackbirds because of their clever eyes and soot-black lashes and their habit of perching on the breadboard and waiting patiently whenever she was putting in the gingerbread, and the name stuck as names will, but the name carried with it no stigmas, no disgrace.

Alek and Debra Knight came to accept their innate separation at least as quickly as the other children did. And as the years pushed them gently but insistently out of infancy and into adolescence and their reputation grew and the world changed around them from one of security and domestic bliss to a globe of Cold War uncertainty and minority suspicion, they found little changed within the microcosm of the Home. Kids got big and got into fights and sometimes kids died, or were adopted and went off into mysterious corners of the city, never to be seen again. But the two porcelain-faced beauties of McEnroy Home remained year after year. And they found with time that while the others who remained were always nice to them and quick to praise them and considered them lucky to be with, none chose to be their friend, for the children were afraid.

2

Wilma Bessell: Bessell the Bitch.

She was a big, muscled woman, strong and pale as chalk as if the sun had never touched her flesh in her whole lifetime. She smiled avidly at the children and whistled constantly as she wandered down the halls of the Home with her open notebook and busy pen. Her eyes were tiny, clever, always bright and full of a mysterious and bottomless glee. A solid woman, she made the children on her floor—the twins' floor—hug her each night before bed. And what a hateful thing was hugging Ms. Bessell; it was like hugging a rolled-up mattress drenched in Chanel No. 5. And when she wasn't walking or whistling or otherwise driving kids crazy, she could usually be found reading old books of immense size on a bench on the playground tarmac, her back to the brick wall of the Home so she could watch the children play. The covers of the books she read were always black with faded gold and covered with long, overcomplicated titles.

Ms. Bessell came to work at the Home when the twins were six, and almost from the beginning they sensed her demure, sometimes suspicious eyes crawling to find them on the playground, in the halls and game room, in class through the wire mesh panes of the classroom door.

No one else seemed to notice. No one but Cook who all but snarled when Debra mentioned her name, Cook who called Ms. Bessell a "hoe-beech" and slammed the door of the old iron oven with a clang of utter authority. Debra smiled and went about repeating the word to everyone insistently—at least until she slipped and used the word on the woman herself and got solitary confinement for a day. Yet not two days later Alek felt those eyes on himself and his twin once more and became first annoyed with it, and then afraid.

Alek, what is it? Debra demanded to know.

Don't look. She's watching us. Again.

The Bitch? Debra's hand never faltered as she copied the lesson from out of their reader. *Stepping Stones*, the book was called, and there was a happy green pond frog on the cover that Alek had always liked, had drawn many times. They did the speaking in the back of their minds, where they could keep it going and use the rest for their work. *Dumb hoe-beech is always watching*, Debra said and turned a page of the book.

The frog on Alek's book smiled up at him, but now it seemed horrible and open-mouthed to him. Sinister. As if it would begin to speak at any moment and say things he neither understood nor wanted to hear from it. *I know*, he answered her. *I hate her. Cook says she ain't for real.*

How?

Alek shrugged, only believing Cook because she was nice and always spoke softly to Debra and sneaked them treats after dark when the kitchen was closed and no one was looking. Cook had said those very same words that very same morning when she found out about Debra's confinement—*She ain't fer real, chile. You best beware the beech, you hear, little bird?* And Alek had nodded dutifully even as Cook grunted and smiled through her bulldog face and wiped the raspberry stain off his face from the tart she had given him.

Maybe she's got an awful monster inside her chewing her all up inside, Debra suggested and it was just like her. *You know? Like in Thriller Theatre?*

Alek bowed his head over his work and did not answer, shutting out the Bitch's glancing smile and gaze. It was Debra's eyes that flashed up, dark and mirrored and full of some black token of warning. She was probably thinking about getting back at Ms. Bessell for the confinement thing by putting earthworms in her shoes or something. He saw dirt in Debra's mind, and squirming living things crawling across an expanse of bluish-white flesh. He shook his head and frowned. But when, finally, he felt brave enough to join her look, he saw that the Bitch was gone.

Debra smiled sincerely, took his hand, squeezed his fingers. The sensation made him wince, made him almost see the worms and the naked earth in her eyes.

Ms. Bessell did not court Debra Knight's gaze after that. She seemed almost afraid of Debra, and for that Alek was grateful and stayed close to her because she was everything to him and she kept him safe with her words and her definite little touches. And because he was certain that as long as they were together and could speak and dream and touch and laugh about the funny names Cook made up for the Bitch everything would always be all right.

3

Later that same week it happened for the first time.

Alek was dressing in the boy's locker room when he thought he heard a gentle whistling rebounding on the dragon-green tiles of the shower walls. He froze solidly in the midst of buttoning up his shirt. He caught his breath and held it tight within himself until the whistling receded.

Then it returned. Louder. Larger.

He looked around and realized he was completely alone, for the other boys had finished showering and gone out to the playground or down into the game room the way he usually let them before emerging from behind the thick white curtain of steam and water. Once, one of the older boys had laughed at him and asked him if he planned on joining a carnival as a Living Skeleton, and since that time he never let the others see his body again. Now he hated that boy bitterly. He wished Debra was near, but Debra was a girl and couldn't be here. Still, he whispered her name for comfort and because the sound of it always made him feel clever. He thought about what she would do in this situation—probably rush right out into the aisle and start chanting one of the funny little ditties Cook had taught her—and did just the opposite and retreated into a narrow niche between two lockers, hoping the Bitch would pass by with her melodious whistling and her notebook without noticing him. Alek closed his eyes, did not feel or think or breathe. And waited.

Footsteps. Whistling, long and musical. Strains of Bing Crosby Then nothing.

Alek opened his eyes.

And there she was looking down on him with small studious eyes. Her frame filled the slight opening of the tiny niche to overflowing. So much so, that for a moment Alek was certain her white flesh—fishlike pale and ugly when he thought to compare it to Debra's cold smooth tautness—would began to seep like Silly Putty around the edges of the lockers and drown him in all its smothery softness like the Blob or something. He thought about what Debra had said about Thriller Theatre, and looking on Ms. Bessell, he saw her the same way suddenly—as something white and dead and as desperate as one of the monsters on television. Her lips were painted overly dark for her face, like someone who had eaten too much raspberry preserves, but between those lips her jumbled teeth were as yellow and mottled as the skin of an overripe banana. The fluorescent lights had made her eyes reflective so they shone like the milky, cataract-filled eyes of a dead woman, a victim of the monster.

"Hello there," the Bitch said as if they were meeting for the first time. She tipped her head and the backlighting threw her shadow like a cold old blanket over his face. "Alek...Alek." Bessell tapped her notebook meditatively. "Did you know your name means 'savior of mankind'? No, you didn't know that, did you? Of course not. Now you do."

Alek said nothing.

Ms. Bessell smiled. She said, "I brought you something," and reached into the side-slit pocket of her dress and offered him the chunky magical wand of a Clark Bar.

Alek wanted to tell the Bitch to go to hell, the way Cook always did, but he couldn't seem to find his voice. Something had eaten it all up.

But Ms. Bessell was a patient woman and held the Clark Bar out to him for some time. "Please, Alek. I want to be your friend. I want you to have this. I promise I won't tell anyone. It'll be our little secret." But when he did nothing after many long wordless moments, Ms. Bessell pocketed the sweet. "No?" she said with a smile. "No: I guess that doesn't interest you, does it? What does interest you?"

Alek watched in dawning horror as the Bitch reached into her opposite pocket and produced a small flashing blue sliver of a razor. A part of him wanted to whimper and beg. And yet there it was, the razor as bright as a cleaver under the harsh glare of the light. Move! he told himself, but his body was fastened into place, his eyes stuck unblinkingly on the shiver and spin of light on the piece of stainless steel.

Ms. Bessell smiled and pressed the metal to the tip of her left pointer finger until the white skin there gave to crimson. Then the dry white hand went out to his face. He turned away, pressed his spine to the back wall and tried to make himself small, but he couldn't escape the Bitch's finger at his mouth, tracing an invisible pattern over his lips and wetting them with the warmth and stink of her substance, lingering on the hard ridges of his eyeteeth. He shut his eyes tight, his mouth tighter; he could hear the other children shouting and laughing down in McEnroy's belly and just beyond it on the playground, so near and yet so hopelessly far away, and all of it muffled by the strangling, rhythmic rasping of the Bitch's breath on his cheek.

For a long time they simply remained that way, like two inappropriate statues hooked together.

And then, abruptly, the Bitch turned and began to walk away, whistling her incessant, stupid songs.

Alek wiped away the foreign substance on his sleeve, waited a moment until the whistling had vanished from the halls completely, and then ran. That night Debra cried for him. Alek turned over in the bed they shared and held her, her bones birdlike and fragile, a familiar mystery of construct, her hair tangling and lost irretrievably with his own. He was afraid, but he trusted his fear to no one but her, because his fear had no name and they were together, but together they were utterly alone. And together and alone they comforted each other and held to each other as if they would lose themselves if they let go even a moment.

So they spoke and wept softly, and between the shelters of their tangled hair, Alek let his special teeth graze his lower lip until he felt the first stirrings of sweetness there and then offered his sister the kiss that was both a pledge and a promise. Her lips were cold and she suckled eagerly at his mouth because it was what comforted her and what they had always done when they grew too lonely and afraid and hungry for something they did not know what. And then, only when her lips were stained crimson, was she able to sleep.

Alek kissed her once more, but softly this time. And he tasted her, tasted them, and the single creature they were in their minds and hearts, a creature so hopelessly different from every other creature here that he sometimes wondered what it was they should be called, what its name was, if he dared ask. Mates, he thought, his hand at her bleak, icy profile. We are mates. At six years of age the concept was almost too distant for Alek to fully understand, yet he knew it to be the only real truth.

4

When the twins were seven years of age, couples began to take notice of them. Debra, particularly, because with her alabaster face and hands she seemed like a pretty china doll that should be arranged on a bedspread or carefully preserved behind plates of dusty glass.

The first time she was to be fostered out she stormed back and forth across their room in her white slip, the fabric thin and fragile on her ghostlike body, her arms crossed and hair trailing after her like a black silk cloak. "I won't go," she stated, not bothering with the speaking, wanting now the gruff pleasure of speech. "I won't, Alek. They can't make me!"

He saw the Bitch grinning in Debra's mind and heard a distant echo of whistling and he nearly shuddered, held it back to be strong.

"They can't make me leave," she hissed. "They can go to hell. All of them."

Alek turned away from the sight of her graceful, pacing rage and studied the box of her things on their bed, the shimmering dark clothes, her sketches of unicorns and the moon and the Raggedy Andy doll he was giving her because she'd lost her Raggedy Anne somewhere in Central Park during a school outing. He looked aside, ashamed, because he wanted to weep and he knew he shouldn't, that he was a boy and he should be strong for them both, the way boys always were on TV. "You have to, Debra. They say—"

"Goddamn them!" She smiled, her hair blizzarding around her savage little face. And he was shocked to hear her say those words and to say them with such power and ease. "I hate them," she whispered, hoarse with grief, "all of them." She began to sob, and he rose and went to her, embraced her carefully, her face sinking into the cradle between his neck and shoulder like two pieces that fit exactly.

Don't cry, Debra, he told her. *It'll be all right, I promise. I'll be right here.*

But you won't be with me. We won't be together.

He thought about her words, and then pressed her back, inspired. From under their bed where he kept his best treasures— a model of The Spirit of St. Louis made of Popsicle sticks, the sockful of marbles he always beat Bobby Watson with at Dead Man's Square on the playground, his banned copy of *Catcher in the Rye* that Cook had given them, an issue of Popular Mechanics all about the Sputnik—and dug out the ring he'd found in a gutter in the street near the Fountain Avenue Dump a couple of months ago. Bobby insisted it was some cast-off junk, but Alek liked to believe it was far more valuable than that.

"Your ring?"

"Our ring," he said because he felt clever the way he did sometimes when he looked at a Picasso picture and could see different stories inside it and make up all his own on paper just from that one look. He turned the ring over; it felt heavy and warm and powerful in his hand. "It's magic. When you look into it, you'll see me."

"That's stupid."

"Is not. Look how it shines. Look how it holds my image."

And it did shine in the dim light of the reading lamp on the bedside table; it shone like a magic talisman in the stories they liked to read by Tolkien and others with their faraway lands and talking swords and beautiful dragons. And in the ring she studied was his own face, as plain as day. "Why is it magic, huh?"

"Well...because something is, you know, if you want it to be. And we're lucky. We're magic. Everyone says so."

"You're so smart." The tears were on her cheeks like splashed gems. "Do you love me?"

"You know I do. I'll always love you." He cupped her face and kissed her, razed his tongue along her teeth so she could taste him and take comfort.

"Debra Knight."

Her precious name sounded so unmusical coming through the harsh gravelly voice of the social worker standing in the door. And behind his impatient, chain-smoking figure were Debra's new foster parents, the McKinneys, a pair of middle-class white-picket people with bovine faces and sympathetic eyes staring at them as if they were two poor Little Orphan Annies. Mrs. McKinney wore her trussed hair under a boxlike hat and Mr. McKinney was dressed in wool slacks and a dull yellow cardigan. They moved almost in sync and looked eerily like mechanical replicas of Ozzie and Harriet Nelson.

Alek narrowed his eyes on them and touched his sister's face once, twice. She caught his hand, kissed it. *My beloved,* she told him, the words as soft and insinuating as a caress to his senses.

"Come along, Debbie dear," said the grinning Harriet replica.

"Debra," she said. *Bitch.* Her fist swallowed up his gift as she turned to her twin and smiled darkly and told him silently, like a promise, that she'd soon be back, soon, and all he had to do is wait. Then she gathered up her box of belongings and followed the social worker out.

Alek did not sleep that night, waking again and again. Afraid. Alone in his enormous bed. He listened to the raspy breathing of the new boy occupying the bed in the opposite corner, hating him. Hating everyone. He closed his eyes and brushed Debra's mind with his own, felt her wake gratefully from her own fitful sleep in a room painted in bright blushing pinks that was all wrong for her in a home set snug and safe behind a whitewashed fence in some upstate suburban town. He put his hand up on the wall over his bed, knowing she was doing the same thing.

I want to fly away, Alek, she said.

So did he.

And then suddenly they were high above the city where the lights shivered and millions of voices whispered, and without ever having left their beds. It was magic, and so easy. It was how the twins learned they could fly. They linked hands and passed invisibly over sharp, lighted pinnacles, the thrill of vertigo tightening their hearts and throats and taking all the pain out of them because they were together now, in the only way they knew how, the only way left to them.

And when Debra dropped in a sudden burst of laughter, Alek followed her to see what had entranced her so. She spiraled down and drifted ghostlike over a great wheel encrusted with hundreds of dark eyes. She dipped lower and then she was beneath the wheeled roof, slipping through a menagerie of painted wooden animals impaled on candy-striped poles, dancing through the strange forest before settling at last with a kind of sigh on the proud arch of the dolphin's back.

Alek watched her from a shy distance, envious, almost afraid because she was so brave, and loving her because she was absolutely everything, the beginning and the end, his life and blood and desire made real. Afterward, Debra returned to him and carried him up over the carousel, and their innocent lovemaking was a dream of fluttery touches and gentle, searching kisses that left him breathless and hungry.

They visited the carousel in Central Park often after that first night, always with Alek drifting at its edge to watch his twin's antics. But then the dawn would come, inevitably, and the dream would end and they would awaken separated, Debra in her dollhouse bedroom fixed by big children playing pretend and Alek in his sterile cage where he could hear whistling walk the halls of McEnroy Home in the early morning like a malevolent spirit waiting on the full moon and the bloodsport attendant thereon.

5

Less than a month passed before Debra Knight was returned to McEnroy Home. The mealy-faced McKinneys were reluctant to elaborate on their reasons except to say that their childless union wasn't quite the torment it once was.

Debra laughed that night as she turned full circle in their room, her bloodred camisole spinning like the scarlet wings of an exotic bird around her legs. Alek embraced her the moment she stopped, and she kissed him and nipped at his ear in playful greeting.

"How did you do it?"

Debra smiled deviously. "Oh so easy, my beloved," she said, casting back her head in delight, shaking out her hair. "I used the

Method, of course."

The Method. The old technique just about every kid at McEnroy used to dissuade a stupid pair of foster parents from adopting you: break a few china plates, clog the pipes, act crazy or just downright rude. But it was more than that. Alek realized that immediately. No foster family sent you back this fast, no matter how badly you wrecked their house.

Debra laughed anew, full of the glee of revenge. "I took their little canary and cooked it. It was absolutely delicious. Mrs. McKinney's expression, that is."

He drew back. He felt pale, a little sick.

But then she looked at him and kissed him again and it was like in all the stories, but with the spell being made and not broken with that kiss, and Alek's love for her was too great for his revulsion and, finally, he kissed her back. But now her mouth was different, her eyes deeper, a shade wilder, and Alek felt he held some strange savage goddess in his arms. What had she learned in the last few weeks? How was she so different?

He tried to search her mind but she shrugged teasingly away from him. He watched her, mystified, when she climbed into the open bedroom window where the summer night wind turned her gown to flames and her hair to a living cloak of sapphire darkness and smiled invitingly and put out her hand to him.

"Fly with me, Alek, pleeeease?" she pleaded.

Out there? In their physical forms?

"Debra, we can't!"

"Why?"

"What do you mean why? We can't! We just can't! It'd make the grownups angry."

"Who cares if the grownups are angry?"

And he opened his mouth to argue, but there was no real argument inside of him, only fear, small and gnawing like a little mouse, and he was embarrassed by it.

"In case you haven't noticed, there is a world out there, Alek," Debra told him. "And I want you to play with me in it! Right now!"

And so he put his hand in his twin's as he must, and that night they played in the dark with their shiny eyes as they would many nights afterward, hide-and-seek and tag and some strange game Debra had learned where you waited until an animal or insect was inches from your absolutely still hand, probing or sniffing it, and you could catch it so quickly it didn't have even a chance to panic.

But with that game and time the wildlife around the Home became boring and Debra guided him to the rabbit holes in Central and Battery Park and to the tenement lots where starved strays burrowed deep into Dumpsters. And she'd learned where the pigeons were and where to find the pond geese by night and the method of catching them and soothing them to silence with her touch and her whispers. At least until the night her little captured rabbit died of fright. Debra cut it open in curiosity and studied its strange and beautiful jewel-like little organs, the jellylike shine of its secrets.

"Do you see?" she said, pointing out its tiny, muscular heart. "Without this its blood wouldn't move. It's like a machine, Alek, a pretty machine." Then she smiled. And quite unexpectedly, she pressed the naked little beast to her twin's lips as if it was a Communion chalice and watched, pleasantly amused, as Alek writhed away from it with a mixture of revulsion and curiosity. She laughed at him, put her finger in the crimson pool and painted his mouth red. And this time when the chalice was passed he did not balk but sipped carefully from the vessel of life, raw and delicate and bitter and wild.

It was a curious thing, not unnatural, exactly, only...unfamiliar. Animals were meant to be eaten anyway.

"I thought it tasted like pepper and flowers," Debra told him afterward.

"What are we?" be asked her in response as they lay down together in bed that night, for though his belly was swollen and warm with their repast, his intellect demanded to be fed as well.

Her mind laughed at him and she called him a poor, miserable philosopher. She turned over and kissed him all over, making him laugh and squirm with the sensation. Finally, when her cold, delicate little lips found the thicket scratch on his cheek, he felt her stop, sip, drink the blood off his shallow wound as if she hadn't had enough with the rabbit, would never be filled. *You know the word,* she laughed.

He thought of the movies they'd seen, the stories in the comic hooks. *Vampires.*

Eww, no. Demigods, she said because she'd learned the word somewhere and it meant something like an angel.

After that it became the routine of their lives. The couples who were comfortable with their safe, beautiful lives habitually fell in love with and wanted the china doll beauty of McEnroy Home to compliment their pristine ivory houses. At least until she produced the red shade of death in their household, after which she was dutifully returned to the Home and to Alek.

Still, the twins were together every night, even in their brief separations, because they could fly. And fly they did, over the city and through it, sometimes as ghosts and sometimes as demigods, but always as mates, and with nothing to mar their dark, perfect happiness but the smiling nightmare of Ms. Bessell and the whistling.

CHAPTER 2

1

The girl was not Debra.

Why had he thought she was? A trick of the light, perhaps, or the fantasy of her doll-like, sensuous face floating before him. Those great dark eyes. But she was not Debra. And Alek understood with all the violence of an epiphany that he was about to die by Debra's doppelganger. Die. Slain by a creature with the body of an angel and the eyes of a Lilith—and yet, he could not move, could not rise, could not flee or start or cry out even as the creature placed her delicate long hands to either side of his head and tipped his face up, her makeupless old eyes boring black holes through his skull and far back into the most intimate chambers of his mind and memories.

So easy for her, she was so old and talented. She saw all he was. All that he had ever done. All his sins. He was naked before her. He jerked once near the end, stiffened like a corpse in the girl's hands. And then he fell away from her and hit the ground at her feet, face to the broken asphalt, prostrate before her because he neither had the strength nor the will to rise. She'd taken it all and he was bereft. He wanted to destroy her—needed to, if only to kill what she'd learned about him—but he would never pick up that sword again. Not now—not when all its tragedies had been revealed to her.

Instead, he remained as he was, cheek numbing against the ground, his eyes open but seeing it all blindly, without purpose or control. All of it. Compulsively. From beginning to end like a horror movie played in fast forward. The blood. Debra. Amadeus. The carousel. The sword. The Grand Testing. He wept. He didn't care now if the vampire reached for him in hatred or in hunger and soiled the floor of the city with his blood. It was all right. It would at least be closure, the edges of his thwarted fate coming together.

He would be with Debra once more—

"Mister Alek? My laws, Mister Alek!"

His eyes swept open, his head angling toward the voice, letting it drag him back to the present. The alley, already tight, stony black with graffiti and night, seemed to shrink further down around the wide, boyish bulk of the figure standing over him with such concern. Eustace. Damned fool. Why couldn't the whelp just let him be? Why couldn't he just let his elder die in peace?

Eustace tugged annoyingly at his arm. "Mister Alek, are you hurt, sir?"

Yes.

"Talk to me, Mister Alek!"

No. Leave me alone.

"Mister Alek!"

No, not Mister Alek. Just Alek, once. Just Beloved. Just that, once, when I belonged to *her*...

Finally Eustace let him go and stumbled back to eye the creature stationed not a dozen paces away from them, watching them. Catlike. Waiting. White-faced Kabuki doll in all her medusan tangles of midnight hair and red eyes and lacy bloodstained dress. Black leather coat. Chains. Too old for her, that coat, and that dress too young, like an old whore had dressed her. How old *was* she? How old could *anything* be? Her hands slid like fragile white spiders down the line of her hip and thigh. Her eyes darkened. Her lips parted silkily. She had fanged eyeteeth, upper and lower, like the mouth of a great cat, like something unevolved and primitive. She was old, old to smile like that with such teeth. She would pounce on them both and tear their throats out and it would all be finished. Him. Eustace. All of it. The end. Fertig.

"Don't worry, Mister Alek, sir, I won't let nothing happen to you, sir, I promise, I double promise!" Eustace drew his sword and parried it at the creature like a poker.

The creature snarled in response and shrank away. Eustace advanced on it, trembling, jabbing at it, winging the brickwork with the tip of the delicate weapon, hooting like a kid driving swine. The creature retreated to the back, stopped, and spun around. Nowhere to go; she'd reached the dead end wall. No fire escape to jump to, no boxes to climb, no windows and no window ledges. Eustace had her boxed in. She put her back to the wall and only watched him approach with wary, unblinking eyes. Her demeanor was distant, unafraid; she seemed to understand innately that the game was almost over and there was nothing she could do to derail this simpleton's prerogative.

Alek eyed the girl. The girl eyed him. Black hair and red dress. Debra...

The ring grew hot on his hand, as if it had been on coals.

Debra. She was alive. But how...?

Alek was on his feet, the sword at his side. He could rise after all, he discovered; he could take up the sword. He did have the strength and the will after all. And he would save Debra this time. It was so easy, so clear and easy and full of truth. Magic. It was like a different soul stepping into him, an older soul, one with all of the answers. A soul he trusted with his life.

He stalked forward, wielding his weapon like a wing, and with that wing he took flight.

2

Sean Stone's eyes narrowed in irritation when be heard the noise for the first time. His chair was cocked back on two legs, his feet propped up on the edge of the Coventable, and he didn't pay it much notice at first because he was paging through a four-year-old flesh magazine with a set of straight pins at hand, using them to spear the whore's tits and faces and alternately to peel back the cuticles on his thumbnails to get the blood to rise. His fingers were an aching ruin, two of the fingernails stripped dead away, and the pinups he was torturing were no longer naked; they were gowned in his blood.

Mom used to hate his habit.

His face hardened at the memory. He realized he hadn't thought of his mother in fucking *years*, not since she'd rode the speedball to the stars over ten years ago. Mom in that black rubber-like dress, beautiful and cold as the Snow Queen in the old fairy tale, white-gold hair down to her skinny ass. But her fragile frame had disguised her strength; her hand had had the power of a brick when it connected with his face, knocking his chronically bleeding fingers out of his mouth.

He used to like her better stoned. She'd put him to bed and read things to him, his storybooks or her Harlequins or whatever she had, it didn't matter, not to him. But then after a while she'd crash, and then she went fucking nuts and cried and screamed a lot about her fucked-up abortion and how much he was costing her in food. Like he ate much, or all that often. Sometimes she'd break things, or try to break him. Didn't work.

But, man, that was then. A lifetime ago, all that shit. A lifetime since he was a little snot with blood and fear smeared all over his face. And he'd evolved since then, changed. He'd gone from bleeding himself to the sticky-furred crawly things in the alleys around Slim Jim's Shangri-La, where they lived and Mom worked, to Slim Jim himself one night. The stupid bastard—he'd caught Sean alone in the apartment, put a stiletto under his chin, unzipped his pants, and told him he was up for his first business lesson. And Jimbo had thought Sean would be the surprised one. What big eyeteeth you have, grandma, heh-heh.

Sheep. That's what all of them were—mortal, ripe, and waiting. Stupid and living in the shadow of the wolf. But now, shit, studying the ribbons of blood coursing out of his thumb, he realized he'd digressed somehow. He sucked his thumb. The blood was good, eased the nausea in his stomach left over from the night before. He felt almost right.

The noise again.

Sean lowered the magazine, but there was no one here except the two of them, himself and Father Amadeus. The Father sat meditating like a Shao-Lin monk at the center of the table, brilliant white hair plaited over one shoulder, claw-like hands resting calmly on his knees. His eyes were open, but Sean knew he was elsewhere. Still as a Buddha, man. Beside him lay one of the books of the Ordinances of the Covenant Sean had thrown down after the Father had lighted out and wasn't noticing him anymore.

He shook his head at the book. Rules. Rules everywhere. Sometimes he really hated the Coven. Well, not the Coven precisely—just them, those sanctimonious assholes skulking around like they were angels of death or something. Doc Book was kind of cool and all, but the others...Takara was just a bitch on wheels and Useless Eustace was like some stupid, piss-assed puppy everyone thought was just darling; he could be cute even when he was being a total backwoods weed.

And then there was Alek. That fuckhead had it coming to him, oh yeah. Heir to Covenmaster or not, Sean was going to take his pound of flesh out of Amadeus's protégé for crossing the Stone Man. Turn your back, you long-haired scarecrow, and wham! You are one righteously dead duck. It was going to be easy, man, easy as taking candy from a baby. Easy as...well, as eating a Slim Jim.

Sean giggled at that and turned the page to a new victim.

Shit, what was it with that noise, man?

Scowling, really bugged now, Sean pulled the earplug full of Cowboys From Hell out of his left ear and kicked down his chair. He leaned forward to study the Father. Like a statue. Couldn't be he was having some kind of seizure or something, could it? The Coven with all its rules was pretty much shit and all, but Amadeus was cool. It was the Father who had gotten his ass out of the system last year, just like magic. And, man, if there was a hell it looked like a foster home, and if there was a Satan he was really a social worker. He owed the Father, and the Stone Man was no ingrate. Weren't for the Father he wouldn't know jack-shit about who he was.

It was Amadeus who taught him how to read and write, how to use a sword and handle the psi without killing himself. The Father said he was a rare thing, not a freak like everyone else seemed to think. He was a slayer, a dhampir, not a vampire like in some fucking stupid Dracula movie. Amadeus's choice in heirs was shit and all, but Sean sure as hell didn't want to watch as the old guy dropped dead or something. The Father cared when there wasn't anyone else to give a shit about you.

Sean passed a hand across his master's face. Nothing. Maybe he ought to just hustle his ass out of here. Go crash in his cell and plug into the Net or something. This was all too weird, man.

Scrubbing at the stiff little hairs on the backs of his hands, Sean was just about to take his own good advice when he heard the sound again. It *was* Amadeus. As Sean watched, transfixed, the Father's eyes brightened, the distant consciousness behind coming fully to the fore, and with it—

"Oh, *shit*, man," he whispered, bracing himself in his seat. He recognized that look. Like Mom's, only it was worse because his old lady at least couldn't turn your mind inside out and mix it up like a machine if she was good and pissed off with you.

A wave of silent white rage slapped Sean's face like a fiery hand. He gave a little squeal of surprise and toppled over in his seat, his skull cracking against the cobbled promenade of the Great Abbey. What the hell? He blinked, hands nesting his bruised skull. Then his eyes widened. Using his elbows as leverage, he wriggled out of his overturned chair and scrambled to his feet, cowering. Cowering, because Amadeus was coming off the table in a savage hiss of silk. His eyelids were lax, his colorless eyes hooded by crystalline lashes, his face pale, writhing, subhuman. His hair actually bristled, rising out of its plait like quills. Like albino snakes.

Standing, he began to pace, barking words that lashed the air of the Great Abbey like blades, words in languages Sean could not begin to guess at. His lips splashed spittle, mantras or curses, spells for all Sean knew. Words that built arches and buttresses and pinnacles around them, an enormous cathedral of noise built up and up toward heaven, a golgotha of sound, of light and shadow, air and bronze...

Sean buckled and collapsed. He crushed his hands to his head in a blind effort to hide from the shattering noise of the Father's unleashed wrath, so terrible it seemed to gain a real presence in the room with them. It rattled the crosswords and sent angry hackles through the tapestries. It smothered the candles in the chandelier and it set the mosaic panels to perilous singing above them. Sean squelched his eyes, but it did nothing, nothing to break the cacophony, the sound as nakedly painful inside his head as out. And when something struck him across the face, he began to cry. He didn't want to be hit, he didn't. He wanted to be good, but he couldn't, it was so damned hard, so damned fucking *hard*...

Sean's whimpering voice hitched, caught on a sob. He moaned, trembled. Afraid. Angry too, angry as all hell now, because he was kneeling here with snot running out of his nose and begging for the mercy that had never come, and, shit, man, he was the Stone Man now, not some eight-year-old turdface. And no one hit the Stone Man. No one made him cower. *No one*, man.

His eyes slit open. And now he saw that it wasn't a hand that had hit him. It was a bat. One of the Abbey's bats. It chirped, fluttered over onto its back, struggling and dying. Not the only one too. The bats were falling all around him. Three big young males lay scattered at his feet, glassy-eyed, their little pink tongues lolling stupidly. A female struggled only inches from him, her suckling, crushed from the fall, still attached to a tit. Dark muddy blood spooled from little velvet ears and from moist, struggling snouts and beaded eyes.

Sean groaned.

This was all too fucking weird, man!

Amadeus loomed silently overhead. His face was a lifeless mask. Blood dribbled out of his clenched fists and from the corners of his mouth where he'd bitten through his tongue. His mouth moved soundlessly.

Or not quite soundlessly, for Sean could just make out the murmured phrase being repeated over and over like a holy litany. Latin. And Sean was surprised to realize he could translate this one by way of all the stupid hours he'd been made to study that shit.

Alek. Amadeus was speaking of Alek.

He called him a Judas.

3

Alek collapsed at the foot of the carousel, wrapped his arms around himself and arched his back. His scream was a sword, narrow, deadly, penetrating, and for a moment all his whiteness of flesh flushed red as though his skin had turned to crystal and his blood shone through like light in a cathedral window. Then he sagged forward, forehead touching the stage of animals like a man whose soul had come out with his cry and left him an empty shell.

"Alek Knight."

His eyes moved painfully to meet those of the vampire. She was seated on the edge of the stage like a beautiful and expensive porcelain doll some child had placed there and forgotten. He did not fear her; what had he to fear as damned as he was? "Eustace," he wept, running his hands through his hair, pulling at it like a madman. "Oh Christ, Eustace. *Eustace...*"

Judas, he thought, a second scream within. *Cain.*

She did not smile, nor did she make any move to take him, now, at his most desperate moment. She did not give him even that. "Why did you kill the slayer?" she asked him innocently.

He wept and did not answer her. And all this time they'd said it was Sean. They'd all but branded the word on the young one's forehead and cut his cheeks to mark him. But it wasn't him. No, it wasn't. Because the real Judas already wore his mark and it was the mark of Covenmaster. How had this happened? *How?*

"Alek Knight, so full of regret..." the creature singsonged. "Regret nothing, for regret is a useless emotion."

"I've sinned," he groaned. *Oh, God, have I sinned...*

"You've sinned before. You mean you've sinned against the Coven."

He closed his eyes and saw again the sword burying itself in soft white throatflesh, the redness and the heat and the scream like a wire pulled tight as a migraine across his mind. And all for Debra. All for this thing. "I'm the Judas! I was to be Covenmaster after Amadeus," he sobbed.

"And do you wish to be Covenmaster?"

"Shut the fuck up. You talk like—*the fucking social workers in the Home!*"

"Debra. You meant to say Debra."

"No, I didn't. Get the fuck outta my head!"

He caught himself, calmed his hysteria. Why in living hell was he arguing with this thing? Why had she followed him? Why was she torturing him like this? *Why?* And why the hell wasn't she killing him or leaving him the hell alone?

"Don't lie to me, caro mio. I've glimpsed the naked side of your soul. You cannot lie to me after such an intimacy." She reached for his hand, and to his amazement he found himself allowing her to take it as she had taken the rest of him, his mind, his empty soul. She held it a moment, watched him with her dark, intense stillness. Then she turned his palm over and read it like a Gypsy wise woman. "You have no lifeline," she said.

"I'm dead."

"Vampire."

"No. Yes. No! You're the vampire," he spat at this persistently annoying little demon.

"And Amadeus?"

"Amadeus is—"

"The greatest vampire," she said. "His eyes are dark, Alek Knight. He knows."

"He'll kill me."

She smiled over his palm. "No. He won't."

He yanked back his hand. "Jesus, who are you?"

She smiled, her face flushing like shadowed porcelain, full of secrets. For a moment the world shifted around them and again she was the Debra clone, the saintly, bone-jarring, sensual image. He almost cried. "I am peace. I am beauty. I am death. But you may call me Sister Teresa."

"I'll kill you," he spat to hurt her, this beautiful little monster with her evil powers, her power to make him do things he would never even think of doing otherwise. "Like I killed a hundred of your kind on a hundred other nights like this one."

Her smile never faltered. "Yes, all right. Kill me too."

He looked at her. He looked away. "I lost my sword."

"Then take me with your lips and your hands and your words. Release me as you released the other—"

"Why are you tormenting me?" he screamed into the dark.

"Torment makes pain. Pain makes you strong; pain also breaks you."

"Is that what you want? To break me before you kill me?"

"Don't be too strong to be weak, Alek Knight."

He shook his head, furious, helpless. Broken. "Go away. Just go the hell far away. Go! I'm giving you a respite, only don't make me look at you another moment."

"And what will you do with me gone?"

He did not answer. Why should he?

"I see," she said. "You will return to your great mausoleum and look on the face of your master and he will destroy you and only your skull will remain to crown your infernal Babel. You cannot allow this to happen, Alek Knight."

"It's what I deserve," he insisted.

"But I need you."

He felt something seize him from within. A memory—Debra's mischievous smile. "What the hell do you mean?"

She took his face in her hands. But now there was no pain, no memories. Only her. Only beauty. Only that. She kissed him with her knowledgeable little mouth as if she would seduce him to his death. She tasted red. Debra. She said, "I am old in the ways of continents and languages. I remember the Black Death. I have walked with the cursed children of Lilith since before the Crusades," she said. "So old, Alek Knight, and in all those years I kept the secrets of the Church." She lowered her eyes. "But then came the knowledge-seekers and the powermongers and they took from me the truth, and that truth they corrupted and scribed wrongly. My work, my purpose, was undone. And the greatest among them built up a cache of lies and perpetuated their power upon which to establish his kingdom—"

He jerked away from her, folded his arms on the stage and let his face fall down upon them. That damned Chronicle or whatever the hell it was. That story again. "Oh Jesus, don't say this. Don't start—"

"You don't believe." She paused reflectively. "But of course— you are caught in the web—"

"What am I supposed to believe? That some fucking book out there exists that can destroy the Coven?"

"Debra believed in the story."

"Debra is dead."

"And you are willing to die for her memory. But are you willing to live for her truth?"

"No."

She took him in her hands once more, turned his face up to her own as if he were nothing but a stubborn little boy. "Do you believe in vampires, Alek Knight?" she demanded.

Her flesh was glass, her teeth slim little slivers of bone, her hair coarse black ribbons that slid compulsively over one-half of her face, making him want to brush it out of her eyes, feel its unnaturalness trickle through his fingers. In her eyes he saw the ages of the earth, truth and fire, darkness and light. Yet of her whole face, only her mouth seemed truly alive, lips full and dark and as changeable as a snake, mocking, sensual, cruel, forever tempting.

He tried to shrug away and failed.

"Yes," she said. "Yes, well, if you would believe in vampires, then why will you not believe that some small part of our history remains? Our kind must have come from somewhere, some Source. And if that Source were divine rather than demonic...?"

"This is a joke."

Her eyes deepened as if his face had suddenly become her oracle. "'Blessed are they that have not seen, yet have believed.'"

He snarled. He yanked himself away from her evil. "So you've read the Bible. Oh fine. Fine. A vampire's favorite pastime. Tell me, Sister Teresa, where's your rosary? Are you wearing a crucifix under that dress?'

She narrowed her eyes. "I despise crosses, Alek Knight. Symbols, they are, of pain and death and injustice."

He met her look with a malicious smile. "Oh? And what symbol would you have?"

She laughed at him. "Perhaps a dolphin."

He cowered and shivered, his back to the stage. He drew up his knees and clasped them, his forehead rocking forward to rest there like a stone. He sobbed, completely exhausted, as the newest snow began to fall, and it was the weeping of children grown too old.

4

A hand shook him to waking. "You were calling out, Alek Knight," said the creature beside him. "I thought it best to wake you."

He looked at Teresa's face shading him like the moon, a face made paler still by the halo of deep night clinging to her form. He unwrapped himself and shied away from her featherlike touch on his arm. Let me go, dear God, please! he wanted to plead, but a wind tainted by the new snow kissed his cheek like a spell and what came out instead as he looked out over the lights of the city was, "I dreamt."

"Yes?"

The words came unbidden, as though of their own volition. "I was in a great hall of some kind, full of the voices that spoke the names of the dead. My coat shone so bright it hurt my eyes. And there were animals in cages so small they could only turn in circles. And pictures...there were these pictures. Portraits, I think. A gallery of them. And they were like Tarot. They were alive. They moved..." His voice trailed away as he listened to the lamenting of the snowbound traffic on Central Park South, the angry vehicles nudging each other like a herd of impatient horses. At the corner a drunk in a watch cap riffled through a basket of trash, oblivious to the snow, hungry...

"Go on."

He licked his mouth, remembering. "The Magician watched me; his eyes could turn the land to white ice, could bleed the earth. And there was another...the Queen of Swords, I think. She was red, her hair, her mouth. But her eyes were green. She carried crosswords and she put them through the Magician's heart, and then the animals came from their cages and I..."

He sank into a meditative silence as he lost the thread of memory. Folding his arms atop his knees, he perched his chin on his arms, wondering why he had told her, wondering what in hell he was doing here in the park beneath the shadow of the carousel with this thing in the middle of the night. Eustace was dead—he was late for his ascension to Covenmaster, and a murderer—his whole damned life falling apart around him—

He felt her eyes burn on his profile, the chains on her coat singing in the soughing wind. "Don't be shy. Talk to me."

He sighed, caught a sob before it could take hold of him. It escaped instead in a plume of steamy white air. He felt utterly hopeless. "What...what do you want to talk about?"

She grasped his arm like a trusting daughter and rested her cheek on his shoulder. Light as a toy. He did not pull away this time. What was the point? "Tell me things. Your Coven," she said, "it is very old."

He nodded.

"Is it true they were the magistrates who hanged the Salem

witches?"

"I don't know. The books say nothing—"

"They wouldn't," she said. "We call him the Mad."

"Who?"

"Amadeo. Amadeo the Mad. Asmodeus, if you prefer. The devil with the white eyes. But his eyes are dark."

Debra's words to him, once, a long time ago. When she lived. When they both lived. This creature. She was beautiful and perfect and she terrified him and he stood up and moved away from her, concealing it with a shrug of stiffness.

She smiled at his uneasiness like the devil she was and flicked the end of her braid over her face like a rouge brush. He had a sudden image of himself laying over her in the dark somewhere, bathed in sweat and passion, his hair in her face, his teeth in her throat...

Her smile grew coy. Her image then. *Her* spell.

He tore his eyes away from her and ventured a step. "I can't stay here, I can't—."

"Amadeus."

He moved away from the carousel, to the edge of the bicycle path. At a distance came the muffled clopping of horses' hooves on snow-packed gravel. He glanced upward. The trees of the park rose bravely against the cold and a future of industry and glass and smog. Far off, the city shown like an expensive set of diamonds in black velvet. The Brooklyn Bridge winked like a collapsing web spun by a spider made all of light and glitter. But here, with his back turned toward her, he could not see the face of his tormentor, nor see her evil smile, nor hear her lasciviously whispered thoughts. He cocked his head up at a sky pregnant with black ice. "He draws on me."

"Blood calls to blood. But where will you go?"

Where could he go? He was homeless rabble now, like the man at the trash basket, no better, and the reality of it stuck in his gut like a blade. The night would pass away in only a few short hours and anything that had seemed safe and temporary in the dark, like the lights on the bridge and all the night sins the city had to offer, would soon be gone with it. He had no real friends to speak of outside the Coven, no one who would understand this thing and not think he was insane. The studio would have been staked out by the Coven by now. And he could never see the dolphins in his bedroom window again—because Amadeus knew, and his blood ran through the Father's veins. They were one.

Where could he go? Where?

His mouth trembled. "He'll find me."

"Of course he will."

He thought of the suburbs, then Connecticut, then farther north. How far north? He didn't know. Who the fuck cared? No matter how far he ran it wouldn't be enough. If he went to Iceland it wouldn't be far enough. "Go away. He'll kill you too. Get as far away from me as you can." He waited, the wind in his coat and a hand in his snow-wet hair, combing it slick across one cold cheek, thinking blankly, wondering what the hell he would do. He waited forever, but when he looked back, she was still there, slender as a bone, doll-like in her simple beauty. She would shatter under the barbarity of his most careful touch, had he dared to touch her.

"Go away," he whispered, hoarse. "It's finished."

She smiled, flashed her ruby eyes at him.

It wasn't fair.

"God damn you," he whispered.

"Walk away from me," she said, "if you can."

She knew magic. Vixen. Sorceress.

It was not fair.

"I can't move," he complained.

"Try."

He went to her. He knelt at her feet. She held the mantle of his head to her breast as if in benediction. "See. You can."

His tears soaked all her raven hair. "I love you."

"You love Debra."

"I want to die for you. Please don't leave me. I love you."

Her fingers burned his cheeks as he expected they would. Red fire to cleanse and to sanctify. Her mouth was red against his, the lightest branding. She licked the tears from his cheeks and chin and left behind only wetness and warmth and the purity of her touch. She kissed him once more, on the side of the throat, over the pulse, and when she drew back her lips wore the paint of his life. His skin flushed inexorably, as if she had set him to burning.

Then she waited, patient, as if for some portent or some vow.

His trembling hands framed her face. All that perfect black hair, those ebony eyes with their scarlet hearts. Red. It was all that was missing, all that she needed to make her a goddess. He kissed her hair, her delicate throat. She sighed and turned her head, offering herself to him now with the same fearless passion she had used to steal away his soul. So unfair. So beautiful.

So perfect.

"I want so much to die for you," he whispered into her hair.

"But I want so much for you to live for me," she answered.

5

"I can't move."

The Circle raised their eyes.

The Father was seated at the head of the table, head hanging amidst a medusan tangle of white long hair, as still as a stone god. On the table lay the two katanas Sean had retrieved from the Village alley at the Father's behest some time ago. They'd fallen crossed, absurdly symbolic: Eustace's beneath and Alek's atop.

"I love you," uttered the Father in a drilling monotone.

Sean frowned. He glanced across the table at the others who had shown face tonight: Aristotle. Takara. Robot. Kansas. Doc Book. Every face was distorted with concern, but only Book was seated far back in his chair, a keen look of understanding darkening his eyes, his sweat-slicked hands laced together on the table in front of him.

Sean smiled. "Worried about your childhood playmate, are you, bro?"

Book returned Sean's look. *Shut up, asshole*, he mouthed.

The Father's voice grew theatrically plaintive. "I want to die for you. Please don't leave me. I love you."

Book's face pinched in understanding. He nodded to himself. *What?* Sean mouthed to him.

Alek, said Book.

Sean narrowed his eyes.

Book sighed and tapped his temple with one finger. *He's inside.*

Oh. Righteous, man.

The Father lapsed into a long, contemplative silence after that, and Sean quickly lost interest. He watched the others look broody and lost and turn their rings and twist their hair and shoot all kinds of sidelong "I told you so" looks at one another. And when it all became too much, too boring, too overwhelming—the tension, the silence eating away at the room like an invisible cancer—he chewed his fingers, his eyes roving over the table and his master and the swords.

It was an amazing weapon, Alek's sword. Mirror-blade, white jade handle as carved as a bone with two opposing hooded asps at the top of the hilt. The serpents were as intricate as a piece of art, all the way down to the scales.

"I knew he was trouble the first time I set eyes on him," Takara whispered. Unlike the others, she sat still enough to rival even the Father. Her black eyes wept light like opals. Her white fist was wrapped tight as rope around the ornate hilt of the wakizashi she favored. She turned the wak in and touched the tip of the blade to her bottom lip. A bead of blood welled up there like a gem. "Even as a boy he had no right to it," she said, those eyes of hers set hard on the Double Serpent Katana.

Her words brought to Sean's mind a curious picture: some gangly, longhaired kid all in black messing around with that sword while all those other lollipop-sweet kids like Wally and the Beaver played with marbles and hoola-hoops or whatever the hell they did way back in the wild and woolly 1950's. Sean laughed. Jaded from the beginning, jaded to the end. "He ain't no saint, sister. He's just a fuckin' queer-o fruitcake. It was just a matter of time before he went tipped—"

"Insane," Takara agreed.

Book shushed them both.

Takara growled at Book.

Kansas flinched and reached for the imaginary brim of the hat he no longer wore.

Silent Robot only stared. Eerie.

"I want so much to die for you."

They all glanced up in time to see the Father's face shatter. "To die..." His hands shot out, knocking the swords clanking to the floor. Then, with automatic precision, those hands spidered up to his face, covered his stupid, useless eyes, his fingers curling into talons in the soft pockets of flesh. The Father uttered a low keening noise to which every pore of the body responded, his cry catching in every corner of the Great Abbey, quaking it to its bedrock and beyond.

Book's dark face paled to sick grey and his knuckles showed white where his fingers gripped the edge of the table. Aristotle and Kansas whimpered and hid under the table together. Takara stiffened. Even Robot, usually as unmovable as a corpse, as unshakable as the manmade, soulless creation which had given him his nickname, blanched and managed to go another shade paler, if that was possible.

Sean cowered in his seat, nearly overturning the chair once more, as the blood ran freely down their Covenmaster's face and tainted the swords at his feet.

6

The water of The Pond was black as oil and the swan at its center blacker still, black, black as the winter sky full of unbroken ice. He was the only one of his flock left and he turned in slow, precise

circles to keep the water from freezing beneath him. It reminded
Alek of a book he'd once read as a young child. He could not
remember the title now but he did remember the story: the prince
of swans was heir to the Pond, but the city wanted to fill the pond
up and build on it and then the water birds would have nowhere
to raise their children. But the prince, being clever, had a plan. At
autumn's end, when his people flew to warmer places, he stayed
behind and entertained the park's children with his clever antics.
The artists and the TV people came from miles around to see him,
and it was they who preserved the pond for the prince and his
people and their children and children's children. But then one
midwinter's night the pond began to freeze, and he turned and
turned to save himself, but the ice caught him up in the end as it
must and by morning he was finished.

At the water's edge, standing on the bicycle path running
alongside Central Park South, Alek tossed the prince bits of sweet
roll he'd purchased at a vender's kiosk on the avenue—the only
food he could afford now with five dollars in his wallet and a cash
card whose PIN number wouldn't work anymore. The swan did
not notice the offering, however; he was too busy trying to live.

He would be gone by morning. The creed of the martyr: The
heroes must always sacrifice themselves.

But he didn't want to be a hero and he didn't want to be a
sacrifice. And it wasn't fair, goddamnit. He wasn't some latter-day
Arthurian adventurer. The sky hadn't opened up. No one had called
him. No lady rose from the lake now with a magic sword and a
mission.

Teresa appeared at his side. "The ice won't be denied," she
whispered.

Heartsick, he looked away from the prince, seeking Teresa's old
eyes in the solid black mirror of the water. "Why do you pursue
this?" he asked. "For what purpose? Even if it were possible to
harm the Coven, why—?"

"Walk with me," she said, "as if you have lived a thousand years
and have no fear of me."

He did. And they walked, going nowhere.

Teresa's eyes pierced the dark with a slow-burning inner fire. He found himself unable to look away. It was as if she were hypnotizing him. No, more than that. It was as if she were x-raying him, glancing through the layers of flesh and bone and blood and for a second time watching all the secret wormy things he kept inside and never showed anyone. And for the first time in his life he did not care because he knew she understood.

"Shall I tell you a story, caro mio? A tale to quell your incessant need to understand all things?"

He hesitated. To know—it would be yet another seduction, of course. She might not even tell him the truth, if a lie was what she needed to entrap him—to use him. Yet he would listen, wouldn't he? For no other reason than because he had no other choice at this point. Nowhere to go, nowhere he could hide from her.

Teresa looked up at the new snowfall. "A story of war, you see, is a story of history. There are the heroes and the villains and the cowards, too. And sometimes there are gods among men, mortal flesh and divine understanding commingled like a man whose blood is mixed with that of demons." She smiled, black eyes flashing beneath winged brows. And now Alek saw the innocent eyes of a young girl, the sleek whisper of a gabardine wimple upon her shoulders, her fingers braided through with rosaries.

"I was seduced from the very moment of my birth, you see," she said. "I was born in Sicily at the end of the Roman Inquisition in the years before the Reformation. I was made by the churchmen, a weapon to be used against the encroaching secularism of the coming age. They fed me slaves and let me drink the blood off the cobbles beneath men and women accused of heresy. I was appalled by what I did, yes, appalled as a good Catholic girl should be, but I did what they told me. Tales of the Inquisition loomed, the dismembering of accused witches, the unimaginable torture of the demon-infested and those accused of acts of vampirism—these things were very real. I was a coward and a murderess but I belonged to them. I put the ring of Christ upon my hand and took my vows and did as they bade me.

"They kept me hungry, and so I did my thirsty hunting with the rats in the peasant slums of Rome and Tivoli. Sometimes I chose my victims and sometimes they chose me. When I chose them they were always newcomers off the boats, the homeless, and those priests who thought to use me for a night and did not know what I was. I was not caught. Through it all, I was never caught."

She was whispering, and now he whispered as well. "You lived in a monastery—this is impossible."

She ignored his interruption. She said, "No. I lied. I was caught, once. Caught by a priest in my act of murder. It was with one of the Castrati. The boy had wandered into my cell in the middle of the night, looking for something or lost. I took him. He was so beautiful and I was so hungry. And there *he* was, watching me from the doorway—"

"A...priest?"

"I flinched. I wanted to make excuses, say something to dissuade what he had seen. I was good at it, but clumsy, you see, but then—" Teresa lowered her eyes. "Then—he was not like the other Churchmen. He joined me. He was another of my kind, created by them. His name was Father Paris. He was a foreigner from Geneva. A priest with the Order of Scribes. And a drinker of human lives. A murderer, like me. He drank the blood off my mouth. And then he made love to me, the corpse still between us. He was so pleased to have found another of his breed, so happy."

He wondered if Teresa realized how uncomfortable he was. He wondered if this was some kind of test, to see if he truly belonged to her world, or if it was a mere exercise to see how long his remaining sanity lasted. If the former, she already had his answer in the flesh he had slain for her not more than a few hours ago. If the latter, it was a test completely unnecessary, for there could be no question as to how far gone he was, to let her abduct him like this.

"I bound myself to Paris. We were secretly married by a vampire bishop by the name of Aragon who dated back to maybe forever.

He and Paris had been working together for years under the cloister of their enemy the Church, scribing the history of our kind's relationship with Rome—what history there was—seeking proof of our origins not as devils but as a people made by the Creator for a specific purpose. I joined them at once, transcribing great portions of their history into Italian, seeking rare texts, stealing documents from the vaults that implicated the Vatican in a conspiracy to purge the entire world of every last vampire once it had purged it of every last heretic. I did anything that might help, anything at all."

"The Ninth Chronicle." Alek closed his eyes.

She nodded. "Aragon," she said, "betrayed Paris. The work he had done was never for his kind. It wasn't to save us from another purge. It was for the Churchmen and their Inquisitors. Hundreds of years earlier the Church had uncovered Aragon's secret and had traded him immunity for his services as a scribe and an assassin. The Church was never so ignorant of us. Aragon had used us to discover the names of all the vampires who had betrayed Rome." She hesitated. "There was a new Purge, a silent one. Many vampires were dismembered, disfigured and beheaded—they were the lucky ones. Many others suffered the same punishment as witches. The burning stake. Sewn into a sack with a snake, a dog and a weasel and sunk in the sea. Ground crucifixion. Other punishing deaths. Unmentionable things.

"But because of Paris's work, some escaped. The Church was faced with the dilemma of hunting down all the survivors, a task that would take hundreds of years to accomplish. But, you see, their greatest weapon was always Aragon. In his pretense for peace with the mortals, he convinced the vampires to formulate the Ordinances of the Covenant. The Coven was established as police to curb the possibility of another Purge and the movement spread on the winds of pure terror and desperation. The vampires saw the restraints of the Covenant and the power of the slayers as the only possible way of avoiding certain agonizing death at the hands of the humans. The Church was never so powerful. And Aragon was never so pleased."

Alek blinked and looked up. "And the Chronicle?"

"It was buried in the vaults of the Vatican, where it remained up until 1962, when the Church began a series of reforms to modernize and resurface its image. In the process, it brought in a number of scholars to comb out and destroy the evidence of the 'darker side of Christianity' as they called it." She narrowed her eyes gleefully. "And one of those scholars was Paris."

"He stole the Chronicle back."

"You know the rest then," she said.

He shook his head. "I know only—" He stopped, the words dying on his tongue, the terror so great a pressure it stopped his breathing, maybe his heart.

"What Debra said?" she asked damningly.

7

In the dream he walked down a hallway constructed entirely of human skulls like the tunnels leading down and away into the arcane catacombs under some of the greater older cities of the world. Rome. Paris. Something slithered over his feet and he looked down and recognized it as an asp. He kicked it away and walked on. And near the end, silhouetted by a sunburst of careening light so great he was forced to squint, he saw a tall, gaunt figure all in black, with reams of glistening silken hair and eyes like white pearls and a smile like a blade. In its right hand he gripped the hilt of a sword, long and terrible, and that sword dripped blood like rain upon the stones of the corridor. In its other hand it held a trophy by the hank of its long, blood-encrusted hair, the unfortunate's face lost in deepest shadow.

And it was then and only then that Amadeus realized he was having The Dream again, the *visual* dream. A dream of sights, of light and shadow and the bruised places in between.

The figure shifted and the chaotic lights he had been half-blocking only a moment ago intensified, set Amadeus's tender eyes to bleeding with the sight of all that light in his life all at once. The deadly black figure laughed and held aloft his prize, letting the light reflect off the disembodied head's marble-white flesh and shimmering white hair and redness of death.

Death.

His death.

His death unrepentant, unabsolved.

Damned.

Amadeus opened his mouth as he had each time upon witnessing the sight of his own destruction and cried out with the horror and the unfairness of it all. The years—*centuries*—he'd spent, saving his own soul, saving his most beloved's. And now this...

But there the dream ended and he awakened trembling and sweating, his sword pointing up at the blinding shimmer of light baking his tender sun-shunned skin, pointing it at the breathy tall figure standing over the baptismal of blood he rested in. And for a moment he almost thought it was Alek and Alek's vengeance and he had a terrible desire to lower his sword and give in, such was his love and his despair. But then, once more, he remembered the great betrayer's work to undo him, to undo all of the Coven, and he realized Alek was not here, was too great a coward to face him yet, and he held the sword unflinchingly on his target.

The figure's hands swept up in a defensive gesture. The light grazed Amadeus's face and was gone. "Shit. Sorry, Father," the master slayer Book whispered in his booming baritone voice, "I thought you were awake, is all. I didn't know..."

His watch—it was only his damnable watch! It was only damnable Book! Amadeus lowered his sword and sat up in the stone crypt, splashing blood to the floor like a massacre. "What do you want?"

"I...there's someone to see you. In the drawing room."

"Who? Alek?"

"No." Book hesitated. "A man, just a man. About sixty-five, seventy. Dressed like a Wall Street banker. Rich bastard. He didn't say his name. But he knew you, he said."

Amadeus ran the blood-soaked palm of his hand over his face. A man. Only a man. But he knew who it was—it could be Joshua Benedictine and none other at this juncture—and the Cardinal was far more than a mere man. And far less. Rising naked from the baptismal, having slept that way, if sleep was indeed what one would call that unsettling interlude, Amadeus began to dress for the audience in his customary black habit, the frogs buttoned so tight he felt like a soldier getting ready to go off to war. He stepped into black boots and slipped the ornate boot knife into place. Lastly, he slid the black wool cloak he favored onto his shoulders and clipped it with a Vatican brooch. Now, regal, and larger for the cloak—and hoping to match Benedictine's personal extravagance— he made for the door of his cell.

At the end of the brick hallway, at the bottom of the cellar steps leading up to the ground floor, lurked Book. His smell was one of unease and discomfort. He was trying to understand this madness, trying to protect his master. And then his pocket pager went off and Book seemed immensely pleased for the interruption. "Oh Jesus, that's probably Dr. Sacco. Damn man never leaves me have any peace, even on my days off. I swear to God, if I—"

"Go to your hospital," Amadeus commanded him, tying up his long hair with a hank of silk ribbon. "Care for your sick. I will need no retinue."

Book hovered a moment more, wanting to help, wanting more to go, to sink beneath the surface of his human life and be just a doctor now, a man. At least for a while. Maybe until all of this was over.

"Go," Amadeus whispered harshly. And so Book went.

"We must assume the dhampir is aware of our plans," Cardinal Benedictine stated after Amadeus had seen the old man in the drawing room to one of the wing chairs near the fireplace. The fury seethed like a nest of snakes in his whiskey-scoured voice and made him drum his fingers irritably against the wooden armrest of the chair.

The two men had not seen each other for years, and yet the

human, a powerful priest out of Rome herself, had made no formal or informal greetings, had not even waited until his host's arrival before breaking open a bottle of Scotch and fetching a glass and starting up the fireplace. And for the next five minutes, as the room warmed around them, their conversation was one of total debriefing. Of course they despised each other as two creatures must whom nature had put natural enmity between. But their ambitions and aims had long wracked that relationship into something unnatural. They were not friends. They did not like each other and never would. But at least—for the moment—they bit back their true thoughts with steel-trap grimaces.

The debriefing was finished. Now came the subjective part of their talk—the part Amadeus despised. He shifted in his seat, the fireplace sweating his flesh under the layers of clothing. He spoke softly, with no attempt to use his voice or mind to influence or otherwise sway Benedictine's mood. The man, in his present state of almost perfect sobriety, would have required too much work. And anyway, Benedictine knew him too well. He understood Amadeus's race perhaps better than any other human being in the Church—or indeed the world—and he would sense the penetration, deduct it rightly as desperation on Amadeus's part, and then there would only be more questions, more trouble.

"I still do not see how this little error could have happened, Cardinal," Amadeus said. "I made him my personal student. He knows nothing that I have not told him—"

"Then someone—presumably Paris's whore—is giving him classified information. God help us all if he puts it all together. There will be a period of darkness the Church has never known before, not even during the Crusades." Benedictine coughed harshly, seemed surprised by the rebellion of his aged body, as if he had forgotten how mortal and fragile it was growing all around him. He cleared his throat angrily.

"I am truly sorry," Amadeus said without emotion.

"Madre. I flew in from half a world away because of this 'little error', as you call it. I had to leave important Council matters and lie to His Eminence himself just to be here, damnit all to hell, and I won't have you treating this thing like some hangnail...!" Again the coughing fit seized him.

Amadeus smiled. He knew the man well enough to know he was lying. Benedictine had spoken to no one before coming here. No one ever questioned Benedictine's work or intentions. The man was powerful. In the last twenty years he had acquired his own private jet and his own retinue of bodyguards. The Papal Council already considered him heir to Peter's seat in Rome—a position that would have undoubtedly fallen to Benedictine's superior, Cardinal Guiseppe, had the man not died some five years earlier of snakebite. The circumstances were a little unusual, but certain men were possessed of almost preternatural luck and even greater allies. Amadeus had done work for Benedictine in the past and Benedictine protected him and his Coven. So he took Benedictine's angry ravings on the chin, as always. As always, he played his loyal dog part, knowing that one day this man would be all that stood between his race and total annihilation.

Benedictine tipped his glass back, the ice chinking against his false teeth. The liquor seemed to stop his cough, surprisingly. And curb his roiling anger. "But we've got to forget about the hows and whys for the moment and do something about the situation," he said, his voice falling soft against the walls of the Covenhouse as his sobriety began to slip. He closed his eyes, savoring the whiskey. "If you cannot contain it, Covenmaster, we in Rome shall."

"I am doing my best, Cardinal."

"Well, your best is not good enough, is it? Where is he? Where is this dhampir? Why haven't you found him yet?" The bottom of his glass banged against the armrest like a judge's gavel. "I thought you were some great all-seeing oracle, some hellishly talented sibyl that saw to the ends of the earth, I thought—"

"The city is large," Amadeus calmly explained, lied, "and even my power is limited. I see the future, Cardinal, not the present."

"I thought he was bound to you, you fucking demon! What have you been doing with him all these years?"

Amadeus closed his eyes. The darkness was the same either way, but sometimes, in times of great angst, like now, he almost felt he could control it. Draw it close like a cloak to hide a shame. The dark, after all, was where his breed originated. And where it would eventually return to, in time. Yes, it would be so easy to find and destroy the whelp. He need only confront Alek, draw his sword, and come home with the whelp's head at the end of it. So easy. And it would save his place in the Covenant, would probably save his own damnable life. But Benedictine couldn't understand the price. He couldn't understand the pain of watching your most beautiful and singular piece of art die at your own hands, your magnum opus. He couldn't understand what it would be like to see the one thing all your life led up to simply crumble away like that. For Alek to die, all that power wasted, all that training vanquished with one fell swoop—it was like Donatello taking a mallet to his beloved David statue. It scarcely deserved imagining.

People like Benedictine, so powerful, did not understand love. People so powerful as Benedictine was did not need it to survive.

Amadeus said, "I must have time. A week at least—"

"There is no time! I told you, we must assume the dhampir knows about our plans, and that would mean he is trying to find the Chronicle even as we speak. Damn you, we can't wait even another day!"

"I want to let him run."

"*What?*"

"I want him to run. To find the Chronicle. If he can."

For a moment Benedictine was silent. For a moment he almost seemed prepared for another bitter outburst. And then reason and understanding set in, warming his ambition like the whiskey warming his belly. The ice cubes swirled around his glass as the man considered the implications of what Amadeus had just said.

Amadeus smiled and halved his eyes. "Yes, Paris's whore knows things. And so does Debra's whore. Who knows where such things may take them together?" Amadeus paused to let all this thinking sink through the human's thick skull. *And I am quite certain that*

Rome will greet you well as you return triumphant from your pilgrimage with their Chronicle under your arm. What do you think, Cardinal? Benedictine let out his breath. The man practically reeked of joy. "A week, you say?"

"I trained him to be my double, Cardinal. Please understand— I must have at least that." Amadeus stood up to indicate the audience was over. Benedictine stood as well. Like most humans, the man, even with all his human power and influence, was still a man standing in the presence of that rarest of creatures—one of his few natural predators. He was trapped under the sway of a cobra that he perceived as a pet. "One week. And I will have your Chronicle in one hand and my wayward acolyte's head in the other. I swear it."

A pause. And then Benedictine said, "Do what is necessary. I will do what I can here to keep the Church from getting in our way. I'll give you your week. But hear well, vampire, you make sure that when you have the dhampir, that you have him *dead*. Is that understood?"

"Of course, Cardinal."

"You sound unsure, Covenmaster."

Amadeus shrugged. "He *is* my double, Cardinal."

"He's not that good," Benedictine said, more a question than anything else.

"Like me," Amadeus said, "he is a king among his kind."

Benedictine considered this. Then the man let out his breath, coughed again, the phlegmatic cough of the perpetually ill. Amadeus thought of serpents shimmering across the hardwood floor of the drawing room. From him to the Cardinal's feet, biting with raspy mouths full of ragged fangs. The Cardinal took a hesitant step back as if sensing this threat on some subconscious level. Yet the poison was already there, planted like a fertile seed in the mortal's tender mind. Benedictine simply would not know it until much later when everything came to pass. He said, low and intimate, "Do not fuck this up. The Purge is only a few years off, and none of us needs a reprisal of 1962. That or...things may have to be done."

"Of course, Your Eminence." And Amadeus tipped his head and clicked his heels in the manner of the old-world style.

Benedictine looked him up and down. Amadeus felt the man's eyes on him like chips of fire. "I want that Chronicle," Benedictine whispered. "And believe me, vampire, you do not want to see me disappointed. I am not as forgiving as my predecessor."

Amadeus smiled evenly and sent Benedictine an army of serpents to track his dreams for the next seven days. "I assure you, Your Eminence, failure is the farthest thing from my mind."

8

He scarcely remembered running from her, his mind and body were in such a state of turmoil. He glanced around and suddenly found himself in Rockefeller Center, alone, walking at a purposeless gait along the path lined with evergreens that led toward the ice skating rink from which he could already hear the needling strains of music. Above the rink stood the golden statue of Mercury in mid-flight. Behind him the giant Vermont fir was naked of lights and had been for over a month. February. No Christmas, no spring. Only cold white and an endless sea of time. Only that. Away from Teresa, among familiar surroundings, their conversation of moments before seemed less real, a thing of dreams, bad dreams, lies. The Church making and using vampires. The vampires trying to unmake the Church. He quickly regained his wits and watched the night skaters sweeping across the mirrored ice and almost felt his own self again.

"Do you want to skate?" Teresa asked from behind him.

He didn't quite start. "They want me—*he* wants me—"

"I'll bet you're an excellent skater," she said, coaxing him toward the kiosk. He let her kidnap him a second time. Apparently their date wasn't over. It seemed useless to resist. They rented skates from the vendor, tied them on, and set out on the ice. There were quite a few people in the rink and they waited their turn for a break in the traffic before coasting in and slowly building up their speed. Alek turned, half-expecting to find the little Italian nun lagging far behind, but instead she cut the turns even sharper than he did and moved up effortlessly beside him. Then she took him by the elbow and broke him free from the herd.

It was as if they were flying, soaring side by side through the cold wintry air, a pair of identical spirits leaving the earth and all its petty problems far behind in favor of another place, a different world. It was a feeling that lasted only a few minutes, but when it was over and Teresa led him to the side of the rink, Alek was breathless with exhilaration. He could feel the summoned blood in his cheeks like roses, hot and blooming, and his pulse ran like a clock in his throat and wrists. So long, he thought, it's been so long since I felt this...

"Where did you learn to skate like that?" he gasped.

Her eyes darkened, reflected all the entwining lights of the rink. She watched a couple fumbling along, find their rhythm side by side on the ice. "The art is open. People learn so much faster. Evolution." She looked at him. "That's what Paris used to tell me."

"He died—was killed," Alek said. "I remember the name."

"He was murdered in 1962," she said, "by Aragon—Amadeus."

Alek digested that. "And you believe this?"

She narrowed her ancient, holy eyes. "Yes, caro."

He heard the lisp of her accent now, the pain in that other life. He stared into the ice like King Arthur awaiting an answer or a purpose. "Why me? Why choose me? Revenge?"

She turned him around so his back was to the crowd, so he saw only her, and slid her narrow hands up his lapels. Very strange that touch, part priestess, part lover. He leaned into her instinctively. "You want to corrupt me," he guessed, "to hurt Amadeus—"

"I want only the Chronicle. That is my revenge."

"I don't have it. I don't know who does."

"You know. You have only to remember."

"I don't understand—" His head swam. "You're using me,

seducing me."

"Do you mind?"

He kissed her mouth in response, drawn to the shine of her skin, the darkness in her eyes. Her mouth was hot, like blood. He touched her hair, worshipped the waterfall of it through his fingers. His heart pounding in his ears, he kissed the curve of her cheek, the perfect line of her throat, her delicate wreath of collarbones. No spell now; only her, only this. He felt her swallow, gasp, heard her say:

"I have watched you. I love you."

He sighed, let her go. "You don't know me. You don't know what I've done—"

But she was not listening now. Her gaze was turned away from him, out over the frozen water as if it were again the Pond where the Prince undoubtedly continued to turn his harrowing circles in a vain attempt to save his life. He heard it now too: Conflict. Human conflict from the street. Human voices. Human noises of pain and surprise and horror as the evil of the city awakened.

"Wait for me." Her hand covered his heart as if she meant to spell him. He watched her as she skated to the edge of the rink and unlaced her skates and climbed the stairs back up to street level. I love you. Wait. But she no longer touched him and that made her sorcery weak, too weak for the sudden panic that she would leave him to suffer alone with these unwashable memories.

Panic-stricken, he went to the edge and tore away his skates and jogged up the stairs after her. He closed his eyes. She wasn't far. Pulling his coat close, he muscled his way through a crowd of people on the sidewalk and up the street towards Fifth Avenue. Halfway there he turned off into an alley between a fenced apartment building and an industrial warehouse. He walked softly on the glass-littered fissures of broken asphalt, shaking his head as if that would clear away the memories of Eustace's death in an alley so like this one. He stopped to feel. She was near. Just ahead, beyond an elbow in the alley, came the resonant high-low of young voices at war. Alek edged around the first turn.

Two black boys were standing over the body of a third boy lying against the brick wall of the building, his head bracketed by graffiti. Spools of blood ran freely from the knife work on the boy's face and hands and ribs. Alek eased himself back automatically into the shadows.

"...no hard feelings now, Jimmy," one of the two other thugs said, a tall youth with a shitkicking expression on his stone-hard face that reminded Alek uncomfortably of the Stone Man. He flicked his steel stiletto closed like a circus trick. "Shoulda known better'n to be in these parts, you mofo wipe-ass. These our streets. You come here, you get the business. Get it?" he said with a savage steel-toed kick to the downed boy's ribs.

Jimmy jerked, wanted to beg or curse, but his pain was too great and he could utter only a long moan through the clots of blood in his mouth. His eyes gleamed black in the darkness; he wanted so much to escape the pain but the blood only ran more swiftly from his ruined body.

"Survival of the fittest—just ask Darwin," a second boy, his white T-shirt spattered with gore under his cowboy duster, added. He laughed at his own clever wit and pulled out a Cuban import, inserted it under Jimmy's ribs, and pulled the trigger twice—*whomp, whomp*—the sound muffled and toy-like against the jerking, suffering flesh of Jimmy's stomach.

Standing in the shadows some ten feet away, Teresa looked on with a shrewd, impatient understanding. Alek blinked and wondered if he was imagining all this, but there she was, motionless and unseen with only the glint of steel in her eyes to mark her position. The two punks turned toward him. Alek slid back a mere moment before they—or Teresa—would have seen him coming up on their blind side.

Like a couple of loosened spirits, the boys shot past him and down the mouth of the alley to where a battered lowrider was double-parked in the curb, hooting like a couple of athletes in the winner's circle. Teresa watched them go. Then she drifted forward like a beautiful plaything brought to horrifying life. She chose not to pursue the two of them; instead, she looked down on Jimmy. The boy was dying slow, his wet, shiny eyes turned up on her, on this lovely angel fallen to earth to frighten off his tormentors. He raised his hand to her face and she took it, fell effortlessly to one knee at his side. She cradled his head and drew his slashed palm to her lips and tongue. She whispered the sacred words of the rosary.

Jimmy closed his eyes. He said he loved her.

She leaned over Jimmy's face, held Jimmy's hand as she kissed the wounds on his face one at a time and took the last of his life through them. Jimmy's hand grew soft in her grip, fingers slackening, curling, lips parted in some final word or prayer. And when she was done, when she drew herself up, Alek saw what a fastidious creature she was with only her radiant flush of stolen life to paint her porcelain face with color.

She turned to look at him. "I told you to wait."

The sound of her voice broke the spell that held him. He stumbled back against a wall of the warehouse. He saw the boy. Jimmy. Whose son? Who would know he was dead?

"Don't," Teresa said. "It makes for useless pain."

"You said pain makes you strong"—he slid down the wall into a crumpled pile—"once."

Her eyes dropped away. She looked at Jimmy, touched his stony, lifeless cheek. "You want to hurt me. I understand."

"Those other boys..." He shook his head. He was not surprised to notice he cast tears from his face with the gesture.

"I will have them in their time," she said. "'For everything there is a season—'"

"He trusted you, goddamn you!" be sobbed.

Vampire, he thought at her with the weapon of his mind. Monster.

She looked up at him out of her dark and hallowed face. "My righteous child, life and death are not always as they should be. He was dying, the life running out of him. But now he will be a part of me forever."

"But he believed—"

"And it comforted him."

"You betrayed him!"

"Him?" She rose up and swayed toward him.

Alek shrank from her, turned his face away until the brickwork burned cold against his cheek. He sobbed. No. It was over. He couldn't go on. He thought of the whelp he had just murdered. Eustace. And the dozens—hundreds—before him. *Hundreds.* He was a hypocrite and damned and he could not help himself. So be it.

He sensed her withdrawal and her sudden misery. So many years. So many faces. How did she live with them all? How the hell was he supposed to? Her voice, bitter and ancient, was as reedy as the rain when it came:

"At least I never denied what I was. At least I had that much pride left."

"*Fuck you,*" he said. He covered his face and wept until exhaustion and fear overtook him and he felt nothing at all.

9

Amadeus caught the rattler by the head, deflected its fanged attack with a deft underhanded strike. The snake recoiled, returned to the bottom of its tank in defeat. Sean saw the black mamba go for an opening. Sleek as an eel, man, yet the Father trapped its black, poisonous head inside the cup of his palm like a man stopping a fastball in mid-flight. The Father crushed its head, tossed the crumpled ribbon of its body aside.

Bitchin' cool, man. Beautiful Saimin—fucking—jutsu!

The Father crossed his wrists and prepared himself for the next series of attacks. He was naked to the waist, his flesh oily white, flawless but for the colonies of bite marks striping the insides of his arms like the needle tracks of the junkheads Sean had known in the system. "Again," said the Father.

Too cool for words. Sean grinned at the slayers watching from across the table. Takara looked interested in the exercise but Book only cupped his chin and looked away. Spoilsport. Sean grabbed up the poker and crawled out across the table toward the big squirming tank. Fifteen in all. Fourteen now—mambas, black and green, slippery coral snakes, pygmy rattlers. He stirred the medusan brew with the poker. The snakes knotted and writhed. The rattlers gave a cold warning whicker of their tails.

He'd noticed these fuckers before, sleeping under rocks in the big tank in a corner of the Father's cell. He'd even seen the Father handling them once, his thumb hooding their little angry heads, coiling them around his neck like the most experienced Kamir snake charmer Sean had ever seen on TV. But they'd been pets— pretty fuckin' weird pets, but pets nonetheless. Or so Sean had thought.

A particularly energetic rattler jumped at him like a spring. No time, man! The motherfucker was gonna—

Amadeus caught it by the throat. It coiled up around his wrist and attached itself to his forearm. Amadeus grunted and pulled it off, thrust it into the tank with its brethren. He spoke softly as he worked the tank, his voice tediously slow and his hands featureless blurs, and Sean listened intently to the words.

10

"Christ, I can't carry on like this. I need a drink."

"You need salvation."

"Shut the fuck up. You don't know what I need. I need to get the fuck away from you!" He stood up violently, only to weave against the wall with disorientation and the pain blooming behind his eyes like a migraine.

He steadied himself. Then he headed down the alley. Out there, on the avenue, came the reassuring sounds of traffic and people and businesses open after hours, crime and pain and life and death, but at least they were human sounds, normal sounds, the sounds the real world made. He looked despondently around at this back alley space he was trudging through like the drunken bastard he was, the garbage littered wide and the rusting Dumpsters and the subterranean skitter of rats fighting over a burger wrapper under a heat grate somewhere and wondered for the thousandth time how everything had gotten so hopelessly fucked up in only a few short hours.

"And now?" Teresa said, following him.

He shook his head. He wanted to rage at her, but he had no strength. "I don't know."

"You know."

"What do I know?" he said. "That I'm a corpse waiting to die."

"You know that with the Chronicle you can stop them. It can be your security, your saving grace."

"I don't know shit on a Tuesday," he said, leaning heavily against the corner of the building. Taxis and limousines coasted by, their windshield wipers screeking rubbery against the rain of diamond-hard droplets falling over the city. Rain now to freeze the snow into marble. He shivered and wondered when the winter would goddamn give it up already. "I don't know where the Chronicle is. I never did. Debra knew and Debra is dead."

"Paris knew," she said. "But Paris never told me."

He put his hot cheek to the soothing cold brick. "Which leaves us absolutely nowhere, Sister Teresa."

"But how did Debra know?" she asked. She took him by the arm, the desperation barely contained in her voice, in her steel-gripped fingers and wide, light-refracting eyes. "Who told her? Who were her friends? You must know something...*anything*..."

He closed his eyes and shrugged. He had resisted her and failed. And now he was giving up. But at least he was giving up knowing he had tried to resist. And giving up, her prisoner completely now, he told her what little he did know.

11

"There is a woman I once knew"—Amadeus deflected a coral snake, snatched the head off a green mamba—"a great keeper of books and strange lore. I think"—he caught the head of that problem rattler, crushed its skull in his palm—"if anyone knows the way, she"—another rattler, a third mamba— "will."

Amadeus stopped. The remaining snakes had retreated to the bottom of the tank. The rattlers were silent. They had given up, all of them.

"Again?" Sean asked expectantly.

"Enough."

"D'you know? You know where he is?"

"Yes," said Amadeus, sliding into his robes. "I know."

"Righteous!" Sean gripped his master by the sleeve. "So when do we—?"

Amadeus dealt him a two-finger cobra strike to the throat.

Sean flew across the length of the table and crashed into his chair, overturning it again. Supine on the Abbey floor, he moaned dazedly, coughed, felt the two tiny puncture marks at the base of his throat. Shit, man, that was going to leave a hell of a scar.

Yeah!

"Hodie mihi cras tibi," Amadeus hissed.

And though Sean did not understand the words, the sentiment was clear enough.

Mine.

12

Night.

Night in a club at 3:00 a.m., the time of the abyss, when the children of men slept and everything was neither here nor there. The club was in the basement of a burned-out cathedral, so most of the light was lost among the old blackened wood girders that rose more than two hundred feet into the night.

Night in the Abyssus. The walls, painted black, crawled with arcane characters and gangbanger badges in red spray paint. On one wall was a religious mural of the Crucifixion done in rusty red and brown tones. The club was located near the docks, so even here the cold fishy stench of the bay invaded, pervading the warmer scents of cheap perfume and melting hair mousse and clove smoke and fresh flesh and blood. The pit in the center of the club was filled with men and women entwined with their brethren, faces flushed with lust and languor, heads thrown back in the grimace that was so like agony.

And on the tiny stage enmeshed in dog wire, presiding over it all like a high pagan priestess, she sang. She was like the victim of a vampire's obsession in silk gown and no shoes and naked arms ringed in delicate wreaths of barbed wire, and she sang much the same way, clinging to the microphone as if the weight of life would drown her damaged soul. She gave strange performances, alternately whispering her taboos and screeching them as if she would tear open the fragile fabric of the night around her and let in every wayward earthbound deity.

They said she was a fallen angel, the infamous Eleventh Scholar. They said she drank the blood of children and offered the kiss of purgatory to virgins.

They said a lot of things about Leigia, not all of which Salvatori believed. One thing he did know for certain was that the boss lady had a thing for Leigia and she was strictly no-go territory where he was concerned. He could respect that. He supposed he had to.

Leigia finished her last set to a sizzling roomwide silence and climbed down off the stage. Sal shot her down a whiskey sour full of cherries, her favorite.

Three o' clock and the Abyssus teemed, just like Sal liked it. Lots of heat and teenagers, more industrial goth than anything else here. Black hair and albino skin, red mouths and smoky grey eyes. Black paten leather and blood-slathered chains. Pain freaks and vampire groupies and, sure, plenty of regular lowlifes and poseurs too. A roomful of Cyndi Laupers and Boy Georges three days dead, a few geeks, the bearded poet type in worn army surplus jackets who quoted Nietzsche a lot, but he liked it; it was home.

Sal drew down a quartet of beers with enthusiasm. He'd been working at the Abyssus for twenty-eight years now and it was a big deal. Talent night Tuesdays and Fridays, industrial metal band on Saturdays, blood orgy almost every night. Boss lady ran a tight ship but gave good benefits, decent pay. She and Empirius had made a good man of Sal, who'd seen nothing but tommy guns and bloodshed and human ghouls high on visceral violence most of his life.

Yeah, Akisha was okay, took none of the schtick the patrons who sometimes got high and rowdy after a band cooled down were apt to hand the barkeep, even going so far as to install a couple of human ghouls at the back door. Pip and Kyle. Wussy names, but Sal wasn't fooled none. Pip was an Outback brawler with Lou Ferrigno's face and Mike Tyson's left hook; Kyle was no better—an ex-Navy Seal, he'd eaten army privates for lunch during Desert Storm, or so the stories went. Some fancy work back there. Yeah, Akisha was a fine woman indeed. And Empirius—well, shit, Sal spat on the floor and crossed himself, first upright and then upside-down—it was just too damn bad about the boss man.

But Sal also knew that when you were living life on the edge the way his breed were apt to do, you couldn't go around hanging your head all day and mourning the passing of every vamp you knew. They died too fast. Faster than some humans, the way the slayers culled the herd

And anyway, it was Saturday and Saturdays were a fine night. Plenty of controlled chaos, lots of overheated bodies and quick smiles. Everyone getting down and ready for Shrapnel's first set, Leigia warming them up, getting them heated and wanting more. Nights like these were goddamn magic. Black lights poured down through a crowd of chain-smoking teenagers and cleaved like purple cream to the base of the raised altar-like stage in the middle of the Pit.

Sal fixed a couple of guillotines and shot them down the bar at the two kids with scarified faces and links of chain sewn through the tender skin of their scalps. One, the androgynous girl, smiled at Sal. Maybe later, sweetheart, he thought to her. Onstage, the longhaired, riveted members of the band were tuning up and getting ready to serve and command their people like a cliché of black-eyed underworld gods. None of that battle-anthem street beat stuff to start with; Shrapnel was a sophisticated barbarian. Kill me, eat me, suck me dry, then do your brethren, my little brothers and sisters. God, but it was too righteously cool for this jaded new millennium.

Sal was shuttling off more beers to the waitress when he saw the dhampir come in. Over the years he'd seen the full gamut of goth, over-painted lips and over-bled skin, that forced worldly look the kiddies put on for their brethren. But Knight was a regular scare, even in Sal's book. Not goth. Not ghoul. Knight was the real thing. And a slayer. Goddamn fucking *slayer*. Knight looked around a moment as if to re-familiarize himself with the joint, and in the shadowy dimness of the club his eyes looked huge, black as sin, as if he were absorbing every last particle of light in the place. Fucking cat eyes.

Sal buttoned up the neck of his white oxford shirt and wondered who was next on the ol' chopping block.

Knight looked his way.

"Shit." Sal stopped shaking the tin cylinder for the kahlua he was making as the slayer headed in a beeline for him. Big guy, was Knight, the typical artist type, long fingers, longer hair. But unlike the other creative fifty-year-old lushes in the Village Sal knew, Knight spent his nights wielding steel and sieving members of his own fucking kind. There wasn't a soft spot in his whole unaging body. Sal's eyes moved self-consciously to find Pip and Kyle.

Maybe trouble.

Kyle nodded, folded his big he-man arms across his grey fatigue tank top.

"Salvatori."

Sal set the kahlua shaker down before he dropped it. "She ain't in," he said automatically.

"She's always in," Knight responded. "Remember what I said about you fucking with me, Sal?"

Sal shuddered and looked away. "Leave her alone, will ya? Haven't you done enough damage here?"

Knight looked taken aback by the outburst.

Sal thought to kick himself. Real good, Salvatori, he thought, you're a total Einstein. Probably it's going to be *your* fucking neck attached to your fucking big mouth on the line now.

But to his utmost surprise, instead of reaching across the bar and making Sal intimate with that oversized pig sticker of his, Knight looked down and away. "Would you buzz Akisha please? I'll understand if she doesn't want to see me."

"Huh?"

"Please." He looked up, his eyes inky. A tear? "I need to see her."

Sal shook his head. Poor fucker. Akisha was great about everything down here—but upstairs was a different matter completely. No one saw her without an invitation, except maybe Leigia, and even there Sal wasn't certain the dame could just come and go as she pleased. It was Akisha's only vanity. And she certainly wasn't going to want to see the face of her blood-bonded lover's murderer. Still, he might as well make a show of it, just in case Knight was hauling that pig sticker around with him tonight. He picked up the phone and buzzed Akisha's office in the loft, the only livable floor in the whole building.

"Knight wants to see you, Mistress," said Sal. "You want I throw him out?"

Damn his courage! Was he going fucking crazy in his old age?

"Alek?" came Akisha's slithering voice.

Sal glanced up at the slayer. "Yeah, big guy, black hair—you know, the one with balls enough to show his face round here after carving up the Master?"

There was a lengthy silence. Sal could hear the static on the phone. He could hear the breathing of the slayer. He could hear his own breathing. It was like a fucking Carpenter film. He'd scream if Akisha didn't say something pretty soon.

Finally: "Send him up to my lounge, Sal."

Well, this is something new, thought Sal. He hung up the phone. He was numb. "Go on up," he told the slayer. "Stairs at the back."

"I know." Knight nodded and smiled, showing the tips of his petite but still impressively sharp set of eyeteeth like they didn't embarrass him any longer. Then, without aplomb, he crossed the Abyssus to the stairs at the back. And it was the damnedest thing—it was as if he'd expected no other reaction.

13

The erotic image of a woman lying on a purple divan, red heat lamps set in the wall giving her flesh a warm, rosy semblance, was the first thing to greet Alek when he entered the lounge. Her upper arms were prisoners of coiled reams of cruel-looking barbed wire, and he felt an immediate and familiar ache in his teeth at the sight. She stared at her image in the ceiling mirrors and reached down to run one bloody hand down the front of her diaphanous white gown. "You came," she whimpered as if drunk or stoned or in some mystical way operating far outside her body. "Akisha said you would. She said...your touch is like steel." She nodded solemnly. "I love Akisha."

He tried to ignore her; even in the red of the lights he could see the razor scars all over her body. Hundreds of artistic markings like tattoos, each one the stigmata of a passage, a passion. A passage toward what? A passion for what?

"Death," said Akisha, emerging from the darkness and into the light of the lounge's oval stained-glass window, the diffused, bluish light of it turning her flesh transparent under her scarlet Jean Harlow-inspired nightgown. "Death and rebirth." Long matching evening gloves covered her arms, and a necklace of flawless white diamonds that had once belonged to Elizabeth Taylor bound her throat. Her spiky-heeled boots hardly made a sound on the hardwood floor as she moved.

Alek looked again at Akisha's girl. She emanated a scent like steel and roses so that he had to make a conscious effort to completely ignore her. "Does she know that nothing you do can make her any different? Does she know how different we really are from them?"

Akisha tipped her head, her pelt-like black hair falling forward to brush the hollows of her cheeks. "Close enough to mate, but not close enough to turn one another?" She arched a black eyebrow, then turned to face him fully and graced him with that rarest of gifts: her predatory smile. "I don't think Leigia knows much of anything right now."

"You should tell her. These children—"

"And lose yet another lover?"

Alek grunted and walked to the room's old-fashioned french doors. He opened them and stepped out onto the balcony where the air was so much fresher and colder and more open. He looked out over the distant mass of Central Park. On the far side he could just see the lights of the buildings on Fifth Avenue. Akisha came and stood in the doorway behind him, and for the first time in years he felt truly old. Like the city, he would live forever, but unlike the city, and Akisha's girl and all the other mortal children in the club downstairs, he would never truly be a part of this world's vibrancy. Not this world—not the Coven's. He had traded in the Church's redemption for the chilled eternity of the rogue. He almost thought he would go and be feeling sorry for himself again, but he found he was tired of growing sentimental over city lights.

The moon was fading fast from the sky and he felt a sudden need to call it back. All those years exerting control and a priest's restraint, and yet, buried deep, he was hungering all along as badly as the worst of his race. He closed his eyes and felt the cold night wind brush his cheeks and wondered what new madness this all would take him into.

"I am sorry about Empirius. About Carfax. All of them. Every one—I can't tell you..." His voice trailed away uselessly.

Akisha reached the parapet rail. She looked out over the city with him. "So it's happened, has it? You've been awakened." Her voice—it was less like that of a seductress and more like a friend, some old friend from the distant past, someone surprised but not really angry to be remembered only now, in a time of need.

She turned to him, the gems gleaming and reflecting the red of her gown at her throat. "Tell me what happened, tell me," she said, sliding back against the rail. Like her choker, her eyes gleamed cold, but in them was the suffering wisdom that came only with long life. The wisdom of sorrowful experience. Akisha had been witness to empires crumbling and returning to life a dozen times; nothing he could say would shock her, or could.

He opened his mouth, and like a confession, he found himself recounting the events of the night leading up to his arrival here at the Abyssus. He spoke carefully and calmly, leaving nothing out, and doing his best to appear impartial to it all. As he talked, Akisha grew serious and thoughtful, but she neither questioned nor interrupted him. And then finally he was done and she stared at him evenly but said nothing. And the silence was too great and he turned back to the city and gripped the rail until his fingers hurt and he said, "I don't know where to go, what to do. I thought of you. I thought of what you did for Debra. You were someone she trusted. I thought maybe...I don't know." He looked up. "Maybe she told you something. Maybe she knew where the Chronicle was or knew who did."

Akisha watched a pleasure boat moving up the Hudson. "I don't know that there's much to know. I don't know that it even exists."

"It exists. I have to find it. Without it...it's just a matter of time before they come. And I can't fight them all; I can't do this alone, Akisha. Please." He heard the pitiful whining of his voice and despised it, and himself for being brought down to this level— begging help from one of his victims. He felt so alone.

Akisha moved closer to him. Her voice was soft and breathy.

"You are not alone. You were never alone. You have the sword. You have Debra."

He shook his head in denial. "I'm so afraid. I don't think—"

"Then don't, little whelp," Akisha scolded in Japanese. "Don't think. *Feel.* Do what you must in vengeance, not fear, never that."

She moved even closer to him, and Alek suddenly wished that she hadn't. She was stirring emotions inside of him and his feelings were quite complicated already. He closed his eyes yet again, putting the veil of absolute darkness between them, but her perfume was all but overwhelming. He thought of hot airless nights heavy with jasmine, wisps of cloud on a full dirty city moon. He could feel the touch of her breath. Beneath the perfume it had a uniquely sweet, carnivorous smell. Debra.

"Yes, do it for her," Akisha whispered and kissed him on the corner of the mouth, the lightest touch, as much a brand of benediction as passion. "Our love for our kin is what binds our spirits to them. They are never very far off. But you knew that already. You always knew that. Avenge her, for vengeance and honor is the only path of the true warrior, my whelp."

14

It was near daybreak when the second slayer stepped into the club. He wasn't like the other, darker, one. This one was a holocaust of whiteness. It hurt Sal's senses to look on all that wintry flesh and hair. Fingernails like slivers of ice. Pale, pupil-less eyes. Black leather coat. Long ponytail of hair. Christ.

The slayer swayed between the sweating, gyrating teenaged bodies like death loosened among a field of wildflowers. He stopped only once to gaze up with a scowl at the grinding, feedback-riddled music onstage, then moved on past.

Sal nodded at Pip and Kyle.

Standby, boys.

The freak approached the bar and put his hands up on the

bumper. His coat parted a little with the gesture and Sal spotted the getup beneath. Not goth or punk. Amish, or those other strange ones, Mennonites or whatever the hell they called themselves. Sal looked the freak up and down. Black wool suit and rabato, white hair tied with a hank of black silk ribbon. What now, fucking Pilgrim undead bullshit?

"A pilgrim I am, sir," spoke the slayer, and his voice was coarse like his big ragged chain-wrapped coat, vaguely accented, "on a pilgrimage."

Sal laughed, couldn't help himself. "Look like Cotton Mather in those threads, dude," he said. "You an Amadeus groupie, or what?" He kicked himself a second time that night. Good going again, Salvatori. You just insulted the slayers' grand master by running your mouth off at this dickface Amadeus wannabe. He might just as well have shit on the Mona Lisa. He knew plenty slayers who went around in chains and bleached cornstarch-white hair and phony Nazi-inspired accents, and most of them had pretty much the same short, sword-wielding temperaments as the king slayer himself. He reached for a glass and began to polish it vigorously

The groupie frowned, ran a hand over his clothes. "A costume? Not in my time. A...groupie? No."

Sal laughed once more. These slayers. He tried to move away from the freak, but the freak only put his long ugly hand around Sal's wrist.

"I must see Akisha," said the freak.

Sal looked at the hand, at the hand's owner. Was he actually swaying a little side to side? Sal shivered, tried to look away, but something was happening to the freak's eyes, something impossible, even by vamp standards. Were they actually darkening at their pit-like centers? Narrowing in some snakelike way? "Akisha's sure a popular one tonight."

"Another was here to see your mistress? Was he a dark tall man with eyes like obsidian and a beauty to match?"

Something hissed insinuatingly and Sal finally mustered enough courage to glance down. A lock of the freak's hair had actually slipped with scaly serpentine grace up the back of Sal's hand. "Who the living fuck are you?" Sal demanded.

"Answer the question."

"Get the fuck outta here before I—"

The thing wound around his hand bit him at the same moment the slayer hit him in the throat. Sal dropped the sauterne he was polishing and rocked back into the frosted saloon mirror behind the bar, his hand and throat coldly ablaze with pain. The mirror marbleized on contact. Motherfucker punched me! Sal thought in some remote self-righteous corner of his mind as he watched a bottle of good Chardonnay fall to the floor and shatter like a body thrown from an enormous height. He punched me!

A girl screamed and he heard the unmistakable *twang* of a guitar string breaking. People looking at him, pointing to him. The slayer smiling demurely. Pip and Kyle doing nothing. Nothing! Everyone watching the barkeep getting soaked in a widening pool of spilt Sangria. Stupid bastards, didn't anyone ever see a guy get kayoed before?

Sal looked down at himself to see what the others were looking at with such rapt interest. Not punched. He wasn't punched. A punch did not leave two gaping holes in your carotid artery through which your life force escaped like a bitch.

The slayer said, looking on him, "The milk of the serpent is far sweeter than the blood of the vine."

Too bad, too, Sal thought miserably as his consciousness leaked away with his immortal life. Boss lady gave such good benefits.

15

Alek took Akisha's shirasaya from the glass display case and unsheathed the lethally sharp blade concealed in the seemingly harmless staff. The scabbard and handle were made from a single piece of rosewood to connect perfectly. He ran his thumb over the engraved mara-tu symbol of the craftsman marking the perfection of the blade and felt a curious sickness in the pit of his stomach. He wondered where his katana was. It felt as if a chasm existed between himself and all hope.

"You are feeling its displacement as a warrior should," Akisha said to him as she went to sit by the side of her blood whore. She placed her fingertips on the girl's forehead, producing an almost visible flow of energy as she put the girl under her influence a little deeper. The girl let out a long, deep-throated sigh as Akisha sent her to another world of erotic shadows and whispery touches. Almost as a reflex, the mortal ran a hand along the inside of her thigh. "Love you so much, Akisha...so, so much..."

When Akisha was assured that she was completely under, she turned her attention back on Alek and became almost brusque. "You should never have separated yourself from it. It will save your life one day."

Alek glanced at the divan where the girl's breath was coming in long heartfelt gasps, her breasts undulating, hands flexing, seeking the imposed image of Akisha's fantasy. Alek scowled.

"Alek."

"I'm sorry," he said. "She's a little...distracting."

"There's little I can do about her right now."

"Are you binding yourself to her?" he asked. He knew that was possible among the oldest and most experienced of the females. In lieu of a male vampire, some could invest their hunger in one of their human lovers or ghouls and let their victim take on the full measure of their madness with usually disastrous repercussions. A messy ordeal, but you did what you had to in the name of survival.

Good God, I'm thinking like Teresa now, he thought.

"I haven't decided yet." She stood up smoothly and with hardly any movement at all. "Are you offering?"

He met her challenging gaze head on, slid the blade of the shir into the scabbard. "I would do anything for you, Akisha," he told her, surprised but not really dismayed by the candid truth of his words.

She raised one quizzical brow. "Would you now?" She undulated closer to him, slowly extended a hand until the tips of her fingers just brushed his cheek. He touched her hand touching his face, kissed it. Kissed her. Gently at first, but with a growing openness he found oddly comforting to surrender to. Akisha. She was more than a lover. A mother. A nurse. A sensei. He opened his mouth to her in the most intimate of gestures and boldly touched his tongue to her sharp petite eyeteeth.

She smiled. "My pretty rogue." She kissed him back and her kiss was a curious mixture of pure wicked vampire and motherly affection. Her hand slid slyly under his coat, awakening aches inside of him that had lain dormant for decades. "Promise me. Promise me you'll return. You'll take Empirius's place. You must give me your word as a warrior."

He hesitated only a moment, drunken on memories and the scrape of Akisha's teeth on the delicate virgin skin of his throat. He could almost feel like a youth again, the thrill of absolute intimacy and the erotic taboo of a woman's tongue. "You have it," he whispered. He lowered his eyes. "If I live that long, that is."

She tapped his chin with her pointed fingernail to gain his attention. She said, thoughtfully, "In 1962 I knew a vampire. He had artist's hands and the most gorgeous eyes, like tarns you could fall into and drown in forever. He claimed to have seen the Chronicle, even held it."

Alek's heart leapt. "Byron?" he ventured.

"How did you know?"

"He was..." He looked away a moment, then back again. "He was Debra's for a while."

Akisha nodded sadly, then looked to the rows and rows of high booked shelves that covered almost every wall of the lounge, bookshelves broken only by the art she loved equally well.

"What is it?" he prompted.

"Byron, he—wait." She stared at a portrait on the wall of her sanctuary as if to resurrect some half-buried memory. She nodded. "Yes, I'd all but forgotten," she said to herself. Her hands dropped away from him and she turned, sensual even in her haste, and headed straightaway to the ladder.

16

The military man bursting with muscles took him from behind and wrapped his powerful tentacle-like arms around Amadeus's shoulders. Great power and constriction. Amadeus felt his breathing hitch to a stop in his chest. The man was very brave, trying to slay a slayer.

Amadeus released his tension and sagged in his slayer's arms. His head dropped forward, then snapped back up, connecting with his slayer's face. The man screamed as his face was broken like a platter by the contact. Amadeus ground the back of his head against the remnants of his slayer's face. The man's grip loosened and Amadeus took him by the hand. He spun the man around and ratcheted his arm up painfully behind him. The man opened his mouth to scream. With a roar and a burst of controlled strength, Amadeus mule-kicked the creature into the bar, ripping his left arm out of the socket.

The wood splintered under the man's fall, the hundreds of ragged daggers of wood impaling him through the eyes and brain like the quills of an acupuncture artist. Blood sprayed Amadeus's face and the tiled floor and blackened the walls farther. The man screamed and screamed and would not die. Amadeus went to him and ground out the back of the man's skull like an old cabbage under his boot heel and the man was silent at last.

Chaos. Amadeus felt it on every inch of his skin. Mortals scattering like the cattle they were, the hive vampires paralyzed with fear. Cries of violence. Shoving and shouting and sweating. The musical artists with their devil-inspired beat dropped their noisome instruments and joined their mortal brethren in the mindless, animalistic stampede to the front door. Useless, all this. Why would the barkeep not simply show him the way to Alek and

Akisha?

Why, he wondered, must every act be accomplished with violence?

There was another scream, and then the fear that had petrified the vampires in the club edged up a notch. As one, they rose, overturning tables, trampling each other, and began to crowd toward the front door. A woman brushed past him. He swung the limb in his hand like a jo staff and sent her flying back into the crowd. The cries grew and the press toward the door surged more urgently forward. Someone pushed Amadeus from behind. His hand snapping out, he gripped the passing man by his ponytail of hair, bent him backward. He sank two fingers into the eyes of his offender, gripped the skull tight and tore it loose from its owner's body.

Instantly he was soaked in a glorious bath of hot, pulsing blood. He felt the tingle of his hair writhing with sentient power as it burst its binds. Someone neared him on the right and one long coiled mass exploded outward and snapped its venomous fangs into a mass of flesh pulsating with vampire life.

Then suddenly there was space all around him and another of the hive watchdogs approached him. Amadeus's serpentine hair rattled ominously. The watchdog punched him squarely in the cheek. Amadeus slammed backward into a wall, felt the plaster give all the way to the studs. He experienced the ghost of pain in his face, a slight, unpleasant sensation in his upper palate as the broken cheekbone mended itself instantaneously and a new eyetooth forced the loose one out. The watchdog came for him again without hesitation.

Amadeus hissed and showed the creature his dripping eyeteeth. His serpentine hair did the same.

"Bloody freak," spoke this brave dead mortal. He took Amadeus by the collar and tried to haul him up off his feet.

Amadeus bit the mortal in the big pulsing vein in his wrist and emptied half the culminated venom of fourteen serpents into his bloodstream. The man released him and fell gasping, paralyzed with heart attack, to the floor of his babylon. He wept like a tortured infant. Amadeus spat a mouthful of venom into his face. Flesh sizzled into a foul smoke as it was eaten up like acid. The man continued to wail, his voice echoing up from a chamber of meatless bone, and this time Amadeus felt no compassion and simply stepped over the man and went in search of the stairs which would lead him to Alek, and, eventually, Alek's accomplice.

17

"Byron painted this in the week before he disappeared. I thought it was just another of his wild abstract ramblings. He was quite prone to those, being of that doomishly overdramatic Dali school."

Alek arched an eyebrow questioningly at Akisha.

Akisha smiled and glanced aside at the solemn, lily-fleshed, ebony-eyed portrait of herself on the wall. "He never had your greatness." She swiveled a little in her desk chair to catch the greenish glow of the banker's lamp on the surface of the framed painting on the desk. "It was the last thing he ever painted; he was quite proud of it." She turned a little more towards the light so he could see it completely.

Alek dug out his wire frames and slipped them on, studied the images scrawled in oily gouache across the thirty-five-year-old canvas. A girl on a floor reading a book before a tipped oval mirror, it looked like. Hard to tell. The painter was less than masterful. The only thing of substance seemed to be the book, reflecting upside-down in the mirror. He turned the painting upside down so he could see the page of the book more clearly. He swallowed and felt his heart hammer expectantly against his ribs at the sight of the words of John Milton. "And he drew this for Paris?"

Akisha nodded.

"What was Byron's connection with the Chronicle?"

"Paris mailed him the Chronicle in the summer of 1962, he said. Byron was connected to an editor at Doubleday at the time.

The book was supposed to go to him for publication. Byron said it was part of Paris's plan to undermine the Vatican's work. He hoped this way the vampires would have complete access to the Church's plans for our race." Akisha hesitated, watching as Alek found her copy of Paradise Lost and used a pocket knife to cut away the fabric at the back of the book.

"For when war was declared," Alek guessed and held up a crumpled sheet of parchment.

Akisha shrugged. "But Paris was slain only a short time later and Byron disappeared a short while after that. He gave me this and told me to keep it safe in the event something happened to him. He was very excitable at the time, in a hurry."

Alek thought about that as he studied the little legends scribed here and there on the sheaf of parchment. "What are these?" he asked, pointing them out. "These little symbols things here and there?"

Akisha shook her head. "I don't know. He never explained much of this to me. I thought him a fool." She looked sorrowfully on him. "I'm sorry. I don't know anything else."

Alek smiled, fingering the archaic language on the parchment. "It's a start," he admitted. "Maybe Teresa can tell me more, maybe—" His voice drained away to an all-over shudder. Cold in here. He glanced toward the big, moon-filled mosaic window. Something wrong somewhere—

"Alek?"

Alek shook his head, stood up and peeled off his glasses. "Did you hear something downstairs?"

"Shrapnel," Akisha said, studying him askance from her seat at the desk, "It always gets a little rowdy when they play..."

Alek scarcely heard her. Someone on the stairs. Slow, disturbing presence. *Intimate.* Amadeus. No. Not Amadeus. Amadeus would not trail him here. Would not. How could he? Their relationship was a curious mixture of bonding and mind play, yes, but even Amadeus could not literally see through his eyes. And even if that miracle were possible, the Father would sooner send agents rather than do this himself. And save that, he would not make a public spectacle of their quarrel. They would have their inevitable conflict, most certainly, but it would be done in private. Not here.

Yet even as Alek watched, disbelieving it, trying to convince himself of the absurdity of the possibility, the door to the lounge opened and Amadeus let himself in silently and civilly, with no pomp whatsoever. He closed the door and set his back to it, his blood-drenched clothes sagging heavy on his tall, upright frame.

Akisha stood up immediately, but it was clear from the way she took her position beside Alek that she was uncertain as to what to do next. "I am Akisha," she said, "I am mistress of this house. I imagine that you are looking for me."

Amadeus smiled wickedly, his bloody dreadlocks shifting horribly across his scalp. He bowed slightly at the waist and clicked his heels together, his dead white eyes pinning Alek squarely. "I am the Covenmaster Amadeus, madam, der Vampir sklavischer. And you imagine wrong. I believe you have something which belongs to me."

Alek took a pensive step back, so overwhelmed by a desire to bolt that it took a conscious effort of will for him to hold his ground. He sought something to say, some excuse for this, something that would make amends and erase all this—but what did you say to the man you were betraying, the man who raised you and gave you a home when you had none, a purpose when you were bereft of purposes? The man who was your father and brother and mentor and the greatest part of you? What did you say? What?

Amadeus drew his splattered leather coat close. "You are leaving now, Alek."

No. You said no.

"I'm not going back with you," he said.

"What?"

"No."

Amadeus stepped farther into the room, tilting his head in surprise. "What did you say to me?"

"No. I said...no," Alek answered, nearly choking on every word. "I need to be on my own for a while, I need...."

Amadeus drifted toward Akisha even as the old shugo warrior woman stood solid in place, staring at him with a disturbing and uncharacteristic combination of horror and fascination. Alek thought to shout something to her, to warn her, but surely she recognized the encroaching danger for what it was, surely. Yet even as he watched like an uninvolved passerby studying a pickpocket in action in the middle of Times Square, he felt the terror constrict his throat and turn his stomach cold. No, Akisha would do something, would fight as she had in feudal Japan. She would react.

If she could.

The Covenmaster's eyes darkened glowingly. His smile grew into the lolling hungry grin of a white wolf. Alek sucked in a breath even as Amadeus reached her and drew his katana from the black lacquered scabbard on his belt.

The bizarre stasis holding Akisha in place broke in that moment. Maybe it was the smell of the Damascus steel, the ring of the sword leaving its scabbard. Maybe it was the look of bloodlust on Amadeus's face or the honest cruelty of his smile. Maybe it was all or none of these things—but Akisha reacted automatically, turning sideways to minimize herself as a target and kicking the Covenmaster's feet out from under him.

Amadeus lurched to his side on the floor, but did not lose his grip on the unsheathed sword. Instead he used the momentum of his fall to carry his steel in an arc across Akisha's legs. Akisha saw and moved, but too late. Blood spewed in a thin, purple line as the katana slit her gown and the flesh of her upper thigh wide like a pair of bloody lips.

With a battlecry of rage and pain, Akisha side-kicked him squarely in the chest, tearing her damaged skin further and flecking her adversary's face with gouts of her blood. But instead of crushing in his ribcage, Amadeus absorbed the kick, grabbed her ankle in one hand and twisted it brutally to the right. Akisha choked through the rending crunch of her anklebones and went down, her landing awkward.

It was all the opening Amadeus needed. Licking the blood off his lips like a lion in battle, he reached out and snagged hold of Akisha's hair, tearing some of it out at the roots as he hauled her back with him to the floor. Akisha hissed, kicking out like a wounded animal and instinctively raising her arms to protect her throat. Amadeus's sword caught her in the upper forearm, ripping the meat wide in a smiling gash. But the need for self-protection was too great for her to leave her throat unprotected, and instead of dropping her arms, she let them take a second and then a third bone-deep strike.

Amadeus was on his feet, roaring. He tore her head back, trying to expose her throat to his blade. Akisha twisted like a monkey and snapped her legs around his neck. She squeezed him like a vice. She twisted sideways, trying to break his neck, but the act had no affect on him whatsoever other than to activate the writhing mound of serpents on his head. A dozen reddish eyes opened. A dozen rattles echoed against the lounge walls. A dozen red, dripping mouths hissed wide and attached themselves to Akisha's legs.

Akisha screamed in agony and let him go, her body sliding and shuddering to the floor at Amadeus's feet like some pathetic human in the throes of an epileptic fit. Her body spasmed, her spine bowing almost to the point of breakage, her lips snarling back away from a bloody white grimace of unrelieved suffering. And then the back of her skull hit the floor once, twice, a third time, and her eyes rolled up in their sockets to show only the whites, and something about that unbelievable feature, that *Amadeus* feature, snapped Alek out of his own horror-inspired paralysis and forced him to act.

"STOP!" Alek crashed to the floor beside Akisha and caught her head before it could smash itself against the floor again and held it in a grip of pure, unrelenting iron. Akisha snapped blindly at him, her eyeteeth savaging the flesh of his hands, her eyes narrow, bleeding slits. Alek groaned as Akisha hiccupped massive gouts of blood that painted her ruined lips like rouge. Christ, so much

blood, she was going to *bleed* to death. What the hell had the Father done to her?

Amadeus tried to take him by the shoulders. Alek threw off his foul hands. *"Leave me alone, you son of a bitch!"* He gathered Akisha's groaning, twisting form into his lap. He looked up, appalled by what he saw. How could any creature look on another's pain with such dead interest as Amadeus was doing now? How could any creature *do* this? He was dreaming this. He could not now believe that he had once loved this soulless creature standing over them, could not believe that he had kissed it with such reverence, drank from it. That was another person, another time.

Akisha's blood-filled mouth opened wide, and for a moment a kind of conscience light seemed to fill her eyes. "Ahh..." was all she could manage. *"Ahhhsch..."*

"Help me," Alek pleaded. "Help her, goddamn you!"

Amadeus's empty stare broke away. He sheathed his sword and went to stand behind Akisha's chair, his hand caressing the back invitingly. "Have a seat, Alek."

He could not seem to stop Akisha's bleeding no matter how he held her or pressed the wounds on her body and face. So much fucking *blood*. How was it possible for one of their kind to have so much blood in her? Akisha gripped him by the wrist. Akisha's hand was cold, colder than he ever remembered it being, even all those years ago when she had first touched his hand in passing. No, oh God, no, please. He could save Akisha, he knew he could. A little of his blood, that was all she needed. Akisha would survive. Like she survived Carfax's death and Empirius's passing. Akisha had survived nations.

"Alek."

"Go to fucking hell!" Alek sobbed, trying to open a vein in his own wrist. "Akisha's bleeding!

Amadeus sighed and came back around, unsheathed his sword, and with both hands drove the steel tip of it into Akisha's heart. Akisha convulsed like a fish around the sword pinning her heart to the floor, vomited a near fountain of black heart's blood, almost said a name, his name, then collapsed to dead silence in Alek's arms.

Alek stared with confusion at the dead woman. Blood. Akisha was all ignoble blood and silence. What had happened here? It was as if he were moving through a dream, a nightmare of some kind, the images refracted, unreal. Only ten minutes ago she had been alive and they had been having a conversation about Byron's work, and now...

Amadeus said, "Your whore is no longer bleeding."

Alek set Akisha's ragged, still warm body on the floor. He touched her ruined cheek. There was blood on her white skin, her black eyelashes. There was blood on the whites of her eyes, her goddamn *eyes*. How the hell had it gotten *there*? He felt numb, as if he were the one dead, as if his own soul were gone with Akisha. Yes, it had gone with her, returned to the fabled web where the souls of the damned and the undying went. He wept tearlessly in gasping dry sobs. Soulless. Helpless. "I'll kill you," he said, a promise.

"I rather doubt it." Amadeus said matter-of-factly and slid the blade of his sword under Alek's chin. The motion brought Alek to his feet, stood him up like a puppetmaster pulling the strings of his creation tight. "Now take a seat, mein Sohn, before I hand you your beautiful head."

Alek saw the lounge in shades of red. Something had happened here, some cataclysm. What? He wanted to reach for Akisha's body, but the sword held him back. He swayed uncertainly. He felt intoxicated, alien to himself and to his world. Amadeus had to guide him to the chair like a small child, and there he collapsed into it with a series of unspent shudders.

"How dare you," said Amadeus, sliding behind him and twining his fingers in Alek's hair. And with one deft yank Alek's head was cranked back to the point of pain and his neck exposed to the freezing cold kiss of Amadeus's unforgiving steel. Alek closed his eyes. His breathing came in fitful spurts as his master's voice growled in his ear.

"How dare you disobey me, you ungrateful little whelp! How dare you!"

Alek's breath hitched, caught. "Fuck you."

"WHAT?"

Alek gritted his teeth, felt a sliver of warmth trickle down his throat from the press of the sword's razor-sharp edge against his jugular. He swallowed and felt the blade sink deeper. *"What part of that didn't you understand, you fucking monster?"*

The sword was lifted away and Amadeus's arm found its way around Alek's throat instead and lifted him from his seat with a disturbing lack of effort. *"Four hundred years worth of my work ruined. Four. Hundred. Years..."*

Alek choked and tasted blood like smoldered steel in the back of his throat. He thought with distant, childlike rage that the heroes in the stories he'd read as a child had never died like this, doing the right thing. Not fair. Not fair at all. Alek sobbed as something broke from him, some runaway rage. He twisted in his hangman's position, clawed at his master's face like a cat.

Amadeus snarled and let his acolyte blight his face with wounds, and still he held him with ugly strength. "The beast runs strong in your veins, beloved, so you cannot be held responsible for your foolhardy decisions. As I have said many times, we are all of two minds. But you mustn't worry." He smiled. "All will be made right again."

"Let me go," Alek gurgled. "Please—I don't want to be Covenmaster—pleeease—"

Amadeus dropped him.

Alek coughed bloodily. But as if in answer to his pleas, a pair of stony hands clamped around Alek's head like a living vice and turned his attention on the bloody mess on the floor at his feet. Amadeus's voice cooed in his ear as if he were only a young student again, learning his lessons. "Now you will tell me," he said, "was the whore's death—"

"Damn you."

"—price enough—"

"Goddamn you."

"—for this?"

"This is between you and me!"

"No, pet, this is between you and me and whomever you choose to involve. And now you will give up on this silly quest, lest your other little whore breaks as well."

Alek gave up and wept silent, heavy tears. For Debra and for Akisha and for himself lastly because he was lost and out of love and he could not, could not break these inhuman hands holding him in place...

Amadeus leaned close, their hair mingling, and touched the pointed tip of his tongue to one of the spattering of tears sliding freely down Alek's face. Alek balked at the contact, thrashed uselessly in Amadeus's iron embrace. Amadeus sighed. "I should release you and then where would you run? Where would you go that I could not feel your heart beating and drawing me on? When you run, you run only into the waiting arms of your destiny. And I am that destiny."

"No—"

"Nein? Is there another destiny?" His hand instinctively found the mark of Teresa's kiss at his throat. Slowly, with excruciating attention to detail, he raked that mark into discord with the tips of his talon-like fingernails and tore his acolyte's skin like paper, sending a new freshet of blood running down Alek's neck and into the collar of his shirt. Alek gasped and let his breath out in a whine of eye-watering pain. "Her? You would leave me and the Coven for a bit of willing flesh?" Amadeus tore his acolyte's skin like paper and sent a new freshet of blood running down Alek's neck and into the collar of his shirt. Amadeus spoke but his words were oddly alien in Alek's ear, like endearments spoken in some foreign language, sweet and distant and full of hidden truths.

"No, no—we are destined, you and I, two halves of a single creature. I have seen our destiny and it is set in the ages of the earth. Let this be our time, beloved. Let this be our stage. You shall be my vessel as you were born to be. Only a moment, Alek. One moment in hell. A covenant and a kiss. This is all I ask of you."

The kiss Amadeus gave him seemed to steal the remaining breath from Alek's lungs, and yet even as his vision reddened and he wondered if he wouldn't simply pass out from the shock and loss of blood, Amadeus pulled his stinging mouth away, pushed Alek's face to the side, his lips brushing like fire along Alek's ear and down farther still, following the shining track of blood Alek could imagine glittering black on his whiteness of throat. He felt Amadeus's hand under his shirt and against his chest, branding him there like an iron, and he lifted his head, or tried to, as if he would catch a glimpse of the heart that wanted to leap from the cage of his ribs and into his master's hands.

Amadeus was growling now, growling in the back of his throat, and Alek felt a white-hot flash of panic. For gone was any trace of the sophisticated teacher and weapons master who had taught him all he knew. In its place was a rapacious animal that could kill him if he chose to. Amadeus kissed the wound he had made on Alek's throat, kissed it again. Alek felt the teeth pierce the ruptured skin of the wound and he gasped, shuddered with the tearing pain of utter violation, yet his pain did nothing to slake Amadeus's hunger, nothing at all, and Alek screamed.

He screamed in outrage, fear and pain. He screamed for Akisha lying dead on the floor at his feet. He screamed for his lost innocence. He screamed for the life left behind and he screamed for the life that had never been his. He screamed, at last, for the soul he had lost to this beautiful and evil man.

And Amadeus, even powerful Amadeus with all his strengths and powers, was forced to give up, thrown from his work by the nauseatingly shrill cry of horror in his ear. Alek pitched forward to the floor at the foot of the chair and twisted around in time to see Amadeus charging him, the katana in his hands. He moved out of the way just in time, the blade whistling inches from his left ear and sinking solidly into the drywall behind him. Alek lurched against the desk and scrabbled to his feet, squaring off to face the master. Amadeus's face was contorted into something subhuman by his rage, the words barely audible as they spilled from his slathered, venomous mouth,

"*Whelp! Judas! Whore! I will kill you after all! I will kill you as I was always supposed to!*" And with one monumental wrench, he pulled the sword free of the wall.

Alek had stuttered in his decision to go for Amadeus. He had failed and failed miserably, failed in a way that there were no second chances. But he would not beg for mercy, not that Amadeus would show him any. There was no going back now, no apologies, nothing to be done about the past. He had won and he had lost, but he refused to give the Coven the satisfaction of seeing his sniveling greed for life. There was only one thing he still had in his power— to die as he might have lived. Free, with the strength of his own repentance.

"You want to kill me?" Alek screamed back, hating the sight of Amadeus, hating the sight of him and himself reflected in his mentor so much so that he decided in that moment to do anything, even die, to escape it. The game was almost over. There was no way he could fight and destroy the master. "You want to kill me, Father?" he repeated and spread his arms out to the sides in Christlike submission. "You hate me so much and you want to kill me? Then kill me."

He sank to his knees before the Father, folding his bloody hands before him as if in prayer, head bowed to accept the killing blow. Above him loomed the Covenmaster, his aura blazing with hatred, but it was hatred frozen with incredulity. He could hardly believe his best student was giving up so easily, walking voluntarily into his own destruction. The sword sliced downward and into Alek's left shoulder, almost staggering him down on his face, but Alek quickly regained his balance, gritting his teeth against the searing hot blow meant to stun, to punish, not kill. Not yet.

Amadeus withdrew the katana, the blade scraping shrilly against Alek's collarbone like fingernails on a blackboard. "I don't hate you," he said at last.

Alek looked up. The Father was backing away as if afraid of

this odd act of submission. The look of incredulity he expected was being replaced by something else, something akin to sorrow. Righteous rage. "Don't ever say I hated you!" he spat. "I risked everything for your godforsaken soul! *Everything!*"

"You took everything *from* me!"

"I had to make you pure! I had to convince them..." Amadeus shook his head in dismay. He looked around almost as if he could not understand how they could be here now, having this conversation. How everything could have gone so horribly wrong overnight.

"Who?" Alek ventured, his heart ramming wildly against his ribs. "Who? The Church?" But when no answer was forthcoming, he rose slowly to his feet and tried to maneuver as inconspicuously as possible around to the desk where Akisha's shirasaya lay undisturbed by the chaos. "Is that it? That's it, isn't it? Teresa's right. This—it's all about the fucking Church!"

Amadeus shook his head.

"It's about the plan. The Purge."

Amadeus's eyes snapped to attention and Alek knew then, knew for sure, that he was right. Teresa was right.

"You—Aragon—you betrayed Paris—all the other vampires—for the Church. You made a deal with them, didn't you? *Didn't you?*"

The Covenmaster's silence and indecision was acquiescence enough. Amadeus lowered the sword to his side. He seemed to know the charade was over, all the masks gone. He closed his eyes and said, "Alek, beloved, know that—that everything I did, I did for love."

"Love? The word rots on your tongue!"

Amadeus ignored the outburst. "Where is the Chronicle?"

"I don't know."

"You know."

"I don't know! No one does! Byron did, but you killed him." He swallowed down a sob as the claustrophobic walls of too many memories pressed into him like a collapsing tomb. "You killed him," he said again. "And Debra. Only they knew..."

The Father's simmering white eyes opened. "Do not pursue this, my whelp. Please..."

"I have to!" Alek shouted, shuddered, and caught a glance of the shir out of the corner of his eye. Maybe if he could just get hold of it, maybe in the Father's present state of angst, maybe...maybe he would have half a chance in hell at life. If he could get there, if he could keep the Father off-balance long enough. He said, "Teresa, Paris—they believed the Church was going to destroy us, all of us. Like in the Inquisitions. And any deal you cut isn't going to be worth shit when they get what they want."

"Teresa lies. And you don't know the Church—"

"The Chronicle is proof! Or why would you be here now? Who sent you? Your masters from the Church?" He put his hand upon the desk. He shook his head. "It doesn't matter. Maybe the Chronicle can protect us—maybe it'll change everyone's idea of what's going on. But when the Church gets it again it's over for all of us, you blind bastard. You, me, anyone you're protecting." Alek let out his breath, almost a sob. He was so close, close enough to smell the steel of the blade. "We're all marked, all our race. And the humans will be the slayers then, they'll—"

Amadeus rushed forward, his eyes frenzied. He gripped Alek by the shoulders and pulled him forward. "The Church protects me and I protect you. I always have!"

Alek spat in his master's face. "I don't want your protection!"

The mad, holy expression on the Covenmaster's face shattered like panes of glass. He slapped Alek, the force of the blow hurtling him against Akisha's desk with all the terrible force of a bird struck down from its perch by a cat's paw.

Alek shuddered from the blow, caught himself, steadied himself, gripping the edge of the desk for purchase. His face stung as if the flesh had been peeled from the bone. He tried to tell himself that the Father was misguided, a thrall of the Church, a victim like them all, but he knew that wasn't true. Amadeus was just lost. Lost because he chose willingly to be. And this would not be the last time Amadeus would punish him. Amadeus would hit him again and again. Amadeus would hit him until his will was as broken as his body and he would do anything, say anything, the Father wanted. Anything the Church wanted. Because a ward of Amadeus was forever...

Through a veil of tears, Alek saw the shirasaya laying on the ink blotter of Akisha's desk. He reached for it—then yanked his hand back compulsively as Amadeus's blade hissed by a mere inch from Alek's hand, leaving a long gash in the blotter and an even deeper groove in the wood of the desk. Alek stood back, the desk between them, and tried to decide what to do before Amadeus—

"Akisha?"

Both slayers turned toward the new voice at once. Akisha's girl was on her hands and knees on the floor beside her lover's body. She must have emerged from her dream place after Akisha's death and now she was staring down at the bloody remains of the mistress in wide-eyed, childish confusion. As if she could not understand how something so immortal could now be so dead. "Akisha?" came the girl's tiny, plaintive voice again. And then her expression broke. *"Akeeeeshaaaa..."*

It was all the distraction Alek needed. He grabbed up the shirasaya, liberated it from the scabbard, and pointed the savage weapon at Amadeus like a quivering finger. "I'm not going back. I won't go back with you!"

Amadeus stood a moment indecisively. And then he laughed. He spread his arms, and in his coat and suit of rude wool clothes he looked absurdly like Jonathan Edwards about to sermonize the American Separatists into hell. "Futile, this. How can you win against the enemy who lives inside your head, who knows your devices even as you do. Remember, beloved, it is my blood you have in your veins. That shall never go away. I will be a part of you forever." He drifted around the desk and toward his wayward acolyte like some horrible, earthbound spirit.

Alek made a sickened, strangling noise. "Don't..."

Amadeus stopped and narrowed his eyes. "You belong to me."

"I don't. I belong to Debra."

"Debra is dead."

"Sometimes the dead come back."

Amadeus swayed closer and put out a long white hand to caress Alek's hair as though to challenge him to do this—to strike his master and teacher. Alek blinked, and for just a moment Amadeus's figure transfigured into something looming and monstrous and shadowy and disfigured, something not of this world, something that had never belonged to it, something unnatural and hideous to behold—

Alek shuddered, groaned at the contact, and thrust the shirasaya forward through the cage of his master's ribs and up into Amadeus's gut with all his sudden strength of panic, up, up further, all the way in, burying the long sword in his master all the way up to the simple rosewood hilt—

And halted.

Amadeus jerked from the impact but his expression remained unblemished by either surprise or agony. Alek saw no defeat there, nothing that could be hurt, could die. Only the prowling rage of something inhuman and unstoppable, petty and rejected. And in that single, still moment of absolute crux, Alek found himself thinking of, not Teresa nor even Debra or Akisha cooling on the floor not a dozen steps away, but of the Prince of swans falling on his ice and dying.

Why must the heroes always die?

"Damnable," Amadeus said. "Damnable whelp. I am finished with you. Go to your sister, Alek. Now."

Amadeus grabbed the sword just behind the pommel and jerked it out of the gaping hole in his gut and drove the hilt into Alek's stomach. Alek barely felt it as he careened over Akisha's desk and hit the pane of stained-glass behind it. The old church glass shuddered, shrieked, struggled to maintain the impact—only a second—then gave it up.

After that there was only the hands of the wind and the sickening vertigo of a two hundred foot plunge to the city floor below. He felt the wind animate his coat like the tattered wings of a great bat. And that made him wish in some final moment of utter desperation that he really could change his shape as the stories and movies professed, shrink into a different creature with membranous wings that could cup and hold the wind and make him fly. Really, truly fly. At last, at long last—

But then he gave up the fantasy and let the darkness have him and hide him and take him down into a place after which no one could follow him.

INTERLUDE 2

1

The holiday season was always marvelous at McEnroy Home, with baskets of donated goodies and shopping sprees and outings arranged by the affluent. At eight years of age, Alek enjoyed the time of the year immensely, the theatre and carnival, the colored lights and the tinkling laughter and the warmth the city briefly embraced.

Especially wonderful were the outings when they toured someplace magic and perfect; it was a chance to feel clever and take Debra by the hand and lead her down through the sacred halls of the museums he read so much about and see the Masters of Old Europe and the timeless gods with beast's heads in their upright, airtight glass coffins. A chance to hunt down and study marvelous quarry constructed of oils and bronze and marble and light.

"Sekhmet," Debra said once in The Hall of Gods and pointed up at the lion-headed goddess. "Battle queen. She killed her enemies without mercy and drank their blood." Debra lingered over the statue, but Alek moved on quickly, eyes averted, because the clever feline grin on Sekhmet's whiskered face was so like Debra's own.

They saw Daumier and Delacroix and Matisse's white-plumed ladies. And Alek stood spellbound before the splattering bloodlike oils of Jerome Bosch, fearing and admiring the images that spoke without moving, the secrets whispered without words.

Afterward, the class was ushered to Rockefeller Center as if they were expected to mingle with the children who came with parents and would leave with them. The McEnroy children, uniform in their grey, state-issued greatcoats, skated between boys in letter jackets and girls in flared, candy-pink tulle skirts, all of it mother-chosen affectations to carefully define character in their children. And the Home children all grey-coated and incongruous, Alek thought, all but Debra. Of course.

As Alek watched, his sister crept up to the benches where the doting parents sat watching the expensive clothing their children had discarded in the warm rush of their expended energy and stole a young teenaged boy's black leather jacket almost right out from under the nose of his father. She smiled and swirled across the ice toward him in her red holiday dress and black jacket as the other Home children looked on with horror and pointed at her. "You can't do that," Alek chided her as she linked her hand through his.

She laughed. Her lips looked moist. "Why?"

"Because."

"Damn because! Don't be such a Puritan, Alek!" She broke away and ran for the center of the pond where she executed a series of death-defying off-the-ice flips and landed on her feet like a cat with a cat's same wicked pride.

Alek watched her antics from a bench, enjoying them and her. He did not understand her thoughts many times, and sometimes could not guess at her intentions, but she was beautiful and clever and he would love her forever, so what did anything else matter?

He smiled and settled back on the bench to watch her creep up like a ghost and steal a link of candy from the pocket of another of the Home children. And it was then, when he was most preoccupied and off-guard, that he felt his hackles stiffen as a melodious whistling drifted to him from behind. A flock of pigeons scattered as the Bitch appeared on the gravel walk in front of Alek's bench. She was bundled stupidly, like some German female spy in a war movie, with muffs on her scrawny hands and little black Gestapo glasses on her pasty face. Smiling, she ambled by in her dark coat as if expecting some secret rendezvous. Alek held his breath and waited. Maybe the Bitch hadn't noticed his presence amidst all the other children, or no longer cared. Maybe she had a new victim.

But after a long, breathless moment Alek felt the hiss of a released breath in his hair, felt a raw, knuckled hand brush his cheek briefly, then settle itself like a spider on his shoulder. Alek heard a helpless whimper gather in his throat. Was there anywhere safe? Anywhere at all? He closed his eyes tight; he wanted to go away, run away with Debra right this minute...

And then, as if summoned, he opened his eyes and spotted his sister skating toward him, hands in her pockets, eyes narrow slits, her posture casual and yet like that of a stalking beast, and the hand quickly disappeared. He sobbed as she settled on the bench beside him, sobbed into her hair, quite surprised with himself, and she held him and allowed for it. And Debra kissed the tears from his face and spoke her savage words of love into his mind, and she seemed so beautiful and angelic to him that he feared what she would become.

Somewhere far off at the other end of the pond a group of Home children had joined a group of wassailers in their songs, and it was then that he remembered how Debra was to be fostered out to the Forsythes for Christmas this year and how they must be apart, and the fear was hard, red as life itself inside him, and he wondered if it would crack his very soul open.

"My beloved," she whispered, her voice soft and strong like the sultry voices of the movie actresses she wanted to be like, but with more truth than any actress, more feeling. "We will always be together. Don't you know? Wherever you are I can see and protect you. I adore you and will love you forever." She kissed him and held him close, and between them, on her hand where it rested against his heart, he could almost feel the warm gold magic of the ring.

2

Alek woke sharply to the shadow-deep night of the Home at midnight. Through the window he could see a moon the color of steel hanging like a weapon in the heavens and casting light in a runner to the foot of his bed. He looked at the moonlight, the cold glow of it, and thought of Debra, Debra in her black coat and blacker hair, how the moon always caught red in the pits of her eyes. It was Christmas Eve, and Debra was gone now to Ithaca with the Forsythes so they could play house and feel pious for the season, damn them. He hoped she ate their dog.

He turned over in bed and pillowed his head on his folded arms. He studied the water stain on the ceiling above his bed, imagining ghoulish faces that could frighten the Forsythes and the social workers and all the other people in the Home who conspired to separate them. He hated them all with the deepest part of his heart and soul and more.

And he had just started wondering if that was all right, to hate everyone so completely, when he thought he heard a whippoorwill shrill somewhere in the city that cowered in the night. Whippoorwill. Someone's dying, Debra would say.

Except it wasn't.

It was...whistling

He sat bolt upright. And all at once he felt the quiet of the Home smother him like a great faulty web falling in, like a dirty blanket, like that, or something worse. He should get out of here, he knew, get help, except there were no hall monitors at this time of the night and most of the staff were gone for Christmas. A handful of kids without foster homes like himself slept safe in their beds in other rooms, but that was so far away. Far away. Like Debra was far away. He was alone, he realized. Completely alone.

The whistling deepened, drew nearer.

His heart throbbed painfully in his chest. It was difficult to think, to even *feel*. He shivered violently all over and found moist diamonds of sweat sparkling on the backs of his hands. He should rise and go to the window, escape into the night the way he and Debra did on countless other nights. Except his body felt paralyzed and alien to him and all he could do was shudder and sweat and chant Debra's name over and over again like a mantra or a prayer for deliverance.

He felt his heart die and his body seize up when the door of his room clicked open. He wasn't moving, only fearing something new and horrible and somehow inevitable. Maybe it was only a late-night bed check by the director of the Home, he thought, staring with wide, horrified eyes at the monstrous shadow eating up the wall, something hideous and unnatural to behold. Maybe if he held perfectly still and didn't say a thing, maybe then he wouldn't be noticed, maybe—

The door closed silently but with great force, like a seal, locking him in with something.

And Alek stopped shuddering like someone had turned a switch off inside of him. Instead he found himself reaching beside his bed for one of the sketch pencils in the tin cup on the nightstand. He drew it close to him and buried it under his bedclothes.

The presence glided toward him and settled in the dark at his bedside. Alek did not look, did not flinch, not even when the dry, ugly hand touched his hair. Don't panic, he told himself—Debra's earliest lesson when they first began to hunt at night and he was so afraid of being caught. Never panic. Panic gets you caught.

"Pretty little blackbird."

"I'll tell." He felt surprised that he could still speak. "I'll scream until they come. I swear it."

The hand on his face, as dead and rotten as the hand of a movie mummy's, dropped to his collar, then ripped the buttons violently from the front of his nightshirt. "And if you make them come, I'll tell them about all the nights I saw Alek and Debra Knight run away and kill animals and drink their blood. I'll tell them about the bloodstained and torn clothing that disappears and the dirt and blood under your fingernails, and if they don't believe me, I'll show them the evidence. And do you know what they will do to you, Alek? They'll take you both and put you in a place for mad kids because they don't understand, and then they'll split you up and you will never see your sister again."

"I don't believe you!" he heard himself whisper vehemently.

"I don't care if you do." The hand, the terrifying hand, slid caressingly down Alek's body beneath the open shirt, and he shivered. "How cold you are," the Bitch complained. "As cold as the dead."

Alek shuddered inside and out. It was all he could do to keep from thinking about her words. "What...what do you want?"

The bed groaned as it took on weight. The hand played over his face, yet he felt no instinct to flee just yet, no need to panic. He only tightened his hold on the pencil under his covers.

"You're a vampire," said the Bitch, as simple as a fact. Her mouth gleamed as she spoke. "Do you know what that means? You'll be beautiful and young and powerful forever. Do you know how wonderful it will be for you? Do you have any idea of what promise the world holds for you?"

No, Alek wanted to tell her, to scream, no it's not wonderful or promising. It's horrible. It's confusing. What they were, whatever it was, was like being locked inside a black box with no light and no air, and they had to keep going, keep living, even though they knew it would probably never end. And the most horrible part of it was that there was a part of them that was real and human, but they'd abandoned it once too often and now they couldn't seem to reach it anymore. They lived inside a black canvas like a Bosch they couldn't take themselves out of and they looked out on a bright, beautiful world that wasn't really theirs anymore, and sometimes that made him want to weep until he was carried away on a river of his sorrow...

He wanted to say these things, because they were true and because they hurt and they might wound Bessell, but his voice was constricted with his suddenly rediscovered panic.

"I want to be like you," the Bitch whispered. She leaned close, close, breath cloying. "I want to be a vampire. Make me into one. I want to hunt at night with you and be a part of your world. Take me, Alek. Bite me and take me with you and I promise to serve you forever. I swear it."

But he couldn't! He didn't know why this had happened to them—or how—but it had, and they hadn't been made by anyone, and the animals they killed only died and stayed that way, just like the Bitch would...

"Please, Alek. I don't want the life that's chosen for me. I want to make my own choices; I want to live my own life. I want—so many things. Strength. Power. Immortality. Make me a vampire and I'll be your disciple," the Bitch whispered. "I will join you, learn from you, help you—"

The Bitch's weight was heavy on him, crushing his ribs, the hands hot and filthy on his skin, and the panic was there again— wild and instinctual—and Alek turned away his face, half to gag and half to sob, but with his head turned he felt the slimy, yellowed teeth at his throat and something broke inside him, something massive and snarling, and in one smooth motion his hand came up under the sheet and he felt the pencil sink into soft, warm, ponderous flesh and splinter off, and after that there was only dead weight and the Bitch's wet scream muffled against his throat, and suddenly the weight upon him was not so terrible, and Alek gathered himself and pushed out with every ounce of strength he had and watched, satisfied, as Bessell grunted and the force of it actually cast her over the foot of the bed to crash against the highboy beside the window. The side of the Bitch's head connected with it with a hearty thump and the woman slammed to the floor just below the window and the bladelike quarter moon.

Alek shook to rid himself of the Bitch's touch and crawled to the foot of the bed and looked down. Wilma Bessell lay in a massive lump on the floor. A little blood trickled from just below her ribs where the pencil had gashed her, and there was an angry red area over one temple, but her breathing was deep and normal. He hadn't killed the woman, thank God.

God had nothing to do with it.

Alek looked up at the window.

Debra teetered on the outer sill, smiling in at him. The snow was a rain of knives out there, and yet she crouched in only her thin red camisole and black leather jacket, her feet bare, lassos of her wet black hair lashed across her face and neck like the long arms of spiders. She tapped at the glass expectantly and Alek wasted no time going to her and swinging open the pane for her lithe entry. "Debra," he said, but she corrected him, saying, "Sekhmet, beloved," and danced out of his hold to study the brained Bitch at her feet.

"She wants to be a vampire," Alek explained, feeling sad and sick and a little afraid.

"The stupid cow, does she?" Debra smiled strangely at him, her eyes black and as shiny as wet leather. She clucked her tongue over the Bitch's body. "Only two to an establishment, I'm afraid," she said tragically and knelt down beside the woman, indicating that Alek should join her. And as Alek watched, paralyzed with horror, his twin kissed the Bitch's forehead, then withdrew a delicate little straight razor from the pocket of her coat and slit the soft pouch of flesh under the Bitch's chin from one ear to the other. The flesh split away from the great vein like a pair of open gaping lips.

The Bitch moaned, shuddered once, and was silent forever.

The blood was astonishing. It painted the walls of their white room like a picture of abstract poinsettias. It painted Alek and it painted his twin in its cloying, metallic sweetness. It did not seem possible a single person could have so much blood in them. Debra laughed playfully and put her tongue to the gush of warmth like Alek had seen other children put their tongues to water fountains in the park. Debra drank in greedy, starving gulps, and when she looked up at him, her face was red out of which glowed only the feral blackness of her eyes, eyes shot through with sad, heckling laughter and the madness of her life.

Debra licked her lips clean and Alek felt his paralysis break. He felt himself sink inside at the sight, almost blacken out. And knowing now, knowing why they'd been left on the doorstep of the Home eight years ago by a nameless, faceless individual who had obviously seen the shadows behind their eyes, but who had not had the heart for proper murder. Knowing now, knowing the name given to her, to them, to their race, and knowing it was not demigod, was not god of any kind. Knowing everything now with the shock of instinct, knowing and sick now with the completion of that knowledge. And it wasn't like in the stories and the movies, not at all. There was no beauty in death, no glory. It was all red and torn and bloody and foul.

Debra smiled invitingly at him, red lips drawing away from hard ivory teeth, a pulpy shred of the Bitch's flesh caught in the corner of her mouth, the mouth he always kissed. And he saw, nearly like an afterthought, that the ring was on her finger and that she had his Andy doll clutched tight by one arm, and these human affectations only seemed to make the horror of her utterly real to him. So when she kissed him with her murderous mouth, then tried to draw his face down to the new chalice she offered, he balked and thrashed away from her, from the horror that was her, from the searing, murderous taste of a dead woman on her lips. He got to his feet and raced to the other side of the room and crouched in the moonlight.

"Alek?" And yet still she came at him, eyes curious as a cat's, words seeking him, touch questing. And at last, with his back against the wall, with nowhere else to go, he snapped and made a pained sound of horror in his throat and struck her across the face. Debra went down. It was not a harsh blow, but it had harmed her in a way no blow could because it came from him.

"*Aaalek,*" she whined plaintively, touching her face where a spayed red mark, almost as red as blood, was taking hold.

He cast a sidelong look at the remains of the Bitch, hating her all the more for doing this to Debra. To them both. He shuddered uncontrollably like someone with a fatal fever, trying to forget all those lessons he'd leant in Sunday School, all those meandering scriptures with their hidden and damning meanings, but unable to, for the wages of sin were death, right? And death—murder— was the worse sin in the world anyone could ever do. He found one of their yellowing back issues of *Weird Tales* lying on the floor beside their bed and picked it up and rounded on her, breathing hard. "Is this what you want, Debra?" he ranted at her like a madman. "To be *this*? Is that what you want? Do you want to be damned?"

"Beloved..." She rose unsteadily and looked at him with her subhuman eyes. Her voice was old, confused, the voice of some goddess exhumed from her grave of a thousand years. She looked at the mess of their room that she had made as if she could not understand his rage. "She—it's the blood of our enemy!"

"You murdered her, Debra!"

"She doesn't count!"

She was closing the black box down on him, sealing the canvas over his face like a burial shroud, because she believed his will was her own and her word the truth. But if she was going to willingly embrace damnation and be a monster like in the movies then she would be doing it alone, without him.

He began to weep, but dryly. "You do what you want, but don't you dare ask me to go into this thing with you! *Don't you dare!*" He threw the magazine at her with its ghoulish, cruel-eyed cover. "I won't do it! I don't care who you are, I won't! I hate you! I hate you to hell!"

Like a somnambulist her arms went out to him. A child waking from a nightmare or only waking to a new one. She looked at him without understanding. She seemed to fall at his words.

But then he caught her, pulling her out of the nightmare, to him, to the shelter of his body. She sobbed, shuddering, her mouth wet and miserable against his skin; she stained his clothes dark with her tears.

"You said you'd love me forever," she said.

His anger and horror were gone. His Debra was crying and tearing his heart to pieces. He made soothing noises to calm her, stroked her hair, rocking her gently in his embrace as her mind sought the cloister of his own. He sobbed with her, loving her and despising her, repulsed and enchanted by her, feeling so close to her and yet so very hopelessly far away.

And after many moments it all seemed to end, not the horror of what she—they—had done, but the shock of it. He suddenly found himself capable of thought and words. "We have to go away now," he decided. "Far away before they find out." And she nodded at his words and let him gather her up, cradling her thin, tired little body easily in his arms.

He took her to the bed and dressed her in warm clean clothes and wiped the blood off her face, and then he changed himself and gathered together a few simple but important things. Their pictures. His Andy doll. Once finished, they padded silent and shoeless from the room that had once caged them, been their home. They went down the vacant corridor, down the flight of backstairs that connected the dorms with the butler's pantry at the rear of the Home, and there they put on their boots and coats and prepared to go out into the wintry darkness of the city.

They met no one on the way, and just as well: Alek was certain he would have commanded anyone to stay back as they left the Home by the door through which they had entered it. And he was equally certain anyone he commanded to do so would have obeyed him without question.

3

"Coelum non animum mutant, qui trans mare current."

The coarse white voice came to him out of the darkness and the dull, weary winter dawn, and Alek's breath caught at the sound as if on a thorn. He untangled himself from his twin and looked around searchingly. Behind them the white wooden horse gently moved on its revolver, clicking forward three paces, then falling back as the wind and snow buffeted it. And Debra, clasped to him where they huddled under the canopy, comforted at last to sleep by his words and this place, moaned lightly.

"Horace," said the voice. "*Epistles.* A favorite of mine."

Holding her tightly, Alek narrowed his eyes and was at last able to pick out the figure standing on the gravel path not a dozen feet from them. The stranger had gotten there, but how? He'd thought they were alone here, and he was certain that with his newfound senses he would detect even a drunkard's feeble staggering. And yet a strange man stood in front of him with a hand resting on the ebony war-horse, his robes so black it—and most of the rest of him—disappeared into the night and made his white face and hands swim ghostlike and disembodied in the dark.

No, he was mistaken: it was not robes the man wore but a long black habit and black topcoat, like something a priest might wear.

Alek cradled his sister's head protectively to his heart. "Are you a priest, sir?"

It was all he could think to say. There were priests at the Home who held Mass and regular Sunday School classes every week. He knew what a priest looked like and what a priest was and what a priest did. You told a priest your evils. And priests hated vampires, he knew that too.

The man who looked like a priest smiled with scarcely any change of expression. "In fact, der Klein, a priest I am. But you mustn't fear. Vampire? You are much more. And much less."

Alek didn't know what to say to that or what the priest even meant. "Those words you spoke," he said, "are they Latin?"

One eyebrow arched and the priest's smile grew. "Bright boy."

"What do they mean, sir?"

The priest stepped forward, and as he passed beyond the shadows the last of the midwinter's moon took and became his hair. It was a mane that fell to his waist, and it was as white as a hundred alien suns, as white as a twilight blizzard. He was too impossible to be real, too ephemeral to exist for very long, and yet he did. An enormous power existed within him that he seemed scarcely able to contain, a power so large it dwelled about him like a retinue.

"They mean," he said as he swayed forward and Alek saw at last the vanishing pale of this man's eyes, "that you have come home, Alek Knight." The priest touched his face and it was like the cool holy burning of ash.

Alek shivered. "How...do you know who I am?"

The priest laughed. "Ah, but now, little knight, I can't be telling you all. A magician never reveals his secrets, does he?"

Debra stirred in his arms. "Alek," she moaned, "what's happening?"

"It's all right." He kissed her hair. "He's a friend." He looked up at the priest. "He's...he's like us, I think."

Debra sat up and sought out the stranger's eyes. And almost at once Alek felt the icy rime of her distrust and heard her stony voice in his mind that said there was no room in their world but for him and her. She turned her face into him. *I want to go away, Alek. Take us far away.*

We have nowhere to go, Debra.

Come with me, children, said the priest in their private language, *and go with your own kind. And go into the open, waiting arms of the Coven.*

Alek narrowed his eyes. "The Coven?"

The priest shrugged. "Is everything. Sanctification. Redemption. Everything."

Redemption. Alek knew what that word meant: forgiveness, for Debra and for himself, for allowing them to slip so far into the dark.

The man uncurled one of his hands like a gift. "It must be your decision."

The man was a priest. A Father.

"And you could be my son," he said, "if you so wish it."

Alek watched as his hand came off Debra's face and was slowly devoured by whiteness. He felt a chill in his blood at the contact that burned him as deep as a vow.

And then the priest pulled them easily from the stage and down into the darkness of his coat. And as a new fierceness of midwinter's snow began to fall he raised the loose, swirling folds of that coat and covered their heads against it as though it was a dark wing under which he had taken them.

4

Amadeus, Priest-warrior.

Amadeus, Covenmaster.

Magician.

His house was a magic castle walled in books and glowing with holy light and the perfumes of beeswax and incense, where the past seemed to crumble away, and where each day was a step in some hallowed stairwell that might take them to the Godhead itself one day. In the Covenhouse rooms seemed to gather themselves and stand starkly powerful around the lone individual, not frightening but surely full of power. The cells of the great house were like spare, individual statements of the soul, and the Great Abbey like some lost temple out of a forgotten mythology.

But best of all, in the Covenhouse, no one asked about your sins.

"Who are you?" Alek asked quite suddenly at Amadeus's feet where the Covenmaster was seated in one of his straight-backed benches. Alek had been working up the courage to ask the question since the very first day, almost a week ago. And now, at last, he felt the courage break free from him and direct his words.

Amadeus stopped reading the ancient words from out of his Catechism, his fingers pausing in the middle of the page where they had been following the old scrawled inking. His blind eyes turned downward as if he could really see Alek there beside his sister and the other new kid, the one called Booker who never spoke very much. "A pilgrim, child," he answered.

Alek sat up, enchanted by this new discovery. "Like on the *Mayflower*?"

Amadeus smiled.

At his side, Debra turned her face away and began to sulk once more, not at all impressed by this wonderfully old young man. Stupid of her.

"And before, Father Amadeus?"

"Before what?"

"Before you were a Pilgrim."

"A pilgrim I have always been, my curious one." He turned the page. It was all he had offered and it was magic and amazing and Alek did not ask again.

"I hate him!" Debra shouted that night, her fists balled in her hair, her filmy red gown billowing under her sublime wrath. "There's something wrong with him."

Alek glared up sharply from the Catechism that Amadeus had lent him to read; it was the history of the Coven, explaining the origins of its Rites and Ordinances, its purposes and designs, the vampire's relationship with the Church and each other, all of it interesting. He turned up the oil lamp on the table beside the fascinating little book as Debra paced past, her hair writhing.

"They're dark," she complained miserably. She did not pause, not even a moment, like a lioness in a cage.

"What's dark?" he asked with teetering patience.

"His eyes."

"His eyes are light."

She paced.

He wants me to die.

Alek scowled up at her. "The Coven doesn't slay their own."

"They slay their mad."

"Amadeus doesn't think you're mad!"

"They hate their women."

Alek heisted. "They hate the unbound, Debra."

"So I have to be bound?"

"The Father said, that in time, maybe Book—"

But she spun around too quickly, one hand darting out to strike the Catechism from the table. She struck the oil lamp instead. The light guttered out, and almost at once the entire table was awash in hot oil.

"Debra!" he growled. "Debra, damnit, look what you've done!" He peeled the ancient book off the table. It dripped despondently, and its words, in ink and sometimes in blood, were quickly running into nonsense on the open page.

"I hate him!" Debra shouted. "And I hate you for bringing us here!"

"What was I supposed to do? Where were we supposed to go?"

Debra crumpled down onto their bed, weeping.

Why was she acting like this, now that they finally had a permanent home? Now that *he* had a permanent home? Or was that it? he wondered. Was she jealous because he was the center of Amadeus's attention instead of her? Because Amadeus said he saw great power and potential in Alek? It wasn't fair, damnit. Why was she spoiling his one chance to be happy?

With a little sigh of impatience he set the ruin of the book aside and went to her as he had always done, and she clung to him and wept to him as if they were still all alone in the world, her hands desperate claws on his back, her face buried in the hollow of his throat. And then her cold lips rasped apart and he felt the familiar dent of her teeth on his flesh.

But bloodtaking was wrong. The Catechism said so. Amadeus said so. A priest had discipline and controlled the beast instead of letting it control him. Amadeus said they were all of two minds and that when you fell too far sometimes you couldn't come back. And then you were lost forever. That's why discipline was so important.

And so Alek moved her face down against the breast of the habit the Father had given him. Debra struggled against him, but he did not relent until she tired and stilled and slept in his arms.

Alek put her to bed and pulled the handmade eiderdown quilt around her and gave her the Andy doll to hold. He kissed her piously on the forehead, then stepped back to watch the gray dolphin light float over her deceptively innocent-looking face. The light paled her skin, made her hair look brittle and ancient. Alek shuddered, feeling for just a moment that he was looking on the face of the unburied dead.

"Debra, what do I do with you?"

He picked up the Catechism and, wearily and a little fearfully, went to find Amadeus and apologize.

The Father was meditating in the shadow of the altar of skulls when Alek found him, a wreath of serpents crawling around his neck, but not biting, never that. He didn't seem at all angry when he found out what had become of his book. He nodded. "It is time," he said, and the sightless eyes set on Alek's face seemed to sink into some other place that Alek could not see. As he watched, Amadeus rose and moved to one of the sets of crosswords and took down a katana long sword. And then the Covenmaster knelt with him, one hand on the ornately carved white jade hilt, the other on Alek's face.

"This sword," said Amadeus, "was forged by the first *jonin*, or ninja-master, Hattori Hanzo, and was blessed by the great Shogun Tokugawa Ieyasu. It is a virgin; it has never been used in battle. It is said that its master would live forever and rule the earth for a thousand years. And it is said the weapon would know its master when it met him and the two would be forged together for all time."

Alek looked down at the impressive forty-two-inch weapon and saw his own amazed eyes reflected in the flawless wave pattern of the blade. Such art, such hungry art. He wondered what power had ordained him worthy of this great thing and was about to ask when he was silenced by the reflected image of the Covenmaster in the sword. Amadeus's eyes narrowed, pale as fired steel, sharp as the deadliest summer lightning. His hand coursed down over Alek's face like rain, touching his brow, closing Alek's eyes and caressing his lids so gently that he did not recoil.

"Truth is brewed in darkness, Alek. This is your first lesson."

Alek nodded, lost in Amadeus's created night. It was like pleasure without pain, like pain without the regret. It was like Debra's sacred kiss transfigured into a touch, a thought, a place of thoughts, deep and intimate, both alien and hauntingly familiar. And in that personal night his hands were captured and set around the hard bonelike hilt of Hanzo's sacred sword.

"Make it a part of you forever, Alek, my Chosen One."

He tried to lift it, but it was so impossibly heavy. "I can't,

Father..."

"You will. I will show you how and you will, my son."

Afterward, even as he slept in Debra's embrace, he felt the throbbing presence of the sword under his bed and heard the Father's last words to him that day echo down into his subconscious like a promise or a prayer.

I will create you.

And five years later, he had.

CHAPTER 3

1

"Alek Knight."

He opened his eyes almost immediately; almost immediately he sucked in a breath of cold, stale air. "Debra?" He wanted to reach for the angelic face floating above him, to touch it, but curiously enough, he had no arms or hands to do so.

"Not Debra."

"Teresa."

"Yes."

He smiled drunkenly. "I'm dead."

"Then I must be as well."

He frowned at the faulty logic of that.

"Alive," she said and kissed his forehead with her sweet, innocent little prostitute's mouth. "Alive."

Her face was so perfect and unnatural and he so wanted to touch it and make her real to him once more. But where were his hands?

"I can't move," he complained.

"Your back is broken."

"Paralyzed."

"For a time."

He frowned at the news; it seemed frowning was all he could manage. "How?"

"You fell. I watched you."

"You were there...?"

"I stood helplessly by the banks of the Hudson and watched you fall. I took you down to the docks, and from there—here."

He tried to turn his head, to see what this place was, but that was too much. "Where's here?"

"A safe place I've brought you to hide you. He won't find you here. Even Amadeus the Mad does not know this city as I do."

He was lying on a bed. He saw a jungle of colorless water pipes and shattered plaster in cookie-cutter patterns, cobwebs like shorn, ancient ghosts, or silk. He smelled old water and rust and the musty befurred things that moved busily in the walls. Above came the gentle clapping of birds with blunt nighttime wings. They were in the attic space of some old coldwater brownstone, he was willing to wager, but as to where in the city was anyone's guess...

"How long...?"

"A long time, Alek Knight. Three days and you've slept them through. How do you feel?"

"I don't."

She leaned over him and kissed his mouth, and it was terrible for he could not feel the essence of her breath on his dead traitor of a body. He heard from far down below, somewhere in the belly of the building, a roar of voices. Anger. Human anger. Something shattered against a wall, and then there were more oaths and cries of violence. Yet he could not force himself to concentrate on them.

He was laying on Teresa's bed, with Teresa hovering near, her flesh white and bare to his touch. Her voice, her scent—they seemed to raise his sensitivity until the room itself throbbed with painfully acute life. He saw something long and slender flash in her delicate hands, and for a moment he thought he was doomed. But then "It's time to heal," she whispered in her scorching Jezebel's voice and she pressed the edge of the straight razor she held in a brimming black line between her breasts as if what she offered him was death and not life itself. Carefully, through her persuasions, he kissed her flesh and tasted her angel's blood. He suckled her and felt her essence fill and begin to heal the ruined shell of his body.

So good. But he was so tired. His mouth slackened early, his body relaxing on the meager mattress beneath him and slowly filling with the things he'd thought he'd forgotten—warmth and chill and dull, wretched pain—as his body came alive around him to torture him for his reckless abuse of it.

He shuddered violently and tried to reach for her. "Teresa..."
"Shh." He felt her kiss his bloodstained lips. "Sleep and grow
strong, my beautiful lost one." Her lips kissed his eyelids to closing
and in time he slept. And when his dreams and memories came
once more they were only of her.

2

"I dreamt things," Alek said when next he awoke to the sounds of
violent activity below. He looked around the attic space and found
her sitting in a rocker beside his sickbed. On a table between them
were packages of vendor's food wrapped in white paper and string.
Like Elijah's raven she had brought him something to eat and helped
him sit up now to do so. He sagged like a puppet against the wall.
His body seemed to have a thousand tingling points of pain.
"You're better," Teresa said. "What did you dream?"
Through a white haze of dust her face was ghastly, perfect,
beautiful. White skin, black eyes, black, black hair, her delicate
body now hidden away by an unidentifiable sheath of some ancient
cloth. It looked medieval, or it was only the fact that she wanted it
to seem that way. Her Glamour. He wanted so to touch her and
make her real in all her dangerous allure, and to his surprise he
found he could. Every gesture of his fingers on her hair and face
was an agony, but the pain was fine; nothing felt worst than feeling
nothing at all. "We were walking on Fifth Avenue in the daylight,"
he said, "and it was spring." He smiled. "All the old Greek vendors
were selling their tulips. And I bought you—"
"An ice cream cone," she said. "And I ate it."
He frowned. "You can't remember another's dreams."
"Another's, no. But yours I see." She kissed his hand, licked the
tips of his fingers like a fawning pet. "I see it the way you've dreamt
it, just like I see what became of your unfortunate friend."
Akisha, ancient Akisha...
"Yes, caro," she said, "I know. Slain by the hand of Amadeus."

Dear God, Akisha—but he'd never meant—

"Yes, I know."

He erupted into shameless, uncontrollable sobs, and she allowed for it, cradled his face to her perfumed hair. She stroked him and let his tears baptize her with their purity, and when it was finished and his grief weak and used up she eased him back as carefully as if he was some fragile, valuable old doll.

She leaned forward, her gown rustling, and wiped a tear from his cheek. "And now?" she prompted.

"Nothing." He shook his head. "It's all been in vain."

"No. Byron's picture. We have a map to the Chronicle."

He laughed miserably. "We have *nothing*, Teresa."

But her smile was clever and ancient and seductive, as always. "We have you."

It took him a moment to understand what she meant. "I can't," he said at last. "I can't."

Down below something crashed against a wall and a woman screamed.

"You will," she said.

3

She found him a flier in the scattered debris of the boiler room. He turned the aged paper to its blank-faced side on the slate she'd propped against his knees. He looked at it, its desolate emptiness, and tried to picture Byron's map there, its simple, exact artwork. Simple, so simple, yet one wrong stroke would skew the whole damned thing out of focus. He took a pen from his breast pocket, put it to the paper, stopped.

"I can't do this," he repeated. "I can't fucking draw *apples* anymore."

"You must," Teresa told him, standing in her medieval gown, her black eyes watching him with a determination that was godlike in its absolute purity.

"I'm a hack, Teresa."

"You are a gifted artist. A Bauhaus in your violent soul."

"I don't believe you."

"Try." Her eyes narrowed, saying other things the nature of which he wished he could pretend did not exist. Do it, her eyes said, do it or you will not walk out of here alive, slayer.

Alek thought of the straight razor hidden away here somewhere in her loft. He looked around but there was little to see, little revealed by the burning candles of the loft and the round portal window that let in only a dire neon light. He lifted the pen and put it to the paper once more. His hand trembled, the pen almost too much weight for it to bear as dozens of lifeless Bosch jobs flitted through his mind. Dark. Useless. Hopeless...

"Then was then," she uttered softly as she took her seat beside the bed. "Now is now..."

He caught his breath, put his pen to paper and began to draw. "Talk to me," he muttered, "tell me things to keep me sane."

"Such as...?"

"Anything. Anything at all."

She was silent a moment. Her eyes glowed white in the dark, then blinked out. And then she said, "I arrived in this city almost thirty years ago, but it might as well be yesterday. I had never been away from the convent until then, but survival has a way of educating you in the ways of the world, doesn't it? Paris was dead by then, of course, and so I had no protection. I soon found as well that I had nothing to offer the city but my eternal youth and body, both of which were greedily accepted. I slept in Grand Central Station my first day in town and sold myself the following night in order to get up enough money to afford a room at a boardinghouse.

"I didn't think much about what I was doing, just did it and took their life and their money, used to lending out my body for a few sweaty moments in Rome, and then returning to it later, when the beast was satiated. The priests had trained me well for the life I was to lead. The only difference between the assembly line of eager men who wanted me and the priests at the Vatican was that if I left them alive, I never had to see the men again.

"And they paid me. Well, most of the time they paid me.

"Sometimes they refused to pay, shaking the money under my nose before stuffing it back in their pockets, daring me to do something about it. Sometimes they grew ugly and slapped me around or tried to strangle me. I never knew who was going to turn psycho on me, but one thing was certain—they all paid for their offenses. One old grandfatherly gentleman put a straight razor to my throat and told me he was the reincarnation of Jack the Ripper and he was going to disembowel me. He wasn't quick enough. Paris had given me a knife of iron as a wedding present and taught me how to use it."

She hesitated. "They always seemed to grow ugly when they were done. Up until then they were usually polite. I saw the pattern emerge. It was always the polite ones who turned on you, as if they were punishing you for their own weakness, making you feel worthless only to feel their own worth again, trying to make you powerless to convince themselves that they weren't powerless against their own sexuality.

"I worked freelance for years before meeting Rapper and his girls. He's a kind man for a pimp, understanding but firm, and he knows how to keep his girls in order with just the right combination of intimacy and intimidation. In all the time I have spent in his stable, I have never known a girl to cheat him. But whether it is fear or love or some alchemical combination of the two responsible for such loyalty, I cannot say. I have come to think of Rapper as the Bishop I didn't dare disobey at the Vatican. He fucks me the same as the Bishop did, but only occasionally, and without the hostility and brutality the Churchmen always brought to my bed. He makes me feel protected, something I haven't felt since Paris..."

She stopped speaking. She was watching him with tears in her eyes.

Alek let his pen drop and tried to pretend he didn't hear the violence downstairs rattling the bones of the old building. "You use him—them—for your Bloodletting," he whispered. "You're letting them take it, aren't you?"

Her eyes blinked closed and a woman wailed plaintively, the sound rebounding against the walls of the brownstone like a gunshot. "The city takes my years and I take its jaded life; I think it a fair trade until the day when I finish Paris's work."

"I'm sorry," he whispered. Nothing else seemed appropriate. He studied his work, felt the throbbing pressure of tears. For whom? For himself? For Teresa and her plight? For his own useless victory? He didn't know; he only knew the map was too good for this foolish whelp to have created. He knew only that wherever she was, Akisha looked down on the work with approval.

He lay back against the wall and rested his eyes as she came forward to take the map from him. She studied it for many moments, but he did not look at her witch-white face. He looked instead at the idiot walls around him. And then he shivered violently at the sight of the portrait dominating the center wall over a long-dead fireplace. He wondered why he had not noticed it until now and could only conclude that it must have been covered by a sheet. That or it was Teresa's Glamour at work on him again, letting him see, but only with the blinders she created.

The portrait was of a young woman of supernatural beauty, raven-haired, with predatory brown eyes so astonishing a critic might have thought the artist had exaggerated their brilliance. Her features were delicate, her skin alabaster, and yet there was an unmistakable look of power in her face. Perhaps it was her mouth, the wide lips painted red, smirking but not smirking. It would have given her an expression of bitter derision had she not been so beautiful.

It was his own face at certain times. It was Debra. And he wondered how in hell Teresa had gotten the portrait. He'd sold it years ago on the sidewalk outside his loft. Sold it for a loaf of white bread and a bottle of vodka. He remembered.

Teresa set down the map and looked at him. Her eyes held the flames of the many candles burning in the room like cages of red birds. And he thought rather absently, angel of fire.

"Angel of vengeance," she answered him.

"Whose?"

"Yours."

"I mean whose angel."

"I know." Red ghosts played over her face and gave her the semblance of life, like marble dutifully painted to seem like real flesh to the artist. Like he had meant Debra's portrait to do. She had fed fairly recently, and now for reasons he feared to guess at, he felt no real revulsion. No fear.

"How did you get that picture?" he asked.

She looked at it. She halved her eyes like a cat. "I knew the owner. She gave it to me. I couldn't believe you would sell it."

"You were watching me? Even then?"

She didn't answer him, and he felt confused by her words, as if he were a child being made to play a game the rules of which had never been explained to him. So instead of understanding them, or wanting to, he moved closer to her and said, "Can you read the map?"

She said, "Things change, they changeth not. The map is written in an ancient text known only to vampires, but I know where to begin—"

"Don't."

She was silent. And then she said, "'Your eyes will be mine.'"

"I'm his fucking spy," he said miserably. "Whether I want to be or not."

"There's something unnatural about him. Something wrong."

"Debra said that."

And Debra had been more than right. How had he not seen what she'd seen? Was he so blind? He could glimpse the life of anyone in this city, could even touch it briefly if he so chose to, and yet he had not been able to see the darkness sunk into the eyes of the one who had known him best. How was it possible to see so far and yet remain so sightless?

Teresa disappeared into the dark for a time, and when she next emerged the medieval gown was gone. It had been replaced by the lethal clothing of the day, a black little slip-like dress and fishnet stockings and a pair of battered Doc Martens. He looked at her cold little streetwalker's garb, the way the material, as worn as it was, slithered like silk over her hips and breasts. Candlelight played golden across the shining twin rings in her lower lip. He stood up and reached for her black leather jacket on the bed beside the map. He held it up in front of him like a shield as she approached him. "You must be cold," he said, offering her the coat.

She shook her head, her hair falling loose and tangled like black lace across her naked white throat. She smiled ever so slightly with her smoky eyes and mouth.

He got a solid grip on the jacket.

Teresa only closed the space between them, saying nothing, everything. Primitive images invaded his thoughts. Making love to her, right then and there, and then going down into the city of humans cowering in the dark to run and hunt among them like a wolf in a field of naive sheep. But it was only her Glamour. Her thoughts. It was.

She grew close enough for him to smell the kill on her breath. Her lips parted daintily; her teeth gleamed white. And then she turned and gave him her back, spread her delicate arms. "Please."

Feeling ridiculous and defeated, he slid the jacket upon her like a queen's royal mantle. She took his hands, folded them around her middle, and edged her head back until her rustling-thick hair brushed his bottom lip. He let his hands linger at her waist for only the fraction of a moment, just until she let him go, and then he stepped back, away. She turned back around with her gifts of death and love and seduction and took his hand. She turned it over as if she would read his fate once more and kissed it, put it to her heart. "Don't leave me, Alek Knight. Never leave me."

He watched the flames caress her face and throat. There was red now everywhere in her divine image. Red in her mouth and eyes. Red reflected on her silky black jacket. Red in her touch.

She was luring him out into the center of her web, weaving the spell of her existence over him the way she had for countless others over countless other centuries. He saw the years in her thoughts, the cities, Venice and Rome and Naples, the names and the faces of her kills, too many to count, heard the innocent words of her seduction. She was a woman after all, and an animal. And woman and animal, she lured the unwary to her with the sweet perfume of the pitcher plant on her skin and the venom in her deadly kiss. And there, in countless alleys and convent cells with the moon a knife in her eyes, she had taken their dark Roman faces to her white breast, given her slender frame over to their ungentle hands, let them kiss the purity from off her cheeks. And she had willingly drunk their smoky, beery, decayed breaths on those nights, because it was what pleased them and what they most wanted from their victim and what their exotic pleasures most demanded. But always it ended the same way, not with the ecstasy of life but the exquisite agony of death and early damnation. It was her power and her gift and she gave it willingly and asked for nothing but their life in return. The creed of the predator. Survival at all cost. But though she offered herself as the venomous fruit of Eden itself there was none that saw her soul, none who glimpsed her age and sorrows and her many painful wisdoms...

No one but Paris, once—

"And you. You see me as I truly am," she said and leaned close so she was touching, caressing all his body with her own, the feeling so acute it was like the skipping of a pulse point in the dark. She rubbed herself against him, and the raw sensuality of it grew, warming, seething, seeming to gain a living presence all about them. And then her mouth was there like wet velvet, like an orchid, and she was kissing him with all her vengeance, and her lips seemed so frail on his, but gathering suddenly in strength, and after a moment's hesitation he kissed her back, almost desperate, the sweetness of the deadly pitcher plant and the bitterness of her venom seizing up the priest inside him. For a moment she changed, and he wasn't at all surprised that she should taste of roses and fire and the things that were red, but it was only her charms at work on him, and

when he tensed at the taste and tried to draw away she changed
again, and again he tasted her venom and her years and the wicked
edge of hungry, unspent desire.

She kissed his mouth, her hands branding his back with fire,
sliding like steel beneath his coat. He obliged her by sliding it off
his shoulders. She undid the buttons of his shirt, he the zipper at
the front of her dress. Her beauty was childlike rather than
voluptuous, but the forbidden allure of it only served to excite
him further, to endear her further to him. He went to his knees,
kissing her naked white skin and the stainless steel needles sewn
through her midriff—she said the pain kept the hunger away. She
writhed and knotted her fists in his hair, drawing his attention to
her breasts, as small and flowering as a young girl's, and the delicate
rings piercing the rose-red nipples. He took one of the rings in his
mouth, the taste of it like blood, and playfully suckled the steel
until it clinked against his teeth and he tasted real blood and the
flush of color and excitement went all through her hands and face.
He closed his eyes and held and worshipped her, drinking now,
drinking her. He wanted her now with an urgency that frightened
and appalled him. She had cracked the barrier of his hypocrisy.
She had let in all the floodwaters of his pain and all his sweat-
soaked midnight dreams. She spoke his name and he stopped
nursing only to kiss her mouth, to bite her gently, to urge her on,
offering himself as a villain and a victim, whichever she most
desired, everything if she desired it, his soul if she demanded it.

Her teeth touched the hypersensitive skin under his chin, broke
it in a brief kiss. The pain was exquisite, more than he could bear.
More than he could endure. It was like a dance, but one he knew
the steps to all too well. Something he was returning to. Beneath
the dress her flesh was like silk. Even the hair at the juncture of her
thighs was not like hair but like fur, delicate kittenfur, satin to his
touch. Her excitement ached in his throat like estrus and he nuzzled
her, seeking her, wanting to bring her the most wonderful and
lasting pleasure. Something to help her forget the years of pain.

She arched into him, the tears in her breathing. "No," she said.

"Please."

"No."

"I want you," he said.

"I can't belong to you when you belong to her."

And with those words she broke her fragile spell and set him free. He looked into her eyes and saw the truth and regret there. Her passion and her purpose. And then he let her go and turned away, walking to the portal window where lay the dusky-greyness of the city under nightfall. And he put a hand to the sucking cold of the plane of glass and wept, empty and unfinished and aching for something with no name and no presence.

4

In his dream he dreamt he was asleep dreaming he was awake. And the white face came to him then, floating, lingering above his bed, close, its breath as sharp and raw as sleet against his cheek. The quilt was drawn away and he felt a long white hand caress him, then cover his heart as if it would take it from him like a red jewel.

Sean Stone...Stone Man.

A burning cold mouth more knowledgeable than that of the most ancient prostitute kissed first his cheek and then his mouth. He shuddered with the contact, could not breathe for a moment. He was being loved with such great power and control he felt himself weaken under his lover's spell. Weakness. In his dreams he was a god, always a god, more than man or vampire. And it was that thing more than anything else—the weakness and loss of will—that told him that this was no dream—

He opened his eyes.

The face above him was like Lucifer's before the fall, lovely, alluring, with cheekbones like planes of ice and hair as brittle and beautiful as springtime frost. Eyes...not colorless as he'd somehow expected, but black, as black as mirrors of obsidian, deep and dark and crazed with life. Lidless and serpentine.

"Father?" he said and then realized his mouth hadn't moved at all.

Stone Man...Man of Stone and Ice...come into the dark with me, to the place where truth is brewed.

The face lowered and kissed him, kissed him again. Sean tasted the mouth, the teeth. This wasn't like that time with Slim Jim. What had he to fear from someone who loved him so much, so fiercely? The cold white kisses on his mouth were more exquisite than death or the best kill. And then the hands were on him, the whole being, and again came the kiss, on his throat this time, burning cold, stealing his breath and his words away. He gripped something enormous and smothering above him, heard it sing to his soul in languages far older than mankind. *Father*, he said, *I don't understand.*

Understand—he has betrayed me, rejected me. He lives still and he has proven himself unworthy to stand in my stead. He will be my Judas and he will try and take my head—

No!

But you, Stone Man—you can be the one promised me, the Chosen of my fold. You can carry the mantle of Covenmaster after me...if you so choose.

Sean felt his heart throb and send blood like a delicate offering past the nursing lips of his master. The Dominato. The Dominato! He wanted so to rise up from his bed and embrace the Father, whisper words of feral love into his hair, all the secrets of his broken heart, but strong hands held him in check. He whimpered and writhed with joy and terror, triumph and frustration.

Be still, beloved, commanded the Father.

The face smiled. So white it was, with eyes so impossibly dark, like deep waters at midnight, and the mouth red now, painted, slathered like a beast after a bloody kill. Sean kissed away all the red. The flesh of the creature was all delicate crystal with veins of fire weaving beneath and a rune stone for a heart, a heart that beat in unholy defiance of its own existence, its own unnatural power.

Power.

Power freely offered.

Power for the taking.

Sean twined his fingers in the slithering, shifting mass of white hair and raised himself slowly up to the offering of power, his mouth creaking open and spiderwebbed with saliva to receive the gift of Communion, this share of power...power never to be hurt again, never struck like a stupid little boy again...the power of the earth in all its truths and lies, its fire and darkness...

The face pulled back and his teeth clacked shut on nothing but thin air. Sean wept with the unfairness of it all. He heard laughter like dropping crystals. *Not yet,* spoke the Father. *First you must prove yourself to me. First you must prove your heart is pure, your spirit that of a true warrior.*

How?

You know how, mein Sohn.

Sean stopped crying and smiled, his mouth bowing like the graceful cradle of the moon, a moon full of blood and laughter. He giggled. *I'll wear his scalp as my battle helmet, Father,* he vowed. *His skull will crown your altar.*

The Father smiled. *Do this, Stone Man, and you will drink from the fount of eternal Amadeus and you will know his power forever.*

Sean giggled again.

5

The world was full of monsters, Edna Filmore was convinced of it. They'd cut you and take your things and your body and then leave you bleeding in the dark.

In the half-light of the subway car, Edna shifted her packages around under her seat so her legs could brush them and she could know they were there. Her grandchild sat on the shredded vinyl seat beside her, her legs drawn up under her as if she was sitting safely in her bedroom and not here in the belly of this steel worm shooting blindly through its dark tunnel.

Roxy wasn't frightened. She was studying the paperbacks she'd bought at Borders with a scowling concentration. Edna could see the cover of the one she had now—a grinning skull with worms through its teeth like dental floss. Disgusting stuff. Really, she didn't know why her daughter-in-law Marilyn let Roxy read all that crap about vampires and werewolves and God only knew what else. It was her son Brady's fault, Edna decided, for marrying that nitwit Marilyn in the first place.

The sub lurched and one of the violet florescent lights decided to catch and hold, buzzing like a nest of irate wasps. The dark pulled itself into its corners and Edna could see, really see now. And somehow that made it all the worse. She figured she'd rather be cut in the dark where at least she couldn't see the instrument or the dirty face of madness above it. She reached for Roxy, tugged her close by the sleeve of her denim coat.

"Gram," she whined.

"You shut up. Come here."

Lord, she hated the sub. She wished they'd been more careful with their money and had had enough for a cab. She wished she hadn't had the damnable pride not to call Brady for a ride home. It was awful. She could smell hell, the soot and dirt, the hot sweat and electricity and the ozone. The workers behind the bleary windows wore Glo-red coveralls like devils or prisoners and were busy clicking maintenance coils together, handling the great vacuum snails hungry for asbestos milk or banging the rails back into obedience like Tommyknockers tapping with their last strength through all eternity for the rescue that would never come. Horrible, all of it. Evil as a book cover.

But it was worse inside. The temperamental lighting illuminated place cards and ancient posters, left when the money ran out and there was no one to buy the space or no one to care. Ovaltine. Beeswax. Jergen's. Skipping, smiling girls. Pigtailed girls cradled on the moon and swinging from the stars. Ancient girls faded to thin, gaunt ghosts and forced to look out with absurd gaiety on a changing world, a changing people.

And the people. Men in watch caps and coats of bursting nylon, women in machine-get faux fur, fake coats for protection against a real world, coats held together by surviving buttons or twine or only sheer luck. Nothing at all like the tailored fashions of the fifties that even the lowest class owned. Even the perfume of caste was different: bad colognes and hair oils and the cloying stench of newspaper blankets. Cheap whiskeys and the dank smell of fear, distrust.

Edna watched it all. It was late and the brave ones slept. Mostly they watched or pretended to read, or read, pretending to watch. She didn't meet any of their eyes. Especially not the eyes of the character across the aisle from them with the black coat and long hair and the eyes that looked funny under the florescent lights. The kid in the seat behind her and Roxy, the one with the skull tattoo on one cheek and the concert T-shirt, stood up under a moment's inspiration and pelted the character's shoulder with a wadded-up mass of soggy brown paper bag. "Yo, Count Dracula, man, you're out early tonight!"

No one laughed. They looked away into laps that cradled newspaper and those that did not. The kid sat down, sulky and disappointed with the general appeal.

But Edna had no sympathy for the character. He was an idiot. He had boarded two stations back with his young girl, yet now he sat alone. His girl was at the back, curled up on a seat and asleep, it looked like, all wrapped up in her leather jacket. She was a lovely little thing, like Snow White in the books Roxy used to read before she got into all that horror crap. But she was alone. Who'd leave their girl unattended in this hellhole of a city? Edna's hand bunched around Roxy's sleeve, despite the agony of her arthritis. A fool would, that's who.

The car jerked, screamed. Steam frosted their window in an intricate, lacy web. Edna heard Roxy's muffled curse as she lost her armful of books. Edna got up. "We're getting off."

Roxy fumbled with her books. "Wait, Gram, one got under

the seat."

Edna waited impatiently, plastic package handles biting into her forearm, as Roxy squirmed under the seat. "Don't go touching anything under there," Edna cautioned. "God knows what's under there."

The car was emptying and taking on, bodies against bodies, apologetic, not meaning to touch. Tattoo lurched against Edna's shoulder as he passed, either pushed from behind or just feeling her pockets.

"*Roxy*"

"In a minute, Gram!"

The character was standing inches from her, Edna saw, watching the surge of take-ons from his dark height. Almost as if he were anticipating something. Or someone. When his eyes narrowed on the last of the new passengers, Edna looked.

Trouble.

The blonde man was slickly casual to board. Man? Boy, really. He had skin like a Greek statue. You didn't see too many young people with perfect complexions like that. It shone like ice where it poked out of his smooth, flared-collared leather coat. Wraparound mirror shades hid the top half of his face and the bottom half was a mass of white grinning teeth filed to deadly points. A vicious joker's mouth. Bones chittered out of his earlobes and trickled along his neck like meatless fingers.

"Roxy, let's go!" Edna pulled her grandchild up.

"But I didn't get—"

"Never mind." Edna drew Roxy under her arm and turned around.

The man, the incredibly tall one, filled the aisle in front of them. From behind, Edna had a perfect view of the mass of leather coat hanging from his shoulders and the glistening, greasy witch's hair tumbling to his waist.

The blonde man made of leather and steel came abreast with the witch-man, their shoulders nearly touching. They faced opposite, and yet their heads turned at exactly same instant,

eyes sidling to meet. It made Edna think of a secret agents'
rendezvous in a spy thriller, or maybe something from one of those
disgusting modern movies, just before the two enemy punks
disemboweled each other with stilettos.

Edna pulled her grandchild close and held her breath.

The blonde man pushed his shades down his nose. His silvery
eyes glittered like steel stars. "Hey there, Scarecrow," he said by
way of some kind of greeting.

The man who looked like a witch said, "Stone Man."

Blondie sneered, "You a dead man."

"I know that, Einstein. So are you."

"Cute, real cute, man. You gonna go down, man—you and
your bitch and your fuckin' mouth too, man. You got that?"

"Whatever you want, you obsolete little punk. When I'm
finished here, we'll have it anywhere you want it."

Blondie grinned with his mouthful of Halloween teeth. "I want
it right here, fuckface."

The witch's hair actually bristled, spiking like dangerous quills;
his mouth was suddenly deep with teeth. "Draw that thing here,
Stone, and I'll shove the blunt end of it up your ass."

Blondie's grin melted away into a soundless snarl.

"You wouldn't, though."

"Sure I would."

"No. You wouldn't."

"Why wouldn't I?"

"Because you're outnumbered, Stone." The witch smiled and
took Blondie by the wrist as Blondie gasped and tossed his head
right, left, right. Snow White, magically summoned, stood at
Blondie's other side, her hand knotted around his wrist. And though
she looked like no more than a child of seventeen years of age,
Blondie's arm seemed to be locked in place, as if what held to him
had a grip of pure iron.

"Lemme go!" Blondie shouted.

The witch only nodded at Snow White. She smiled. Together
they pinioned Blondie's arms against his back.

Blondie snarled. His face was full of the light of pain. "Let go of me!"

"No," said the witch.

Roxy gasped in Edna's hold. "Way cool, Gram!" her little voice scorched Edna's cheek. "Vampires!" Edna only held to her grandchild, hating the sub, this city, her own helplessness. Between them were mashed Roxy's horrible novels. Roxy laughed. "It's just like in the books..."

"Let me go! Get your bitch off me! Let go! *Let GOOOO!*"

Blondie thrashed, but he was powerless to break their combined grip on his arms. "Keep it up, punkface," the witch rasped as he cranked the boy's arms an inch further, "and we'll be sending you home to the Father *sans* arms."

"*Eat yourself!*"

The witch and Snow White cranked Blondie's arms an agonizing unnatural inch further. Blondie went down on his knees with a cry.

"Say 'uncle'," chided Snow White.

"*Eat shit!*"

Another inch. Bones began to squeal alarmingly. "*UNCLE, UNCLE, UNCLE...!*" wailed Blondie.

They let up a little. Blondie gasped and sagged between his two tormentors. Snow White dabbed playfully at the shining track of drool on his chin. "Good boy," she said. Then her touch turned wicked and she gripped his chin in her long black lacquered fingernails. "You are a good boy, aren't you?" A trickle of blood ran from Blondie's chin, gaining strength when Snow White forcefully nodded his head. "I do hope so. You don't want to know what I do to *bad* boys."

Yet it was the witch that Blondie turned frenzied eyes on. "He wants you, man! He wants your fuckin' head bad, man!"

The witch sighed. "Really, Stone? Thank you for that enlightenment. What would I do without him, Sister Teresa?"

"I honestly don't know, my knight."

"Reeeal bad, man!" Blondie's shades were askew. His hair was crazy. He looked utterly possessed. "And I'm gonna get it for him! I ain't no turdface no more! I'm a big man now! You lookin' at the next Covenmaster, man!"

The witch shook his head. "Good God, I know Amadeus is mad, but I didn't think he was just plain stupid."

Blondie's eyes bulged in mindless rage.

The iron worm whistled alarmingly and the witch tipped his chin at Snow White. "Would you do the honor of disarming the big man here, Sister Teresa?"

"Of course."

Edna expected a stiletto, a Buck knife at most. Not this. Snow White passed the narrow body of steel to the witch. Not a toy, Edna could see that. Not a prop, either. The commuters' eyes turned down respectfully, inward or into laps, in steeled expectation of the blood and screams that must come, making themselves cold and prepared for it.

Blondie only laughed, his tongue lolling like a rabid dog. "Go on, Scarecrow, go for it! Go on, you mofo, because, man, you ain't gonna get a second take!"

The witch's eyes narrowed to bloody slits. He forced Blondie down into his seat.

"Wassamatta with you, man?" Blondie screamed as his shiny eyes rolled up to meet those of the witch. "You fuckin' chickenshit or somethin'? *COME ON, MAN! DO ME, MAN! DO ME!*"

But the witch only leveled the sword at Blondie's throat, the tip caressing his collarbone, narrow blue ice catching the light of the fluorescents above. "I want you to live, big man," said the witch, his voice huge and uncoiling in this small place. "Live, Stone. Live to bring the Father this message: tell him Debra is coming back, and tell him she's mad as all hell and she's going to kick his ass all over Creation. Tell him that, big man."

Like a kid, Blondie stuck out his tongue.

"Big man," whispered the witch, "the Coven's going down and you're going down with it." He stepped back gracefully, almost catlike, a dance, the sword pointing at the punk's heart, his eyes unwavering, cold. "And by the way—do yourself the courtesy of staying on this car until the next station, Stone, or I'll be sending your empty, brainless skull back to Amadeus in a box."

Blondie hissed like a vampire in one of Roxy's books.

The witch didn't notice; Snow White was pulling him down onto the platform with her. Then she slammed the sub door closed.

Blondie slouched in his seat, seething like a bemused brat. He began to methodically ravish his fingernails, snarling at anyone who dared meet his gaze.

In a moment the car would snort and pick itself up along the line, burrowing into darkness again. Edna sat down and pulled Roxy to her. She realized it was too late, the line already whining, the worm awakening. They would ride it to the next station and there they would get off, escape this underworld of sword-wielding maniacs and call Brady to come get then. Anything but to be buried alive here with the mad and the monstrous.

Blondie snarled in his seat and lapped at his bloodied fingertips.

God, the world was full of monsters, Edna Filmore was convinced of it, utterly convinced.

6

Down here no one looked twice at them, even when they stopped in the middle of the terminal and turned to study the wall together. All white tile like some universal latrine. The dull little lights burned ineffectually high overhead, and under them Teresa began a ritual dance of hands across the hard scales of the tiling.

Alek touched the wall further up. "Nothing here."

"Give me the map."

He pulled it out of his coat and let her take it and spread it against the wall. She traced a pen line with her painted fingertip. She shook her head, tossed her long loose hair back. "We are not yet there, caro."

"Far?"

"Not very," she said, rolling up the map.

The white tunnel ebbed downward and came out in a maze of corridors pitched in darkness under their mostly broken lighting. Here the emptiness lay like a spell, and though there were still posters, the walls were in fact made up mostly of arcane gang graffiti. At the foot of a dead escalator, as frozen as a dinosaur made of metal bones, they stopped.

"Here," Teresa said.

"There's nothing here." Alek stared at the flank of mocking white wall.

Teresa unrolled the map once more, studied it. "Byron," she whispered, "what the fuck were you on...oh *hell*."

"What?"

"We're not at the right elevation. Too high. There must be another floor."

"There is no other floor. This is the sub for God's sake."

"Collapse and surface deposits then." She looked up scrupulously. "There must have been a quake."

He touched the wall as if he could know by touch if the Chronicle rested there beneath the mortar and rock. "This is useless. Let's go."

"I want to know the story," she complained.

"There's no one to ask."

"We'll ask him."

Her cattishly aglow eyes cut through the darkness to a corner bench and its token hobo, his overstuffed shopping cart at his side, his folded blankets of newspaper on the floor, ready for use against the night's subterranean chill. All of it like a Norman Rockwell piece gone bad.

"Don't," Alek told her, suddenly and completely afraid. "You can't."

"Of course I can," she said. "Don't you know? Old men and young girls." She moved purposely toward the hobo and Alek followed dutifully behind, armed with words that disappeared when the hobo folded down the comics page he was reading and eyed them both. Alek saw a scraggly-bearded mouth part in surprise at the pale, beautiful little doll-like woman watching him in her soft black halo of tangled hair and china-white face.

"Well, now," he said.

"Hello," said Teresa.

The hobo smiled and scratched at his shadow. The faded flannel-grey eyes inched upward to find Alek. "Yours, fella?"

"Yes," said the girl.

"Lovely thing." He brushed the loose threads of black over her brow, chucked her under the chin. "Daughters always are."

"No," she said. "I'm not his daughter. His sister, his lover, more."

The hobo frowned, then laughed. Here in this place below the earth in the dark and the tedium and the loss without sense or end, her story was funny. "Who're you, dolly?"

"Something very unlike you." She tilted her head like a bird of prey. "We seek the lower level here and the door through which we might find it. Have you seen it?"

The hobo's eyes grew lazy and unblinking. He did not flinch at her words. "A door into the deep earth."

"Yes. Where is the floor that was below us?"

For the first time Alek really saw the hobo: grey skin and eyes the same. His face was whorled as if the weight of flesh and time was too great for his bones to withstand. He spied the naked skull in the hollows of the man's eyes, the cavities of his cheeks. "I remember a door," he said.

She slipped up into his lap and he received her as easily as a grandfather. "Tell me the story about the door."

The hobo coughed, sputtered against the web of phlegm in his lungs. He petted her head like a favorite child. "Time was, the door was open to below, where the beast usta run, back when the city was beautiful and thought it would go on forever. And in that time, was me and my brother Davey. We worked the rails below and we was the damn best and the damn finest. And we weren't 'fraid like them all, 'cause the line ran and we ran and the damn fool city ran, and it was all gonna run forever, you know."

He paused, as if for effect.

"And then?"

He studied one of the dirty white walls as if to find his story in it. "Me and Davey worked everyday and real good, 'cause we was the best, dolly, the best. But then this big rattler came through and turned the tunnels to shit and rubble. Me, I was out gettin' supplies. Was Davey hitchin' the line when she tore through like a mad bitch."

"Was Davey trapped?"

The hobo's eyes floated back in their sockets as if to see something far inside, far away. "Three days we work, me besides 'em all, pickin' and diggin', and Davey tappin' and tappin', and me goin' on and on, for the sound, for my Davey. And yellin' whole time: 'I'm comin', Davey. Little while yet. I'm comin'. Hold on, Davey, hold on.' But it stopped, dolly. It stopped. Davey didn't listen to me. The tappin' stopped and the silence was white. All white. Me, I carried Davey out on my back. He didn't listen. The silence was all white."

"And the door to the cave-in?"

"Healed her all up. All gone. Built her over. Healed her. Couldn't heal my Davey, though." A dirty grey hand rasped past the wall behind him. "I come here now'n talk to Davey. He don't answer, though."

"Thank you."

He smiled, and it was the smile of a young man, a man thirty years old. "Sure, dolly. You a good girl. I know."

She smiled too, and it was ancient. "You miss Davey, don't you?"

"I gonna see Davey again one day."

"Yes, you will," she said. "You can, you know. Now."

"Really, dolly?"

"Yes." Her eyes blinked black, glittering in the forced light. She nestled against his soft, filthy clothing and kissed his cheek.

"How?" His voice was a rattle, weary and desperate.

"Kiss me and Davey will come for you."

"Magic princess."

"Yes."

No, oh God, no, not again. Alek turned his back on them. And then he was walking, walking, the clocking of his boot heels on the scarred, ancient tiled floor an empty drumbeat, beating, beating a little faster, faster. The beat became a pounding as barbaric as the angriest music, and now the walls leaned in, falling down on him in their suffocating purity, falling in to crush him, to bury him alive here a hundred feet below the earth...

He was running full tilt by the time he reached the great felled escalator. He tried to climb the long slain beast, but his legs were water and they spilled him onto the second step. He covered his face with his hands and rocked and felt a wet mask of grief gathering there. And the punks and prostitutes and the few late-night commuters who passed him on the stairs watched him curiously and pointed and whispered to one another but did not ask him about his misery.

7

"Alek Knight."

Still he knelt on the dead stairs, but now there was no pain. There was nothing. He was a husk, a chrysalis, finished.

"It is near morning," she said from behind.

Her presence closed in on him like a shadow, and the fine hairs of his neck came alive. "Don't, please," he pleaded.

She stopped. "Why are you mourning?"

"Don't act innocent, bitch. It doesn't become you."

It would come now, he knew, a cry of rage that would rattle the skeleton of his sanity apart, a flash of anger like an open-mouthed furnace at his back. He tensed, expecting it, yet all he heard was the purity of the unbroken silence around him.

"I am not Debra, Alek Knight," she whispered with her perfect sense, "you are. And you would do yourself a service to remember that."

He pulled his fingers through his tangled hair. "I hate you sometimes."

She laughed at him. "What a strange creature, priest, to believe that all things are trapped within the perimeters of conception and death."

She hesitated. She was being wise and playful with him, making him the fool with her philosophies. Eventually she tired of the game, however, and she sighed. "He's with Davey now."

Alek shook his head. "Jesus, I can't *think* like you."

"You don't have to." And all at once the mocking wisdom was gone and her voice only seemed frail and so very human. "I don't want you to," she whispered. "Spare a little hate for me."

"That's an awful request."

"It is what the man in you feels and I think it is that that I love best in you."

"You love that I'm weak?"

"That you are strong enough to be weak, to change. You are so evolved, so better equipped for this world than I."

He smeared the mask of tears on his face. "God help me, I wish there was a way out of this. I want to be dead or finished with this."

A muffled, echoing male laugh came out of the darkness: "That *can* be arranged, pardner."

Alek turned at the sound of Kansas's savage Midwestern drawl and glanced around the tunnels, up the curving spine of the elevator, down the branching corridors. Fuck. There he was. There *they* were—a pair of faceless silhouettes standing against the wall twenty yards behind them, anonymous as shadows.

"Where are they?" Teresa asked, spinning on her heels.

As if on cue, they peeled away from the wall and started to stalk casually toward the two of them. Because of the partial shadow thrown by the doorway of an unobtrusive service elevator, he still could not make out their features, but their long-coated forms conveyed an archetypal air of doom: undertakers, Nazis, vultures. Slayers. His paralysis broken, Alek got to his feet and frantically scanned the sub tunnels for an alcove or an exit sign, any means of escape, anything at all.

Nothing.

He retreated a step, but there was nothing so spare as even a shadow to hide in. The fucking lights overhead shone down on them both like spotlights.

"I don't see anything," Teresa admitted, though the two shadows were as plain as day to him.

He swallowed. He understood the game now. They planned on staying on the periphery of everything, making the kill quick, like a pair of African lions on the prowl. He and Teresa weren't safe, not even in public. Not anywhere. Not anymore. Metal shimmered blue. This was it.

"Madre," Teresa whispered under her breath. And now she too saw them. Now. Because they chose that she should. "I can see them, but only from the tail of my eye."

"It's Takara. Her Glamour." He let out his breath in frustration. The terminal was down the tunnel the two slayers were emerging from. For them it was up the elevator and onto the thoroughfare overhead or nothing. He drew his sword and made a sweeping arc over his head. Buzz and spit. The long fluorescent light clapped dark and filled the tunnel with the stink of ozone. Alek grabbed Teresa's arm and dragged her with him toward the escalator. "Maybe we can shake them."

They all but flew down the dark, empty passageways, their heels clocking against the floor and walls like the explosion of gunshots in this close place. "Keep your eyes open," he said. "Tell me if you see them."

"There!" Teresa said, spotting them standing near a news kiosk just ahead of them.

They switched directions and headed down the corridor back toward the terminal. He spotted them in the entrance of a darkened and gated gift shop. They doubled back and saw the slayers yet again, lurking in the shadows around the pay phones. They seemed to be everywhere at once, anticipating their every move. Am I paranoid? Alek wondered. Am I imagining all of this?

"Stop!"

Teresa glanced up. "What?"

"Just stop!" he shouted, pulling her up short. "Do you see them?"

She glanced around. "No."

He looked back, gasping for breath. "Takara," he said again. "Her damned Glamour. They're *not* everywhere. They're just trying to get us alone into one of the branch corridors."

Teresa looked on him with perfect understanding. Then she turned like a soldier and headed back toward the terminal. Alek followed. He didn't know how much she understood about their methods, but obviously it was enough for her to want to turn their own technique on them. Minutes later they were standing at the gate again, waiting for the train to dock and open its doors to them. For some reason the arrival was behind schedule; the train wasn't there some five minutes later when the electronic board announced the line.

He was feeling hunted again, but he knew he had to ride it out. There was no turning back. Here, crushed in with the take-ons, was the only place they were safe. He glanced around, looking for the coats. "Fuck. There they are."

Teresa discreetly withdrew her sharp, ornate knife from the top of her Doc Marten, a knife that gleamed black with a band of rusted pit-marks under the hilt. Iron. Deadly to vampires. And to slayers.

"It's no use," he whispered. "They'll follow us onto the train and do us there."

"With all these witnesses...?"

He caught the gleam of predatory anticipation in two pairs of emerging eyes. "Doesn't matter. Everyone's expendable now."

He didn't know what was going on in the minds of the two slayers, but he was certain if he forced their hand all hell would break lose. In the worse case scenario, they would break the Covenant Laws, disrupt the mortals' world, kill Teresa and forcibly abduct him right here in spite of the crowd. At best, they might all

die together locked in mortal combat. Either way, this was the end
of the road.

He waited for Kansas to go for his gun, and sure enough, he
pulled his hand out from under his duster and stretched it out, the
modified Glock shining like a small cannon as he pointed it
accusingly at Alek.

Alek pointed. *"Gunman! Down!"*

True to form, the people standing on the platform, most of
them New Yorkers born and bred with the fastest reflexes in the
entire country, went down with a communal shout as iron slingshots
sprayed the empty space where their heads had been only seconds
before. The ammo tore the opposite side of the sub tunnel to roaring
tatters. An innocent went down, a few more were lifted by the
barrage of Kansas's high-impact bullets and forcefully shoved over
the edge of the platform and into the track to die slow agonizing
deaths. Those few unfortunates changed everything. When the
gunfire didn't let up, the remaining people on the platform decided
to stay. Alek used the cover to drop over the edge of the platform,
the fingers of his right hand digging into the concrete apron, his
left hand locked around Teresa's wrist as she hung suspended over
the track. He gritted his teeth resolutely and waited until the gunfire
stuttered to a halt.

There was a terrible, prolonged, whimpering silence as the
people writhed in shock and the slayers regrouped. He heard
beneath the constant hum of violence and electricity the distant
cries of panic, police ban radio, and the slayers' clocking feet shifting
on the cement apron, trying to decide if they had the courage to
leave or stay, and completely unsure as to their targets' whereabouts.

Wordless, her face flushing with the work, Teresa suddenly
gripped his forearm and began to inch her way up the ladder of his
body. He opened his mouth to whisper the word *no* to her. She
kissed him in passing as she clambered to the top of the platform.
Alek shook his head vehemently. She ignored him; she gripped his
shoulders, jiggled herself for purchase. Then she reached up, up to
where a boot heel half hidden by the hem of a long dark coat

protruded over the edge of the platform and snagged Takara's ankle. She inserted her iron knife into it like a child taking a first enthusiastic stab at a Halloween Jack-o'-lantern.

Takara screamed shrilly, her mile-high, hot-tin-roof jump ripping Teresa right off Alek's shoulders. Seconds later the screaming was joined by a brief burst of gunfire that ended abruptly on the resounding subterranean *klak-klak-klak* of empty chambers. Kansas swore violently and Alek recognized his opportunity. He reached up and found and grabbed hold of a black flapping bit of duster as Kansas leaned over the edge of the platform in curiosity. Alek let go of the apron and his weight yanked Kansas off balance. His stomach lurched as he and Kansas fell hard to the maintenance walk beside the rail some ten feet below. Kansas's Glock spun and ricocheted off the track and into the dark; Kansas himself let out a low, pained moan, a sound muffled by a charge of screams and combat noises ringing out from the platform as above the ladies engaged in battle.

Hard to notice these things, or concentrate on them. Pulsing waves of agony were shooting up and down Alek's left leg from ankle to hipbone from a knee fracture on the iron rail. It wouldn't heal soon, that. He gasped for breath through all that smothering, mindless pain and rolled away. Get up! he told himself. He got up, stiffly, and too late. Kansas was on his feet, drawing down on him with a pair of vintage Colt .45s. The bullets ripped into the steel and concrete all around Alek, scorching his hip once in passing, but none finding a home inside of him, no Wild Bill Hickok was Kansas. Alek snarled, used his good leg to kick out with all the anger and agony boiling inside of him and knocked Kansas's feet out from under him.

Kansas went down firing all twelve rounds. *Klak.* More empties. Growling like a beast, Kansas kicked Alek in the face, his spurs ripping a gash in Alek's cheek, kicked him again in the ribs. Alek grabbed the slayer's foot the third time around and twisted it violently to one side until the bones snapped and crunched and the foot was thoroughly useless. Kansas roared and threw the empty guns at him. Alek rolled away and came up on his good knee, Sean's sword drawn and at the ready. The cowboy laughed and used the wall to pull himself to his feet. He drew his own sword. He seemed to be of the mind that even with one broken ankle he was still a better swordsman than Alek.

"I reckon you shoulda stopped while you were ahead, *pardner.*" He smiled at his own wild wit. "No pun intended." And with that mischievous grin still on his pain-riddled face, he used the wall to gingerly inch forward.

The rail rumbled and quaked. Alek tasted the blood in his mouth from the gash on his face. He pulled himself up onto his good side, leaning heavily against the wall for support, and hefted the sword into a perpendicular bar across his throat. He smiled and waited for Kansas to amble toward him across the service walk. The train was riding like a line of lightning to his left; he could feel its heat, smell its electricity.

Kansas swung his sword experimentally. Then he tested his foot, stepping down on it carefully, finding it healed enough for the job ahead, and started to charge Alek, his steel sitting on his shoulder like a slugger. He smiled. When the slayer was less than a couple of yards away and the train a blazing wall of suction at his side, Alek let the sword go, let it stick in the side of the train like a strange Excalibur in its rock. Kansas opened his mouth to scream as he realized what was coming, but it did nothing to stop the train as it carried the sword's edge through his throat and vocal cords and spinal column, shearing his head away and leaving his body to wander a moment in confusion before toppling into the line and under the wheels of the train. "Not your *pardner,*" Alek whispered and raised a hand to deflect the gush of red meat and gore and debris kicked up by the train's passing.

And so much for the wit, Kansas, he thought as he freed his boot knife. The handle was almost too slick in his bloodied hands. He wiped them on his coat, gripped the curling ivory in a death grip. First he sliced the knee of the slacks, then the knee itself. He bit down hard on the lapel of his leather coat, bit down so hard his teeth cut through the material like needles as the blade split the blackened skin and a freshet of gangrenous poison smelling for all the world like spoiled meat exited the half-mended knee in a spill of black blood. His head swam and his vision doubled, and for a tenuous moment he wondered if he wouldn't simply blacken out. Then it was gone, just like that. The blood ran dark crimson and he felt the first stirrings of serious mending. Better. At least he could stand, if not run. Could stand and fight for Teresa if she so needed him.

"Whelp," came a raspy voice from behind him. *"Betraaayer!"*

Alek maneuvered around so that he was facing Takara on the walk. His heart hammered at the sight of her standing there, disheveled but very much alive. It was true that right now he was still almost completely crippled by the fall and in no condition whatsoever for any extended sparring match with the Japanese Tsunami, as her peers called her, but Takara likewise was injured, he saw after a moment's inspection. The hilt of Teresa's iron knife protruded from her stomach, Takara's bloody hands wrapped tight as rags around it, her eyes fever-bright, her face aflame with the invasion of pain.

Alek opened his mouth, but what came out over the roar of noise was a weary laugh. "Dying to live, Takara."

"Fuck. You," she enunciated. And with a wicked smile: "I would have brought your little whore's head down here with me, but my hands are busy."

Alek shuddered as the pain returned a tenfold and seemed to twist inside of him as if it were a knife in his own belly. It made a labor of his breathing. He tasted blood. "Takara," he growled, trying to stand on his bad leg and failing horribly, "Prove yourself a smarter little slayer than Kansas and go away. We both know you never deserved that sword." He knew he could have chosen his words better. He could even have convinced Takara that he meant to give himself up. He could have. Why should he? Teresa. Dead. Dead by Takara's hands. He wanted that hand. He wanted her fucking head. He wanted *her*. Alek watched in amusement as rage darkened

Takara's face and her black Asian eyes widened and filled with mindless fury. She shook her head, bloody-black foam spewing from the corners of her mouth.

He turned the last screw. "You're fucking dying, bitch, doesn't that prove it to you?"

Takara screamed, the blood in her mouth like a wet nettle around her words: *"Take you with me!"*

"Take me then, Takara," Alek whispered. "I can't stop you." And he was probably right; he couldn't have stopped her, even in his half-mended condition. He couldn't have stopped her if he had wanted to, which he did not. Hate was an amazingly potent elixir. But hate also made one careless, made one lose focus and control. And as Takara let go of the knife in her gut and drew her still-bloody wakizashi and struck, she left herself completely open for counterattack. Even if Alek had been a warrior of only moderate ability, he could have stopped Takara's charge—Takara, a dangerous creature at any other moment than this, when she had lost all control.

There came a pain like ice in his stomach and groin—and then he was run through with her sword. He bent over it, vomiting with the force of the impact, and Takara came in close to him, using both hands to drive the blade in deeper to the hilt in his belly. Alek threw his arms around her and they clutched like lovers, there on the line amidst the carnage and the ozone. Hands on the sides of Takara's head, Alek drew her close and whispered in her ear. "What a victory for you, Takara. Won't the Father be proud?"

She hissed through her clenched, bloody teeth. *"For the Father, traitor, for the Coven...!"* Her face was slick with pain and effort as she dragged the blade up, widening the wound she'd made. The motion bought the pulsing vein in the side of her throat to the top of her white keisha skin. She tried to draw back, to survey her work, perhaps to finish him off by beheading, but she found herself stuck in his embrace. Her weapon was steel, not iron. It was she who was dying, after all. Alek smiled as the slayer recognized her mistake. What had seemed the weak, dying last gesture of her prey now revealed itself as otherwise. Alek gripped her by the hair and dragged her closer still. She struggled feebly, forgetting her sword, kicking and trying to dredge up one of her illusions. There was no time. There was no strength. The iron in her system was poisoning her blood. The fear in her heart had already poisoned her mind.

"You never deserved that sword," Alek whispered through a mouthful of teeth. "And now you will know why."

And then his savage eyeteeth tore into the flesh of her throat.

8

The blood of the kill revived him, gave him the much-needed strength to slide himself off Takara's wak, to climb to the top of the walk, and to fall down upon the concrete apron like a half-drowned man with the good fortune of having been vomited up upon the beach by the ocean. In his fist he clutched the bloody wak Takara had forfeited upon her untimely demise. He smiled, but it was a smile of desolation, his teeth stained with the slayer's death. A part of him was ashamed by his act of barbarism, yet he couldn't help but imagine how proud Debra would have been of him.

"And I."

He looked up, past the haze of blood and spent war, and spied Teresa's perfect face shining down on him, the eyes that looked strangely lighted from within, the mouth so animated it might spill all the secrets of the ages upon him at any given moment. Her clothing was as tattered and bloodied as his own; like his, her hair was wild with disarray. But she was alive, and she smiled cattishly.

She was alive as he was.

"Too proud to admit I had bested her," she whispered.

"Why...didn't you kill her?"

"You needed the nourishment," she said.

9

The two swords kissed like crossed lightning. Sean squinted against the sparks that briefly lit the Great Abbey, the altar of skulls, and his master's face. Recovering, he pushed against the Father's sword and felt him give, but it was all a ruse. Amadeus moved with the fluid, boneless grace of a snake, his face stern but otherwise without emotion. His blade slid down, holding Sean's back until the guards met. He ducked and spun, controlling his student's blade with his own even then, turning to face him, but now slipping inside his sword arm. It had been one swift, unbroken motion from the moment they clashed, and he completed that movement now as he brought his katana around, stopping just short of decapitating Sean's head, and rested the sharp of the blade on his collarbone.

Sean gave up. He dropped the sword of the slayer Alek Knight and whimpered and fell into a quaking bundle, arms steeling his head against the sword that must fall. It would be the gentlest whistling in his ear, he thought, followed by a pain that would not be pain, that he would not know long enough to be pain. He waited for it.

Nothing.

He hurt. He hurt bad. His eyes ached from his fearful tears and his chest from the greedy amounts of chilled Abbey air he was swallowing. The bones in his arms rang from the continuous clashing of his master's blade. "Spar with me," Amadeus had said in a dead white voce sotto when Sean had returned alone, the only survivor of that shitpile of a mission. And he had known what the Father meant. Spar with me. Only it wasn't going to be just any sparring match. It was going to be war, a massacre, hell on earth. The Stone Man's remittance for a mission well fucked up.

Knight was still out there somewhere. And Takara and Kansas, two of the best and oldest slayers in their Coven, were dead. Did he deserve anything less?

And now pain swelled his body and challenged the seams of his skin. His bones were dust. His blood was heated to a fine red mist.

He was dead and he didn't know it yet. And now the Father would finish what he had begun.

"Sean," said Amadeus, "pick up your sword."

Sean's breath wheezed in and out of a ribcage that had grown too small for him. "No more...please...I can't, I fucking *can't*—"

Some cold thing touched his face, and he whimpered like a whipped dog and dropped forward onto his face. He crawled away on his belly, his blistered, bleeding fingers finding purchase in the cobbles and carrying him along until he felt a shadow hide him. Shelter. He huddled under the Coventable, cold, painfully afraid. And there, oblivious to the other slayers, Book and Robot and Aristotle watching from the shadowy nooks of the Abbey, he sobbed like an eight-year-old child and pushed the back of his hand across his nose to wipe away the drivel. But it clung stubbornly to his face and he could not seem to rid himself of it any more than he could his memories or his fears.

He sobbed with frustration and the sob lengthened and became a long dry howl that was answered against every stone wall of the Abbey. It rippled the tapestries and rattled the stained glass windows. The crosswords over the priest's door clattered down noisily.

"Sean."

He wept.

"Sean."

He covered his face with his hands, splitting his fingers to see out.

"Hush," said Amadeus. As he watched, the Father went down on his knees and pushed his weapon aside. One of his long thin hands unfurled like a spider toward him.

Sean looked at the hand. "I'm af-fraid..."

The pale eyes of the Father narrowed. "You believe this exercise to be a punishment for your failure to bring me the rogue?"

Sean shrugged, licked at the blood on his tattered index finger. "I...I fucked up righteously, man, I know that," he said, and his voice was too young, too whiny, and he hated it. Hated himself.

Hated his mother and Slim Jim and Alek Knight and all the other fucking people who had ever made him feel small and afraid. All but the Father, who had been different. Once.

"You think things have changed? That I am not the same one who came to you in the beginning?" And the Covenmaster's beautiful leonine face was so honest and puzzled and hurt that Sean felt his fear simply wash away with the Father's words. "You think that you have failed me for all time? That redemption is beyond your agile hands?"

Sean looked at the offered hand poised to receive him. Tentatively, he put his own into it and felt the dry white bones close gently, firmly over it. Amadeus rose and drew Sean out of his hiding place. Up, up they went into the soothingly warm yellow lights of the chandelier. And when they stood, close now, so close their shoulders nearly touched, Amadeus drew his acolyte's wounded fingers to his mouth, licked at their bloodied tips. He paused with his lips freezing against Sean's palm, his hungry eyes unwavering from Sean's face. "You are my creature now," he whispered. "Mine, as nothing before has been mine, as nothing will ever again he mine. You belong to me, Stone Man. You are my own. And I do not slay my own."

Sean's eyes fluttered dreamily at the Father's words, and he felt the last threads of his fear and his failure fall away. His lips parted dryly and the voice that came out was new, different, a voice he'd never heard before. "I would...would do anything for you, Father, even...even die for you," he confessed.

"I know. But I want you to live for me. Live to take the head of my Judas." Amadeus smiled and kissed the tips of Sean's fingers, each one in succession, like a ceremony. Then his lips fell away and Sean stood alone once more. He shook his head as he came back to himself with a resounding thunderclap of despair going off in his heart. "But...what if I can't do it?"

"You will. I will train you and you will. Alek is weak. He will never be one with the sword because there is a part of him that will always despise the sword. But you, Stone Man, you have a talent for the sword for your love of it, for your love of battle. You are my Chosen now, my champion."

Sean scuffed absently at the floor with the toe of one worn sneaker, studied the cobblestones and the pattern of ancient bloodstains between them. "Am I as good as Alek now?"

"Better. A thousand-fold better."

"Really?"

"I am no liar."

Sean smiled.

Amadeus nodded at the fallen sword. "Pick up the weapon. We begin again."

Sean shook his head. His smile melted away. "I can't. That sword's way heavier than my old one." He massaged his arm thoughtfully. "And it makes me feel...I don't know, funny when I hold it."

Amadeus frowned as he retrieved his own sword. "How do you mean?"

"Like..." Sean shrugged. "Like it doesn't like me or something, you know?"

"No, I do not know. It is only an instrument. Pick it up," he commanded, assuming a light combat stance, feet shoulder-wide, sword leveled against his forearm. "Pick it up and make it a part of you."

Feeling the eyes of the others burning on him like unseen little flames, Sean went and retrieved the sword. He picked it up, holding it as he was taught to, and yet again he felt the familiar *wrongness* of its weight and feel in his hand. Like it was alive, a living thing, a pet left in the hands of a stranger with whom it has no relationship and no interest in being with. Slim Jim had had a dog like that— a big black motherfucker named Animal that hated anything that moved. The beast used to bring ragged pieces of unidentifiable flesh back to the Shangri-La like some dogs brought home branches or balls. All of Jimbo's girls were afraid of Animal, all but Sean who had never given a shit how big he was or how many people he'd taken down. Jimbo turned Animal loose on Mom once, and that had been a farce, hadn't it, with Mom screaming her goddamn head off and ramming a broomstick at Animal's head. And where would she have been were it not for Sean spotting her stiletto on the nightstand and using the psi to send it through the back of Animal's left eye, hey? Now for some reason he recalled that incident. The sword—it was like somebody's watchdog left with him, obeying him (reluctantly) but hating him with all its guts and more, if that were possible. He thought about all the things Alek had said on the sub and began to wonder if there weren't some truly fucking weird things going on.

"Father?"

"What is it?"

"Who the hell is this Debra bitch? Alek said she's coming back, whatever the hell that means."

"Little time," Amadeus said. "We fight."

The Father parried an underhand strike. Sean met the sword the best he could. Steel shrieked against steel and slid away. The rebound of the lunge nearly put Sean on his ass. Luckily, he hit the back of the Coventable and caught his balance against it. He leaned over to catch his breath. "Do you...do you know where those two are?"

"Not yet. But soon. Denn die toten reiten schnell."

The slayers hovering at a distance shifted like shadows and whispered to each other, their hushed voices like the beating wings of the surviving bats in the Abbey.

"Denn die-what?" Sean said, eyeing their glowing white distant eyes.

Amadeus smiled and struck savagely once more. "'For the dead travel fast.'"

10

Asleep she seemed younger, more vulnerable, and he had to remind himself that it was only her spell. Her Glamour. Her power to change reality to suit her needs. Sitting on the mattress beside her with his back propped against the wall, Alek skated the chunk of coal over the blank side of an old flier in staccato bursts of black. It was good, the purest thing he'd drawn in years. But that too was her spell; certainly, her face had had the power last evening to stop curious commuters all the way from the subway to the street.

"'The Devil hath power/To assume a pleasing shape,'" she said suddenly, coming alive at his side and turning over so the shadows were off her face.

"Dante?"

"The Bard. I detest the goths." Her black, unnatural eyes were open now, and sitting up she was once more a great, perfect doll, sinister and animated.

"Dante believed that all the world's devils go back in their box in the ground during the day," she said, stretching like a cat, skin taut over strong muscle and deceptively delicate bones. Unlike him, she slept naked, unashamed—if, indeed, shame had ever been an element of her spirit, even as a young woman. He seriously doubted it. Her flesh was pierced in some places, scarified in others, the scars an art in themselves that drew his eye again and again. Yet nothing about her repulsed him anymore. Quite the contrary...

She looked on him as if reading his thoughts. Her skin, her hair—white satin, black silk. But unlike her clientele, he had touched her not at all while they slept at either ends of this common bed. It wasn't that he didn't desire her, oh no. Even now he did. Particularly now as she all but offered herself up to him like a living sacrifice. But she was right. To love her, to be beloved of her—how could he keep the ghost in the picture on the wall from intruding?

"Tell me your thoughts," she said.

"I wish I could be with you, inside you. A part of you." Another thing that had changed. He no longer felt self-conscious about speaking his thoughts.

"I dreamt that you were," she admitted.

He touched her face, gathered her hair behind her head, kissed her, sliding his tongue against her teeth. She kissed him, tasted him. And then she turned away on the bed. But the sight of her slim back and white skin was his undoing. He didn't think. He crept behind her and slid his hands across her slim girlish waist, then cupped her breasts and toyed with the metal rings as his hungry mouth found its way under her ear and along her throat. She mewled delightfully. His hand dropped over her stomach, stroking. He pressed against her, his heart beating so hard it hurt, wanting her so much he felt he should die.

At first she responded, accommodating him, and it was as if his heart had been relocated to his groin. Desire grew and encompassed all of him at once, making his clothing an inconvenience because it controlled the hunger his body had. If only...but then she unlaced his hands. "No," she said, "He reaches down from above and she stands below with wings outstretched and Alek Knight hangs between two devils, the white one and the black."

The words turned his passion cold. He let her go, got up and walked away from her, lest she see his despair and his rage. The white devil. The devil with the white eyes. But they were so dark, so tainted with his six hundred years of blood, his wrath of holy fire and the twisted lies of his life.

"I'll kill the bastard," be whispered, leaning against the wall of the loft. "This is all I'll endure. This is *it.*"

"Vengeance."

"Fucking *war*. He killed Akisha and he killed Debra. I've carried this so long. But not anymore." He grimaced, tasted copper like a Eucharist of metal on his tongue. The taking of the Host before battle. He turned around and spotted the chains Teresa kept on her coat. He grabbed them compulsively and began winding them about his arms. "I'm going to make the prophecy real. I'm going to serve up the motherfucker's head to the Church and whatever god he serves."

Teresa narrowed her vixen-eyes on him like a high pagan priestess bestowing a benediction upon a favorite warrior. "You would spit in the face of Lucifer." She smiled. "At last."

She picked up his sketch, but he took it from her. The lines were drawn so perfectly to scale, the graceful curve of her cheek, her breast, her black, beautiful alien eyes. He crumpled the paper in his fist. Beautiful but insubstantial like all the work of his life.

He could see. Finally.

Awakened, as Akisha called it.

He wanted to be with Teresa, but he wanted this war more. He found his coat and put it on like the battle armor it felt so much like to him. He adjusted the leads in his coat to accommodate the weight of Takara's sword. Lastly, he found the map and glanced at the spot circled in red ink. Tonight's destination.

There was no pain now in his knee. There was no pain anywhere in his body but in his heart. He set the map aside and turned to study the picture hanging like an angel over the bed. He felt his smile mimic that of Debra's. Devious. Predatory. Secretive. The look of the ancient and the wronged and the powerful. He felt taller and as dark and manifest as an open abyss.

Tonight the city was his.

The city and the hunt.

11

Sometime after midnight he was standing with his back pressed to the alley flank of the Empress as if he would read the song of her walls. And of all the off-off-Broadway opera houses, surely she had the darkest of melodies. Both celebrity and scandal, she was certainly a piece of work. Alek had read somewhere that she'd fed the tabloid well at the turn of the century, back when social angst was as fashionable as padded corsets or Derby hats. She'd petered off after that, then gained a little recognition as something of a sordid vaudeville stage frequented by soldiers on leave during the Second World War. She'd been little better than a boulevard rattrap in the beginning, but she'd transfigured with each transferring of hands—theatre to museum house to antique emporium to government record house to temporary Department of War Defense outpost. On and on...until she'd come full circle in her cycle.

Well, she wasn't *quite* the same. Gone were the hosts of preening, posturing members of society lining her stairwell of crumbling cantilevered stone, the women in fur and jacquard, the husbands in spats who carried canes with beast's heads of real silver, all of them there to see and be seen. Now only the poor and the bored and a handful of aspiring Thespians attended her nightly amateur productions, attracted to her history or only the sinister smile of her cornices.

The scarred bricks were cold against his shoulders, stubbornly thick and secretive. Still, if the Chronicle was anywhere it must be here. It had to be here. He looked around tentatively and tried with the whole of his being to feel this derelict Eastside block full of Pakistani grocers and Asian nightclubs and abandoned rail yards. A few doors down, in the doorway of a deli, a black man in a tattered green field jacket scalped a roast chicken with enough coke stuffed inside of it to keep the Forty-second District on their toes for the next three months. Further on a lonely woman in a coldwater flat cried herself to sleep. Alek tried to reach beyond these human tragedies, looking for the supernatural cancer in the body of the city that would indicate a slayer or two.

So far nothing.

He didn't feel relieved. If they weren't here now, they soon would be.

The bum sleeping behind the meager protection of a Dumpster at the back of the alley turned over and muttered something whiskey-soaked and incomprehensible. Alek ignored the man and tipped his head back against the wall. Overhead the stars flitted like stop-signals in and out of sight through the choking blanket of nighttime smog. "Nothing," he whispered. "I think we have enough time if we don't dawdle. Maybe."

Teresa said nothing, only gazed up at the abused cornices with their wicked Corinthian relief as if she were wondering about its secrets the same as he. She breathed in deeply, taking the air and all the data it carried in through her sensitive Jacobson's organ, seeing the unseen the same as he, but with a process more natural than he was used to. Finally she said, "You dread this game, caro, yes?" She started down the alley.

"I'd like to dig Byron up and kill him again. Yeah," he muttered. "I'd also like to get my ass down to Port Authority and get a one-way ticket on the longest line out." He rubbed his arms nervously and started out after her. "But I guess we need that goddamn book first."

They followed the antique iron guardrail to the back stage entrance. On the stoop they encountered a punk heavy dressed in a tuxedo that looked scarcely able to hold in the force of the man's raw gym muscle. The man in the tux reached out and thumped the plain of his palm over Alek's chest, halting him. His piggish eyes shrank still more in his ruddy, bald face. His bicycle Mohawk stood up proud and blue like the quills of a particularly threatening and unusual porcupine. He eyed Alek with contempt. "No way. No one goes back there without a pass. 'Specially not bag people like you, you read, homeless? Soup kitchen's down da avenue."

Alek looked down at the hand holding him back. A colorful viper tattoo meandered along its meaty back, lending a dazzling three-dimensional illusion of the snake creeping out of Tux's sleeve. He thought absently of Erebus, another hulk of a creature, and the damage he sometimes had to deal the man to get past. His hand came up, ready to snatch and break the man's arm, to tear his hand off at the wrist if he had to. Because he could. Because, really, this was the only way to deal with these types.

"Caro."

He stopped and dropped his hand, remembering Teresa's Glamour, the spell so easily woven by her—the power that protected them from Amadeus's all-seeing eyes in her nest, the power that had beaten back even Takara's illusions long enough for Teresa to plant her knife in the slayer's belly. Alek turned his eyes up into the punk's face. "Please," he said, gaining an impression of the man's ill-defined anger being artistically channeled into this bizarre job.

"We need to go inside."

"Wassamatta, you stupid? Scram. Don't make me angry..."

Alek narrowed his eyes. Anger. Anger was innocent death, the broken chain before its time, anger was a thousand voices calling for the blood of Aragon, a monster, a man made god by the Church and unchained among the weaker masses like a wolf among sheep. Anger was the covenant sealed between creature and creator when all the vows were broken. Anger was a strike to the face, not wounding but as sharp as a drawn sword...

Tux fell back against the back door and slumped down, leaving the way completely open for them both. Alek stepped over the man and into the wings. The expression on his face might have been religious agony, but Alek did not look close enough to know for certain.

12

Twenty minutes after his blackout (the beer; it was the beer and the fucking hot suit) Richie Bellini was back on his feet and hitting the skinny blonde duck with the bad makeup job square it the chest with two fingers and telling him to piss off if he knew what was good for him. Bone-headed bums. When were they gonna learn that the Empress wasn't a country club for the homeless?

The kid in the long black coat with the long yellow hair looked down at the fingers in his chest, looked back up at Richie. Like so many punks today, he had smart-ass, fuck-me-why-don't-you eyes. Snowy grey, they were, almost pale. Albino? No. Albinos had pink little bunny eyes, didn't they?

"Don't touch me," the kid whispered.

Ooooh, a real badass, this one. Yeah, uh-huh. Richie Bellini, in the course of his long illustrious career as gypsy, roadie, punk and brawler, had bounced bigger fish than this one, and he knew for a fact that he was going to have one righteous time giving this kindergarten brat the beat down. He put on his ugly bulldog face and sneered, "You just hustle ass outta here. You hear me, asshole? Go home to bed before your mommy and daddy start looking for you." He punctuated each word with a good, hard threatening prod of his fingers.

The kid continued to stare down at Richie's fingers. *"Never...touch...me,"* said the kid, his whiny, nasal Bronx voice digressing into an upper-lip-raising snarl the likes of which Richie had only ever heard from a well-tempered vintage Hog engine set to run. Richie saw the kid's pearly little teeth, and for just a second he thought maybe the kid was an extra with tonight's troupe— except Richie knew that the Bard was on the run tonight—R&J and *not* the Scottish Play—and that the guys inside weren't in need of anybody who looked like he'd just dug himself out of his own goddamned grave.

What was it with these brats today?

Richie was just about to take the kid by the collar of his really cute Dracula coat and high-fly him out into the street (couldn't weigh that much, the kid, pathetic, anemic, from the look of him) when a hand as long and pale as a latex glove clamped down over Richie's wrist and suddenly burst apart the knob of little wrist bones.

The kid laughed like a maniac as the viper's head was severed from the rest of its body. Richie felt only surprise at the sight. In all his years as a road warrior and then a heavy—and God knew there were plenty years there—he'd never come up against a punk that was so white and ridiculously thin and so fucking *strong...*

Or so looney-tunes, either.

Richie meant to laugh this off like everything else, though what came out was really more like a good, healthy scream of pure, unadulterated horror. A distant part of Richie's brain considered that in his whole forty years he'd never screamed like a pansy before and that his reputation was good and ruined now.

But then Richie's pride was saved when the kid cut off his scream by dragging Richie toward a wolfishly open mouth whose stage teeth were far, far too real.

13

"Where are we?" Alek asked.

"Beneath the orchestra pit, I believe." Teresa studied the map by the muted light of the sole bulb shining in the center of the ancient, musty womb that passed for the Empress's prop cellar. "God but I think I agree with you. I'd like to kill the bastard again myself."

"Paranoid."

"What?"

"Byron was paranoid. That's why he did this," Alek said. Paranoid. Like I am. He unsheathed his sword and went to hover at the bottom of the cellar steps, testing the weight of the new sword in his hand, learning its contours in the dark in the event he needed it. At the top of the steps the door was sensibly closed. Beyond it, actors' muffled voices were natural and even. Feet stomped to the natural rhythm of script. A drummer hit a bass drum in dramatic fashion, the sound like muffled, far-off thunder.

He glanced around the cramped space, the sawhorses and busts and pasteboard weaponry and racks of moldering costumes. Here, below, he tried to tell himself there was nothing to fear but an avenging army of dust bunnies. And yet he shivered.

"Someone coming?" Teresa asked him.

"Or I'm just spooked."

She moved wordlessly to one wall, brutally shoved aside a clothes rack, and put the tips of her fingers against its plastered face. "Here."

He checked the cellar door again and saw only a thin bleeding of light around the edges. He sheathed the sword and went to the wall, touched it. "Drywall."

"Can you break it?"

He nodded. "Have you read it right?"

"I'm certain."

"But shouldn't there be a regression here?"

"Perhaps they've plastered it. For aesthetics."

Her voice sounded thin and desperate, too old and far too young at the same time. And why anyone would worry the appearance of a cellar was a mystery to him, but saying it was over would be giving up and giving in, wouldn't it? Instead, Alek went to the place Teresa had indicated and pressed his palms flat to the wall. He gathered his strength, sensed the broken grain and the living chitter of mice behind the skin-thin barrier, and *pushed—*

Plaster crackled and fell into depressions as dust wintered the chilly air. A piece like a massive jigsaw came away in his hand and he felt his heart skip a beat, then stop altogether. This was it. This was the place, damnit. Renewed by hope, he punched through the exposed stud, felt the satisfying crack and splinter of decades old dry wood. He put his hand into the hole he had made, felt around...encountered it. His fist came out of the crevice in a shaking, powdery fist. Flagstone. "Christ," he said. "Why would a theatre company flagstone their fucking cellar? What the hell kind of thinking is that?"

Teresa was silent a long, dark moment. Then she sighed as if from the bottom of her very soul, the sound eerie and resonant in this close place. "They wouldn't," she said. "But the government with its banks of wartime secrets would."

"*Fuck!*" He punched a second bowling-ball-sized hole in the stud next to its sister but did not feel the pain course through his hand, though he bled well enough. He leaned against the wall and closed his eyes against a headache he suddenly couldn't shake.

"There is still one more possibility. Come. Let us waste no more time among this mockery." She turned, graceful and maddeningly calm, and began to ascend the steps.

14

"You weren't planning on leaving without sayin' goodbye, were you, man?" Sean called from his vantage point on the metal catwalk circumventing the backstage. Alek looked up, anticipating the sight of the punk's grinning eyes and saluting sword, anticipating them the way someone might a badly reoccurring dream complete with closets and bogeyman.

He did not expect the body, however. It fell bonelessly to the floor at Alek's feet, fell like a sack of potatoes with exactly that much life and weight to it. Perhaps it had been human at one time. It was difficult to tell. Now it just looked like a train-wreck victim with a blue Mohawk.

Alek danced back a step, out of the widening pool of viscous mixed fluids.

The little shit smiled down at them. He put his free hand on the safety rail. Then, hardly putting any pressure on it at all, he leapt over the edge of the catwalk and landed in a crouch and a little *whoof* of air, one hand spayed flat to the rutted oak floor, the other bearing the weight of the Double Serpent Katana readily to his inner arm.

The katana, thought Alek. *My* sword. The little *bastard...*

The backstage being an abandoned junkyard of cables and stacked sawhorses and carpentry and mechanical tools, no one was there to notice Sean's grand Shakespearean entry. Not the actors, off in the wings watching the play, nor the propmasters who were also the actors. They were alone. Alone.

The eyes of the Stone Man narrowed to bloodless silver blades. Madness there—worse, sane hatred.

Alek stepped back, almost mincing.

In response, Stone Man straightened up, a six-foot tinkering tower of merciless bone and steel and squealing paten leather. He moved differently. Alek saw that at once. He had that loose-limbed liquid grace one only found in some of the oldest and best-trained warriors—the catlike beauty of a born predator, a born slayer. He twisted his head unnaturally, like an amphibian catching a fly, and flicked his tongue out at them. "Miss me?"

Teresa edged sideways toward the wings.

Sean licked his lips and smiled at her. "You look delicious, babe. I hope you've got some pussy left over, 'cause after I'm done cutting up your boyfriend here I'll be all yours!" He laughed, a riot of obscene snuffling, choking noises.

Alek drew the weapon under his coat, but Takara's tasseled, feather-light wakizashi felt about as much protection as a large kitchen knife. "You want to cut me, you little shit?"

Sean grinned obligingly. "Whatever you want and wherever you want it, you said. Well, I want it here. I want it now!"

"Careful what you wish for," Alek whispered.

Sean lunged, made a cross-handed slice meant to take a layer of skin off Alek's face. Alek sidestepped him and tried to roll the punk off his shoulder. He'd always been better in close-up—the curse of the long-limbed. It wasn't the advantage most thought it was. Even an endlessly legged spider winds up its prey, Amadeus once taught him. And it was that lesson he tried to use. But something happened this time.

Sean caught himself before the throw, swung his blade around so he was *inside* Alek's sword arm. Alek changed tactics at the last moment, met Sean's blade with his own as it came back around, skidded off it too quickly in his haste, and heard the tell-tale *screek* of his blade breaking against the tyranny of Hanzo's blessed sword. It stole the pathetically light Japanese dicer from his grip and the meat from his hand. Alek dropped to the floor and rolled out of the way of Sean's crosswise strokes.

Blood on the floorboards now, too bright and too real in this place of makeup and make-believe.

Sean's whinnying filled the wings, undercutting the beat of the bass onstage.

"First blood," Alek whispered, finding his feet and binding his hand with the belt off his coat.

Sean came at him again, swinging his sword like a kid up to bat. Alek flattened himself against the floor under the assault of the swing, dove for Sean's middle. Sean hit the floor on his back with a graceless *ooff!* of breath.

Sean twisted around and was on him inside of a moment, no quarter given, no punches pulled, real streetfighter mode this time, all clawing fingernails and snapping teeth. A fist landed on Alek's mouth, another on his cheek, blackening his vision. He shook himself, and when he could see again the sight that greeted him was hackle-raising: Sean loomed above him, his mouth cranking open impossibly far, the unnatural snakelike incisors descending like needles. And then the jaws snapped closed around Alek's throat like a steel trap. Christ, he'd been practicing. He was using what was at hand. He was getting good—

Sean thrashed like a Rottweiler with a chunk of meat in its jaws.

Alek gasped, heard the material of his coat collar snarl, felt his flesh shred between Sean's jaws. He was good—but no master. Not yet. Alek snarled, the sound guttural with the blood bubbling out of his nostrils and foaming through the corners of his mouth, and brought his hands together in a thunderclap over Sean's ears. There came a muffled *pop* as air was forced down both Sean's ear canals at the same time. It shot his equilibrium to hell. The trap loosened around Alek's throat and Alek, choking, gasping, finally able to breathe something other than blood, pushed out at his slayer.

They went over like a pair of wrestling alligators locked in a death roll. Harnessing momentum like once he had beneath Wilma Bessell's assault, Alek launched the Stone Man off himself. Sean flew back into a sawhorse, destroying it utterly. He groaned, sat up. He looked, for wont of a better word, simply pissed. He let out his breath in a hiss, got to his feet, shaky but not defeated, and began to circle Alek like a jungle cat searching for a weakness in its intended prey.

Alek got to his feet and watched the Stone Man circle, keeping a dozen paces between them at all times, keeping Sean always to the front of him. "You're good," Alek spat bloodily upon the floor. "But you're still a dickless little whelp."

Sean lifted his sword. With a wet, frothy snarl, he flicked it at Alek's head like a circus dagger.

Alek used his coat to deaden the blow of the blade. The sword clattered down no more than a half dozen feet from the toe of his

boot. He tried to grab it up but the sword skittered animatedly
out of his reach.

No...

Again he went for it; again the sword jumped like a living thing
toward Sean, making Alek feel ridiculously like a victim of a Charlie
Chaplin short, the Derby hat that always seemed to get away and
all that. Sean laughed hysterically at the sight and clapped his hands
together.

Alek hunched forward, ignoring the heckling, all his
concentration on Hanzo's blade, the engravings he could feel even
now in the palm of his hand. Akisha said it was a part of him. And
because it had drawn Debra's blood he knew this to the true. The
sword jittered nervously, tried to skip away, being drawn as it was
by Sean's powerful mental persuasions. But it wasn't Sean's sword,
goddamn it! You should never have been parted from it, came
Akisha's whisper. The sword will know its master, said the sword
master Amadeus.

You know me! *You belong to me...!*

He threw himself down on the floor, reaching for the hilt,
reaching for it the way a child might reach for a particularly shy
pet, reaching for it with his hands and his mind and his heart.
Reaching—almost—and—

"*Shit-fuck!*"

—the sword bucked away from him as his fingertips brushed
the pommel. Alek jumped to his feet and let out a roar of frustration
as the sword slithered away, kicking up sparks on the buckled
hardwood floor, sliding with uncanny ease into the mold of Sean's
hand. Then Sean was on his feet, laughing riotously, leaping at
him and sending him reeling backward through the stage curtain.

Romeo was onstage, enraged by the recent death of his friend
Mercutio. He was rushing his evil cousin Tybalt with drawn sword
when the two slayers broke through the curtain. Romeo's pasteboard
sword glanced off Alek's shoulder and bent like a rabbit ear as he
and Sean broke between them and cut a jagged, crazy line toward
the apron of the stage. Tybalt swore, his face crumpling in angst at

their blatant upstaging, and tried to take hold of Sean's arm and drag him off the stage.

It was Tybalt's mistake. Laughing still, grinning all the while, Sean dragged his sword back over his right shoulder, clearing Tybalt's head from his shoulders like a man knocking an apple off a barrel. Blood exploded across the stage.

"Oops," giggled Sean, "dropped something."

Alek hissed like a cat, like the blood loosened from the stump of the man's neck. *"Bassstard..."*

Sean grinned at him with surprise and shook off the headless body clinging to him, kicking it into the orchestra pit and sending down a rain of blood like anointment on the heads of those in the first two rows. "Like you ain't?" He chopped at Alek with the murderous sword.

Alek recoiled, skating the blood and the metal cables of the stage, jumping nimbly away from the silver whistle of death falling across his throat. Sean's second slice caught Romeo at the side of his head as the actor was turning to run, shaving away a portion of his cheek it a flap and exposing his molars on the left side. Romeo screamed out of his mouth and out of the side of his face.

Blood painted Alek's face like makeup, blinded him: Tybalt's, Romeo's, his own. The floorboards under his feet were iced with spilt blood. He stumbled out of the path of Sean's downward assault, sensed the floor skating out from under him, but he was unable to stop his fall. He went down, the back of his skull cracking against the iron stand of a strobe light.

Darkness poured in. The house was white with silence, but through it all Alek felt the crashing peal of laughter and the whicker of a quick overhand strike, a finishing strike, the coup de grace—

Faster than the human eye could see or follow it, he took the strobe's stem in his hands and blindly wrenched it forward like a shield. Steel glanced off iron and made the strobe sing in Alek's hands, sent the vibration and the heat of the poisonous metal shooting through his hands and all the way down to his elbows. He threw the strobe stiffly away, his hands burning cold. Above, somewhere amidst all the darkness, Sean was howling like a wounded animal. Alek tossed his bead, shook away the remaining darkness, and looked...

The Stone Man was on his knees at the end of the stage, the sword forgotten, his hands sheltering the portion of his face that had suffered the sword's ricochet. His bottom lip had been shaved off, his nose clipped. Sean tossed back his head of blood-washed blonde hair and screeched deafeningly like some damned beast out of the Abyss. The clamshell lights rimming the apron crackled and spat in winks of bursting blue light and pungent ozone, then went dark. Cables came alive and twisted like tentacles around the props. The backdrop split and fell away like flesh off bone. With a final little cry Sean tipped sideways over the edge of the orchestra pit and was gone.

Shaking as if with palsy, numb beyond pain, almost beyond terror, Alek dragged himself up in the midst of the blood and the carnage, the war and the strange silence. He squinted out at the audience through the smoky violet lighting and waited. Then, all at once, the audience began to applaud. Alek weaved with confusion and unbelief as the sound redoubled his shuddering like a leaf in a tempest. Idiots. Did they think this was a performance? Part of the fucking *play*? Something flambant neuf? He felt sick. Sick to death. Sick almost to the point of passing out.

From behind him came the rusted bells of mad laughter.

He turned around, slowly, dreading this, dreading it all...

The Stone Man emerged slowly from the pit. He was a horrorshow of scored tissue and awry bloody hair. The remnants of his nose hung like beaten meat from his face. His left eye was gone, the socket swollen with a yellow fluid as thick as curdled cream. Still he grinned, slinking up onto the stage like a serpent from out of its hole. "They love me," he garbled. "I was born for the stage...and my face"—he touched the ruined red soup of his face—"my face is my fortune!" He screamed laughter.

It was too much; Alek backed away to the end of the stage. Mad. Sean was mad. The Coven was mad. Their whole fucking race was mad.

"Don't go, Scarecrow!" Sean cried as he climbed to his feet on the stage. He weaved uncertainly as he turned to face the appreciative audience and the falling flowers, and swept downward in an elaborate bow which liberated the fragment of his nose from the rest of his face. *"They haven't seen our encore yet!"*

Encore. It took Alek a moment to realize what Sean meant. The audience had risen in an ovation, most of them punks and goths and poseurs with weird tastes in theatre to be sure, but among them only two figures were moving. Moving toward the stage. Aristotle. Robot...

Alek ran. Velvet curtains crashed away as he ran from this boogeyman made of steel and bone and blood, ran from the slayers quickly closing the distance between them. He ran like an animal sensing death, ran blind, numb to all feeling but one, but terror— hair-raising, bone-cold, all-consuming terror. And there, in the alley behind the Empress, he encountered the ten-foot-high security fence, jumped against it, smashed against it, and did not move. It was enough. He hung there, crucified. He was so tired, so damned fucking *tired*...

"So full of despair, are you? You said we would always be together. Did you lie, beloved?" came a seductive little voice from just beyond the fence. Through a mosaic of tears he saw red; Debra had come back for him at last. She stood waiting for him in the alley just beyond the fence, and she was wondering if he had lied to her. He had done many, many things, most of them horrible, but he had never lied to her. Never in all his years. He promised to love her forever. He promised.

His vision cleared. Not Debra. Teresa. Not again. He wanted to take her and shake her and scream into her face. She was cheating. She always cheated and tricked him. But there wasn't time. He could hear them approaching, the clocking of slayers' heels on wet concrete, the brush of long coats, the hiss of drawn blades, and he remembered what waited for him if he did not move. He moved. He climbed, awkwardly but with determination, over the top of the fence, then dropped to the other side like a man slipping into an abyss.

15

Were this not New York City one would almost think it was ten in the morning instead of ten at night. The sidewalks were full of people, walking from parking lots towards the glamorous lights of Broadway, or making their way toward the bars and restaurants that ran in storefront chains up and down the streets. Among them, visible only to those hungering for what they had to offer, stood those selling illicit wares, illegal substances, putting on their lines, sometimes snagging a respectable-looking passerby. As he walked these streets with Teresa, being as casual as his look allowed, it amazed him to realize how many ordinary people burned with unmentionable desires.

I will leave one day, he thought solemnly, I will go away but it will not be me going. I will be somebody else when that fateful day arrives. Because if *I* went, I would die. And he wondered how many others had such an obtrusive thought-loop. But on the other hand, there was no way he could stay here if he failed to find the Chronicle, no way at all. And yet he would. Because for all the grime and underlying violence and ugliness, this was his city. And he had absolutely nowhere to go. Damned if you do, damned if you don't.

They waited at the light, staying in the shadows of a bank building, prepared to make a left on Forty-second Street on their way home. Teresa's home, rather. A block away rose the corner of the high-rise housing Covenant House, its facade lit with flood lamps like a beacon to runaways everywhere. Alek remembered that about a decade earlier its founder, Father Bruce Ritter, was accused of having sex with several male youths. He resigned amidst scandal and disappeared from the public eye without being prosecuted. And without ever being seen again.

The Church took care of its own.

The light changed but he made no move up Forty-second. "They're here," he said, and Teresa turned, looking for all the world like any other working girl but for her eyes, her crystal-gleaming, night-piercing eyes. He saw her stiffen and knew she'd seen it as well. The slight rush amidst the crowd, the bit of turmoil as figures waded through, cutting a skirmish line to the front.

Slayers.

The light had turned to red again, and now the slayers emerged fully to the fore of the waiting crowd. Two of them. The one was a petite male with a sly fox-like face. Aristotle. The other, Robot, would have been as nondescript as a balding, middle-aged banker were it not for his sheer size. The man had biceps as big around as Alek's thigh and outweighed him by more than sixty pounds. His black wool topcoat looked ready to split at the seams from the sheer muscular bulk and hidden hardware the man carried. Both Aristotle and Robot turned to look on him at the same moment. Robot's expression was unreadable, as always. Aristotle smiled ever so slightly with only his eyes and moved aside to accommodate the third member of their little unholy trinity.

Stone Man.

He stood with both arms loose and slightly spread, a monster, a living monster. He was naked of weapons, but his posture more than made up for that—shoulders slightly hunched, chin pointing at the ground, eyes—one eye, anyway—turned up and showing all white at the bottom. Typical vulture stance, just before the creature leaps from a tree limb and eats the eyes out of a dying desert animal. The other eye was sealed shut with running fluid. His face ran like a blood pie and everyone who looked upon him turned pale and backed away. His little army surrounded him, providing the stage set for what Alek hoped would be some ill-conceived power play, a few obscenities thrown, maybe a boyish tantrum before departure back to the Covenhouse, the memories of Kansas and Takara's untimely demise still rolling around their fearful little brains. Then again, Kansas and Takara had taken their frustration out on the whole of the subway, so maybe there was going to be more. Maybe there was going to be fireworks. Or a nuclear bomb.

Alek felt snakes twist in his stomach the moment he spotted Aristotle reaching into his coat. "Down!" he almost barked, and then felt a wash of relief that he had hesitated as Aristotle withdrew a box of Camels and pulled one out with his teeth. He waggled his eyebrows at Alek like Groucho Marx making a joke. Robot did not reach for the iron throwing knives Alek knew lined the insides of both sides of his coat. Sean did not move at all, as if waiting for some cue. Cold carrion comfort. So they were here to bring him back alive—or at least intact. But that didn't mean they weren't going to have their fun first. Oh the joy of the hunt, Alek thought as he and Teresa began to casually shove through the crowd, working fast but not so fast they would attract a cop's attention. No one ran in New York unless they wanted to get caught.

Walking medium-fast, breathing cold through his teeth, Alek's mind and inner sight jumped to a passing pedestrian heading in the opposite direction. Sure enough, Sean and his soldiers were on the move now.

"Don't look back," he whispered as they turned up Forty-second Street, past a city-subsidized apartment building and a corner store selling baseball caps and T-shirts. The hair on the back of Alek's neck tried to crawl down his back. They were walk-running now as fast as pedestrian traffic allowed, trying not to look like targets. Trying not to look suspicious.

Again his mind jumped, this time to a street musician in a doorway across the street.

Sean was not running. He and his soldiers were walking with predatory grace to the center of the street, en masse. He was laughing, a low rumble more felt than heard, like the prologue to an earthquake that could decimate an entire city block.

Limos and taxis shot past Alek in the slushy curb on their immediate left, their glass shivering. He saw his eyes in the trembling passing glass, his young, frightened eyes. He saw them squelch as something like a muffled explosion seemed to build in the canals of his ears. Then they were too far past the musician for his piggybacking to be of any more service. Again the rumble like the street or something beneath it was awakening. He spun around.

A fire hydrant exploded as Sean crossed its path, spitting out a bloodlike gush of furious white water that soaked the street and the traffic and four dozen pedestrians before they managed to escape its wrath. Sean laughed. And still he walked, the acoustic rumble following him like a peculiar second retinue. Behind him, a sawhorse in the curb slanted sideways as the tarmac heaved and made a manhole cover quake and dance like a gigantic fallen quarter. More laughter, amped up like an electric guitar ringing on a high, screechy A note; it made the street crack and smoke with his steps as if he were some hellspawn spat upon the earth to set waste to it.

The ground buckled under Alek's feet, the walk sliding upward like a tombstone shoving itself up toward the earth. Alek grabbed a lamppost for security, slid around sideways off the rearing concrete and set himself down beside Teresa in the street. She worried her bottom lips, her eyes fixed behind them.

"What is it?" she whispered.

"Psi..." He lost his train of thought at the blaring sound of a rampaging car horn. A taxi headed for them, the cabby leaning on the horn. Alek grabbed Teresa by the arm and pulled them both out of its path. It roared by, all hot rolling exhaust and flying paper. Sean grinned as the cab headed dead-on for him and swept his arm outward as if to swat a fly. The quake that followed shimmered across the street like deadpan heat. Brakes squealed and an apocalypse of white light flickered off the windshield of the cab, briefly illuminating the cabby's expression of mortal, uncomprehending fear. Then the cab was off the road, was up on the walk, past it and through a stand of meters, the nose ramming like a bullet into the picture window of a lighted 24-hour Korean deli. The vehicle slammed to a crunching stop, half-in, half-out of the face of the building, teetering, the horn blaring incessantly like a siren with no shut-off.

All bets were off this time. Pedestrians scattered like ants, which was the only advantage of an otherwise awful situation. Teresa hovered in the street, taking it all in, then chose the largest group of panicked escaping pedestrians to join. Alek followed wordlessly. They were thinking alike. The longer they kept to the tatters of the crowd, the harder they would be to follow. Unless, of course, Amadeus, that bastard, were tracking him by blood and feeding his slayers the information. If that were true, then they were truly doomed and there was nowhere they could hide for long.

He saw shadows flickering from the corners of his eyes and he decided he didn't want to contemplate that possibility. Maybe, he thought, by staying with a larger, more mobile crowd, there would be fewer casualties this time. Even the trinity of evil on their heels could not possibly kill every citizen they encountered without the police and maybe a full SWAT team first descending upon them. Could they?

They reached Port Authority and Alek felt his heart start to sink as the lights and the noise inside the station hit him like a fist to the midsection, staggering him back half a step. I don't want to go in there. I don't. Death there. He leaned against a wall to steady himself. Teresa pulled him by the arm. "They're coming, caro."

A security guard from across the concourse looked up from a newsstand and eyed the panicked crowd curiously.

Alek took a deep breath. There were crowds of people rushing back and forth, seeming to loom towards him and then just as quickly receding. Above echoed the huge vaulted ceiling and all around them came the relentless lights reflecting off the white floors and walls like ice reflecting the heat of the sun. Light poured from ticket counters and shop windows and fast-food restaurants and departure gates. Too much. He felt sick and dizzy. He glanced around for an escape route and saw they were directly across the street from the Church of the Holy Cross, its orange brickwork making it look more like a factory than a church. He grabbed Teresa by the sleeve and looked toward the church sitting there like something in disguise, something afraid to admit to what it was.

He felt Teresa's muscles stiffen in response when an explosion and the acrid stench of a broken gas main down on Forty-second reached their senses. The air felt charged around them, hot, like a summer night with the air stifling and full of the threat of lightning. Sirens seemed to fill the night with panic. He saw the shine of them in her eyes. "Will they follow?" she asked, eyes flicking to the cop who had dropped his copy of *Veranda* and was heading out in the direction of the commotion.

He glanced down the street at the smoke and the chaos that arched like a living wall between them and the enemy. "Pray to God they don't," he answered her.

Moments later they stopped at the wooden double doors of the church and looked up at the stone visage of a saint on his plinth standing outside like a sentinel. Alek didn't know his name, but the face of the divine mortal was somewhat familiar, pale and broody and vaguely carnivorous. He tried the door of the church, praying it was open, the back of his neck hackling with the sounds of the encroaching heat and violence, and found to his utmost surprise that this time his prayers were answered.

It was the first time as a grown man that he was inside a church and he did not know what to expect, if the ground would quake, if God would strike them both down when they probably had no souls. The collective power of the votive candles was like a solar flare as they stepped inside, and for a moment he was truly afraid. God *was* striking them both down as soulless creatures fool enough to enter His sacred dwelling place. But lightning did not strike and the ground did not open up. They were alive.

He let out a sigh of relief, and then reminded himself that most of the legends about his people were wrong anyway. Garlic, wooden stakes, silver—these things did shit against vampires, so why would a church be any different?

He squinted against a massive, shifting, reddish darkness that made him feel as if he were wading through a great watery womb.

He saw terrible stained-glass images of violence and Stations of the Cross crowding the walls like the markings of some alternative Coven. There were dark wooden pews, but no table. The ornate raised altar was of wood and stone and brass and nothing had died for its construction. He detected incense, as in the Abbey, and beeswax, but the cloy of human warmth and sweat was new and unfamiliar.

They were alone, or nearly so. A drunk lay asleep on a back pew, and somewhere far above in the choir loft someone tapped inexpertly at an organ. They seemed oblivious to the horrors going on outside the doors. Or used to it. Alek shivered.

And then there was the young priest. He turned away from the tiers of candles he was lighting to remove his chasuble and watch as Alek and Teresa walked down the aisle to the altar front. He was a handsome man with coal-black Latino hair and eyes to match, a square, honest chin darkened by the shadow of a strong beard, his lips tight and stern but oddly devoid of the sour ecclesiastical sneer Alek had come to associate with priests and slayers—that look that came with decades of denying the flesh. And if their overall appearance or the blood on their clothing frightened him, the priest did not show it. Perhaps he'd seen worse. Perhaps he'd stood at the mouth of hell itself.

Alek stopped toe to toe with the priest and looked into his dark eyes. The priest tilted his head and blinked questioningly. For some reason, a surge of shivering guilt rode Alek's flesh to the bone. *Vampires believe no more in heaven or hell than mortal man. No angels or devils make themselves apparent to us, no matter what the paperback lies say.* Empirius had said that on the night he died, died believing in his God no more or less than any human priest. Alek's mouth moved but for a moment he could find no words to speak. He felt like a little boy at the bench of a god. He felt as if he stood in the doorway of the Abyssus once more, watching its dead lord lap blood from his little stone altar.

And then the words came, unbidden, in a torrent of dry sobs. "Bless me, Father, for I have sinned," he said. "I've killed...so many.

So goddamn *many*. I've put the dead in their grave, and the living too—I've—help me—" The words beat at his brain, made his head swim.

The priest hesitated. His eyes and posture spoke of interest and suspicion, but no fear. Invitation. But no judgment. He opened his mouth, then closed it. Again a wave of discomfort washed over Alek, a guarded feeling like being stalked in an alley when the shadows weren't working to your advantage. They said confession was good for the soul, but that was a human cliché. Vampires had no souls, or if they did, it was composed of a vastly different substance. He told himself Confession would do him no good.

Then the priest nodded as if understanding these things innately. And then he spoke. "When I was eight years old I drank the blood of my infant sister. That was in 1746. That is my Confession."

Alek swayed on his feet. He felt numbed.

"It is my gift, to conceal," continued the priest. "It is the reason the Coven has never darkened the door of this church. Until now."

He didn't know what else to say. "I'll go."

"Don't." The priest frowned, and Alek saw it then, the endlessly weary creature hiding inside a habit and a human's skin. He reached out with one hand and made contact. Some object, cold and heavy, was pressed into Alek's palm. A key. "To the vault below," said the priest. He nodded at the angel-faced little prostitute sitting in the front pew and watching them both with her great dark eyes. "You'll be safe here; the Coven will not find you this night. I promise."

"Thank you."

"Do not thank me," said the priest without a smile. "Only promise me...promise me that you will use your gifts for some good in this world."

Alek held the stern even gaze of the ancient young man and then nodded his head once like a vow taken.

16

The slayer stood at the frozen midwinter's window and touched the immortal dolphins in their static flight, the twilight somber on his face like a mask, the glass cold as bone under his fingertips. His breath plumed in the darkness with his sigh. Booker closed his eyes and heard the harsh, whispery echoes of precocious thirteen-year-old children, chosen brothers, at war with one another:

You can't go, you can't!

I can't stay, Book, not now.

Has he given you the Rite of Blood?

What kind of question is that?

Answer it.

That's none of your fucking business!

Silence.

Then: *You never told me.*

Book opened his eyes and tore open his tie knot. Hot as all hell in here, he thought, watching the steam of his exhalation frost the windowpane opaque. He started drawing a little dagger on the pane, was molding the hilt into the form of a dolphin when he finally noticed the hem of his London Fog was smoking.

"Fucking *shit!*" he hissed and beat the blackening material out, feeling like the biggest damn fool on the planet for letting the psi get away from him. Goddamn walking Zippo, that's what he was. No fucking discipline...

He almost laughed at that. He was the one always going on about discipline like some wise-ass Shao-Lin monk, giving Alek all those pained looks about his drinking problem, all that advice. Fucking hypocrite. Yeah, that's what he was.

Flame-free, he checked the time. After five. Sundown. Shit. Somewhere out there in the city Alek was on the move. Alek, a rogue. God, but that was impossible. Debra had been a rogue. Not Alek. Alek wasn't mad. Just headstrong.

Just a fool, he thought, rubbing at his prickly arms. He undid the garroting tie at his throat completely, then ripped it off, afraid it might catch. What had the fucking fool done? The Father had given them so much, a home, a brotherhood.

Book knew how it was. In 1958 the Father had stolen Book away from a group of white-jacketed Dr. Jekyll-types who sat him in a room all day and made him set playing cards on fire. He'd been alone back then, the memory of his mother and his little brother Tyrone's scorched bones lying mixed in the debris of their Eastside project still fresh in his mind. No father had ever claimed him, and after a few years Book had pretty much figured out why. His life had been an almost perfect carbon copy of Debra's and Alek's and Eustace's and Sean's and all the other slayers', the same patterns and problems repeated in gently diverse ways.

But the Father had taken them away from all that. The Father had given them education and a purpose. Maybe that purpose seemed strange and violent at times, maybe they were asked to do things which frightened them, even appalled them sometimes, but it *was* a purpose, damn it to hell, and Book knew from hard long experience that purpose was what kept you sane in this life, no matter how long it was. He'd seen people, mortal and otherwise, die for less.

Purpose was the glue that kept the masses together, his mother once said during the Movement.

Purpose kept you alive, when there wasn't any reason to go on.

The pager in his pocket buzzed him.

He ignored it.

Purpose, he thought.

And what purpose existed behind the kind of insolence and insult Alek was heaping upon the Coven? Book closed his eyes, trying to see through the film of Alek's insane actions, but all he saw these days when he closed his eyes were memories. School. Parties. Slayings. Alek. He saw a big strange old Colonial house, a door swinging open on a cell with this tall, white Brooklyn-born boy with Asian-black hair and eyes, a boy and his sister. A boy with no hope in his eyes. A boy years older than his body. A boy who could have been Book himself. A boy who became his *brother,* for chrissakes. A boy who believed in their purpose, a boy who sacrificed damn near everything for it. Like him. Just like him.

When the device in his pocket persisted after several minutes, a regular five-alarmer this time, he took it off, tossed it to the floor and stepped on it. Fuck Doc Sacco, he thought. Fuck them all at St. Vincent's.

He glanced sidelong out the window, the city tinted grey through the hazy blue glass. He gritted his teeth. Aberration. That was what Alek was, an aberration, an ungrateful child. There was no purpose to this. It was all mindless *passion*...

He was pacing without knowing it. It was so clichéd, he hated it. Pacing. So hot in here, he thought as he unbuttoned his coat. Over on the nightstand sat an old rag doll with a ratty worn face. He went over to it and picked it up.

The moment he touched it the doll combusted into a mass of tattered cloth, stuffing and roaring red yarn. Cursing, Book threw it down into the wastepaper basket beside the bed. The flames sprang up, blue in their heat, then died down. The doll burned fitfully for a second or two, then dissolving into white smoke and debris.

He closed his eyes as he fought to put the endless gout of psi back in the fireproofed box of his mind, like the Father had taught him. He hissed through his teeth, concentrating. Threads of sweat tricked down his brow with the effort of control...control...

Boooker...

He shook his head. He opened his eyes.

Oh Boook...

He looked sideways at the miniature pyre burning at the bottom of the basket. This was ridiculous. What, was he hearing voices in his head like some kind of fucking psychopath now? He shook his head, but an image came to him with all the shock of memory. He was no more than fourteen, showering, the water a roaring curtain between himself and the rest of the world. Yet the figure penetrated it. At first he thought it was Alek; then a pair of delicate female hands broke through the curtain and touched her white fingertips to his naked chest. He saw her face, eyes flashing black beneath winged brows, a wicked, inviting smile...

Debra...

With a roar, Book threw the basket against the bookshelves, the flotsam of burned stuff filling the room with an acrid, hellish stench.

God help him, he had a sword. And he had another weapon locked none-too-safely inside his mind. And he had no trouble using either one, so help him. If Alek and dead Debra wanted to play Crispy Critter with him then that was just fine, that was just...fucking...*fine!*

The stench of crisping fabric and scorched bone gathered in his nostrils and mouth and throat...

He nearly gagged with it all, with purpose.

He turned from the window and rushed from his brother's cell with scarcely a thought, but an entire mission simmering inside of him, taking form. Yes. He knew what to do.

Downstairs in the library he found the rolled-up map. He unrolled it, studied it, then turned it upside down. The map made no comprehensible sense to him, of course. Byron, the clever bastard, had drawn it in a code few knew. So he took it with him to the desk, booted the computer he and Alek had added to the Covenhouse in the mid-Nineties, and sat down to write an email.

Ten minutes later the letter was sent and Book started the waiting game, his finger drumming over the desk as he watched the evening light turn soft through the stained-glass windows. In time the light bled away to a dense wintry darkness. Nightfall. It seemed forever and a day before he was alerted to a response:

Oui, not impossible, but I must see the map. —*J.P.*

Book pursed his lips over the letter, then scanned the map in and sent it along. Then he waited some more, hands bridged in front of him, chin resting atop it as the first hard snow of the season began to whirl against the windowpanes. There wasn't much time. Soon night would fall and the Covenhouse would come alive. Soon the hunt for the hunter would begin again. "Come on,

Frenchie," Book whispered, straining to hear every sound in the house. He got up. He paced. He fumed and heated the room like a goddamn propane heater He was straining so hard to hear everything he nearly missed the little You Got Mail announcement.

The Metro, most definitely. Are you hunting him? —J.P.

News travels fast, thought Book. But he wrote back: *Thanks. And yeah, I am. Isn't everyone?*

17

It was another typical Braxton show being played out for another excited wannabe who believed himself the center of attention. Alek moved among the humans, sipping nothing in passing, nodding at none of the empty comments and praises, the de facto center of attraction if for no other reason than because he looked like none of them. He looked like what he was, instead. A tramp. A rogue. A rumpled, longhaired, extremely tired slayer. He looked like hell itself, and the crones who haunted these parties to see and be seen with their cowed husbands turned away as he approached, their diamonds still burning his eyes. He had thought of waiting until after the show, but, Jesus, they didn't have that much time left. Not anymore. Not with Amadeus so close. Not with the Stone Man practically on their heels these days. Braxton would just have to find time for them.

Hot in here. As usual. Alek undid his coat and stopped a waiter tricked out in a black tux like some cheap Hammer film-style vampire, and said, "Do you know where Charles is?"

"Charles, sir?" came the hesitant, heavy-lidded, Jeevesque reply. The boy looked positively puzzled.

Alek shook him. "Charles Braxton. The man who employs you?"

More querulous frowns from the boy. Alek decided not to push his luck anymore. He let the boy go. If he intimidated the waiter, the kid was liable to call security, and then there would be serious trouble to contend with. Too late, old man, he told himself. Already a couple of plainclothesmen were swimming toward him through the crowd like a pair of idle hammerheads. Holding up his hand in a sign of surrender, he backed out of the room.

Apparently deciding he was more than a minor threat to aesthetics, they followed him out to the alley. They looked a little unreal, these two. Sort of like Abbot and Costello doing the Keystone Kops thing. Abbot's magnum was real enough, though. He stepped through the back door and put it in Alek's face while Costello with his paunch and self-satisfied looks unclipped the police ban radio disguised as a cell phone on his belt.

"You don't want to do that," Alek said.

"I don't wanna kick your ass between your teeth, boy," Abbot answered in a northern redneck drawl that did little to support his Bud Abbot image, "and I won't, jest long as you stay right there. Here?"

Alek grabbed the gun and turned it on the man, the man's hand still attached to it. The wrist bones sounded as noisy as a kid smashing down a bowl of corn flakes with a spoon. Abbot screamed hoarsely. Costello pulled out his own little cannon. And maybe he was a born-and-bred city boy the same as Alek, with nearly the same reflexes, but that didn't make him quick. Nothing could, just right then. Alek mule-kicked him in the groin, doubling him over and sending him into the side of a Dumpster with a hollow thump.

Costello groaned, scrabbling at the asphalt and his lost toy. Teresa stepped out of the shadows and gripped him by the back of the coat and bashed the back of his skull against the side of the Dumpster again. Costello finally slumped down into dreamland.

Abbot continued to wail irritatingly. Alek wrenched him over so the man flipped onto his back on the pavement. He put his booted foot over the man's face and was just about to rub it out like old cabbage when the voice at the mouth of the alley caught his attention.

"Don't do that to Lenny. He's slow, but loyal."

Alek looked up.

A woman stood there, a stark black outline burning against the streetlights of Madison Avenue. Alek tried to put the voice together with the outline and failed horribly. Presumably the woman had followed him here from the party, and that meant she knew him or had business with him. For a moment, from the angle of the outline, the easy, angled curves, he almost expected Akisha to step forward, fully reformed and beautifully alive. But then the figure shifted, came a number of steps closer, and Alek finally recognized the woman.

Not Akisha. Not one of his own.

Mrs. Tahlia Braxton chuckled a little in that gravelly Lauren Becall voice of hers like he had said something witty or wise and took a long drag from off her cigarette. She frenched it as she came over to study her downed man. Charles's powerful wife was dressed in an outfit typical of her style, a white linen jumpsuit bare at the throat and arms, a torc of silver with a red tiger's eye around her naked throat. No coat or stole. Alek thought she must be frozen to the pavement, but she showed nothing of discomfort as she prodded Abbot in the side with one white designer boot. The boots had platform heels and Mrs. Braxton stood nearly as tall as Alek himself, so the heels must have made her feel like a giant. He had only met the White Bird as they called her twice at these parties, but both times he had come away with the feeling that Braxton's better half was just that—smart, suave, a regular iron hand in a silk glove. Now was no different.

"Get up, Lenny, and take Morton down to Emergency."

When Lenny did nothing and only continued to stare up at the two of them with lemur-eyed fear, Mrs. Braxton tossed her cigarette aside and lifted her eagle-eyed attention on Alek. "Get this sot to his feet?"

Alek got Abbot up, trying not to make it look like too easy a task. God knew what she'd already seen; he didn't need her asking him where all his Superman strength came from. Between himself and Teresa they managed to get the Keystone Kops to the curb and into Mrs. Braxton's waiting limo.

Mrs. Braxton directed her driver to St. Mary's, then shivered and turned. She opened the silver monogrammed cigarette case in her pocket and lit a smoke. She rubbed at her arms, seeming to feel the cold at last.

"Look, Mrs. Braxton—"

"Tahlia."

"Tahlia," Alek said, "This is a mess."

Tahlia shrugged like it was no big deal. "I expect it from your kind."

"My kind? I'm just trying to find Charles. I—"

"Dead."

Something jumped inside of Alek. "Charles is dead?"

"For the last fifteen years. Haven't you noticed, dear?"

He watched her, mystified. This was the last possibility, according to the map. Maybe Tahlia knew more that her cantankerous husband. Or maybe it was just desperation pushing them on. Probably it was desperation. Alek thought about Teresa's words this evening as they left the rectory of the church with its bloodred candles and pale saints and haunted priest. *One last hope, mio caro. One last hope...*

Tahlia waited expectantly.

"I...don't know how to put this," Alek said.

Tahlia's eyes narrowed. An older woman, but she had the most ageless face Alek had ever seen on a mortal. She was as near to omnipotent as any human he had ever known, and he reminded himself that next to nothing happened in this town without Tahlia Braxton's approval. She was quite literally a one-woman mob, probably capable of committing murder itself and getting away with it. And here he was, begging her interest.

He said, after a long breath, "I really don't know how to ask you this, but do you—can you—I—"

"We were lovers, Byron and I," she said.

For a moment the world took a half-turn around him. He looked out at the rough beginnings of a savage midwinter's storm gathering in the form of chrome-colored clouds above, the missions and soup kitchens locked tight against the night on distant 79th

Street, wondering when the world had gone another level of crazy around him. Finally, he looked again at Tahlia. He swallowed, felt the curious edges of fate or coincidence brush past his shoulder like a wing. "Excuse me?"

Another cigarette. Suddenly he saw the worry and the past, some secret sorrow, take root in Tahlia's storm grey eyes. She said, "This—it's about Byron, right?"

Alek shivered, but not from fear. "How do you know that? Or dare I ask that question?"

"You dare," she answered him levelly. "But dare ask it inside, won't you? I'm freezing my ass off here."

He nodded. He moved to open the alley side door for her, but just as he did so, just as he was about to follow Tahlia inside to discover all her secrets, another shiver. And then a dark, bone-slender figure moved out from behind one of the Corinthian columns at the top of the museum steps. It had begun to snow. The figure stood maybe a hundred feet away, but even were the storm a living holocaust of white, he would have been able to identify it alone by its feral, saint-like posture. With a tip of his head the man started down the wide Roman steps.

Alek said to Tahlia, "Will you give me a moment?"

Without a word or change of expression, Tahlia walked inside. No answer. But her posture, the turn of her shoulders, said a universe of things. Be quick. We have much to discuss. Teresa started toward him, but he held up a hand. Wait for me? She nodded and he turned back.

Book, standing on a step halfway down the stairwell, sank his hands into his coat pockets and looked over his shoulder at the banners hanging on the face of the Metro. He sighed as Alek approached, his breath pluming in the darkness. A moment of silence passed. And then he said, "I remember a time when we stood at a window and you shouted at me, and I think the entire house shook for you." He laughed. "I even remember your face, your expression, that Brooklyn-born don't-the-fuck-get-in-my-way look you were wearing. Funny the things we remember."

"I don't have a sword," Alek said, stopping a step below his brother, their gazes even.

"But the house shook. It was yours. It was always yours."

"The house was his, Book."

Book sighed once more, looked at him, past him. His flesh was beaded with the sweat of his unreleased energy. Alek watched the falling snow melt off his face and shoulders in tiny, running rivulets of moisture. He was an island of suffocating warmth in the midst of the cold night. "Do you really believe I want to kill you, brother?" he asked.

"Yeah."

Book laughed miserably and the heat was gone. "Should know better than to try and outfeel an empath. You fuckers know other folks' feelings better than your own."

"But you won't do it. Yet."

Book snorted, looked away. "I should. I'm really thinking about it, Alek."

"Don't try. You don't want to find out who's better," Alek said and watched the wounding of his words. "It'd kill me, but I'll cut you down in this war if you intercede. I want him, Book. I want his head."

"He gave you everything, you bastard."

"What he gave me was corrupt and spoiled."

"This is madness!" Book laughed viciously, turned his back. "Debra's madness."

Alek moistened his cold, cracked lips. They were perched on the ledge of the world now, teetering, ready to fall. And now, with no voice and no argument, he was forced to explain to this man what he could not explain to himself.

"He saved you from Debra," Book said. "Christ, Alek, he saved you from yourself! Do you know what would have happened to you if he hadn't intervened? Do you have any fuckin' idea what you'd be today?"

"I wouldn't be a slayer."

"No, you'd just be out there on the streets ripping throats out."

Alek breathed in a mouthful of cold, bitter air. He tasted steel and acid and the coming war. "So he takes us in, so he gluttons us with books and art and music, so what? So fucking *what*? It's still there, Book. The madness. You act like some fucking virgin. You mean you never think about it—killing something? Maybe someone—?"

"Course I think 'bout it! We all do, damnit. But thinkin' don't make us animals, the doing—that's the problem. But that's why we have the Coven, the slayings—"

Alek harrumphed. "You think killing all those vamps takes it away? You think you'll wake up one morning and it'll just be gone like a virus or something? All the killing used up? I think we're stuck with it forever. What do you think? You even *have* an opinion of your own anymore?"

Book let out a raw breath. "I think you're crazy as bat shit, Alek."

He felt numb. Nothing could penetrate him now. Nothing at all. His armor was fully forged. "He killed Debra," he heard himself say in a scorched voice too full of years and sorrow. "It was all his game. He killed her so he could have me all to himself. He even bent the prerogative of the fucking Church to have me. And believe me, there's nothing pure in his intentions, Book, nothing at all."

Book looked appalled, as if his brother had spoken against God Himself, uttered the blackest profanity. He shook himself, looked everywhere. "You know what we are and you know what it means. You know what it's like to belong to no one and nothing. The Coven is everything, brother, because it's the *only* thing." He shook his head. "Goddamnit, I don't want to watch you die, but I don't want the Coven to die either. And if you kill it, you bastard, I'll kill you back, I swear to God I will."

Alek nodded, turned away his face and let the storm buffet his profile to numbness. He watched the limos skim down Fifth Avenue like black sharks on their way to a mass feeding frenzy. "I suppose then it's going to he different the next time we meet. We won't be brothers anymore."

"Can you accept that?"

"I suppose I have to." He blinked the snow from his eyes, wiped it from his cheek and throat. "He's killed, Book, you know. The innocent and the guilty. He killed Akisha. That wasn't sanctioned. It wasn't even necessary. Sean's a killer too."

"Casualties of our war, Alek Knight."

He felt cold. "I just wanted you to know."

"I know." Book laughed again in utter despair and drew his sword. A bone-handled tachi, it reached an easy forty-six inches. He turned and set it against his brother's collarbone. It gleamed there like the dirty white ice at his feet, utterly real. Cold.

"You'll be celebrated a thousand years," Alek said, watching Book's eyes and not the sword. "They'll put your face in the Abbey. Hell, they'll probably make you Covenmaster." He felt nothing. "Is that what you want?"

Book's lips quivered back in a silent snarl. He looked ready to spit venom like the legendary Lilith who had created them out of Adam's wayward seed. But instead of striking, either in weapon or word, he dropped the sword to the packed snow at Alek's feet and started down the remainder of the steps.

Alek picked it up. "Book?"

Book turned around. The snow melted and ran away from his feet in a widening pool like stop motion photography or some sort of special affect. It ran slowly down the stairs of the Metro. Bubbled. Boiled. "I don't need a sword to do you. Remember that."

Alek said nothing, did nothing.

"Take it," Book said. "Maybe it'll save you. Maybe not." His expression fell from anger to utter neutrality. He said everything and nothing at all in one long tragic glance. I love you. I hate you. Go to fucking hell, you damned traitor—

"Book," Alek finally said, anything to break the silence and the cold and the unnatural heat weighing in on them both.

Book looked back.

"Did you tell him I'm here?"

"What do you think, brother?" Then he turned away, and on

the ledge of the world Alek watched him walk away and shrink into a silhouette down on Fifth Avenue, a bit of darkness against the pale foot of the Metro.

"Damn you, Book." Alek snuffled, breathing in the white claustrophobic air and the bitter snow and cold and the deep heart of midnight. He waited for at least a single tear to fall, but it was stubborn in the end. And after a few moments he gave up and started back up the stairs.

18

She was waiting for him in the Wallace Wing for Modern Art. He saw her as the crowd parted for him.

And then he saw the painting hanging on the wall behind the roped-off area, the painting Tahlia Braxton was studying so intently. It was a woman with chains upon her face and her arms upraised to an encroaching storm, a stainless steel apple in her hand.

"I like your work," Tahlia said.

Alek looked around the hall, the people, but they might as well have been alone because no one looked his way this time.

Tahlia lowered her gaze, looked up at him piously from beneath her feathery lashes as if he was some interesting painting or sculpture to be appraised and categorized. Alek felt a curious mixture of relief and gratitude, as if the matter of his talent might end there. But Tahlia had other plans. From the tone of her voice he was almost certain she was merely being polite. "But I think you are greedy. You play at feelings, yes, but you also hide behind them."

Her bizarre critiquing of his work caught him off-guard. His head jerked up and he almost completely forgot his reason for being here. "What...do you mean?"

She indicated the painting with a flourish of her hand. "Art is suffering. Every great artist suffers. It is the human condition that makes him suffer—loss, sorrow, the futility of love, the fears of mortality. You have painted loss. But the loss you paint is a sham and of little consequence. You paint darkness, but it is the darkness you imagine men feel, the darkness you believe waits for them at the end of their lives. It is not *your* darkness. The only work which almost touches your brilliance is this one. You are greedy and you keep the darkness and the loss and, ultimately, the beauty, to yourself. You keep it within, afraid to expose it to the sun. And because of that greed, because of that petty need to hide your beauty, you will never be great."

She spoke quietly, earnestly, without condescending him, and Alek knew in his heart that she was right. He also knew that she had studied his work, all of it, for this painting he considered his best. He had poured everything he had at the time into the image. But there was also the uneasy feeling that somehow or other he had traded on misfortune to create it, like a fascinated bystander at the scene of a gruesome car accident.

Tahlia shrugged noncommittally. Again as if his fears and agenda were plain for her to see. "An artist is a vampire, Alek, did you know? He drinks the pain and sorrow out of the wounds of others and turns that pain and sorrow into immortality. And when you do that you raise a monument to his or her memory. You make your sufferers truly immortal."

She started walking down the hall, her heels clocking on the exotic tiles of the floor. He followed her. They were joined by someone he hadn't noticed in the room with them until now. And as they emerged from the preening mass of people, he found Teresa walking beside them both like a great animate artist's doll.

"You have," Alek said, watching Teresa, "an unusual perspective, Mrs. B—Tahlia."

"Perhaps I am more like you than unlike you. Even for our obvious differences." She snagged two glasses of wine off a passing tray and offered one to him.

Alek hesitated, the fear of being bated somehow hovering near. He took the wine and held it. "I'm not sure I understand what you mean," he said at last.

"You choose to be evasive." She stopped when they had reached the primordial wing of the museum. It was less crowded, and propriety seemed to fall away more easily. She boldly put her hand over a yellowish skull on a plinth; it was a great feline skull, extinct, with saber teeth, but she touched it like a pet she had once loved. "We could play that game, yes. But I rather doubt you have much time left. The Coven is closing in on you."

His head spun. For a moment, yet again, he almost felt as if Akisha were again with him, motherly and protective, yet a brutal predator to him as well. "Who are you?"

"Tahlia Frencesca Braxton," she answered.

"No—*who* are you? How do you know Byron? And the Coven? What do you know about that?"

She smiled. Demure. She drank her wine. "You seek the Chronicle. Paris's Chronicle. Am I right?"

Alek said, "How can you...?" He shook his head, mystified.

Tahlia nodded and sucked back on her smoke with careful passion. Then she halved her eyes like some wily cat. "Oh, this is before your time, my dear. I was a regular wet-nose myself when I knew Byron. A debutante, if such a thing still existed in the forties. Long time ago, back when the dinosaurs ruled the earth."

He looked up, staring at the erected skeleton of a suropod suspended like a cage of bone far overhead.

Tahlia tipped her head, again catlike. A secretive woman, but full of secrets she could no longer hide. Or chose not to. "Of course you won't find anything in those artsy books on Byron. He was a cartographer in the French army, did you know? He also raided tombs in Egypt and pyramids in South America. Later on, he played the tragic eccentric painter, all right, but within reason. You see, Byron didn't care at all about upping his piece value if it meant drawing every goddamn slayer down out of his hole like flies to a carcass."

Alek was frozen to the floor with fascination.

Tahlia smiled her wide, toothy, movie-star smile. Suddenly she became the White Bird again, the cat no longer. "His exhibits were on loan here"—she indicated the museum as a whole—"and Byron came following after. What folks today call a tour. Only they called it abroad then. Anyway, Byron told me everything about Paris and the Coven—about the coward who calls himself Amadeus. Byron used to wander the galleries after closing, sit and study the frescoes. And could Byron talk. Said he remembered the Bastille, the Occupation. Napoleon, Hitler—they were all the same to him. When you were as old as he was it all starts running together, he said. Only art bookmarks time." She glanced around. "He pointed to a hundred different pieces he'd done under a hundred different names. He used to laugh he'd died a thousand deaths a poor, proud painter."

Then she nodded to herself. "And me...well, I guess I was his Renfield. At first. At least until the night he started showing me the basics of watercolor in his Village loft and finished up showing me other things." She fell to a meditative silence and watched the floor, her eyes alight with memories, some sweet, some so sad they were a palpable emotion between the two of them, like the fragrance of a woman's skin, the brush of silk.

Alek closed his eyes, opened them. He wandered closer to the woman, examining her mature but in no way unbeautiful face. The lines there were not imperceptible, but instead of aging her as they should have, they only gave her a mysterious character. She was like one of his own, but not. She was mortal. Wasn't she? "You can't be in your seventies. It's not possible."

"Seventy-six," she said, reaching for a sip of wine. "The blood of his kind...it acts rather like an elixir on human tissue, did you know?" She smiled, but now somehow infinitely sadly, as if she'd been asked to speak of the dead. Her hand grew utterly still over the cat skull. Still now, she was like a work of art saying much by saying nothing at all. Then the portrait came alive. The portrait said, "We both expected him to bury me. We never expected we would have only thirteen years out of an eternity. Thirteen years..."

Teresa approached the human woman and took her hand from off the cat skull and held it prayerfully between both of her own. Was this possible now, this icon? Predator subservient to prey? But it was. It was.

"Love is dangerous," she said. "I am sorry for your loss, but all of us here have lost someone."

Tahlia narrowed her eyes, set her wine aside, and sealed the icon with her second mortal hand. "I married Charlie—I don't know, I suppose I thought it would help me find the answers I needed. The names of the people involved in Byron's disappearance. Charlie knows so much of this town. But nothing ever came of it." She smiled sweetly and sadly. "Byron was not a man you would have liked to know, sister. Too old. Full of bitter drink. And I fear some of it has rubbed off on me."

"I know the one you seek, cara," Teresa whispered, her black lashes skating her white cheeks as she dropped her eyes.

"I'd heard a name once, a woman, Deb—"

"Amadeus."

It was enough to slay her speech. She looked ready to protest, but Teresa chose to gift her with her attention again and something in Teresa's eyes stopped her. The truth.

"Debra—was Byron's lover for a time, but never his slayer," Teresa said.

Tahlia hesitated a moment. Then she nodded, numb perhaps straight to the bone. Alek could feel the shock pouring off of her in freezing-hot waves. It was like an epiphany. It was like death. Or a bizarre rebirth. He couldn't imagine it—to spend your whole life in the revenge business, chasing a woman who was already dead.

Unspent tears gleamed in Tahlia's eyes. She glanced querulously around the room as if searching for something or seeking an escape. "I am sorry. I'm a foolish old woman. And a bad hostess. If there's anything I can get you—?"

"There is." Alek withdrew the handmade map and gave it to her.

Tahlia looked it over for a moment. Then she looked up.

"It's Byron's work, Tahlia."

"I know. You do wonderful reproductions," she said.

He took a deep breath, wondering how to phrase this correctly. "Then maybe you know why I'm here."

"You're here for the Chronicle," she said, and Alek felt his heart skip. "Byron told me. He said he had it, that someone would come for it one day. But no one ever did." Her husky smoker's voice faded to a whisper. Then nothing. "Debra," she said the name, finally. "Who was she?"

"Just another victim." Alek looked aside. His voice, when it came haltingly a few moment's later, sounded to himself like a lone wind through a tunnel of rocks. "Tahlia...Do you have it, still? The Chronicle? Did Byron give it to you?"

She will say no. For a moment he was absolutely sure. She will say no, that Byron died before he ever gave it to her. She will say no, sorry kids, he didn't, and that will be that.

"Yes."

Alek started like a man kicked. His heart fluttered. "You have it? You really do?"

Tahlia hesitate, but only a moment. Then she moved robotically to one of the glass-encased display cases and removed a small key from her pocket. She opened it and for several moments studied the archaic tomes spread out on blue silk under moody lights. Then she chose the brown one in a broken leather cover. The book had been there all along but he had never noticed it in detail, never realized its significance.

Tahlia said, holding it, "I made up a story about how I had gotten this book. That it was an antiquity I had gotten in an auction in Rome. I didn't want Charlie to know. I still don't." She looked up at him. Not imploringly, but with comradeship.

"Your secret dies with me," he said. "I swear it."

The book was unaccountably heavy in his hands. And now Alek felt such relief and long-stayed fatigue he wondered if he wouldn't simply fall to the floor in a faint. He didn't know what they would find when they translated the Chronicle, did not know if it would really be enough to save him, but here at least there was dated, living proof of what the Vatican had planned for the

vampires, proof that the Coven was a useless mental fixation, a
Judas goat that would one day very soon lead all the others to
slaughter.

He looked again at the title-less, innocuous book. For a moment
he did nothing but stare at it, the swirls of dust on the battered
brown leather cover, the mark of fingerprints on it. And then he
looked up at Teresa, to share the happiness.

But her face was a bitter mask, her eyes stormy. He tried to tell
himself that this was a moment of joy and discovery, but already a
chill had taken root in his belly like a little worm. The blood slowed
in his veins. He hated that look on her face, hated her for having it
now.

She shook her head. And then she lowered her eyes.

"Is that why he died?" Tahlia whispered.

Alek gave in and opened the book. Latin. He read the first
words on the first page to himself.

In the beginning God created the heavens and the earth.

He touched the ancient page, concentrated on the words as if
they would change before his very eyes.

In the beginning God created the heavens and the earth...

In the beginning...

No. That wasn't true. This wasn't real. They had worked for
this. They had bled for this.

But was it a joke, then? A joke with an evil punch line?

In the beginning God...

"Alek?" Tahlia.

"There is no Chronicle," he said. Or at least, none here. None
in the States. None that Byron had possessed. Paris...what had he
done? Was it still in Rome, then? Did it even exist at all anymore?

Teresa put her hand on him. He retreated from the contact and
snarled through his nose and his bitter, tasteless mouth. He
narrowed his eyes, felt the beauty of his own monstrosity seize him
and blacken the pits of his eyes. Other patrons moved aside. He
would be ugly then, ugly like the monster at the end of the story
when it sheds the final level of its humanity like a bad skin. Like a

snake. Like what he was, under the man. The snake. The monster that could scare even the most sophisticated and jaded back to their childhood fears. He would be ugly because it was what he was, had always been, would always be.

He scarcely recalled his next move, only dropping the book and escaping the heat and glare of the museum, the people, the human people. He needed the cold. His city. He ran mindlessly. He found the door and started climbing down the steps, but the steps rose up like a mountain of marble constructed with the sole purpose of tripping him up. Climbing it, he lost faith and fell to his knees. So he gave in and crawled like an infant down them, like an animal, and managed to make it to the bottom where the storm had picked up and he could feel the scorching cold battering him like voices from the past, voices that would live forever, immortal. He wanted to fly, to be lifted by the power of the storm and the voices, but he was too heavy and earthbound.

He fell. Broken. Finished. There was white now in his hair, and he thought with giddy amazement, I am Amadeus after all. As was foretold, as is preordained. We really are one. Why do I care?

The book. The useless book.

Written for Man. For the Chosen of God.

Not for him and his. Not for his kind.

Not for the vampire. Never that.

Why am I fighting it?

And she found him like that, the little whore, found him weeping at the foot of the Metro with his hands over his face and tearing through his hair, weeping with the black humor of complete irony and his forgotten pain. And he looked at her over one shoulder, spitting frozen strands of his hair away, in complete abhorrence of all she was. Fucking whore. That was what she was. Monster. Medusa who bad bewitched him. Eve who had led him astray.

Lilith.

Cunt.

"Caro," she spoke softly, coming toward him. "Beloved—"

He exploded. "Don't say that!" he spat. He tried to rise, failed. *"Don't ever fucking call me that, you fucking bitch!"*

She frowned and reached for him, and he cowered, bared his teeth in a treacherous smile like an animal trapped in its warren with no hope of escape. He was cold, cold as death, and it was dark and her face glowed pale and as perfect as the cold Valentine moon overhead, a moon that never left, that would keep him in its lunar spell forever.

But she was not Debra, had never been Debra. Debra was dead. And now, at last, so was he.

She loved him, perhaps, but what she loved was dead and loveless. "I never asked for you," he told her with enormous honesty and articulation. "I'm not like you! *I'm not like you at all!* I hate you, I hate you to death, to hell!"

She recoiled. Perhaps she wept or died under his words, but what did it matter? It was his craft to destroy, his obligation. It was what Amadeus had fashioned him for, his only purpose

He was a slayer.

A machine built for only one purpose.

He was an angel, a harbinger of death.

And like a machine, he wept tears of blood.

INTERLUDE 3

1

His dreams were full of blood and trouble and he woke from them gratefully.

He woke but did not open his eyes.

He woke beneath the weight of a heavy tome.

He woke sensing intuitively that it was their birthday today, his and Debra's. Valentine's Day. The day of their birth, thirteen years ago.

He wondered where Debra was, wished he knew so that he could say to her what he was thinking, so she could share his odd emotions of memory and mourning with her. But she was never around much anymore, rushing here and there with those musicians and biker-types she seemed to favor to his company, lingering only long enough to fight with him or taunt him and call him a slayer—though, in fact, he had not yet even presented a single offering to the altar, hadn't even yet experienced his Grand Testing. Still, the word slayer came off her tongue like a freshet of deadly poison profanity.

Slayer. What are you afraid of, slayer? What do you want, slayer?

In the last five years Debra had tried shamelessly to lure him from the arms of the Coven to the world she'd said she'd discovered beyond its walls, a world alien and strange and ugly and full of things brief and breakable.

And the other slayers talked.

Debra knew the city hives a little too well, those of Carfax and others. She knew Akisha, Carfax's chosen mate, a little too well. She had taken him to the club a few times and Akisha had given him looks from across the room, but he just shuddered and made for the door. At home, Debra dueled in cruel words with the

Father and others of the Coven. She treated her people like her enemy. She treated the vampires in the city like her fucking *family*. She tortured his brother Book with teasing touches and obscene promises and her sinisterly lashed brown eyes

In five years Debra had learned nothing. Become nothing.

And now she was gone. Today. On their birthday.

It was their fight last night, he knew.

"It does exist! Byron says and Byron knows everything about everything!"

He had been in his cell, oiling his sword, when she started, burnishing it with a cloth and making a mirror of the blade. Trying to avoid the coming fight. Debra was poised across the table in her silk camisole, the fabric like a sheer red mist around the new, demanding angles of her body. A body she no doubt used to get Akisha and this Byron character to do whatever she wanted them to. And what tricks did she ask of them? What games did they play in those underground leather bars? He couldn't help but wonder about the black painted walls of the Lower Eastside club called The Abyssus that she so favored. Better to hide bloodstains?

And Byron. What the hell kind of name was Byron anyway?

"Alek."

He looked away. This does not concern me.

"Look at me, Alek."

He looked at his sword instead.

"You bastard," she said, her voice coarse now, the roundness of womanhood tainted with the fury of childhood still. "You fucking bastard, how could you think those things?"

He looked up at last, looked her up and down. The way she painted and pierced herself up these days, she reminded him of the dollar whores that hung with the pushers and pimps on the wharf near the Hudson. How else could he think?

But where he expected a fury of grief and tears and pain at that thought going out to her, there was only pity, black and cold. "No, beloved," she whispered, "you may put your most impure thoughts aside. I am not sleeping with Byron or anyone else. Though perhaps

I should. How would that make you feel to know I was? How would you feel to know I was selling my body?"

His fingers bit into the hilt of the sword until the blood fled from his cuticles.

"Why don't you look at me anymore? You know my face; you know my body. What are you afraid of, *slayer*?"

She snaked narrowly across the length of the table that was all that separated them and all that saved him from her. She seized his hands, and by consequence his sword dropped uselessly to the table. "What are you afraid of, little Puritan?" she asked once more and pressed his hands to the cold poreless flesh of her face that was so like the stone skin of some savage goddess stolen from her sacred garden. "This?"

No. Of course not.

"This?" she asked in a little hiss as she moved his hands to the new perfect fullness of her breasts under the gauzy material.

Still he did nothing, felt the whole of his being tremble with silent fear.

She smiled with divine wickedness. "How about this?" she hissed and lowered his hands further, down over her belly, down further—

He jerked and stood up away from her, his chair toppling. How he wanted to harm her in that moment, but what could he say that she would believe? What could he call her that she would not laugh off?

She came around the table, stalking him like a predator, and trapped him against the wall of his cell. She put her hands on him, kissed him. He resisted her at first, and then he did not. It seemed pointless. She kissed his mouth, licked it like a puppy licking the lips of her beloved owner. But not like a puppy would kiss.

And then her hands were on him like her kisses, her hands on his lower back, and then lower still, cupping his backside and pressing him against her. And he felt something alien surge inside him. Felt it grow and gather like a bad storm. Felt it pull at his insides until they ran.

"Don't you love me anymore, Alek?" she whispered against his mouth in her aching, breathy little girl's voice.

"You're my life," he told her honestly.

She kissed him again, but lightly this time, at only the corners of his mouth. "Then be with me. Believe in me. Believe in Byron. We can leave here tonight and go and have all kinds of adventures." She smiled, dropped her voice conspiratorially. "Byron says he has the Chronicle. He says no one will dare oppose us with it. Come with us—we can have so much fun!"

He touched her rosy, flushed cheek with sadness. "The Chronicle is a story, Debra. A joke. Byron's just leading you on."

Debra hissed and dashed his hands away from her face. "It's real! Damnit, Alek, the streets whisper the story if you'll only listen. It's not a story! It's all real!" She took a deep breath, composed herself, and said, "The humans will kill us, Alek. Soon. Because they don't understand. They'll never understand! And it won't matter then what name we put on ourselves, dhampir, slayer, it won't matter! We're marked, do you understand me? Marked."

He narrowed his eyes at her, at this foolishness she'd nettled from her restless jaunts into the city underground, foolishness she was no doubt being fed by underworld life forms who went around calling themselves names like Byron. He knew his catechism. He knew the words of the sacred Covenant by heart. "Amadeus says it's a myth," he tried to explain. "A story, Debra, contrived by the vampires in their fear of the church. There is no Chronicle. The Father—"

"Damn the Father!"

"The Father says—"

"Fuck the Father!"

He let her go. This was useless. It was 1962 and the whole world was mad with ideas. War. Peace. The Summer of Love. More war. Everyone was just fucking out of their mind. He went, solemn, back to his seat and began to shine his sword once more.

"*Slayer*," Debra hissed as she dressed herself for the night. "Go on and draw the blood of your own people, Alek. Bathe in it. Drown in it for all I care. Go on and stay here in this cage and be the pet of Amadeus the Mad." She faced him in her leather coat, links of bone growing from her ears, her eyes dusky with makeup, her lips a bitter, brutal red gash as she leaned forward and breathed in his ear. "But be warned, beloved, there will be a reckoning, a Dies Irae, and it will be sung at the Requiem Mass of the Covenmaster Amadeus, the betrayer of all our people."

And then she stalked artistically away.

And now, awakening, he realized that she was gone. Out at one of her haunts. On their birthday. Where was she? He wanted to—

I'm here.

He gasped and felt the thin, perfect weight upon him that was not some large tome.

Alek opened his eyes.

She was astride him, her knees locked around his hips. She had undone the buttons of his nightshirt in his sleep and her nakedness and heat was soldered to his own as natural as two old links. Her face came up from where it had been lying in the hollow of his throat. Her hands flashed out, greedy and powerful, and pinned his shoulders. She peered down at him from under her sooty lashes as if to observe him from an enormous height. She smiled. She breathed on his face, his throat. "Happy birthday to you," she sang softly as her eyes deepened, blackened. "Happy birthday to you. Happy biiirthday, dear beloved, happy birthday to you..."

He tried to utter her name as if in doing so he could stop her, seize her up in mid-stride, but her mouth was too quick to cover his own and kill the sound. He felt her mind touch his in an intimacy that was new and frightening, and he tried to think of thoughts to anger her, to make her go, but nothing came, no argument, no rebuke, only an unformed plea for completion. She kissed him and he shuddered fiercely beneath her work, the shell carefully placed around him by five long years of Coven practice, that shell with its volumes and Rites and ordinances, its music and art and study, suddenly cracked open and allowed all the doubt and dread and passion to pour into him like strange waters.

His hands sought her back as she leaned over his throat, kissed and licked a seamless path to his lips, her hair tenting them in together. He held her, crushed her to him, body and soul. He shuddered once more, but what she'd destroyed now was the barrier of his own self-consciousness. He lifted the heavy veil of her hair away from her face and kissed her, his teeth hard at her lips, for the first time in years freely admitting his need for her, for the completion she brought to him. He feared her and he feared he would lose himself in her and would disavow the Coven, but the fear of dying without ever knowing her was far, far worse. And then she was kissing him back and the past and the future were as unreal as shadows, vanishing into only the now, and now there were no rules, no Covens, no names for what they were, no distinctions, no borders drawn by philosophers' hands to separate them from the Children of Eve or the Lilith.

What am I doing?

His eyes fluttered closed under the assault of her mouth, and he realized all at once that they belonged to all the races, all at once, impossibly, like an ethereal enchantment. She growled deep in her chest, her lips yielding, then demanding of him, fitting his as if they were only one body. Her hands slid under his shirt, down further, bold arcs of fire over his chill, a sacred dance across his naked flesh until his body came alive under her like a separate thing.

What what what am I doing?

And when he ventured forth to do the same, to trace the sacred lines of her perfumed flesh, her arms, her breasts, every delicate bone, first with his fingertips and then with his lips, he felt her thoughts, her eagerness, the hunger bottled up inside her all these long years. And his own. And together that one voice abolished the last of reason and Amadeus from his mind.

My life. My blood and flesh and strength. Impossible to say whose thought.

Reaching, he laid his palm to her cheek, touching her carefully, as if she were as delicate as she seemed, and inside the intimacy of the touch he sensed the edge of some shadow, some shade of grief buried deep within her, as if she knew their love could only end in goodbye.

"It's all right, Debra," he told her. "I'm here and I won't let us be apart."

Her eyes looked wet, impossibly far away. "You can't know forever, beloved. Don't try."

"I don't un—"

"Quiet, beloved. We have no future and no past. Only this. Only now."

He could make not a sound, could not even move, when her lips brushed away and rested at his temple and he felt her fleet pulse under his mouth, the rush of her blood like the voice of the ocean in his ears. Hesitantly he kissed her throat. Then, afraid he would hurt her, he gathered her breast in his hand and kissed the delicate rose-tip, first with his lips and then with his teeth, and the yolky, familiar taste he'd not known in a lifetime of five years pooled into his mouth, keening his senses, narrowing them to the point of near pain, where he felt certain they could fly from the very skin of the earth if they so desired.

Debra gasped and moved against him in her delight and her need. "Fly with me, Alek," she pleaded in her sweet little voice, hot in his ear, impossible to deny. "Tonight. Before it's too late, before—" Her voice cracked on such a sigh of joy and pleasure he found he had no words to deny her. Found he had no heart to.

So much to say, to tell her, show her...and if she left him, what then? What would he be without her? He didn't know, didn't want to discover what. So he let her go and told her yes, yes, beloved, because he must and because he chose to, and kissing her, disentangling himself from her, he prepared to leave with her that very night.

2

"You can't go, you can't!"

Alek packed the last of their things in a single suitcase, his and Debra's favorite books and clothes and sketches, Debra's doll. He touched Debra's ring at his throat on its chain, the one she had given him before leaving last night, and looked up. It was early evening, just after practice in the Abbey, just before dinner in the dining room, and Book stood by the dolphin window, the diffused bluish light of dusk on his cheek and white cotton oxford shirt, giving his upper half the all-over look of grey marble, a statue scarcely alive. But his eyes moved, blinked, fluttered with disbelief.

"For chrissakes, Alek—"

"I can't stay, Book. Not...now." He tossed aside his skein of too-long hair and forced the last articles into the carpetbag, shirts and trousers, no habits, a pair of scissors, no sword. The sword remained wrapped and untouched under his bed. Almost a shame, it was such a beautiful piece of art, but where would he need it? "You don't understand what it's like. I belong to her, it's—hard to explain."

"You'll be just *like* her," Book argued. "The Father says. You'll *turn*..."

But Book didn't understand, couldn't understand. Book was homeless without the Coven, family-less. Book was the Father's son; Alek was only his resident.

And, of course, Book didn't have Debra.

"Turn into what?" Alek asked, angry now, angry for a target. "A fucking bat? Fucking Bela Lugosi?"

"You know what. Christ, Alek, you can't just walk out!"

"Keep your voice down!" he hissed, sitting on the suitcase to squash it and latch it tight.

Book flared his nostrils and looked at the window. Hot in here suddenly. Alek wished Book would cut it out with that shit. Did he want the bedclothes to go up?

He stopped fiddling with the latch, narrowed his eyes on his chosen brother. "Look—"

"Has the Father given you the Rite of Blood?" Book demanded, turning back around.

"What?"

"The Rite of Blood," Book repeated, sounding angry, betrayed. "Have you tasted his blood?"

Alek lifted the suitcase, almost did not answer, then set it down. "What kind of question is that?"

"Answer it."

"No."

"You have."

"It's none of your fucking business if I have or not!" Alek shouted, momentarily forgetting to hush his voice. He shivered, held perfectly still, held his breath and wondered if the Father would stalk in at any moment in a storm of black robes and white hair and find him like this, in the midst of betrayal. But Amadeus did not mystically appear and Book only continued to look wounded, ever more betrayed. They'd never kept secrets from each other, the two of them; they were brothers, damnit, but this thing—

"You never told me," said Book.

Alek hefted the suitcase and this time did not set it down. "It doesn't matter to me," he said.

"It matters to him. You belong to the Father. He'll hunt you down."

What did he care? He'd shared blood with Debra. But in that case it was different; the blood was Debra's, belonged to her. With Amadeus it was only borrowing. Amadeus understood that. "He won't hunt me," he retorted, and his voice sounded very brave and sure to himself. Like the cheer of a Viking before they went into battle, he thought. Why shouldn't it? "He loves me, he said so. And he's always let us come and go."

"He lets Debra come and go."

Alek shook his head and walked in his street clothes to the door of his cell. Why was he arguing over an already done act? Useless. The pact was sealed with their blood, his, Debra's. Not borrowed, born. He'd promised Debra to love her forever and he had to keep his promise. He twisted the doorknob and spoke without turning. "You going to tell him I'm gone, Book?"

"I don't need to, brother," he answered.

3

Under the white scythe of the moon he walked. He walked through the park, toward the familiar shape of the carousel, toward Debra and her Byron. He was supposed to meet the two of them here for their midnight rendezvous and flight from the city.

Byron was an artist and Road Hog, said Debra. He had connections wherever the road went. Byron, the modern gypsy. And where would they go? Anywhere, said Debra. Once she arranged it they could travel to Hollywood and be actors in big films, or go to the South and the swampy warmth of sinister New Orleans where Byron said all the creatures of the night were. They could go anywhere, do and be anything. Anything at all.

And they'd be together forever.

They could love each other forever.

He reached the carousel and saw that it was still and vacated, with only the ticking of the revolver and the soft thunder of the wind caught in the canopy to greet him. Where were Debra and Byron? He stopped and looked around, searching for some clue.

There, on the opposite side of the carousel, was a trike. Byron's?

Alek minced around the big wheel of animals to the other side. Yes, a trike, grey and silver. He touched it and looked up, wondering where everyone was.

Byron lay, stretched lean, on the track between two horses, his head turned aside and his eyes watching Alek with something akin to amazement, offense. Yet they saw nothing at all. Alek felt his heart lurch into his throat. He swallowed it down. He was certain it was Byron, ponytailed black hair, black Gypsy eyes, too tall for his thinness. It might have been himself at twenty-five or thirty, and so it must be Byron whom Debra seemed to trust.

He wasn't dead long. The carousel ticked forward a little on its revolver and the moon, which before had seemed pale and elusive, illuminated the torn bloodless throat, not vampiric in appearance but purely carnivorous. And again the angry, surprised eyes.

Alek dropped his suitcase.

And ran like hell.

4

He reached the Covenhouse, let himself in, and went immediately down to the Abbey. It seemed the most logical thing to do somehow, though in fact he could not recall really considering any other option in his short, furious flight home. The Abbey. There was sanctuary there if nowhere else, a place for him to hide, alone, and think and stifle his fear and try and understand what was going on. Perhaps a place of divine revelation.

He tripped on the forty-fifth mason's step and fell into the Abbey, prostrate on the floor. He could not move. He wept soundlessly though he felt curiously devoid of emotion.

He shook and felt like a fool. Debra's fool.

After a moment he climbed to his feet.

He was not alone, after all.

So.

Amadeus stood waiting on him at the foot of the altar, dressed all in his black, the negative mane of his hair tinted gold by the holocaust of candlelight filling the void of the Abbey with its warmth. The chandelier had been lit for ceremony.

And there on the altar, in the shadow of the golgotha, lay Debra and Hanzo's blessed blade. Alek swallowed and steadied himself against a sudden rising tide of panic. It was horrible, the sight of her laid out like that. Almost like a funeral.

"You had to know," said Amadeus without moving. "Verstahen. Sometimes it is necessary to be cruel; often it is the greatest kindness of all."

Alek steadied himself, walked the promenade to the altar, drawn by the sight of the womanish girl in her black and red lying on the dais. He touched her face, moved the medusan tangles of hair from her still features. Her mouth was dirty red, her hands the same; her eyes were open and she breathed sharply, but she reacted not at all to his contact. Was she alive? Was she dead? Somewhere in between? Something brutal as a serpent and bitterly poisonous twisted inside him, choked the words in his throat like venom up from his bowels.

"Father...what...?"

"She came here to find you," Amadeus whispered. "Her young man was not the savior she expected. He wanted her but not her lover. And when she insisted, when she grew too bold, he threatened your life. He did not understand the nature of the beast."

No. Not again. Not again, goddamnit!

He said, softly, "Debra?" And shook her.

No blinking, no answer. Nothing. Nothing at all.

He sat her up and looked at her. Belladonna eyes, black as quags. Nothing there. But she could not be broken. If she was, he would know. Should know. But now as he touched her mind he felt only the presence of her absence. No wrenching or bursting. No sense of severance—only a void, deep and black and utterly still, as if what he held in his arms was dead but undeparted. Filled with the Abyss and the Lilith they all feared so much.

Undead.

"Turned," spoke Amadeus. "Her Bloodletting has crushed her mind, taken her from us—"

He shuddered, shook her violently. *"Debra!"* he screeched.

She looked through him.

"Debra! Look at me!"

"*Alek.*"

He stopped shaking her and looked at the Father as Debra's spent, weightless little body dropped onto his right shoulder. For a moment, looking upon Amadeus, the light behind him and silhouetting his darkness, he resembled something else, something gaunt and almost misshapen, something with pale filmy eyes. And in his mind, Alek again saw Byron and Wilma Bessell as they both had been, throats raw and open, screamless, eyes flat and seeing nothing, depthless, and Debra overtop the carnage with her similar eyes and her mouth slathered red like the open, hungry jaws of a lioness.

Debra. It wasn't fair. Why had she not listened to the Father, to him? Why had she not bound herself and learned her lessons and been good? They were children born of an unholy union, said the Father, and punished for their parents' sin. The sins of the father and all that. No, not fair. Not fair at all. Why did the sins of the parents have to be visited upon the children?

So the Father wept for them both. "Show her then, Alek, her beloved, the kindness that birth withheld her."

Alek held her fiercely, and yet there was a second, curiously harsher pain in his soul. It was like a muscle stretched too far and aching in release. "We don't slay our own," he repeated their creed, the words oddly foreign in his mouth, a sob, wet and almost soundless.

Amadeus moved out of the light and a little ways away, as if his presence here amidst this catharsis suddenly embarrassed him. "Debra is no longer our own. I think you know that. I think you know what she is and what must be done," he said with a gentle ache in his voice. "She has let the serpent in and now she is poisoned." He shook his head, looked away. "Come and be one of us, Alek. Be one of the alive. Put to the grave the dead and make it so that our cursed half-existence is not repeated."

The Grand Testing. The final vow, sealed with blood.

He turned and looked at the sword lying innocently before the eyes of a thousand unseeing victories. A virgin. Like himself.

But it wasn't supposed to be like this...

"Turn now," said Amadeus, coming forward to lift up the sword and offer it to him, "and you turn indefinitely, for she will sink you unknowingly into the Abyss until the light is an anathema to you and you become one of the hunted."

He looked at the beautiful weapon. Amadeus. Debra. The Chronicle. The Coven. Blood and light. Darkness and fire and the eternal living damnation of a soul with no prayers and no escape.

He promised to love her forever. And love was selfless. Love was peace, closure.

He took the sword from the Father. He looked at his reflection in the steel he kept so oiled and polished.

"Alek," asked Amadeus.

"*No!*" he wailed, turning away. "*I can't!*"

But Amadeus was not looking at his outburst and betrayal. He was staring at Debra.

Alek turned.

She was almost upon him, the teeth almost in his throat.

Amadeus...

He didn't think. He slashed the edge of the sword across the tenderness of her carotid artery and she fell back hard against the altar. Like a rag doll.

No...

He hadn't meant to hurt her!

He dropped the sword, abhorring it now, finally, and dropped to one knee. He caught his sweet, wicked sister's head before it could hit the floor and tipped it forward, momentarily stanching the overflow of blood down the front of her dress, the blood that was everywhere, the blood that was his. He coughed, tasted her loosened blood in his own throat. She was drowning. He tried to suck all the blood she was drowning on out so she could breath, but it did nothing. Nothing. It was only a kiss in remembrance. His kisses fell on her still, soulless black mouth. He told her that he loved her, that he was sorry, so sorry, but the dark light just faded from her eyes.

What did you do? What...?

He was shaking when he stood up. He was shaking uncontrollably. And yet he felt nothing. The Abyss was gone. He looked at his fallen, bloody sword. He was surprised to find how light it had become. It had grown into a part of him over the last five years and be could wield it now like a wing.

CHAPTER 4

1

Alek dreamt, and in his dream he stood in the crawling shadow of the altar of the golgotha with Teresa before him as still as a stone statue in his arms, his sword at her exposed throat. And the Father said, at a distance, "Show her then, beloved, the kindness that death withheld her." And at those sweet evil words, Alek saw his own eyes in the steel of the sword and spoke her name, Teresa, Sister Teresa, and dropped his weapon and buried his face in her shoulder. And with his lips alone he took her, drank her, became her, slowly, painfully, each long swallow of her darkness a labor. And Amadeus roared hoarsely, and the altar at their backs fell to pieces.

Now came a river of skulls, an ocean of them, some ancient, the skulls of Separatists and Colonists and Tories, some little older than he was himself, some younger. And under their assault he was smote and buried alive. And as each of those living horrors with their feral, cheated emotions covered him he felt himself weaken, becoming more a part of the hollow beast, until, at long last, his will was gone.

Hands had him then, two pairs. They dragged him up, and finally he looked upon his saviors and slayers, their flesh flawless as ice, their black deathlike coats and long hair and opal alien eyes and the studded silver torcs they wore about their necks that he had never noticed on a slayer before. The slayers hissed his name with their black, unfurling little snakelike tongues. They hissed between themselves in their old language and dragged him free of his prison of bones.

He fought them but he was a toy in their able hands.

"My children, bring me the Judas," crooned a dry, scouring

voice.

The creatures jerked him up, held him high and tight and immovable between them. One of the creatures dragged his head back by the hair to see. And there at the head of the Coventable sat the Covenmaster. And the Covenmaster was Sean Stone in black habit and white hair. He cradled the mystical Hanzo sword in his arms, but the hilt was changed now, not white jade. Obsidian, tainted. Alek looked his master over with wonder. Sean's body was innocent of trinkets, and the purity of the image was the most horrible sight of all.

Had he *ascended*? Had this lunatic become Covenmaster in his place through the Dominatio?

Sean's smile was demure, his pale eyes devoutly crazed. And when he spoke, his voice carried a vastness inside it that went far beyond his years. "I am the Covenmaster Amadeus," he said.

Not the Stone Man anymore. Of course. He had become the Father as Alek was once meant to be. He was the shell. The...host?

"I am Amadeo, Asmodeus. Aragon. I am the Chosen. I am der Vampir sklavischer. I am Covenmaster. Who are you?"

"Alek," he heard himself stammer. "The Slayer."

Sean/Amadeus laughed and Alek recognized the music of the ages in his hollow voice, the boom of the crashing sea, of thunder, the whirr of insects, the creep of a snake and all things elemental. "All this I command. All that you see is mine. Tell me, what do you have, Slayer?"

Alek's voice came unbidden, without thought. "What I have is what I am. Free." He tossed back his hair to show the lack of a torc about his neck.

Sean/Amadeus smiled with his hybrid of a mouth. "Then you have nothing. Your freedom is a lie. Your life has been in vain. And your love is bitter, Slayer. You are nothing. You were always nothing." He nodded solemnly at his Children.

The creatures smiled eagerly. Together they drove Alek to his knees and pinned his arms to his back until his body was striped with pain.

Alek choked and cursed the name of Amadeus in the oldest languages of the earth. Yet still the slayers forced his head down, down. And now he saw the currents of ichor lapping in mirrored waves at the pedestal of the Coventable. The creatures pressed his face to the substance and he breathed in its coppery sweetness and its venom. So foul. He tasted the Coven and his master's kisses. He screamed and the ichor filled his throat, choked off and stole his final breath...

"Enough Amadeus. Begone," came a savage little whisper out of the dark.

Amadeus was gone and his Children with him. Just like that. Like magic, an enchantment.

Alek gasped and came up like the drowning man he was. He drank in a greedy mouthful of untainted air and turned to find the owner of the new voice. His true savior. And in that turning the dream turned as well as so often dreams will.

He stood alone in the dark, alone but for a tall woman in a black silk gown and veil. She was as narrow as a stalk and standing at a distance like a mourner at a gravesite, an aura of angel light on her sapphire hair. Savior, he wanted to say, My sweet savior. The woman in her mourning veil and gown beckoned to him, and he rose up immediately and started after her as she began to walk away.

She walked fast, taking long strides, and he had to hurry to keep up with her. But after a moment he drew abreast of her. He so desperately wished to see the unearthly face of his angel, but her layers of netting veil concealed her features completely from him. All he could see were her eyes. Red, he thought. Red like roses. Like blood roses.

"You saved me," he said.

"Oh yes."

"Why?"

"It waits on you."

"What waits?"

"You know."

"The Ninth Chronicle? The Chronicle is false."

"It waits on you, the false Chronicle."

He touched her arm. "Who are you?"

The woman stopped. "Don't you know, beloved?" she asked and turned to face him and drew away her veils like a bride of the night. She sighed and looked on him with such gentle grief. "I lied," Debra said. "I saved you for myself. I was always a selfish creature, but you know that, my most beloved."

Strange that he should feel no fear or astonishment. Only love— love and regret and the sweetest sorrow he'd ever known. Debra. Yet not Debra. Yet her nonetheless. Some new and different Debra. An older Debra. The woman Debra. Her face ached beauty and love and her image wounded him like a sword.

He whispered her name like a prayer, the deepest part of his soul begging him to reach out and touch her pale perfect cheek, if only to prove that she was real, that she was really here now, with him. Yet he held back in the end. He'd failed her, failed her so often in so many ways. He didn't deserve this reunion, if reunion was what this was.

She smiled with infinite sadness. "You never failed me. You promised to love me forever and you kept your promise."

Alek hesitated a moment and contemplated her words. Then he slid to his knees and wept, utterly destroyed by the strength of her absolution. "I believe now, I do. But I can't do it," he wept to her feet. He kissed them. He laid himself prostrate before her like a repentant at the feet of a saint, his body wracked with sobs. "I can't find the book. I don't know what to do, Debra. I can't—"

"Hush. You can't find your way because you do not have the proper map." She touched his hair and he looked up. She was smiling sadly and offering him her hand. "Take it, Alek. Fly with me. One final time. Fly with me, beloved, as if we are still children."

"I don't understand."

"Then don't."

He hesitated only a moment more; then he placed his hand in hers.

They flew, fast and high over rivers of obsidian punctured with stars and silver monoliths corkscrewed into deadly points. They dropped like a breath, soared through darkness and through light, and where they passed he saw day birds on their wires and ledges and high places pluck their heads from beneath their wings and fly with them. They flocked around the twins, guided and escorted them, above and below and all around them, so that everywhere Alek looked he saw nettles of starlings and pigeons, the loose brotherhoods of crow.

Debra? What is this?

Your spectators, beloved. They wait on the final conflict. They stand at the door you seek.

And that door?

She looked down upon their most sacred altar.

He looked as well, and he saw and suddenly he knew. *There.*

There, she agreed. *Byron hid it there in his last moments. Because I told him to.*

But that's so easy.

Yes, of course.

Alek felt that familiar stir in his chest, that thrill. He wanted so to spiral down and touch that sacred, magical place, if only momentarily. To visit it with her like children with his young hungry heart, to adventure there, to be with her, to be young and silly and free and full of the power of the night. But now she was pulling him back, drawing him up with her, up and away, as easily as smoke caught on a thorn of the wind.

Debra?

Hush, beloved. There will be time for what you must do. For now let there be only this. Only us.

She drew him to her completely, her arms around his neck, her face buried against his throat. And real, oh yes, all of it. He sensed the demanding friction of her breasts against his chest, her soft, thick, feathery hair real, wreathing them both like her black veils and skirts as they drifted together on the current of the night wind. And when he kissed and worshipped the redness of her mouth and stroked her breasts and the long line of her thigh through her gossamer gown and saw the light of mischief and desire in her eyes, it was real, every touch and every sigh. Real, all of it. Real though they clung as ephemeral as wraiths above their midnight metropolis; real though only one of them truly lived.

Impossible, he thought. *I dream.*

Perhaps. But dream with me now, beloved. Make for us some strange new world and in that world make love to me. I've waited so long.

Alek smoothed away the veil of her hair from her face and kissed her desperately, fiercely, his mouth and body giving, taking. Wanting. And there, she tasted the same, the blood of some immortal saint and the dew on roses at midnight. So good and sweet. His love. *I adore you, my beloved, my mate,* he told her. And then he made their sacred world and it was down in that infinite other place, a place of light and shadows, color and darkness, that he laid her down and he loved her.

2

Sean dreamt, and his dreams were all red steel and full of the memory of pain. Pain that bloomed and stretched and turned him inside out, absorbing him, until he was the pain and the pain was him and Sean Stone was only the dream...

He awoke in blindness and in the echo of pain, in confusion. He mewled and pushed himself up against his bed's headboard.

His face ached. He touched his face and remembered. Remembered Doc Book's work of putting him back together again, every screaming, sutured inch of it—and before that, what Alek Knight had done to him on the stage of the Empress. The rage, the unfairness of it all. Oh, run while you can, Scarecrow, he thought, 'cause you are mine, man. Mine. The memory hurt like pain, like a migraine to all his face...

But there—the pain was going away. Sean found the abrasive end of the sutures and pulled the silvery-red threads from his face one at a time. Then he touched his pretty face, and sure, there were still stitches of pain and a general tenderness, but at least he was *whole* again.

Oh yeah.

A mirror—he needed a mirror. He took the sword—Alek's sword lying beside his bed—by the hilt and found his face in its burnished body. Yeah. Gorgeous. He looked like a million bucks again.

His tongue rasped across his fully self-restructured teeth and full pink lips. Two bright silver eyes blinked back at him. Whatever else all those slayers bitched and complained about like sorry-for-their-own-asses antiheroes, being a vamp, (even half a vamp) sure as hell had its advantages. Now if only he wasn't so damned *hungry*. He looked around absently, as if something here could satisfy him. Maybe he'd drive through Mickey D's tonight and pick up that juicy little window girl who always blushed and giggled and bleated like a sheep when he winked at her.

How did that song from Cutting Crew go? "I just died in your arms tonight," Sean sang and giggled, fell back to the mattress, still giggling, rolling with it.

And that's when the body of the whore fell off his bed and onto the floor. He hadn't even noticed it there, until now. He looked over the side of the bed, at the redhead's greying face and empty, ceilingward stare. Her throat was gone. Not just chewed and sucked, man, but fucking *gone*. Her head literally hung by strings—the spinal cord, a few ribbons of bloodless flesh and tendon, not much.

Jesus.

Had he done that?

He tried to remember what had happened after the Empress. The march. Trying to catch the rogue. Sucking a few pedestrians in passing to keep the psi going and deaden the pain in his face. The blood. The screaming. But not catching the fuck. Coming back here. Alone.

Alone.

So when had the whore come into play?

Mein Sohn...oh what has become of you?

Sean jerked, remembering now. Remembering...the android-like woman hovering near like some kind of sacrifice...Amadeus...he shuddered again, more violently...Amadeus feasting on her, not like some monster in a Hammer film, not some two-second Christopher Lee quickie, a love bite and a few sips. *Feasting*, man. Like a fucking animal. The blood a sludgy black rouge on his face and chin and throat and chest. The flesh gnashing, the cartilage crunching audibly between the subhuman teeth. Jesus, those *teeth*...

And then those teeth, that searing hot mouth on his, not biting, but offering the gift of raw red copper-iron strength in a liquid regurgitation of life itself—

Sean swallowed, giggled hysterically and drew back away from the sight of the whore, his fingers on his mouth, feeling the obnoxious crust of dried blood, his and the woman's, all over his lips and teeth and chin. He looked again at the body of the woman and realized he had to make a physical effort not to get down on his knees and bury his face in the awful remains. He bit the ham of his hand to stifle the insane noises his mouth was making, but the action only made him grunt and quickly open his jaws. His teeth felt sharper, more prominent, if that was possible. Was that possible? What the hell was possible anymore? He was some half-human freak living a nightmare inside of a nightmare. And now he had drunk the life out of some cunt who could have been his fucking mother!

Quite abruptly, the whimper gathering in his throat died at the sight of the black bathrobe cast over the foot of his bed. He centered his attention on it because it wasn't his, it was the Father's, and it was something else to look at other than the corpse congealing in a pool of black gore on his bedroom floor. A corpse that had been violated worse than anything that Sean, even with his extensive experience at the Shangri-La, and with Slim Jim, had ever seen.

He crawled like a little boy to the foot of the bed. Curious, he touched the fabric.

Not a bathrobe. A habit.

Put it on, Sean.

With a cry of surprise he leapt from the bed and looked around his room, at the concert posters on the walls, the storybooks and bone collections and CDs scattered wide, at the open-door armoire of falling-out clothes. But no one was hidden here among his things. He was alone.

Put on the habit, beloved, said the voice inside his head more directly.

Oh. Only the Father and his hocus-pocus. Well...all right.

Sean slid out of the sheer, blood-stiffened nightshirt the Father had dressed him in and shrugged into the habit, struggled with some of the little hook and eyelets, gave up on the rest of them, the ones nearest the small of his back where he couldn't quite reach. He stretched and moved around the bed, trying to get a feel for the material and using the bed to block his view of the corpse. Out of sight of the whore, he found he could think a little more clearly. He went to the full-length mirror on the backside of his armoire door. There was a little too much drag in the hem and sleeves of the habit, but otherwise it was a pretty righteous fit. Quite nice, actually. Quite... impressive. The black did him up well, gave him that same big, pale Reaper look the Father had.

He looked closely and realized that even his eyes looked weird. Too light. Pale, whitish blue.

He opened his mouth and looked closely at his teeth. Sharper.

All right, man, now what?

You must be pure. The trinkets—be rid of them.

And almost immediately, without thought or mitigation, Sean unscrewed his facial studs and earrings, broke the wires of teeth around his neck. The pieces shattered like bone on the cell's floor. He touched his face with wonder. What did he look like barren of his trophies? He knew he felt infinitely more powerful somehow, feather-light and capable of flight. Strange and wonderful. Was this the reason the Father chose to live like a fucking Spartan? Alek too?

He attention returned to the mirror and there he was witness to the birth of a new person. He touched the loose yellow silk of his jaw-cut hair, toyed with the idea of letting it go. Long. Rock-musician long. Long enough to plait. Long like the Father's was long. He saw himself then: long pale hair and black habit. Pale, somber eyes. A priest? Yeah, a priest. Or at least, priest-like. He though yet again of the whore, and suddenly the thought of living like a priest didn't seem like such a ludicrous idea after all. Before the mirror, he genuflected in the invisible presence of his Coven. "Welcome. I am the Covenmaster Stone Man," he stated, tasting the words and grimacing.

That really sucked.

Inspired, he went through the gesture again. "I am the Covenmaster...Amadeus. I am the Chosen. All that you see I comm—"

Yes, my son. The new temple of Amadeus.

Sean choked, caught in mid-bow, stiffening like a little boy caught doing something obscene to himself. He blushed in the face of the Father's shining laughter, lovely and pious and faintly mad.

The Father was pleased.

Come to me, beloved, commanded the Father. *Enter me and become...*

The music of the voice drove the dizziness of his hunger away, drove the nausea of the image of the dead girl on the floor away. It was like in the beginning. This was the lovely coarse voice of the strange man he had found sitting on the sill of his State Institution dorm room one night upon awakening, eyes like white fire in a face as pale as the full moon which had beat down upon them both. That night the Father had come to him and had known him by name and had spoken those words low and so intimately to him: *Come with me and come into the arms of the Coven, mein Sohn, into those arms which love you best of all. And who could love such a thing as you but one of your own?*

Yes, who? His mother? His mother was dead. And better off that way. Better dead than a slave to a neverending procession of strange men night after night. Better dead, he thought with a sideways glance at the dead whore, than a victim of a monster.

And so, without hesitation, Sean let himself out of his cell and started down toward the Great Abbey. He did not feel the cold of the twisting corridors carrying him along, nor the stone steps under his feet, meeting them so graciously as he descended into the beauty and immortal secrets of the old house. The Abbey would receive him and there he would see his beautiful, white-faced Father waiting on him, speaking low the words he so cherished. The words he so longed to hear. *My love...my own.*

But when he arrived he found the Father did not sit in his usual perch at the head of the Coventable. Instead, he was kneeling on the dais in the shadow of his altar, the wedge of his pressed hands resting at his mouth, his sight miles off.

The chandelier had been lit as if for ceremony, its whitish power bruising the stone walls of the Abbey and blushing the strong old faces on the tapestries. A halo of it circled the Father like an angelic laser of light. Sean took in the sight, the lit candles, the shining stained glass, the Abbey itself vacated but for the two of them and a handful of surviving bats irritated to restless flight by the alien impinge of light. Slowly, almost fearfully, he walked to the nave, then up the steps to the dais, so that the two of them, himself and the Father, existed in the Altar's shadow equally.

Sean knelt down and looked aside at the Father.

Amadeus spoke.

"Alek knows the location of the Chronicle," said the Father.

Sean shuddered but did not show it. The Chronicle. It was half their problem. Their other half, of course, was Alek himself. But the idea, suddenly, of the two problems coming together, converging—Alek actually getting the goddamned Chronicle—hung like a dooming storm over Sean's thoughts. That lying piece of shit book was probably enough to totally undo the precarious relationship they already had with Rome. Or so said the Father. "Shit. Where?"

Amadeus told him.

"There. Christ, that's dumb."

"It is fitting. It is the place of beginnings, and it is just that it be the place of his defeat."

"Is he there now?"

"Nein. His is with her in a place that is closed to me. I know only that he makes love to her, that he drinks of her power and her passion."

"That Roman whore—?."

"Not her. The other. The first."

"Who?"

"Debra."

"Who is Debra?"

"Death."

Sean's flesh hardened as if touched in every place by a steel sword. He scratched at his collar, his sleeves. "What...what do we do?"

"Prepare. When he is finished he...they will come for me."

"Shit."

The Father was silent momentarily. And then he said, with purpose, "I have been doomed by a prophecy I have no power over. Death has marked me. But I refuse to die at the hands of an infidel."

Sean shivered. "What...can I do for you, Father?"

"Vel caeco appareat."

Sean said, "'It would be apparent even to a blind man.'" And then he laughed, amazed with himself, that he should understand the words.

Amadeus nodded. "Then too, my beloved, you know what must be done."

"Ah...well, no."

"Take me."

Horrified, Sean looked at him.

But the Father only said, breaking his pose and reaching for him, framing his face in his long hands and kissing him with sad passion, "It is time, nein? You have been awaiting this. Your desire.

The Rite of Covenmaster is yours. Drink of me and be complete. Drink until I move within you, my beautiful slayer."

Sean hesitated, groaned, shivered. He wanted to protest, but then came his master's lips on his throat, caressing his thirst, his need, his hunger to be...more. More than some little whore's punching bag, more than Slim Jim's young prey or Alek Knight's rebellious little acolyte, more than the Stone Man. More than a punk stereotype with cotton between his ears. More—

But he would be *what?*

And all at once, Sean was afraid. Amadeus had lied. He was not a vampire, at least not the kind he had come to understand as real. Amadeus was not a victim of Lilithine blood, a subspecies of the human race. He was less, and more. A servant to strange forces, stranger understandings. A demon, a wraith. A beast and a priest and both borne of a savagery Sean had never known in all his life on the streets. Hungry. Starved. Incomplete. And some part of Sean's expanding intellect tried to reason this out, what Amadeus was with what he did, and failed.

After this Communion, this passionate exchange of blood, what was he—Sean—to be?

What in hell was he to be?

Then came the cold kiss, the stab of bone-sharp teeth, the hiss of an uncoiling nest of snakes all about them. And in the spinning private cloister of Sean's mind he heard the answer: *You will be everything you have always wanted to be...and everything you have ever feared. You will be Amadeus.*

"But..." He gasped. That mouth. It was on him, in him, a living thing, separate from the Father, with its own hungers and desires. Sean shuddered yet again, nearly collapsing against the Father as he sank his teeth deep into the flesh of Sean's throat, feeding from him in lapping swallows, stealing back the strength and red life that he had given Sean earlier. Yes, he understood how that had happened now. What drove it. What had driven them both to destroy the girl. The hunger...nothing was like it in the whole world, nothing at all. Love was like that hunger. And now it was as if he were being loved by some underworld god. Hades. Satan. Set. It was as if he were being eaten alive by a cannibal lover. The girl...she had known this and willingly endured it. The hell that was heaven...

Through the veil of passion and overwhelming pain, Sean fought for his thoughts, his fears. "But...I only...only wanted to be something...more."

The mouth let him go. The beautiful and blood-slathered and unkind teeth let him go. "You will be everything."

"Everything..." Sean murmured as Amadeus held him close and stroked his throat, kissed his mouth and the chains of his tears, laid upon his face his bloody lip prints until the touch and taste and scent of life was so great, his hunger so far greater, he thought he might weep or die or simply implode from the force of it. Sean leaned into his master, felt no desires but that for giving in. The choices had all been made and be understood innately that the time for protest was over. It had ended the day he took the Father's hand and escaped the dorm with him. It had ended the day Slim Jim died and left a child with blood and mucus all over his face sitting on the floor, afraid to move, to even breathe.

And strange that in this moment of which he'd dreamt so long and so hard that his thoughts be filled not with images of Amadeus, nor even his mother, but of Alek Knight.

Alek. He had run. He'd escaped this.

Why?

"I will make of you a god on the earth," the Father whispered against his mouth, pushing him back onto the altar like a sacrifice and slitting his habit with one talon of a fingernail and laying kisses to the nakedness beneath. "A god whom none will again harm. No more hurt. Eternal and unstoppable and accountable to no god for your sins." Each phrase was punctuated by a kiss, a bite, until Sean felt his entire body shudder like a marionette on short strings.

"No sins," Sean repeated, and he was not surprised that he wept keenly into the frost of his master's hair, the sight of a dead man's shredded bloodless body glowing at the center of his mind

like an ember. And the woman—the woman torn like a doll. The
pain and pleasure became one entity within him. "Oh Jesus, Father,
I love you. Save me, please. *Please* save me." The words did not
seem foolish and they did not embarrass him, and as he worshipped
his master's face and hair with his kisses he felt his terror lessen.
His soul and savior and power, he thought. He embraced the father,
opening himself up in every way to his savior. How he wanted to
die for Amadeus, crack his soul open upon the rock of the Father's
divinity.

And when pressure at the back of his skull brought his kisses to
the Father's throat he scarcely knew it or cared.

"Drink me," Amadeus invited. "Drink me and become."

Sean kissed him deeply with his every passion, kissed and licked
at his master's throat and the thin glass of flesh that was all that
separated him from his eternity. His teeth ached and his mind
screamed. And when his time came and he could hold off no longer,
Amadeus held him fiercely and crooned to him in languages he
could not fathom.

3

Book dreamt, and in his dreams he walked upon a red desert full
of white skulls. They were ancient things beneath his feet, those
skulls, thin as eggshells. And where he walked they shattered, and
where they shattered came the angry red geysers of their ghosts.
The sky above him was cramped and low, a mocking backwards-
running river of blood. Horrible, all of it, like something Alek
might paint on a good day. Fucking Dali. Where the hell was the
exit?

Book walked on, searching, but he did not hurry, because to
hurry would mean to burst more of the skulls under his feet. He
walked on and he kept his eyes steady on the flat, hellish horizon
far ahead, for he knew if he looked down he would see the millions
of empty, screaming eye sockets beseeching him, and that would

be too much; that would drive him mad.

He walked in that hell for a thousand years. He walked until he came upon them. And stopped.

Upon a bed of bleached bones they loved. Book watched them without shame and without revulsion. It was only proper after all that on their wedding day they should have a witness. They were both naked but wreathed in red silk and the pearled sweat of their effort. He saw the pale narrow serpent of Alek's back, and he saw Debra beneath him, alive, a woman, innocent and seductive where she clung to her mate, her hair a mystical web of darkness spilling out and out around them, encircling them, binding them together. Forever.

Book envied Alek his angel. He always had.

And from his angel Alek drank, her precious blood lighting his flesh from within like light though a crimson window. And slowly, as Book watched, Debra grew frail in the arms of her twin, her flesh and bones giving, cracking herself apart for him, to give and to nourish him. Spent at last, she was all red silk and sand in Alek's hands, her hair like the dark pelt of a fine kill.

Book frowned. "You've killed her," he said.

Alek looked up at him with his narrow, flushed-red eyes, and Book then knew his mistake.

Alek said, *"I have become."*

And Booker Jefferson jerked awake to the flickering, cinematic darkness of his Lexington Avenue penthouse apartment with its Klee originals and French lithographs and sunken Jacuzzi whirlpool. On the flat TV the Saturday night silent film was on, Fritz Murnau's classic, *Nosferatu.* Lousy joke. Book stared at the blueness of the screen, at Count Orlock moving like animated death toward a victim all lily-skinned and innocent. He looked away, at his pale, grey, characterless furniture, the weepy neutral carpet and colorless walls. Again the lithographs, every one a mint and worth more than most blue-collar workers made in a year.

On the floor by the door was his imported seven-hundred-dollar London Fog where he had carelessly dropped it on entering, and he thought somewhat absently, When the hell did this happen? When did I go from being a tenement homeboy to fucking pampered Donald Trump? When the hell did I stop being an in-your-fucking-face street-smart kid like Alek?

Alek. He touched his brow and found it misted wet. His hand clenched into a fist, trembled slightly, and dropped onto the wooden armrest of his chair. He split the mahogany finish like kindling.

When did we stop playing street ball and getting subs down at Arnold's Soda Shop, he wondered, and going down to the Hudson in the summer and walking around the old rail yard with our shirts off, looking for fun, looking for trouble, looking not to be bored—

I have become.

Become what?

Debra, of course. Fucking idiot.

He rose up from his fashionably anemic furniture in his rumpling of fashionably anemic Armani suit and Italian shoes and began to circle his psychotically tidy living room, seeing it and smelling the five spice curry in the take-out boxes on the coffee table, seeing the movie and knowing it was there, but feeling only a white, heavy silence like a veil all over his thoughts.

I have become.

And what have you become, Book? Other than a rich, snobby pain in the ass like all the folks you and Alek used to make fun of down on Central Park West, hey? What are you other than some black-boy-made-it-good stereotype with plenty money and an internship and a Jag and about three hundred dead vampires to your fucking name?

What the hell are you?

And there, trapped inside his silence and his questions, Book circled the room once more.

4

Sometime after midnight, the Covenmaster of the New York City

branch of slayers rose to standing on the altar's sacred dais, the
sand of the spent host crunching under his heels and a deep long
Abbey breeze casting the few remaining white crystalline hairs like
spider's silk against the altar's thousands of bony faces.

The skull in his hands crumbled away. Not even that remained.

The Covenmaster let the bone dust fall between his fingers, and
then he put out his hands to see the grinning wall of dead bones.
"Exegi monumentum aere perennius," he said and smiled. The
shell was finished, the creature reborn once more. He took away
his hands and explored his new body from collarbone to hipbone.
So strange to be young and new again. Each time it was a new
experience, but after so many years, so many hosts, it was an
experience he grew accustomed to very easily.

He went directly to his cell and shook out his good homespun
clothing, put them to his face. In his imagination he could still
smell in them the salts of the Atlantic, and the pitch and greenwood
of the great ship. He remembered his covenant with the church
and he remembered what it meant. He was tempted to dress himself
in these clothes, the collar and the cloak and the Quaker's hat—
but to do so, he knew, would be to be conspicuous and to
undermine all his work this evening thus far. Instead, he went to
Sean's cell and found among his things a T-shirt and jeans and his
slayer's coat made of leather. He found the whelp's wrist blade
with its intricate little mechanism, and this he strapped on his
forearm and tested the slide of the blade using the knowledge
inherent to the temple. Satisfied, he armed himself with a sword as
he had always done in the past before a great mission. Not his
sword. Hanzo's sword.

Alek's sword.

Alek.

Yet would be their time.

Using the mental link he shared with all of his children—yet
none so strong as it had been with Alek—he summoned the
remnants of his Coven down to the Great Abbey. They came and
sat like weary children. Aristotle fidgeted in his seat and thrummed

his fingers as Amadeus explained his instructions to them. Robot said nothing, of course.

The shadows of the skylight grew long. Nightfall. A hunter's moon rose. And finally, silence fell across the Abbey.

Aristotle said, "So, like, when did God die and put you in charge, whelp?"

Amadeus, who had been standing near the altar, was crouched atop the Coventable in front of Aristotle, his wrist blade under the whelp's chin before all the words were out of his ignorant mouth. "About an hour ago, actually. Cross me not." He smiled.

Aristotle was aghast. He swallowed, his throat working against the instrument pressed firmly against his carotid artery. And then he gathered what little wits he actually had and said, "What—oh, Jeezus Christ—he was right—the Father was right—someone really did kill him—"

Robot was on his feet, coming around the table like a train. Without removing the blade from Aristotle's throat or otherwise turning away, Amadeus sent his messengers out, heard and felt them wrap like Punjab lassos around the bulk of Robot's body and lift him quite literally off his feet. Robot sucked in great, greedy mouthfuls of air, the only sounds of terror the big mute was capable of making, and flailed uselessly in the grip of Amadeus's medusan retinue of servants. They rattled irritably and tossed him away like a child tossing a rag doll across a room in a fit of temper. Robot crashed to the floor, stunned and nearly broken.

Amadeus's blade snicked back into place. And then he stepped down off the table, lithe like a cat, and cast his blind gaze down upon the Coventable. It trembled and rattled a moment as if under the spell of a lunatic séance. Then it turned end over end and splintered into shards against the far wall.

The tapestries rippled as if touched by invisible ghosts.

The altar moaned dryly.

Amadeus felt the vibration of the shattered wood through the floor and up through the soles of his feet, and he knew Aristotle felt the same. He asked, "Do you believe in your heart that the

Sean boy is capable of these kinds of miracles, *whelp?*"

Aristotle, frozen in his seat, still as a statue, said, "No...Father."

Amadeus drew the wild tangles of his hair back into a tight halo around his head. He smiled and let Aristotle see the old Lilithine blood rise in his eyes. He showed the whelp the tips of his saber teeth in a savage smile. Then he gathered his coat close to himself and went to the great oaken double doors and with a single stabbing look blew them open to the above and the night and the city cowering like a collection of children afraid of the dark.

Wind whistled down the corridors of the old house like whispered promises. Like voices from the distant past.

But when the others remained as they were, Amadeus turned back to them and said in a measured voice. "Let's get it on then, man."

5

The Slayer awoke in a world of white cold. He blinked up at the rearing architecture—the gargoyles with catlike faces, the stone children grasping to cornices—and frowned, wondering where he was, what world he had landed in. He shifted his weight, cramping his back on cold stone. Pungent tobacco smoke warmed the white cold.

And when a chill came to his temple he gasped. Where was he? A hand. But whose? Very dry.

"Mrs. B—Tahlia," he guessed.

"You got it, kid." Through the haze of her cigarette smoke her face shone like a white jewel, like the visage of some wartime songbird he'd long forgotten the name of. She was encrusted with white wolf fur, the snow on her eyelashes making her seem like the Snow Queen in some long-forgotten fairy tale.

Alek tried to rise. He was lying uncomfortably on the steps of the Metro, apparently, half-covered in a snow blanket. But his body hurt in too many places—his hip, his ribs where he'd fractured one in his fall on the steps—and he gave it up after a moment of effort and too-much pain and lay back down.

Tahlia undid the buttons on his shirt, took a wad of kerchief-wrapped snow and pressed it against his side. The immediate pain took his breath away. After a moment or two, Alek found he could speak. "How—?"

"I found you, but couldn't do much more than keep the snow off you. I'm strong, but not strong enough to haul your bulk inside, let me tell you. You're goddamn heavier than you look."

He groaned and tasted cotton in his mouth, a hollow ache in the pit of his stomach. His body was mending, but it was running out of juice again. He was hungry. He ignored it. He concentrated on the stinging ache in his side instead. How do you know where I need it, Tahlia? He made a face—he felt like he was breathing through ground glass—and decided not to verbalize his musings.

"I have my ways," Tahlia answered and smiled at her patient's astonished expression.

Alek carefully shook his head. Byron's blood had worked mysterious miracles over Tahlia's mortal flesh, that was for sure. "More to you...Tahlia...than I thought," he managed.

"But of course," Tahlia proclaimed with her big false pride. "I am a veritable jungle of talent, don't y'know." She winked. "An old jungle, granted, but that fact need go no further, right?"

Alek laughed and that hurt too. "Help me up?"

Tahlia eased him into a slumped sitting position on the stairs. And when she was certain her patient wouldn't slide, she pulled a small silver whiskey decanter out of her pocket and unscrewed it, offering it to him.

Alek put it to his lips, then away. The smell of the alcohol was unbelievably offensive. How could he have ever drunk this stuff in the past? "Tahlia," he said, holding onto the decanter to be social, "exactly how much to you know?"

"Know." Tahlia lit a cigarette, her hands cupped around the flame to keep the snow from killing it. "About art, a lot. Other things, some. I do know that Amadeus is a bastard of the first school. I know last time I seen Byron was the winter of '62 when the worm set his dogs on him. I do know what the Father's dogs can do. I know I never seen Byron again after he took to his heels." She stroked her chapped bottom lip with tragic ease. "I do know I want you to kill the fucker for me and for Byron and mostly for yourself."

Alek looked out over the winter-wrapped city. It was so white and perfect and pristine, he might have thought they were alone in this world. "I don't know if I can do that, Tahlia. I don't know if I'm good enough."

"Then you ain't never gonna be free of him, are you?"

Alek set aside the decanter of whiskey and pressed his face with both hands. "My God, Tahlia, if you knew so much about this, about me, why the hell didn't you tell me anything when I was younger?"

Tahlia gave him a sidelong look. "Well, for one thing, I didn't 'know' much of anything. All I knew about your people was what Byron told me, which wasn't much. And after he was gone, I knew nothing at all."

"But you knew about the Coven. You knew what I was." He looked up, and then dropped his gaze apologetically. "No, that's wrong. I'm not your responsibility. Jesus, I'm treating you like some parent that didn't come through for me."

"And if I had told you," Tahlia asked, "would you've believed me about the Coven? Would you have believed the words of Tahlia Braxton over Amadeus?"

He said nothing and tried desperately not to feel like a complete fool in her presence.

Tahlia touched his arm. "Kid," she said, "we all gotta get where we're going in our own time. No rushing it. Besides, I always knew you'd figure it all out one of these days. Was always there, y'know. I seen it. Your girlfriend seen it too." ·

Alek's hands dropped away as a sickening dread filled all the empty places left inside of him. He sat up, his eyes skating over the whole of city, what he could see of it, the white veil of it. "Where is she? Where did she go?"

Tahlia's gaze flickered toward the street where cabs skidded through the slush.

Alek stood up, then weaved uncertainly as the world twisted sideways on him. His ribs throbbed, his head ached—but there, already all the discomfort was fading. "I need to tell her...tell her what I know."

Tahlia stood up to steady him. "Whoa, kid. Know what?"

He looked down into Tahlia's upturned face, her small, brilliant, quizzical eyes. "The Chronicle," he said, "I know where it is. The real one."

Tahlia's smoke dropped out of her teeth.

Alek smiled and lowered the hood of Tahlia's white coat, leaned over and kissed the side of Tahlia's cheek. "Thank you," he said. "Thank you for everything, Mrs. Braxton. I mean it." And then he escaped Tahlia's hold on him and went down the steps and into the blizzard of light and snow.

The storm begun earlier was dying and the wind lisped through the narrow straits between buildings. A sheer white rime of snow had gathered on parked cars and telephone wires and well nigh everything else that was static and unable to escape the gentle wrath of winter.

Alek stopped on the walk outside the Metro and glanced around at the rubbernecked traffic and the homeless cowering back in doorways, trying to determine which way to go. He chose a direction at random. And for the next hour of nonstop walking he felt out of step with everyone around him. They all—or most of them, anyway—seemed so damned purposeful, these people. So driven. He watched them in amazement, realizing that he used to want to be one of them. One with them. No more. He stood in the middle of the mad bustle of Grand Central Station in wonder at how he could have lived such a false life for so long without seeing behind the stage-prop scenery at the barren futility of it all.

A face in the crowd. His lifelong dream. To just be an Everyman. And now? He was a rogue. A slayer. No, The Slayer. Yes.

The new knowledge clung to him like an epiphany. He waded carefully into the crowd in some half-hearted attempt to catch the sub. But the sub to where? he asked himself. Back to Rapper's building? Someplace else? The Empress? Rockefeller Center? Where? Where did Teresa go when she wasn't with him? To his horror, he realized he had no clue, none at all. She might have flown to the moon, such was his helplessness right then. To know— to have the knowledge she sought for so long, the whereabouts of Paris's Chronicle—but of course his damned stupid, passionate outrage had to intercept all that. Critical mass at the most horrible of times. He'd been cruel and cretin and she had learned to hate him. She had walked away, but that was fair and just, wasn't it? It was, after all, what he had struggled to achieve only an hour ago. He felt a stab of regret under his heart. Regret, of all things. Useless, that emotion, Teresa had said in a time when she had believed he was her guardian angel. But regret changes nothing—

He leaned against a lamppost and tried to think, to imagine where she would go. If only she would feel for him, feel with his special blood-born senses the new surge of hope, of knowledge, in him, maybe she would come get him. Or at least tell him where she was.

There was an interesting thought. If she could feel his presence anywhere in the city as she said she could, could see his dreams even, then why couldn't he? He had done it once before, when he had followed her from Rockefeller Center. He started walking again. No real direction, just walking, letting the streets take him up and down. Where are you? Tell me where you are. Broadway. He looked at the signpost. Are you here? Is this the reason I've chosen this direction? He kept walking, looking, feeling the cold and the feelings under the cold. He heard his heart, heard the rush of his blood, imagined it drawing him to her like a strange compass.

He found himself standing at the door of the revolving bar at the Marriott. He went inside. Nothing. But near. Now he felt it. Subtle. Like the ache in his side. He passed through the bar to the left and found himself in the lobby, standing amidst the red plush carpet sea between the visitors to the city and the haggard bellboys. The night clerk looked just as haggard and a great deal less trustworthy. "Can I help you, sir?"

He already knew Teresa was somewhere in the building, probably on one of the upper floors from the feel of it. What he didn't know was whether she had created any obstacles to his seeing her. "Did a woman check in here? About this tall? Very pretty, with long black hair? Brown eyes?"

The night clerk looked annoyed. "I'm sorry. You are mistaken."

"I'm not mistaken." But he saw now. The man was used to these midnight rendezvous, escorts and their clients, and like any good New Yorker, he let people make money and kept his mouth shut. An admirable quality at any other time but this.

"What room?"

"Excuse me?" The man shuddered, but only a little.

"What. Room." Alek narrowed his eyes and *pushed...*

"1010, sir."

"Thank you."

6

The first discovery that Alek made on entering room 1010 in the Marriott was that Teresa wasn't alone. A human male was with her on the bed, powerfully built and probably attractive from what he could see of the intruder by his bare, ebony back and baggy-khakied ass. Bald head. Six-hundred-dollar sneaks. Some battle-rap type Alek would probably have recognized from an MTV video had he cared to remember. Maybe even a nice guy in some other life. Right now, only an intruder. Alek went to the bed, faster than either one of them could react, gripped a fistful of the man's pants seat, and peeled him off of her.

"Whadda fuck!" Homeboy ranted as he pedaled his legs and pinwheeled his arms. After a moment of intense effort, Homey managed to twist his head back on his short, bullish neck. He

showed Alek his double row of pearly-nice, Hollywood-capped teeth. *"I'm goan fucking cut your balls off! Put me dooown, motherf—!*

Alek put him down. Hard. "Get your clothes and get out of here," he said distractedly as he watched Teresa sit up on the bed. She was dressed in a black lace slip and garters and stocking with stalks of butterflies embroidered along the backs of her legs. Her motions were fluid, openly inviting, and Alek had to swallow down an urge to turn back to Homey and rip his goddamn head off for seeing her this way. He felt like a jealous, irate husband in a Jane Austin novel. Gentlemen, take your pistols and ten paces...

Homey obediently went for his shirt on the bed—then grabbed Alek by the arm instead and swung him around and tried to land a four-ringed knuckle punch to his face. Alek caught it in his fist. Held it. He looked Homey in the face and felt the man's pulse tick with useless, angry energy. The man sneered.

Alek sneered back. *"I said. Get. Out."*

"I paid good money for the cunt," Homey said. "You her fuckin' husband or *what*?"

Alek let the man's fist go. He grabbed him by the back of the skull instead and thrust his own weight against the prick. The impact sent them crashing into the wall beside the bed. He felt the drywall groan, give. Homey's skull banged against a stud. The vase of fake orchids on the nightstand beside the bed rattled, danced, fell over.

Homey blanched, choked.

Kill him, he'd like to fucking *kill* the motherfucker's ass.

Alek let go of his head and stepped back.

Homey looked down and stared at the forty-six-inch ceremonial tachi sword slung up tight under his balls with wonder for where it had come from and how fast it could have found its way there.

From one brother to another, thought Alek, and smiled with genuine malice. "We want to be *alone*," he said, raising the sword ever so slightly. "Get it?"

Homey put his hands up in an authentic I-give-up-man gesture and reached for his shirt for real this time. Without putting it on—or for that matter even reaching for his wallet lying on the nightstand beside the overturned vase, an act that would have made him cross the path of the tachi—Homey backed away to the door and opened it behind him, slunk out backwards, gold chains a-jingling, grey-faced, defeated.

"Put the Do Not Disturb sign on the door, won't you?" Alek asked.

Homey took the sign with him and slammed the door.

Alek put the sword down.

Teresa crossed her legs. Though her face had hardened from the moment of his arrival, she seemed to be having trouble maintaining it now. "He and his friends have a lot of money, and he could have recommended me," she said.

Alek said nothing. He watched her face, all of it cold, unbroken ice, all reflection, as if she were doing her damnedest to hide what lurked inside. She looked away. "My time is money. And I would appreciate it if you would leave now."

"You gave up on me," he said at last.

She looked up. "You gave up on you."

He opened his mouth to say...what? Suddenly his whole being rebelled against this and he had to take a step back, away from the slayer in himself—that Amadeus-made creature with armor as black and hard as beetle shell. Silence roared up between them like an icon to his pride. But pride, like regret, was a useless emotion. He broke it. "I'm sorry I disappointed you, beloved. I'm sorry I made you hate me. I really am."

She tilted her head. She flushed. "Don't be so stupid."

"Am I? Stupid?"

"You are if you think I could hate you." She dropped her eyes, her lashes like ebony fans on the marble-white planes of her cheeks. "I wish that I could hate you. I was angry, caro. You angered me. No one has angered me in a long time."

He approached her. She lay back on the pillows of the bed. He covered her with his hair and strength. He touched and caressed her freely. He wound strands of her hair like silk around his fingers. Then he kissed her with all the fierce hunger of his passion, kissed her, unafraid at last of that passion, kissed her until he heard his twin's contented sigh echoing up through the tunnel of his soul. How Debra would have loved this. She and he and this beautiful witch, touching, a living trinity of emotion not unlike what she had once desired between the two of them and Akisha. He broke the kiss, kissed her again, and again, said to her, breathlessly, against her mouth, "I'll never disappoint you again, I promise. I swear it..."

"Your eyes." She touched his face and shook her head. "You're different. What have you seen?"

He smiled mischievously, brimming.

Her dark eyes brightened. "You know."

"I was shown."

"Where then?"

"So close, so, so close. Yet a lifetime away." He studied her face. Loved her eyes. The planes of her cheeks. Her eyelashes. Her rare smile. He kissed them all. He loved the strength and determination in her heart, the wisdom locked in her mind. Loved her...not just as a lover, he realized, but as a student loves his sensei, all but worships her. As he had loved Akisha. As he would always love Debra. "Come, fly with me. Let me show you."

"I will...but..." She shook her head with wonder.

"What is it, Teresa? What?"

She looked deep into his eyes. "What are you?" she whispered.

He stood up. "Complete."

7

How immortal was the altar. In almost thirty-eight years it had remained unchanged. It perhaps bore a modern skin of graffiti and its red and gold paint was weak and its brass rings a long time lost, but at its soul the altar remained changeless. The fellowship of animals remained in their painful stances, heads tossed back as if in the death rictus of poison. So many years and its milky canopy mirrors still reflected the swarm of city lights and the rise and fall of the deathless sun.

Things change, they changeth not.

On the icy gravel path, Alek stopped. They were alone. Lone worshipers at the altar. Few New Yorkers ventured this far into the park at this hour. Rather, even the insomniacs and insane would be staying to the gravel paths near Central Park South and along Lexington Avenue, waiting for the sun to burn off the mist and some of the cold and chase away all the monster they knew dwelled in the dark.

He shivered quite suddenly and wondered if it was only the cold, looking on the barren benches, the night's worth of garbage clustering on heat grates, the rats squirming through the wire baskets on their early-morning foraging trips.

"Here?" Teresa said, creeping up beside him.

"Under the carousel. It's all he had time for before..." Another shiver. Cold. Danger. Or an echo of danger. Perhaps.

Another slayer. Not perhaps...

"He's here," Alek said.

"The Stone Man."

"Not Stone Man."

She withdrew Paris's ornate knife. It gleamed dirtily in the coppery sodium lights surrounding the carousel.

"Won't you go back?" he pleaded. "For God's sake, the sun—"

"I want the fucking Chronicle."

"You'll be blind in half an hour."

"Then let's do this already and quit arguing about it." She looked at him challengingly. She had opted for heavier, darker clothing this time. A wool coat and hat that made her look like some princess out of a Russian novel, black shades that wrapped around her eyes nearly completely. Not that the meager black fabric and plastic would help. In less than an hour the sun would crest and turn her world into a watery red inferno she would no more be able to endure than a naked man could bathe fully within the sun's unrelenting rays and not collapse, blind, from heatstroke. But trying to convince her to wait until nightfall was impossible. Trying to make her wait for him to return from this even more difficult. He knew. He'd been trying to convince her otherwise since they'd left the Marriott.

"Killing yourself won't be avenging Paris, you know," he said.

A crow called harshly and she looked up. The firs and the naked, narrow-boned maples writhed alive with a rich dark foliage of day birds. He felt a shiver that was not fear. She turned away, met his gaze with such open hostility he found it incredulous that this was the same woman whose words had moved him so only an hour ago.

He spoke again, but now as if from great height or distance. "The running animals...and a midnight sun. He saw this." He closed his eyes. "'And the Covenmaster would not know another rising of the day.'"

Teresa looked cynically upon the carousel animals. The revolver moved, out only laboriously, and not two whole inches. The stage protested even that. "The carousel has not turned in ten years, caro."

He breathed in the cold and the steel and listened to the gravel crackling like bone dust under his feet. I don't want to be here, Tahlia. I don't want to be doing this, Byron, my mapmaking friend. I want to be elsewhere, away. I want to be safe. I want to be hidden somewhere in the shadows of the city and not here, not now. I don't want to know if I can beat him. I don't care to know. I just want to be finished, *finished*...

Debra sighed and laughed. Afraid, Slayer? Are you a coward as well as a murderer, then?

He opened his eyes.

The carousel clicked forward three paces and displaced shadow. And momentarily, before sliding back under a cloak of darkness, he saw it—a dark paralyzed mount with a figure sitting sidesaddle upon it. Still. Waiting for him.

Like in the beginning.

They had come full circle.

So.

Above a blackbird cackled and rattled the air with its voice. Teresa drew cautiously back, back off the path like some pre-recorded ballet, recoiling but not retreating. She manhandled her iron knife and looked at him, her eyes luminous and full of night and understanding. "I would stand with you, but I know my place as Noah and Moses and Jesus knew theirs. You must go alone. Otherwise he will make me a pawn to make you do what he wants."

He nodded.

"He will try to kill you," she said.

Again Debra laughed, but like a wraith, sneeringly.

Afraid, *Slayer*?

"He had that power," Alek answered. He went to Teresa and took her knife hand, held up the lethal little weapon, touched his tongue to the edge. He felt no pain. He did taste his own coppery sweetness. The final host. It would bleed slow for hours and keep his battle hunger up. He touched her hair but did not kiss her, not now, not when he wanted to touch the anger and the emptiness in his childhood heart. Finished, he walked, alone, toward the altar.

The night wind blew his hair back, blew open his coat.

The dark horse ticked forward as if summoned to meet him. And now it did not slide. And the master of the horse appeared fully, unshielded. Just like that first time in the cold and the dark, but now his face was turned down and away and a wide round Quaker's hat concealed his beautifully awful features.

Alek mounted the stage and stopped. He narrowed his eyes on the silent figure and waited.

After a moment the hat was tipped back on the blonde head. Tiny filed-sharp teeth grinned up at him, gleaming like pearls in the dark. "Hey there, man." The slayer's coat slit open to reveal an old Radiohead concert T-shirt. Alek flinched back, lurched against the dolphin at the sight of the spineless little prick that went around calling himself the Chosen.

"Drunk again, sailor," snickered Sean. He lounged back on the carousel horse as casual as a great black cat. "You know, man, you look righteously disappointed. You were expecting, maybe, like, Count-fucking-Dracula?"

"Amadeus," Alek answered uncertainly. "I was expecting Amadeus."

Sean pouted. "Real shitter, man. As it turns out, the Father's busy making excuses to the Vatican on his fucking *knees*, man. And all because of fucking *you*. So looks like you gonna have to make do with *me*."

Alek recovered, leaned around a pole. "Fine. This should take about five minutes."

Sean narrowed his eyes. "Fuck *you*, man."

Alek narrowed his eyes in return. "Where are your ghouls, whelp?"

"My children are here."

"Your *children*?"

My children, bring me the Judas...

Alek sidestepped. Not right. Something wasn't right here.

He eyed the Stone Man closely, flesh thin and translucent and almost blue in the moonlight, earlobes naked of their decorative arsenal of steel and bone. Where were his trophy teeth on their wires? His leather jacket and his chains?

"You've changed, haven't you?" he said.

Sean smiled crookedly as he eased himself down off the horse. "Maybe I'm assuming my role as Covenmaster."

Suddenly, the dream—

Sean with his master's eyes, his master's smile.

I am Amadeo...Asmodeus. I am the Chosen. I am the Coven...

"No," said Alek, looking around nervously. "You're lying. Why are you lying?"

...the sword with a blood-blackened hilt. All that you see I command...

"Who the hell are you?"

Sean snickered. "The Stone Man."

Alek shook his head. But what had he expected, a transfiguration? The face was unchanging, offering Alek nothing. But the mind...a book suddenly, pregnant with history, with time, its words twisted into the languages of other places and other people and scribed in blood. It toppled, that book, tumbled over, its pages opening like wings in flight, its words clear and sharp and utterly false. Ugly. Such pain. A twist of the soul. And inside the private chamber of Alek's mind, at the very height of understanding, a seeping voice like a whispered battle cry:

Memento mori, beloved.

Amadeus's hand, which was Sean's but not Sean's, flickered out. Alek saw a brief glimmer like the sun before it strikes the horizon. Then a bloom of scarlet burst heavenward and splashed the dark horse's paralyzed flank. It painted the Sean-thing, his hair, his empty lifeless face. Ideograms of blood splattered across Sean's shades like a talented and disturbed child's artwork.

Alek tottered back in defense, but too late. There was a narrow, unfelt pain in his throat. He put his hands there and felt a fast, cold spring. He looked down at himself, at the red life that was his but was also Teresa's and Debra's racing out of him and embracing the ground, turning the snow pink as candyfloss at his feet.

On the stage the Sean-thing was standing, sliding the dripping wrist blade back into its secret sheath. The thing cocked its head sideways, a curious animal, an artist fascinated by his work.

Alek knew then. He understood everything, or suspected it. Sean would be laughing at him; only Amadeus drew blood piously. "Father," he whispered in words and blood because it was true, because it was *him*, it was Amadeus...

The wrappers were ripped away like some final disguise and Alek saw beneath, saw the serpentine eyes, and looked away. Before him the park rocked a little to and fro as if the entire world were perched on a great swinging, cosmic pendulum. He shivered, felt so cold on the inside, white cold, cold as silence. He gripped the wound at his throat, but it was an action entirely reflexive. He could no longer feel his outer shell, only his insides, his veins and arteries as they began to collapse in line and shut off odd portions of his body. Taste was gone. No hands. He felt a terrifying lightness gathering under his heavy coat.

He swayed.

"Look at me, mein Sohn."

He did.

"You are dying," said Amadeus in Sean's voice and cadence. And yet Alek recognized the Father's harsh accent. "The blood is the life after all and the life runs out of you. Will you try and catch it?"

He tried, but it ran obstinately through his fingers.

Powerful, hulking arms took him from behind. Not Amadeus. Too great, even for the Father. Robot. The enormous ball-breaker of a slayer gripped him firmly around the waist and kept him upright on his knees, not unkindly but with enough strength to prove he had no intention of fucking around if Alek started to struggle. Alek did not struggle. There was no strength left to struggle.

Breathe, blink, look up—no.

A shadow...

No.

Teresa stood on the edge of the bicycle path, eyes riveted on his struggle, oblivious to the shadow slinking up behind her. He opened his mouth, but nothing came out of him but blood and a mewling kitten-like noise. His eyes instead went to the shadow, widened. Teresa turned then, but it was over already.

Aristotle turned the million-candle-power halogen lamp on her. Teresa screamed and hid her face.

Aristotle giggled like a schoolboy playing a nasty prank.

Teresa turned away and reached blindly for escape, but Aristotle was there and she went down on her face instead, Aristotle's knee in her back.

Amadeus nodded.

And then everything happened at once.

Alek balked the moment Aristotle, the bastard, started to pick

Teresa up. But Robot was having none of it and tightened his hold on Alek's waist until Alek was certain his newly-mended ribs were going to be crushed to powder in the slayer's massive hands.

Aristotle lifted Teresa into a fireman's carry. Teresa hissed and whipped around like a cat, her hands reaching for Aristotle's eyes, missed, tore a flap in his cheek with her fingernails. Aristotle cursed, swung around, cracking the back of her head against a tree trunk. Teresa slumped over his shoulder, as still as the dead. Cursing still, Aristotle carried her semiconscious body over to his master, a dog eager to please.

"The little whore," Amadeus muttered and gripped Teresa's face in one massive hand, his fingernails cutting black furrows in her white face. "Open your eyes, little whore."

The pain revived her. Teresa's eyes fluttered. She worked them open. Her body shuddered, but the pain was too much for her. She sighed, almost a word, her blinded eyes bleeding slits.

"Paris was a fool," Amadeus whispered and backhanded her across the face, knocking loose her hat, knocking down her long, long hair, knocking her off Aristotle's shoulder and to the ground like a lifeless lump. "Alek *is* a fool..." Again the hand, and a spurt of blood too dark for anything human broke from between her split lips. *"You cunt..."* He took her by the face, took her again, took her so hard he lifted her off the ground like a child's doll.

Kill you, Alek thought to Aristotle, standing nearby and watching, the eager-dog look plastered all over his bleeding geek face. Kill you like Takara. Rip you fucking *apart...*

He tried to lunge with what was left of his strength. Nothing. And now Robot scarcely held him.

Amadeus turned around and said to Robot: "Hold him up so he can see."

Robot did. Proudly.

A real challenge, eh, Robot? Holding a semiconscious man upright so he could watch a woman being tortured? You're such a *man.*

Amadeus flicked his wrist. Again the blade, glowing like an evil blue light, ghost light—

Again the lunge. Alek felt it surge through him from some dark inner place of strength. He moved, made it a foot.

Amadeus noticed. "Hold him, God damn you!"

Robot tightened his hold on Alek, grabbing him by the hair.

Sssliiit.

A fistful of Teresa's beautiful hair fell in a heap of silky ebony at Amadeus's feet. The Father's eyes stayed barren, no feeling there. Just an act of fucking barbarism, like anything else in his life. He went to work again, again he robbed Teresa of her wonderful hair. And when he was done there, her hair cropped, he went to work on the front of her coat, slicing away the buttons, shucking the material off of her like a hunter skinning some great animal of prey of its pelt, so that she lay on her back on the gravel path in only her black slip, her neck and arms bare to the cold and her assailant. Alek could not help but think of her stories, the freaks and psychos she had endured, beaten at their own game. Did you know it would end this way? he wondered. In this ignominy? Again her eyes fluttered and the muscles of her neck and arms tensed as she tried to swim to the top of consciousness.

Amadeus reached down like a man about to touch the cheek of a sleeping woman, and instead struck her with the sharp of the blade. Alek shuddered, pain felt. The marks were like tar on her cheek and throat. A profanity. A sin. All that white perfection marred like that—

Alek coughed and wiped away the blood that came off his mouth. Then almost suddenly he gave in to a vast urge and went down in the cold snow and cold blood mingling into an icy pink froth all over the altar. He knelt, his hands over the maw of the wound at his throat as if he would salvage what was left and hold it in long enough to fight one last time, one last time for her...

It refused him and only raced away.

He forced up his trembling eyes, made them focus through the gathering crimson dusk on the Sean-face with its black Amadeus eyes. Its unfeeling eyes. Empty eyes. Voids. "Why—you—doing this?" he asked with painful effort of clarity. "Why can't you—let me—be?"

"Fool's philosophy," said Amadeus as he used his booted foot to kick Teresa over, and then brought the crushing weight of his heel down into the small of her back. The bones of her spine crackled like kindling. Teresa let out a long, gasping breath. "Things cannot *be*. Things must be made."

"Hate—you."

"Hush." He kicked her back over onto her broken back. "I drown in love for you."

"You're filth," Alek spat bloodily. "A plague—hope the prophecy—puts you back—in hell!" And with final, near-impossible effort, he broke from Robot's iron grip and crawled past Amadeus, toward Teresa's desecrated body.

Amadeus stepped on the tail of Alek's coat. "Foolish, my beloved. The prophecy has been rendered null."

Alek strained, but his bones were water, his blood air, and he collapsed with his face to the snow inches from Teresa's paralyzed hand. "Not true."

"It is." Amadeus took a fold of his coat and jerked him back like an evil dog on a leash. "Amadeus must die for the prophecy's sake. I am not Amadeus, I am der Neugeschopf—a new creature."

No!

"I am a hybrid."

Nonono—

"Crucify the whore, my slayers."

—NOOO!

Aristotle stretched her out on a patch of snow, arms out, legs set neatly together like someone in mid-dive. Teresa suddenly came alive and snapped her jaws around his arm as he was drawing back, and Alek felt his heart leap at the sight. "Bitch!" Aristotle spat. He cracked his fist and Cornell college ring against her cheek. More blood. More. Robot came next with a leather bag and set it down. Planned this, then, they had fucking *planned* it—

The slayers withdrew a mallet and a pair of iron railroad spikes.

Alek tried to shrug free from the skin of his coat, saw himself do it, escaping it like a moth from a cocoon, escaping it to wreck hell on earth on these fucking barbarians, but Amadeus took a fistful of his hair and wrenched brutally back. Alek fell in a crumpled, bloody heap.

He closed his eyes, buried his face in the snow and blood.

All through the work, Teresa made a series of long ear-splitting noises, not human, not vampiric. Throat-scorching wails like nothing he had ever before heard. Like a soul being torn apart, spiderwebbed by a force it had absolutely no control over. The cries beat at him like a hammer, a fist to his heart and senses, rattling apart his sanity.

Then she fell silent and Alek opened his eyes, blinked them clear of tears. She was staked to the earth at both wrists, staked and held by iron spikes and waiting the coup de grace punched through her heart to stop its immortal beating. The old-world method. The method used before the eastern slayers lent the west their katanas and their mercies.

Amadeus stood staring down at her, the last spike in his hand. He was speaking, speaking low and intimate the words of the old Rites of exorcism. The nonsense. The gibberish in Latin. The unholy inversion of Last Rites. He crouched low, the words "Fucking whore" on his whispering lips, and Alek closed his eyes a second time.

Teresa screamed, inside his mind and out, over and over like a machine.

Alek lay motionless, spent at last. His body was elsewhere and all he was now was what he could feel and what he could think, and what he thought was how immortality was such an ephemeral thing. So tired. So old. All he wanted was to rise up and fly, fly, out into the night, because it would make the grownups angry, and who cared if the grownups were angry? But Amadeus was straddling his body as he had Teresa's a moment earlier and he was pinning Alek to the ground like yet another victim and now flight was quite impossible, wasn't it?

Amadeus kissed his mouth and the chains of tears on his face. "Why have you done this, my most beloved?" he spoke to Alek's heart. "Why do you struggle? You clung to me once, a child in your fears and grief."

Alek shook his head, once. "Deceived—me."

"I created you," Amadeus hissed. "I loved you best, you ungrateful child. Who could love you but I? You came to me a devil and I made from you an angel, and how do you repay my work, but with deceit and betrayal. I should destroy you for your sins, nein? But I am overcome with love for you still." Amadeus smiled, drank the blood from off his child's cooling lips. "I created you. And I will create you again." He touched Alek's heart, wholly rejoiced. "There—only a beat away."

Alek spat the remainder of his blood into his master's face. But the beads of blood on the Covenmaster's lashes were simply blinked away like red tears. "My journey's end," he said. "My true temple."

NO! NOT YOURS!

Amadeus kissed him once more, almost sweetly, his sharp little Sean-teeth lancing Alek's tongue, gagging him. And within the wet, private universe of Alek's mouth he tasted of Alek's blood like a Holy Communion. *I will not die,* he said. *I refuse it. You were always in my visions, Alek, you who will be the greatest among my slayers. I will not be cheated of my promised one. Your psi will make me omnipotent; your body will make me eternal...*

Lied to me! You said you would be no Orpheus. You said you would preserve only the Coven!

I am the Coven.

No, no, nononononoNOOOOOOOOO...

"Hush," Amadeus whispered as he combed away the ropes of hair clinging to his acolyte's frozen cheeks, kissed him lightly, almost fondly. Kissed him hungrily.

Alek felt nothing, every touch a distant ghost. Every thought foreign, lost in memory...

"Yes, yes." Amadeus undid the rabato at his throat and pressed the edge of the wrist blade to the small triangle of white flesh there. A red crescent like a smile appeared, and Alek's dead body convulsed with horror. He closed his eyes. No, no, he wouldn't, he *refused*—

"You lie in the cradle between life and death, beloved."

No. And again no. He wasn't afraid to die, not like Amadeus, not like his Father, who knew nothing, had learned nothing. Coward. He locked his mouth.

Amadeus cracked his palm against Alek's cheek, rocking his head to one side as if he were again a child. Steel in his mouth. Ichor. Bitter heart of war, love turned to venom, spillage, bad vintage. Amadeus kissed him savagely, shattering the flesh of his lips with his teeth. He framed Alek's face inside his stony hands. "You will honor my will, Alek Knight," he whispered and ran his fingers over the tears and blood on Alek's face, down his throat and over his heart. Under his coat. The touch. No. But it found his most vulnerable places, it stroked his weakness, and he couldn't help himself. He arched against his master like a puppet with its wires pulled taut. The fire was there as always, the goddamn hunger that no amount of slaying vanquished, the desire that was always and eternal...

Amadeus leaned low so that Alek's mouth was pressed to the freshly opened wound and circled his arms around Alek's back. Blood rouged his lips and cheeks, bubbled up his nostrils. He tasted life, survival. The sweet sharp crimson fruit of paradise itself—

"Drink," said Amadeus, moving against him with the most persuasive friction, an ancient whore who knew all the tricks. "Let me create you. Let me fill you and complete you with the life as I was always meant to do. Drink, Alek. Drink until I move within you."

No, he thought to himself, *no, goddamn you, don't you dare give in*, even as the memories and the night and all the horrors brought jewels of agony to his eyes. He tried to blink them away, but where was his strength? Where was Debra? And did Teresa forgive him? Could she? So near, they had been, so fucking *near*—close enough nearly to touch the Chronicle.

He groaned and wept as his body betrayed him and he licked his parched lips and bit the sweet wound, bit into it, seeking. Like water on a fire…no, wine in the throat of a dying man, a victim of the sun and desert—

"*Yes, yes, my love…*"

Alek strained and drank, afraid to move, to lose even a drop of precious life-giving blood. He clung to his master and maker and drank. And he drank, wondering what creature he and Amadeus were writ to be and who had set the benediction. He drank, wondering what part of himself, if any, would remain and if he would have the will above that other entity to remain and fight. He drank, wondering what he would feel as he slid down into the belly of the beast and he hoped to God and to Debra and to Teresa and to all those whom he had betrayed that he felt absolutely nothing.

8

Inside his white soundless sphere, Book stopped in his pacing as if struck by an invisible barrier. His eyes moved analytically around the room, yet he recognized nothing, identified not a thing, as if the world around him had suddenly decided to alienate him.

On the muted television the lily-faced heroine embraced a beautifully horrifying Count Orlock, offered herself up as the sacrificial lamb for all the good of a 1920's mankind. Book could not find the metaphor and so he took up the remote and changed the channel to MTV.

He watched artists sing about their sorrows and felt himself drift, lost among it. He groaned and tossed the remote to a cushion of his fashionably colorless love seat. He turned full circle, the room too large, turning too fast. Where was Alek? His brother when all the brothers had gone, his best friend in all the world and fucking beyond? He had to find him—had to.

Why?

Didn't know why. Had to—
Where? The city's a big place, fool.
Silly—he knew. Of course he did.
He knew as if he had always known.
The beginning place.
"Your empathy must be rubbing off, brother," he said and reached for his coat lying on the floor.

9

Tahlia cast the cat skull across the full length of the gallery. It hit a gorgon-face shield like a missile and clattered to the floor in shards.

She turned in the empty hall, surrounded by the relics of all things dead and destroyed and gone forever. The bones and shields, the spears and skeletons, the armor and parchment, the swords and maces, as if an army had fallen here and scattered their debris everywhere.

She looked around, bewildered. She had fought this war too long.

They all had.

Exhaustion displacing rage, Tahlia slumped against the wall under a Valazquez, a somber painting of the death of Socrates, one hand in her sweaty hair and the other over her heart. You are long over the hill, Tally, whatever the face may say. Gonna give yourself a heart attack. Yeah.

"No!" she answered, and strange this voice: it was not her own. It was the voice of some other Tahlia, some younger Tahlia. The voice of the woman who had sat up all night in a cafe on Columbus Street listening to bad beat-generation verse and rattling her glass and stomping her feet with the best of them as the rest of her withered and curled up like an old rose and died inside. The woman whose heart knew that Byron was never late, never in all their thirteen years late for one of their dates, and that being late tonight meant something more than *late*. The woman who knew these

Beatniks and their lousy poetry but who was too much a coward to admit to it. The woman who had drunk herself into a Vermouth-inspired stupor that night and then drove home to her converted loft apartment in the Brooklyn Heights and cried herself to sleep and stayed, aching, in that bed for three whole days, nursing the horrible knowledge she had like a disease. That woman, the voice of the woman ages younger and not a little feral with emotion, a voice armored in steel and war and all the things that were lost forever.

This new-old Tahlia sobbed, "It can't end this way, kid. Please, please don't let it end this way." And that Tahlia went to her knees in sobs on the floor of her husband's gallery with the relics of war all around her.

10

The moon rose and the carrion birds came. Slowly her wounds bled and steadily her pain increased. It seemed as if the night wind were on fire where it touched her body and the sky was full of screams. The sound of the birds squabbling over her bloody flesh—her wrists and her face and her bloody barren womb where the Covenmaster had chosen to send the final spike instead of her heart—was enough to drive her mad. The birds polluted her mind as badly as her body. All she had to look forward to was the rising sun, when the world would turn red and the pain would be over. She hoped it was soon; more, she hoped she felt nothing.

Time wore on. Breathing on her broken back was a nightmare. Existence itself was a greater horror. How she prayed to die, then—not for the first time but never with such vehemence. She cursed God and Lilith and Paris and Alek Knight and all those who had sent her down this path of destiny to be here now in this living hell. She wept, feeling a horrible void of self-pity opening up beneath her and sucking her down its great length. Where was grace now, now that she needed it? Where was mercy? She had not disobeyed her God, nor her destiny. Only they had conspired to set her up against an invincible foe. There was no hope for the world, she realized. The slayers were worse than the monsters they hunted. And they were spreading across the face of the earth, slowly, calculatingly, maiming and destroying, making a barren No Man's Land of her people's world.

Her people. They would never know the secret of their blood now. The secret of their true origin. Now, with the Chronicle back in the hands of the Churchmen, they would never know safety again.

The birds found her inner secrets through the hole in her loins and she heard herself scream inside her mind and out, heard the ringing echo of her own tormented, skybound curses.

And that was when the man came and stood beside her in her darkness and her agony, the man in the cleric's robes. Not robes like now, finely crafted and sewn with threads of gold. This was a cleric of the Reformation, the Renaissance. The learned, worldly cleric in rough black robes and a tarnished papal cross that was all he had to denote his statue in life. He was tall and lean, his long, white-blonde hair combed back carefully over his ears. She looked at his beautiful hands, his piercing black, pious eyes, and felt her heart stutter inside of her. She had forgotten the light he could emanate despite his darkness. The beautiful torment of his touch, his kisses. She had forgotten...so much. "Paris," she said through numbed lips. "Husband..."

He put one finger to his lips. Shhh. He smiled. *My beloved. My wife.* His eyes flicked aside to where she thought the betrayer Aragon must be standing. It was so hard to tell, pinned to the ground like she was. Lost in the dark the way she was. "Someone might hear," he whispered in his native Dutch.

"Take me home," she gasped in her native Italian. She could not remember Dutch. She could not remember anything, her pain was so great.

"Not yet," he said with gentle patience. And then he looked on her with such love that she could not find the pain anymore. It was as if he had eaten it all up with his gentle, wanting gaze. "My Teresa," he said. "Will you give up on yourself?"

She shook her head no.

Paris smiled and beckoned to her. "I'm waiting."

"I...no, Paris..."

The others might have heard her, except that Paris had cast the birds away and their escape was like thunder. She was sitting up, her hands torn and frayed to rags but set like stone around the end of the railroad spike protruding from her womb. She gripped it, her hands burning like hot wax around the cursed metal, and pulled the spike from her belly. It came out of her like the scream she dared not utter. She lay down

again, if she couldn't simply pass this cup by. If Paris wouldn't simply forgive her and come get her.

Will you give up on yourself, my Teresa?

Somehow she managed to sit up again, to climb like a staggering victim of battle to her feet. Her back was partially mended, but her hands bled. Her womb bled. She was hungry, so hungry. The iron's poison was still in her veins, but perhaps it had lost some of its potency. She took one step, and then another. She saw she was coming slowly upon the two who had crucified her. They were mere fuzzy black images, her vision was so bad. She closed her eyes and found she could track them better by their warmth. The slayers, the small one and the bully, stood a dozen paces apart and were busy watching their master twine with Alek Knight on the ground before the carousel. She was closest to the bully. She withdrew Paris's knife.

It felt heavy in her hand, but to give up now...Paris would never forgive her. She took yet another step.

And then she was upon the bully.

11

She never did like the cross.

A silly, stupid thought, but the one that gripped his mind in the moment before it happened. Over the Father's shoulder, Alek watched the assault. Such a small, weak-looking creature, and yet when provoked she was like a battalion, unstoppable and extraordinary. He watched her sink the knife into the back of Robot's head, through skull and blood and grey matter, all of which exited the wound she made in a loose, chunk-filled geyser. Robot made a sound—a peculiar sound like a cobra taken from behind by a weasel, perhaps the only sound he had ever made in his whole long life—and dropped lifelessly to his face a mere dozen yards from Aristotle. And yet, so captivated was Aristotle by the Rite before him, the whole assault went completely unnoticed by him.

Teresa dragged Robot's body back into her arms, pulled the knife loose from the sucking cavity of the slayer's skull and put her mouth there a moment, taking some nourishment from the wound. Then she took a few shambling steps forward, and, with her resurgent strength, plunged the knife into Aristotle's back. Aristotle wasn't so silent. Aristotle screamed bloody murder, falling to the ground and scrabbling at the gravel path like a cockroach someone had impaled on the floor of a Bronx tenement apartment.

Amadeus jerked away and turned. *"You,"* he whispered the word like a snake hissing a warning. His eyes, black as wet leather, black as sin, narrowed to mere slits in his white face. And then he let loose with a torrent of almost tangible psi force.

The shockwaves rippled out like a block of mortar cast into a peaceful stream. Alek felt it in those first seconds, the web of terrible force spinning out like a net, the threads of living violence collapsing the foliage around them, trembling the earth and seeking its victim. Carnage. A canopy of rickety maples crackled inward in a cavity, pulverized as if a great and invisible giant had passed there. A cannonball of wild energy ricocheted off the street between two stalled cars, shattering the asphalt, then crossed the avenue like a skipping stone and burst against the face of the Metropolitan, tearing down the Horses of San Marco banner. A small awry sphere buffeted past Alek and bounced around the inner canopy of the carousel in dreamcatcher pattern. And in that moment he thought of himself and Sean in another close place in another time with Sean's psi a demented wraith seeking its return current. Alek saw the force go to Teresa like a speeding subway train, like a trained pit bull terrier set loose on its hapless victim. Teresa raised her arms, but it would not be enough, never be enough...

Alek closed his eyes, opened his mind to Amadeus's stolen psi. He called to it sweetly and softly. And like a fish it sought its birth fount.

The energy struck Amadeus squarely in the chest. Not like a fish. Like an iron musket ball.

The force split the two of them apart like a hammered bone. It struck Amadeus from the stage and cast Alek in the opposite direction, into a steel panel of the carousel house. He tumbled down as a crushing darkness pressed in from every angle. There was pain in his skull and eyes. His stomach, Jesus, his stomach. Alek blinked and then dropped over into the track, touched his face to it in agony as the venom churned like steel knives in his belly. He tried to feel himself, who he was, but himself was like a distant character he no longer had any interest in. Red, searing pain. Black despair. Loss. It was as if those two colors were the only ones left in all the world. To die—perhaps then he would be free of this pain. He arched and slammed his face against the floor of the carousel. The pain lessened, then came crashing back like a tidal wave. He fell to his side, immobilized by it.

Time passed and he seemed to recall an image of an angel descending upon him. A dream. Perhaps.

From far away he tasted once more the shed blood of a goddess. Achingly sweet. Foreign but potent. Before his mind even knew it, his body was hungrily sucking up the substance. A swallow. And then another. Pain. But it was a different pain, it was the pain of mending. The itch of recovery. After a few moments the flow lessened, and at first he thought it was because his body was running out of blood, but then he realized it was because his body was healing, turning back on its own strength, which should have been impossible with so much of the master's blood and will inside of him. Yet after a moment or two his vision cleared and he was able to see clearly again.

Teresa lay beside him, feeding him her own blood from her cupped hands.

He shook himself. For a moment he thought it meant she was recovering. But then he saw that her horrible wounds had not healed at all. Her eyes halved, registering his sorrow but smiling even now. Even now, with her hair cruelly cropped and her face a map of half-healed scars, she was alluring and ancient and provocative. He wanted her, even in her curtain of red death.

"Only enough life—for you," she said.

He pushed her hand away. "No..."

"You are only hope." She forced yet more of her blood down his throat, feeding him from the gaping red wounds in her body, splashing it over his lips, forcing him to feed by stroking his throat like a child might a sick kitten. And it was suddenly as if the current of her life and the many lives she had taken and made her own began to overwhelm the invading will. Alek gasped and swallowed, and then he felt it die slowly within him. A warm silence stole over his body. He was certain the Father's venom had been nullified in his system. Yet inside he was still in torment. Even as he sat up, Teresa seemed to lose strength and lay back down. The wounds in her body were massive and black with gangrene, the rot of the iron shot almost entirely through her system, and he cringed because he feared that if any more of her flesh was eaten up by this cancer that he would see her heart beating, or slowing down. He tried to open a wound in his wrist, to drip blood over her parched and broken lips, but she stopped him.

"Too late," she said. She shook her head.

Another death. Another death he could not bear.

"No," he moaned.

She raised her left hand and touched his hair. "Are you so afraid, caro?"

The tears on his face were like splashed red gems. They would stain his skin, he knew, and he would carry those scars for the rest of his days, out into the world where people could see them. The slayers. The humans. The ones in between. All of them. He wanted to bury his face in her chest, but he was afraid he would hurt her more. So he took the hand she touched him with and he kissed it. His voice was choked. "You shouldn't have done this. I'm not worth it, beloved."

That amused her. "I do what I want. And you do what you must. You are more human than you know. More human than me...or him. You are the new breed...hope. Yes." Her eyes focused on the stars, her breathing harsh and painful to hear. A spasm shook her body and he heard her heart skip as she began to die.

Sobs racked his body. "Don't...*please...*"

She looked at him with her usual impertinence. "...coming."

He looked around, but there was nothing to see. No one coming. No one that he could see, at least. His heart hammered. "How do I stop him? Teresa! Tell me what to do!"

"Her," she gulped, "she knows."

"Who? Debra? You mean Debra?"

"She always knew." A convulsion suddenly gripped her, and her body arched up off the floor. His tears were a river. All those deaths, all those years of the sword, had not prepared him for this. To see another lover die. Yet Teresa, with her failing strength, pulled his hand down and touched her tongue to the tip of his finger, a gesture so final and yet so erotic he felt the need for her to the very pit of his stomach. "She knows how—" A sigh escaped her lips and her eyes brightened like church glass with the sun setting behind it. Inside her chest he heard her immortal heart stop, but there was air left in her lungs and she said in that special soft voice of hers, "Mio amante, il Cronaca..."

The Chronicle. Even in death she wanted the Chronicle.

Those were her last words. She was gone, back to the fabled web from which all their kind were reputed to come.

12

The world began to move like a filmstrip before his eyes. Alek stood up with Teresa's body cradled in his arms and wondered if the rage and the sudden loss had made him mad. No. He sensed heat and life. From deep inside the carousel came a rusty long growl, the snarling of locked gears frozen for too many years turning over, sparking to life, the carousel trying to move, enlivened by a stray bit of Amadeus's psi.

The irony of it all. He laughed. Didn't the Father see? He hadn't cheated the prophecy after all. The animals *were* running, and the midnight sun *would* shine and this was to be the last night the world would tolerate the existence of a monster.

He jumped to the ground and set Teresa's body down. He stood up. He felt nothing. "Where are you?" he whispered. "You coward, you son of a bitch, where are you?"

Nothing. Goddamn *nothing*.

No—something. Something moved toward him in agonizingly slow, movie-mummy steps. Some*one*.

He waited. After several minutes the figure closed the distance between them. And in the sudden flashing lights of the carousel the being was revealed fully to him.

Aristotle, the iron knife still in his back, dropped to his face at Alek's feet.

"Please..." He scrabbled at Alek's booted foot like a digging dog. "I don't want to die." His tears and snot had turned to ice beneath his chin.

Alek picked him up by the collar of his slayer's coat.

Aristotle hung limp and shuddering in Alek's hold. "It hurts..."

"I know," he answered gently. He looked into the suffering depths of Aristotle's eyes. "She hurt too."

Aristotle shook his head. "It hurts so bad, so bad..."

Alek narrowed his eyes. "You hurt her. You *watched*."

Aristotle's eyes widened as if he understood what was about to happen and had decided it was worse, far worse, than having an iron knife stuck in his back. He tried to move, but the poison was too deep in his body. It was no challenge at all for Alek to drop the kid to the ground and take his jaw firmly with one hand and to sink the fingers of his other into Aristotle's mouth and with one rending jerk to tear the top half of the slayer's head off his spasming body.

The body flopped, bleeding and dying like an eel dry-drowning on the ground at his feet. Alek watched, unfeeling and unmoved, until the body lay still and twisted in the crimson snow.

Memento mori, Alek...

Alek turned at the slithering sound of the voice in his head and felt steel lick pass his cheek and draw blood like a vampire's kiss. He lunged away from the thirsty Hanzo blade and slammed into the carousel stage.

Amadeus stepped out of the dark.

Alek stood, rocked sideways, fell to his knees, then stood again as the king slayer moved in for the kill. Too much. Too fast. He dropped below the slashing blade and loosened Book's tachi from his coat all in one fluid motion as Amadeus closed the six-foot gap between them and tried to take his head. Above came a muddy rendition of "Stardust" like a roar in his head. Seething, ferocious with hate and full of broken music, Alek waited—waited until the king slayer was within reach, waited until the Hanzo blade began to fall, waited until the last possible moment. And then he swung the sword at the beacon of pale face and hair.

In one impossibly graceful gesture, Amadeus changed the course of his weapon in mid-fall, blocked the incoming blade with his sword, reached and took Alek abruptly by the front of the coat with his free hand and threw him shuddering into the stage again.

More pain, but dim and distant this time. Alek got halfway up and met the Covenmaster's blade over his upturned face, the swords screeking down to the tsubas, holding, holding. Alek tried to push but there no leverage. Amadeus smiled and held the swords in place—what was he waiting for?—and then unbalanced the fragile crucifix of blades and stepped aside as Alek pitched forward.

Amadeus slashed his sword but Alek rolled out of the path of the descending Hanzo blade.

Alek found his feet. His tachi slapped willfully around to meet Amadeus's sword edge to edge. They slid off each other, not war but ceremony. Alek danced back, then up to the stage, slipping between the animals for protection. He eyed this man, this thing he scarcely knew, and yet knew too well.

This thing that wanted him. This thing that was trying to kill him.

"Why?" asked Amadeus.

"I loved you once," he whispered above the dull roar of the great whirling toy protecting him from the Father's blade, "but you took everything from me, you fuck, and now all my love is turned to hate."

Amadeus hissed like a beautiful reptile. "What I took you gave me freely, you little whore." He smiled without emotion. He showed the tips of a pair of horrifying teeth. Not vampiric. Predatory. The teeth that had ended the life of Byron and a hundred thousand others, for all Alek knew. "You drooled for me, for your passion, you *bled* for me." His smile grew, a leer the likes of which Alek had never before seen. "You belong to me. And you will *die* for me. Come..." He gestured like an artist inviting a subject into his loft. Like a vampire welcoming a virgin sacrifice.

Alek was no virgin. The draw of their common blood was powerful, but it wasn't enough. He held his ground, pointed the sword at his master like an accusing finger. "So the church will absolve you and make you their favorite little dog again?" He shook his head. "All those people you killed, all those fucking *people*. Akisha and Byron and Paris and Teresa. And you did it for the fucking *church*." Again he shook his head. "I think I hate you because of that more than anything. So don't call me a whore, you hypocrite. At least I didn't sell my soul to the Church. At least I have that much pride left."

The white eyes narrowed. Amadeus twisted his head unnaturally to one side. "I serve the Church and you serve *her*. We two are equally guilty of our passions."

"At least when I say I did what I did for love, I'm not a lying cunt," Alek said and threw his weight against the blade through a break in the animals.

Amadeus met and deflected Alek's sword and pushed him aside as if he were but a toy, as if he had no weight at all. Alek landed on his feet, turned, swung the blade slantwise for the Father's face, missed, but there—against the fire of violence there was a kind of spark, an unholy burst of white light and a milky expulsion. Amadeus stood back, his sword with its attached hand at his feet. He smiled and Alek saw no real blood come. Only milky whiteness, only writhing shapes, sinewy shadows in black ichor...

"Christ."

"I'm afraid not," said Amadeus, stooping to retrieve his sword and hand. He replaced the hand and the white, bloodless flesh mended itself almost immediately like slick white dough. "Very good. You forget nothing. Now again," he said as if this were but a simple sparring match.

Monster. Half-thing.

They came together again and again, Alek strong, Amadeus older, stronger. The sparks they made were like embers glowing through the darkness. There was no way of winning, not fairly, not against a man who lived by the sword. Alek feigned left and threw his shoulder against the master. The two of them went down in a tangle of arms and legs and teeth and swords. The Hanzo blade came screaming up for Alek's throat. Alek palm-heeled it flat to Amadeus's chest. The blood of our enemy, he thought and exercised the weapon so much more natural to his species: he bit deep into his master's throat, shredding the minor artery under Amadeus's ear, growling and foaming the blood back out of his mouth and nostrils. He shook himself, thrashed, tried to peel the flesh away from that one vulnerable spot in a great wet chunk.

Amadeus clapped his hands over Alek's ears and the burst was like an explosion in his head, the headache like a volcano. Stunned, Alek let go and tried to back away as the whine of tinnitus filled his head and made his teeth ache. But something insinuating slithered into the cup of his ear and along the back of his neck. Something else sank its needlelike fangs into his shoulder.

Alek grunted and batted at the halo of death trying to enfold him. He jerked away from the rearing, ember-eyed serpents, sliced at them with the tachi, or tried to, but the tachi was too long to work in such close quarters. The serpents lashed out at him as one, a net of hissing white horror, slashing the flesh of his face, his hands. He couldn't decide which was a worse noise, the cacophony of the carousel or the deafening, unwinding rattle of the serpents trying to slice him to pieces. Finally, he lifted the tachi high, serpents at his wrists and around his neck, and tried to bash his master's face in with the hilt. Amadeus caught it. Twisted it.

The snap of wrist bones was like an explosion in Alek's ears. He felt nothing. Nothing but helplessness as he relented his hold on the sword.

Amadeus slapped him away, and again the ground met his back jarringly.

"Sssilly boy," Amadeus said, rising with a smile and reaching for the Hanzo blade on the ground beside him.

No you don't!

Alek reached for it with his one working hand. The blessing of the *jonin*, he thought, the sword that knew its master...

Amadeus growled as the sword skated away from him and into Alek's hands. His face looked as ancient as some gift off his golgotha. He crept backwards away from Alek and smiled again a little as if from courtesy.

Alek climbed to his feet in his shredding of clothes and hair, the sword at the ready. He tasted blood, his mater's, his own. The war lust was on him now like a fever. Kill you, he thought, kill you by any means necessary. "I will kill you," he whispered through the false carnival of lights and music. "Like you killed the others, demon. How many are there? How many wait for you in hell?"

Amadeus stopped crawling and went down on his knees in a gesture of seemingly complete surrender. "Fulfill the prophecy, my beautiful ssslayer," he invited. "Absssolve yourself." The thing, creature, un-thing, smiled and looked at him as he approached. Amadeus looked past his eyes and into his brain to the place where there was always sight for him...and showed him the numbers, the souls who had perished at his hand, and the number was no hundred or thousand as Alek had suspected. He was wrong. Alek saw them all and there were a screaming, writhing *million*...

The plan had worked perfectly, of course. Alek felt their anger, their million-power rage, their mindless, immortal fury, and screamed and slashed his katana too early and without half of his strength.

Something happened, a spark, a scream of air—what? Alek knew only that his sword could not penetrate Amadeus's power. Hitting him was like hitting an invisible glass barrier. With nothing more than a look, Amadeus shoved him back down to the ground. Icicles of laughter impaled his wounded mind and made him cringe—Sean Stone's heckling, stolen and transparent.

Alek shook once, violently, and looked up.

As the animals undulated and turned, he saw Amadeus standing against them, against the hellish whirl of light and sound. As he drifted forward there was an insinuating *snick* under the roar of the music. The switchblade again. As long as a wakizashi, it pointed down at the ground from his sleeve. Some awful enigma, thought Alek as he recovered, this ancient man and his modern weaponry.

"You broke my heart," explained Amadeus as he charged forward and brought the weapon down in a glittering blue arc.

Alek, seeing it out of the tail of his eye, jerked sideways, and instead of penetrating his sternum, the perfect blade sank into his shoulder, making his body explode with pain and simultaneously pinning him to the ground.

The Father bent low, his face white, a mask of envious hurt. He wept. He said, "Does it hurt?"

Alek coughed blood, shook his head, felt only dark, deep pressure gathering from within. "Fucking bastard, you killed Byron...made me kill Debra. Your spell...you did it to her. Always your game. Why did you hurt her?"

"You loved her," said Amadeus. He twisted the blade, sending shards of pain pulsing deep within Alek's body, then withdrew it slowly. He licked its greasy red single edge and smiled painfully in his tears and rouge of blood. "You kissed her and touched her and put your filthy, unrepentant hands all over her. You would have run away with her. How do you think that made me feel? Did I mean so little to you, Alek?"

Alek closed his eyes. His body was stone, immovable. The pain was there, but it echoed emptily. Where was his sword? There. Maybe ten feet from his outstretched hand, the steel all blue light, the hilt like a white bone. Too far, God help him, he had no fucking strength left. "It wasn't any of your business," he whispered. "Why me? Why do you care? Why won't you let me go?"

"I love you," Amadeus answered and stabbed him in the opposite shoulder.

Alek convulsed as if by the force of the impact alone and felt the katana slide into his hand, sleekly, like a serpent. The weapon more than anything else seemed to respond, seemed to animate him and power his dead right hand up in a lashing silver arc.

Amadeus fell away and seemed to dissolve into the dark.

Alek sat up, rose up as if full of white fire, pain, purpose. He smiled, breathed through his teeth. He felt the Abyss yawn open in the center of his heart, felt it swallow the last whispers of pity or fear or pain. They, the two of them, he and Debra, had been born for this, this work; they had been set in the Covenmaster's way. The knowledge sat within him in some dark, hidden place deeper than instinct or memory. Debra knew. Had always known.

Like Teresa had know.

And now, at last, so did he.

The katana jerked up over his head as if alive and clashed with his Father's falling blade. Alek turned, a half pirouette, and met the Covenmaster's ground assault.

Amadeus grunted and broke away.

Alek followed, feinted right in an attempt to force his foe to circle around so the checkerboarding of carousel lights was out of his eyes.

Amadeus ignored the feint and went in like a surgeon.

Alek beat it off and countered.

Amadeus simply faded back. Coward.

Alek stepped into the lead and again attacked in their dance of death, shifting his line in midmotion.

Amadeus followed the line of the blade, deflected it.

The swords clashed once more, shearing their edges and casting ruby-red sparks into the night. The two men came together corps a corps, and then thrust each other away.

Jesus, thought Alek as he caught his balance on a park bench. He battled himself.

"Yes, beloved. Yourself," said Amadeus with an unwinding hiss, a narrow-eyed smile, a step forward. His hair writhed and rattled, the serpents all over his face and shoulders like trained pets. Whatever humanity he might have used to cover his awful stigmata was gone. He was all clattering claws and white bloodless skin and leather-black eyes and tortured serpent-hair. A monster. A beast. "Your blood is in me. Your mind is a book. So easy. You cannot win, do you see? You cannot defeat an enemy who can anticipate your every move, who knows your heart better than you. You cannot fight yourself."

"You're not me!" Alek spat bloodily.

Amadeus struck.

Alek did not recoil but blocked it. Sacrament in steel. He bared his teeth, rotated the sword, first one way and then the other, yet the swords would not divorce themselves. Die, Amadeus had to die! The beast had to die! He thrust with both hands against the hilt of the sword and was met with only unabsolved agony, the Father's hands, his weapon and mind, cold and diffused, light through an uncolored pane of glass, heatless light changing steel to bone and bone to dust.

Amadeus shoved him back and he crashed into a park bench, flattening it to timbers.

Alek stood up and encountered suffocating pressure, unbelievable weight. Amadeus's psi slammed into his shoulders like a dropped sepulcher stone and the raw force of it drove him back down to his knees.

"Yesss." Amadeus nodded. "It is as it should be. Kneel, Alek. Kneel and receive your Communion."

Alek stiffened, strained a moment, sought an escape from the impossible weight, almost—but too great, too big. He lunged to his knees. He wept to the earth under his chin. He could not rise, could not fly. Impossible. Debra. Where was she now? Where was his strength? He was failing her again. He always failed her...

Then came her indignant voice in the chamber of his mind, so close he could almost have reached out to touch her cheek: *Will you give up on yourself? Will you?*

"I can't..."

You can. Or you would not have been the one Chosen.

"I don't have the power."

You don't. But we do. Slayer.

She was there in front of him. He saw her in her black and red and he saw her reach for him and put her hands over his where they lay upon the hilt of the sword. He felt no pain, felt only the void of his own strength, taking, transforming. He tried and the sword came up where his body would not. He looked down. Debra's hand was gone but her ring flashed on his hand. The ring. The enormous holocaust of carousel lights was in it as the Abyss was in him now.

He turned a little to catch the light, then a little more to direct it.

Amadeus hissed when the laser of light struck his face, fell away in pain, his tender eyes boiling with light.

The weight melted off his shoulders and Alek sprang up like a shoot reaching for its life-giving light. He leapt his master's paralyzed figure, turned in a crouch and slid the blade silkily along the backs of Amadeus's legs. Amadeus fell, twisting, to his knees. He stared directly at his son and acolyte and slayer. His face was carved from angry white stone, unlife made flesh and imbued with a mask of twisted human expression, hate, love, helplessness...

I pity you, Father, Alek thought but did not pause in the deed. You've learned nothing.

13

It was over.

Alek felt the pagan Pentecostal fire leave him and he let his sword drop. He fell to his knees and blinked against the narrow aura of dawn clinging to the carousel's silhouette and blushing the bellies of the cloud beds overhead as they unraveled and drifted away. The birds were leaving, their voices calling softly to the dawn.

He felt tearless, not changed, only...finished.

The ring on his hand, Debra's ring, clinked to the ground.

He picked it up, understanding.

He turned his eyes out of the sky and rose, shrugged off the aged husk of a six-hundred-year-old mummified corpse holding him in its embrace as if Amadeus would not be denied his temple, not even in death. The headless body toppled and scattered to dry silt the moment it touched the ground. Finis. Fertig.

Standing tall, he watched the shimmering swirls of dust as the new open world received the remains of the Covenmaster. Night master. Black king. No more. It dusted the tarpaulin of the carousel, glinted on the dark horse's hindquarters like dappling. And the dark horse, like the dolphin, like all the rest of the carousel animals, was slowing, the wildness gone out of him at last. The carousel chuffed and wheezed asthmatically, the music cranking down, the lights of the carousel's battlements winking uncertainly, then going out forever.

He breathed deeply and smelled scorched oil and the pungent friction of the revolver grating, resisting, its momentum and its life gone. The carousel at last was truly dying, giving up its immortality.

Amadeus's remains were gone when it finally heaved to a dead halt.

Ashes to ashes. Dust to dust.

He walked amidst the battlefield, seeing the decayed and unrecognizable bodies, the remaining hair and clothing the wind was shoving away into the corners of the city. Robot and Aristotle. Teresa. Amadeus. A bum in three coats ambled past, but he did not see, did not look. Or chose not too. Alek found a perfect skull of palest ivory laying on the ground, and picked it up. The last vestiges of its white hair blew against his cheek, blew away.

The first dead of the Covenmasters. He held the skull like a precious gift. The first fallen of the Covens. He cupped the skull in both hands, was almost saddened to find no last impression in it. There was nothing. Amadeus's emptiness had been complete. He would exist damned in the dark with whatever god he worshipped forever.

Alek turned back around. Abruptly, he paused.

A man stood watching him from beneath a crystallized fir. Not a bum. He looked tall, though actually he was not, very; it was his slenderness which created the impression. He had a strong, agile figure in his tight-belted longcoat. And he would in fact have seemed strong, even invincible, except that his face looked older than the skull Alek now held in his hands. How long had he stood there and watched in his paralyzed silence?

Too long, said his oily black eyes. Too, too long, brother.

"He—the Father—he took me from this godawful place for mad children," Book told him from afar, his whisper a scorch. "It was in the beginning, y'know, after the fire—I was burned and they thought—but I—he..."

"He was nothing," said Alek, "and what he made was nothing."

Book looked at the skull in Alek's hands. He said nothing for long moments. He literally wrung his hands. Somewhere a bird called. A whippoorwill. Book laughed. He said, "No, no, you were supposed to be Covenmaster after him, brother—you—you can still be—you can—"

"No," Alek said. "I can't."

Book narrowed his eyes. In the refracting light of the creeping dawn they looked more white than black. Empty except for the rage, the sudden childlike, mindless rage.

And now too long denied.

Book snorted, the blood hectic in his face, and let the storm break.

The hairs on the back of Alek's neck stood up as a silent, enormous bolt of death broke from Book's mind. The passage of burning air warped the white winter air like ozone; it singed Alek's nostrils; it filled his throat with smoke, his eyes with acid. He might die or he might live, but certainly he would burn for Book, for his pain.

Alek closed his eyes and steeled himself...and felt a phantom warmth on his cheeks.

And then his brother screamed, double over with that scream. Sweat striped his temples as he called back the psi, let it fall back on its source in all its fury. He hugged himself, struggling to balance that fury, flesh smoldering, the cuffs and hem of his coat blackening, curling. He turned aside his face and snorted whitely. He shivered, sighed, and then the heat was gone. Only a master could do something like that. Only a master. The look he offered Alek was one of sick fear and bereavement veiled with courage. It was as if he were asking questions. What have you done and tell me how to live with it. But there were no solutions, no answers. Only more questions. Only that. Freedom was a beautiful monster, after all.

Book straightened up and casually sank his trembling hands into his coat pockets. He looked only once more at Alek, impenetrably, "I told you I didn't need a sword to finish you off," he said. And then turned away and let the white hands of the firs receive him.

Alek almost followed him in pursuit. Book, his brother, his fucking brother, man. But the war and the damage and the coarse beauty of the new day were too much, and he felt at last the delayed weakness of his body strike and nearly crumble him on the spot.

Yeah, he wanted to follow Book, turn him around, scream into his face. He wanted to make it up to him. Somehow. He wished he could umake it all. But in the end he simply limped away from the carnage like the very young or the old.

14

He crouched low to the floor of the carousel house and took the tarnished ringbolt he found there in his good hand. He pulled, but the trap door would not give for him at first. Spent, he was too spent, like a child within reach of the brass ring but too wounded from defeat to claim it.

Strength, he thought. He put both hands upon the ring, his living hand and his dead one, and jerked the ringbolt and heard the trap grind up with a rusty groan. He studied the thick dusty square of darkness that was revealed. Where did it lead? Middle Earth? The fabled Abyss?

Licking his mouth, he slid on his belly, backward through the service trap, felt with his feet for the rungs of a ladder. There was none. He held his breath and dropped. The fall was short—just after his head was below the house floor, his feet struck dirt and he stood straight. He looked around and found he stood in a cramped, close little room full of cogwheels and cables, belts and pulleys that were the mechanized entrails of the carousel. Smoke twisted lazily around his shoulders, smelling of things cooked and dead and finished. Alek squinted through the choking mechanical gloom broken in uncertain shards of stolen light, looking for a clue to the Chronicle's whereabouts. Looking for anything at all.

A girl laughed. He did not know who it was, but he turned and started in that direction.

Halfway to the wall, the toe of his boot hit something and sent it sliding a few inches. Not many. It was too heavy for that. He knelt down and found the box lying there in a track of thirty-year-old dust. Just a plain black jewelry box. Nothing inscribed in the age-blackened wood, nothing peculiar about it at all.

He cracked the fragile wood against the cement floor of the service space, heard and felt the entire box splinter apart. What remained was priceless and beautiful and a wonder to behold. And it was with wonder that he read the first paragraph of the first browning, archeological page of Latin.

> The supposed history of the vampire as a species, as recounted in documents discovered at Athens, Rome, commences in approximately 14,000 B.C. According to the work's hellish author, this period was a time of visitation by beings from the Underworld who are generally referred to in the vampire texts as lamiai, but who are also identified as The Medusans. The lamiai/ Medusans are alleged to have come from a common source, that of the Void or Web, depending on what text one consults. It is also alleged that they not only visited Earth regularly, but that, to this very day, many of the Medusans have in fact taken up residence amongst the vampiric population in cognito...

He closed the yellowing, mismatched papers of the book. With this, he realized, he could probably destroy every last slayer. He tried to imagine what Teresa and Debra and Paris would say, the joy they might have known at holding the book in their hands. But at the moment he could find neither the joy nor the sorrow. He started slowly up the stairs to the newborn world waiting for him. For now there was only the work of the Slayer and the fear gathering in the streets of the world as the Covens fell one by one and the dead slept and told no tales of the shadow that had crossed their path, silently, with an angel's sword.

EPILOGUE

A letter from His Eminence Cardinal Joshua Benedictine, Special Attendant to His Holiness and Chairman of the Vatican Historical Council to Father Adamas Bodine, Representative of the New York Branch of the Vatican Historical Council, postdated Present Day:

Brother Adamas:

Unfortunately it seems my late mentor, Cardinal Guiseppe's, worse nightmare has become our reality. Yes, the rumors you have heard are correct; the white angel has in fact fallen by the wayside. A sad, unfortunate thing, to be sure, but we must remember that the hellspawn did serve his purpose quite well, even at the end.

Why, were it not for our angel, how else would we know of this incredible new talent which has materialized in your great Mecca of civilization almost overnight? I am sorry to say that whilst visiting your city some seven days ago to look in on my now-fallen angel I did not have an opportunity to study the history of the One that we now discuss, though in fact—as they say in your country, even today—voices do carry.

Still, none of this alleviates our present dilemma. The vampire Paris and his fox-like agents have managed to outwit us yet again, even from beyond the grave. Again the Ninth Chronicle is lost to us. And so, like my mentor before me, I find myself imploring your fastest aide in getting back our property. Time is of the essence, as Cardinal Guiseppe once said, and time, it seems, is quickly running out for us.

I will do my best to stave off any interference here at Rome, but you must be quick. Use the many resources we have mined over the years to find and study this rogue. Gather all intelligence and send it promptly back to *my attention only.*

Be warned, my brother: do not be seen by our rogue, for I fear he is in many ways twice as deadly as his teacher. For my demonic angel it was a matter of holy passion. For this rogue it is almost wholly carnal revenge.

I fear for what path all this must lead us, as men of God, down. But I also revel in the opportunity to be such a profound weapon as we have obviously been called to be. Remember the proximity of the Purge and keep your faith strong in our Lord and the divinity of our mission as you set yourself to these tasks. Remember, as well, that it is a Holy War that we fight, and that we are apt to encounter many strange and powerful warriors along the way.

God be with you and yours. I will be in contact again.

Yours in Christ,
Joshua

Printed in the United States
1317500002B/22-27